Perilous Siege

C. P. ODOM

OYSTERVILLE, WA

Also by C. P. ODOM

A MOST CIVIL PROPOSAL

CONSEQUENCES

PRIDE, PREJUDICE & SECRETS

PERILOUS SIEGE

ISBN: 978-1-68131-030-5

Cover design by C. P. Odom
Layout by Ellen Pickels

Dedicated, as always, to my family,
especially my dear wife, Jeanine,
for putting up with me when
the writing bug gets its claws into me
and I go into hyper-focus mode

Introduction

While history is often regarded as a mere a collection of facts, people, and dates, a closer inspection reveals that many events could easily have had dramatically different outcomes. What if, for example, Julius Caesar had heeded the warning of the soothsayer about the Ides of March and stayed home from the Senate? What if Britain had won the Revolutionary War and kept control of the North American colonies? Then there's the most intriguing supposition to ponder (in the US at least): What if the South had won the Civil War?

These speculations have been explored extensively in the alternative history genre of science fiction in which the usual approach is to restrict the historical change to a single critical event or decision. All subsequent happenings hew as close to the demonstrated characteristics of the characters and their situation as the author can manage.

In my three previously published novels, all set in the imaginary world of Jane Austen's signature work, *Pride and Prejudice*, I've used a similar approach by changing a critical point in the storyline (Jane does give us quite a few, after all) and then continuing from that point, trying to keep the characters true to her novel.

My approach in this present novel was partly similar and quite different at the same time. I tried to maintain Austen's characters and their motivations, but I stirred the plot by mixing in the idea of a limitless number of parallel universes and bringing in a refugee fleeing an apocalyptic doom in the near future of our own world. Naturally, I used artistic license to have my refugee familiar with Austen's works, so he quickly discovers he has been transported from imminent death in his own world to a world populated by real-life, flesh and blood Austen characters. This puts certain limitations on what he can and can't do since he obviously can't say, "All you guys are fantasy creations from a writer back in my world! You shouldn't exist!"

Now, one might say, "Wait a minute! Didn't Mark Twain do something similar in *A Connecticut Yankee in King Arthur's Court*? My answer is a qualified yes, but his was a comedy and satire against romanticized ideas about chivalry contrasting with the ingenuity and democratic values of his visitor from the future. Also, his character is put to sleep by Merlin for 1,300 years and wakes up in the modern era of Twain's time. In my novel, I'm just trying to tell a story, and the refugee can't get home. The path through the infinity of universes is strictly a one-way trip.

A tip of the hat does go to Andre (née Alice Mary) Norton, a science fiction and fantasy writer whose books were a staple of the local libraries where I spent a lot of time in my teenage years. In one of her most famous novels, *Witch World*, she used the mechanism of the Siege Perilous from the King Arthur legend to transport her hero to a parallel world—the world that would be a fit for a person who didn't belong in this present world. When I first devised the bare bones idea for this novel, the Siege Perilous instantly popped into my mind as the way to get my protagonist from our world to the parallel, fantasy world of Jane Austen's most famous characters. I know Miss Norton didn't conceive the Siege Perilous—it is a legend, after all—but I have to credit her for giving me the idea.

All these thoughts were in my mind when I crafted the following tale although I also had fun imagining some less likely possibilities without (hopefully) causing the affected players to break character too dramatically. I will leave it up to the reader to determine how well my efforts succeeded. Above all, have fun with this modest effort. I did when I wrote it.

— *C. P. Odom*

Prologue

//

Behold, the day of the Lord cometh, cruel both with wrath and fierce anger, to lay the land desolate: and he shall destroy the sinners thereof out of it.

— Isaiah 13:9

\\\

Tuesday, October 10, 2045
Cornwall, England, 0830 hours

B ack to your beloved chick-lit, Gunny?"

Major (brevet) Edward McDunn, USMCR—one-time Gunnery Sergeant McDunn, USMC—looked up at the tall, lithe brunette. In woodland camo battle dress with corporal's chevrons at her collar-points, she gracefully squatted beside him. PFC Smith stood behind her wearing his usual expression that always made McDunn want to reach for his wallet to make sure it was still there. Unlike the duo, McDunn's battle dress was desert issue, shades of brown and tan rather than the green and brown more suitable for the Cornish countryside.

He gave Corporal Sandra Desmond what he intended to be a stern expression. She was one of several original corpsmen of Bravo Company and was now the only surviving unit corpsman of a greatly depleted second battalion of the equally depleted Second (Tarawa) Regiment, the advance element of the Marine Expeditionary Brigade (MEB). But his expression, as usual, had no effect on his irreverent corporal, causing McDunn to sigh in fond resignation.

Corpsmen get away with murder in the Corps, he thought—*always have, always will. Assuming there still is a Corps, of course!*

"By this time, you should know better, Dancer," he said mildly, waving his electronic tablet at her and responding to her jibe with equal, if strained, lightheartedness. "*Pride and Prejudice* is a classic of English literature and is not, by any stretch of the imagination, reserved solely for those of the female persuasion."

Sandra rolled her eyes expressively, the mischief in them plain to see.

"Anyway," McDunn said, warming to his topic, "I haven't read this story in years. Haven't had the time."

"And you have the time now?" She grinned wryly, gesturing toward the raw earth fortifications to their left and right.

"What else do I have to do? I inspected the troops and equipment at 0530. Everything's done that can be done. Everyone's dug in, communications are set up, and we've done all the contingency planning we have the resources for. In a situation as stark as this, everyone knows what to do. The troops don't need me spooking around them, wasting their time. Why shouldn't I get reacquainted with an old friend?"

"But you *have* read it before, right? And you've read all the other books by the same author?"

McDunn responded to Sandra's sly look with an expression crafted into inscrutability by a thousand late night poker games. "Well, yes," he finally admitted. "They were a particular favorite of my sainted grandmother."

"Chick lit, like I said! But don't worry. I promise I won't tell anyone."

"Thanks ever so much, Dancer," he said sarcastically. "Except Smitty here, of course."

"Any time, Gunny, any time," she said, giving him a crooked smile and patting him consolingly on the shoulder. "And Smitty won't tell anyone because he knows what'll happen to him if he opens his mouth before I tell him to."

Then, before he could think of a suitable rejoinder, she abruptly changed the subject.

"I've got good news, and I've got bad news, Major. Which do you want first?"

McDunn sighed and powered down his personal tablet, securing it in its ruggedized case before taking a USMC-issued tablet from the field pack at his side. The tablet wasn't really his. He had his own issue tablet, the version given to all enlisted men, but he hadn't used it in months. It was buried somewhere deep in his pack.

This one he'd inherited after their first engagement when Gunnery Sergeant McDunn, USMC, became Captain (brevet) McDunn, USMCR, commander of Bravo Company in a battlefield promotion—an officer and a gentleman though he hadn't any idea how to command a company, much less be an officer or a gentleman. Commanding the weapons platoon of Bravo had been something he knew how to do, and he had done his best.

Sandra looked on quietly as he powered on the device and went through the security protocols in his steady, methodical manner. Her quick eyes flitted approvingly over his rugged frame, much sturdier than her own. His face matched his body, tanned and weathered with crow's-feet at the corners of his eyes and deeper brackets at his lips, despite his youth. Both features owed as much to good humor as they did to grimness though the situation at the moment was grim enough to make even Pollyanna despair. He looked older than his twenty-three years, but she thought his face was one of the ageless ones. It would look the same at sixty as it did now.

As though any of us are going to see sixty! she thought in despair, feeling the familiar knot of grief in her chest at the thought of what they all faced.

She didn't so much fear dying herself, but she ached at the thought of McDunn's death. She had said as much in the privacy of her prayers, wishing desperately he might somehow miraculously survive but not able to convince herself he would.

At least he doesn't suspect how I feel. If we'd had some time, any *time at all, since coming to this godforsaken country, I might have found a way to talk to him—to let him know how I feel. But it didn't happen, and it's too late now. It would just distract him when he needs to focus on what we're facing. When we all do.*

Her thoughts were no more visible on her face than were McDunn's but for a different reason. In Sandra Desmond's short, arduous life before joining the Corps, she'd become highly adept at dissembling and concealing her emotions. It had been a survival trait on the streets of New Orleans, and those who didn't learn the lesson invariably came to bad ends. She'd learned *and* survived.

McDUNN WASN'T OFFENDED BY SANDRA CALLING HIM "GUNNY" EVEN though he was now an officer. A major, by God, even if it was only a brevet rank—temporary during the current emergency unless or until permanently ratified by higher authority. But all those who were left from the original Bravo Company usually called him Gunny. He didn't mind it in the least.

He actually had been a real, sure-enough gunnery sergeant once, a feat rather remarkable for a marine who was barely twenty years old and on his first enlistment. But it was a feat possibly explained by almost four years of intense combat in various locales around the fringes of the embattled United States, engaging a bewildering variety of terrorist and paramilitary groups trying to exploit the turmoil roiling the entire continent.

The Corps had been significantly impressed and had offered to send him to college and then to OCS, but he'd wanted to be a civilian again. He'd wanted to go to college on his own nickel, chase girls, drink beer, and go to football games. He'd done his time, and he'd seen all the combat he ever wanted to see. He'd wanted the freedom to make his own decisions rather than have them made by the Corps.

College had looked much safer than the Corps, and so it proved for two years and a few months while he completed his degree in industrial engineering in record time and headed off to graduate school. The first indications of impending disaster had been the appearance of the Blight bioweapon in Middle Eastern croplands near the Iraq-Iran border. Then the long-dreaded nuclear attack from Iran had exploded with the launch of twenty medium-range ICBMs aimed at Israel. While eighteen of the missiles had either been intercepted or gone astray, two detonated above the economic and technical center of Israel.

Israel's counterattack had been devastating, and Iran virtually ceased to exist. After that, the whole Middle East exploded in a series of retaliatory strikes, and much of the area and its oil-producing capabilities were devastated. Almost unnoticed in the middle of the nuclear catastrophe had been the satellite imagery showing the spread of the Blight as brown areas grew to eclipse green croplands.

With population centers devastated, radioactive fallout posing unknown hazards, and croplands disappearing, millions of refugees began to flee the Middle East. The overwhelming majority of them headed toward the countries around the Mediterranean, most of which had little remaining military capability to resist the surge even if they'd had the political will.

This included America's long-time ally, the United Kingdom, whose new king had appealed for US military assistance. His military had become a shell, almost completely depleted by successive governments attempting to buy votes with money the government no longer possessed.

Despite the horrifying news screamed from every media outlet, McDunn had still been rather shocked to receive a special delivery letter in January at his Texas A&M grad student office. He'd ripped it open to find that the president had declared a state of emergency and thus recalled him "to active duty in the USMC for the duration of the present emergency plus six months."

His discharge, evidently, hadn't been as final as he'd thought, or so said a lawyer he consulted.

And here I am, he thought tiredly. *Back in the Corps and part of the under-strength lead element of the mostly non-existent Marine Expeditionary Brigade, sent over to help the Brits stave off the oncoming horde of refugees fleeing from what's left of the Middle East as well as what seemed to be an equal number of radical terrorists from any number of European countries. And all of those, refugees and terrorists alike, appeared bound and determined to make a new home for themselves in Merrie Olde England by the tried-and-true method of taking it away from the present owners.*

His tablet gave a *ping* at the conclusion of start-up, and he looked up at Sandra and Smitty, who were waiting patiently for him.

"Sorry," he apologized. "So, let's have the bad news first as usual."

"It's both good and bad. Smitty got a full ammo loadout from what we laughingly call our supply section, and we just passed it out. Here's yours." She passed him an almost empty canvas bag that clinked with the sound of rifle magazines.

He looked inside and counted twenty fully loaded M-36 magazines—six hundred rounds—plus ten grenades.

"A full loadout?" he asked, looking up. With ammunition so scarce, they'd been getting half-loads for a couple of weeks.

"Yup. Full load of ammo *and* grenades. Like I said, Smitty and I passed it out."

"Okay, that's really good news. What happened? Did we stumble across another old Brit armory?"

The expression in her eyes penetrated his understanding, and he sighed.

"Okay, I should have known. You said the news was good and bad. So what's the rest?"

"The bad news is the ammo we just got is all the ammo remaining. All of it. The cupboard is bare."

"All gone?" McDunn asked flatly.

"Yup. There's no need to hold back anything for a rainy day. If we don't survive today, there won't *be* another day. If we do survive, we'll have to try to scrounge weapons and ammo from the enemy—the dead ones, of course. I'm sure none of them will be interested in surrendering, not that we'd accept it. Not after what we learned."

"Yeah, I know. Man, I hate kamikazes! But all the ammo! I knew it was coming, but I'd hoped it wouldn't come quite this soon."

"The group who hit us last week soaked up a lot more of our available firepower than we'd hoped, even with everyone on semi-auto as much as possible, as well as using captured AK-47s until they ran dry. Anyway, Sergeant Cleary—excuse me, *Lieutenant* Cleary—gave me the latest poop about what's coming at us."

"Yeah, the colonel passed it to me also. We don't know a whole lot about this latest group. They somehow took out our drone—our next-to-last one, by the way—a lot farther out than they should've been able to, so all we know is there were a whole shit-pot of them heading our way and about thirty-five klicks[1] out as of three days ago. Probably about six or seven klicks away now, from what our patrols could see. The colonel doesn't want to commit his last drone until they get closer. And no more patrolling. Our forward lookouts should be enough. It's not as though any of these barbs have any military smarts. They just come at us and keep coming unless we kill 'em."

"Anyway," Sandra continued, "the colonel ordered Cleary to go ahead and hand out everything left from the last airdrop. After we got our stuff, Cleary and his two men grabbed their pieces[2] and chicken plates[3] and headed over to Third Bat. They're even worse off than we are."

"And God knows we're plenty bad. Second Bat started with 970 effectives, and now we're down to 74—about the size of two platoons. But Third Bat's somewhere around 60. Actually, according to the book, neither of our

---

1 Kilometers.
2 Rifles.
3 Body armor inserts.

so-called battalions should be able to function with this many casualties."

"I'm shocked, *shocked*, to hear you say such a thing, Gunny! I know your reverence for the official *Marine Manual*. You'd probably be reading it right now if you didn't have your chick lit."

They both shared tired grins before McDunn cocked his head at PFC Smith.

"Anything else, Smitty?"

"Nah, Gunny. I mean, sir!"

McDunn shook his head with a smile and waved him on his way. Smith was a lifetime marine, and he'd been up and down the ranks. He'd even gotten as high as sergeant once, but that was in combat. Out of combat, he was a handful: drinking, fighting, gambling. Combat stripes soon disappeared once back at base. But he was good in combat. Short, skinny, and mean—a good marine. In combat.

Turning to Sandra, McDunn said, "During my first hitch, we used to joke about anything worth shooting was worth shooting twice, because ammo was cheap while life was expensive. Now every round is worth its weight in gold."

"Yeah," she said with a humorless smile. "I know what you mean, even though I'm just a pill pusher."

"Oh, you're not too bad with your piece, Dancer," McDunn said with a grin and a wink. "Your personnel file says you qualified as Sharpshooter. Not as good as Expert, like *moi*, but still better than in the old days before they moved your MOS[4] from the Navy to the Corps. That must have been weird, to have squids[5] handing out Band-Aids to us grunts. Though I've heard the old-timers talk about how much marines used to love their corpsman and how corpsmen never had to buy their own drinks on liberty."

"When I was going to Pharmacist Mate School in San Antonio, the Navy lifers used to talk about working with 'those lunatic jarheads.'[6] They didn't seem to miss the old days much, even if they do have to buy their own drinks these days. I don't suppose the colonel's heard anything from the States, has he?"

McDunn shook his head. "Nope. Communication's completely gone. Six months ago, we had dozens of ways to communicate worldwide, but now

---

4 Military Occupational Specialty
5 Sailors in the US Navy.
6 Nickname for a Marine. It's considered derogatory coming from anyone who wasn't in the Corps.

nothing works, including our military commo. Our equipment depended too much on satellite comm, and it looks like none of the commsats[7] are left. Now we can't raise anyone at all."

"Bummer."

McDunn had to smile at her use of the ancient term, but much of the old stuff had been reappearing, showing once more the cyclical nature of life.

"Bummer indeed. Remember how we found a few old-fashioned radio sets during our retreat? Excuse me—*our retrograde movement*. Trading space for time."

"Call it like it is, Gunny. Retreat it was. I thought marines never retreated."

"They do when they're up against zillions of barbs."

"Why do you always call those guys 'barbs'?" Sandra asked, her brow furrowed. "Everyone else calls 'em 'ragheads' or worse. Usually a *lot* worse."

"Because it's the more accurate term. It's not that I'm offended by derogatory and profane name-calling, you understand. I don't give a crap for the sensitivities of depraved animals who want to cut off our heads. But as an engineer, I prefer accuracy over sloppiness. These guys really *are* barbarians. The real thing. Tribalists who hate civilization and want to tear it down so they can go back to living like they did centuries ago. The fanatics aren't even a majority of those we've been fighting. More of them are from European countries than from the Middle East."

"Well, they all fight the same," Sandra said bitterly. "No tactics or anything. They just charge us until we drop 'em. And they all yell the same kind of stuff—a weird mixture of Middle Eastern and European curses and stuff."

McDunn shrugged. "That's about it. They all seem to have a blind, unreasoning hatred of civilization. Wherever they came from, they just want to tear it down and kill all of us. The whole idea of civilization being a good thing has been breaking down for decades, and this is the end result. They've become berserkers, ready to die for God-knows-what. So I call 'em barbs because it's what they are."

"And you're right about them really, really wanting to kill us all."

"With a passion, Dancer, with a passion. Another thing to note is the way all of them are young men, even those from the European countries. They evidently left their families back home to die, and their plan is to enslave all the British men and take their women. Very antediluvian. Everything's

---

7 Communications Satellites

breaking down."

"Antediluvian? I've never heard that one before."

"It means primitive, archaic, out-of-date."

"Ah. I thought your degree was in engineering, not in English lit."

"Nothing says I'm only allowed to read comic books just because I'm an engineer," McDunn said mildly. "Anyway, once we ran into these bastards and saw their numbers, we had no choice but to back up to keep 'em from surrounding us. At first, we really *were* trading space for time, as the military tacticians would say, until the rest of the MEB arrived. Then the Brigade and all of Camp Lejeune disappeared in the Massacre—more than twenty nukes going off within minutes of each other and no idea if it was done by terrorists or by some kind of cruise missiles. It's interesting nobody claimed credit for it. Nobody we know of, that is. Communications with the States was pretty hit-and-miss afterwards.

"So there we were, on our own, but with no relief expected and only a couple of resupply airdrops to keep us going. So we had no choice but to continue *retrograding* toward the west coast of England, trying desperately to contact someone—anyone—back home to request either reinforcement or evacuation. Neither alternative looked worth a diddly-dam, so now we're at Cornwall, right at the tip of the peninsula, and there isn't any more room to retrograde. Trading space for time stops working when you're out of space."

"Unfortunately, very true, Gunny. But the word you used, anti… anti-devolution."

"Antediluvian."

"Where'd you pick it up? From college?"

"Nope. From reading adventure stories like *Conan the Barbarian*."

"Ah! I've heard of him. What were you studying in college?"

"Industrial engineering, drinking beer, and chasing girls."

"I can believe it," she snorted, "except I think you got the order backwards."

"Perhaps so," he said, smiling.

"I'll bet you wish you were still back there instead of here."

"Well, somebody had to be here. I wish it hadn't been me, but I shouldn't have been as surprised to get my call-up as I was. Despite everything President Davis has done to rebuild the Corps, it's still a ghost of what it was in my grandfather's time."

A shadow crossed his face, and he said, venomously, "That is, the Corps *was* a ghost of itself. Now, with the Lejeune nuke taking out the rest of the MEB, including all the jarheads pulled in from the west coast, there might not be anything left of the Corps except a few shreds here and there."

He took a deep breath to soothe himself before he continued. "Anyway, when I calmed down after opening the envelope, I knew it was because the brass figured out they were going to need some grunts who'd been around the block. They needed to balance all those newbies I saw coming in just as I was getting my discharge. At least, they gave me back my old rank. Being a gunny again was a lot better than being a PFC."

"You *were* a gunny, but only until Captain Edranger bought it in that first firefight outside London. Then you were *Captain* McDunn."

"*Brevet* Captain McDunn, Dancer. Damn. I hadn't thought of Edranger in a while. Good man, good officer. But unlucky. Gotta be lucky sometimes."

"Yup. Everyone was really glad to hear Colonel White make the announcement. We all figured you could show those two new-mint butterbars[8] what to do at the very least."

Her face clouded up in remembrance, and she muttered, "Except those two didn't last too much longer than the Captain."

"What a foul-up this has been from the get-go," McDunn said, his face grim at the memory of the long, cruel retreat to Cornwall. "Good intentions but really bad intel and no reason for it. The sats[9] were still up when the brass was planning things, and it seems like none of them had any idea what we were heading into. Even if the entire MEB had made it over here, I don't think we could have stopped the barbs. Not in the long run. Not without massive resupply and reinforcement."

"The people here being so helpless didn't help," Sandra said quietly. "Even when we tried to pass out captured weapons, they just didn't seem able to summon the will to make any effective resistance."

"The politicos had longer to work on them than in the States, and it was bad enough there. Even a decade and a half of political indoctrination back home wasn't enough to keep Americans from finally rising up and throwing the bastards out and putting Davis in. The Brits seem really nice, but they could have used a lot more mean, nasty types."

"Like us, you mean?" Sandra said, smiling.

---

8 Second lieutenants. The name comes from their rank insignia, a single gold bar.
9 Satellites

"Yeah, just like us. People you wouldn't take home to meet the folks but good guys to guard your back. I remember a quote from some Brit about people being able to sleep safely at night because rough men stood ready to do violence in their name. Who was that? Kipling maybe?"[10]

"Don't ask me, Gunny."

"No matter," he said, dismissing the idle thought with a wave of his hand. "How'd we get so far afield? What were we talking about?"

"I think it was the older radios we found."

"Yeah, right. Even after we got a few of them working, all we could raise were a few ham radio hobbyists in the Midwest. They promised to try to pass the word to the higher-ups, but we never heard anything, and now even they don't answer."

"I still wonder who took out the sats. I know it wasn't us."

"Nope. We frittered away most of our military capability during the bad years. But most everything, even the commsats way up in geosynchronous orbit, is gone now. No GPS either. *Someone* obviously had the capability to take 'em out, and my money's on the Chinese. But they've got bigger problems right now. The people are starving to death, and they're certain someone is to blame. The last we heard, the Blight was spreading through southern China like gangbusters, and the food riots looked more like wars than riots."

"You think the Blight came from Iran? We know they started everything going downhill by nuking Israel."

"Probably was Iran. At least, the satellite imagery showed the brown areas centered on their croplands and spreading out. But the Blight was actually in full swing even before the nuke strike. It was just that crop failures in the Middle East have been such a normal occurrence in recent years, no one considered the possibility of a man-made bioweapon at first."

"Why on earth did they launch it?" Sandra said, shaking her head.

McDunn thought for a minute, reaching up to comb imaginary dirt out of his bushy and rather unkempt moustache, a habit of his while thinking.

"My opinion, for what it's worth," he said finally, "is the bioweapon didn't get launched on purpose. My bet is it got loose through carelessness. Their tech capability—and their discipline—wasn't nearly as good as they deluded themselves into thinking it was. Their biotech might have managed to create

---

10 Actually, it was George Orwell, the author of *1984*.

the thing, but it wasn't good enough to keep it under control. Look how long it took them to develop their nuclear capability."

"Fat lot of good it did them," Sandra said acidly. "The Israeli's intercepted most of their strikes and retaliated, and Iran ceased to exist."

"True, but then Israel got hit by several more strikes. They got most of those also, but several got through. They got hurt badly, and now they have to worry about fallout and the Blight. I'm afraid the whole Middle East and a good part of Europe bordering the area is either already gone or is on the way out."

"That sounds like you think the whole world might be coming to an end!" Sandra said incredulously. "I've never heard you this pessimistic!"

"It's too late in the game to fool ourselves, Dancer," he said, letting his weariness and despair out for the first time to the one person he was certain he could trust. "The whole world has screwed up royally this time, and it may not be able to recover. What if the Blight spreads to the Americas? The military wasn't the only thing we Americans degraded during the bad years when the fanatics were trying to redesign our whole society. Both the physical and the biological sciences took a hit as well. The folks back home might have no more success stopping the Blight than anyone else."

"And that's assuming there are any folks back home. They may all be dead already, which is why they don't answer us."

"The colonel thinks there've been some more nukes, but I'm kind of dubious," McDunn said. "I lean toward the possibility everything's breaking down toward anarchy or even civil war."

"That's a horrifying thought. I really thought we were on the way to rebuilding things, at least up until the Massacre. Still, I can't help getting angry with whoever or whatever's left stateside. Even if they can't hear us, they ought to know we're still here and could send ships to pull us out."

"There may not be much left since the nukes took out most of the east coast. There can't be many ships left, even if they wanted to get us out. There weren't many available to bring us over here, not after twenty years of deliberate neglect. And with virtually all of the government, including the heart of our military, converted to ash, who's left to get our messages, much less respond to them?"

"I have this dream," Sandra said, looking at McDunn wistfully. "We hear jet engines and look up to see a flight of C-17's sweeping in."

"I'm afraid that's even more doubtful than the ships," McDunn said, shaking his head dolefully. "The Air Force general in Oklahoma who arranged the last drop told the colonel he was scraping the bottom of the barrel for it. Now, he doesn't answer either, and with half of his C-17's getting hit by SAMs from the tanker before they even dropped their load, who'd be willing to stage a repeat? We're lucky we got what we did. Those Air Force pukes showed real *cojones* to keep on coming when the smoke trails started filling the skies."

"Damn the Iranians," Sandra said venomously. "It must have been them on the tanker, but who'd have ever thought they'd infiltrate a tanker before we even got here? It looked like it was abandoned, and we sure never saw any signs of life."

"At least we found a use for the old Javelin we'd been hauling around since we ran into the barbs outside London."

"I was amazed it still worked," Sandra said.

"Not half as amazed as those bastards had to have been when they saw it launch. I don't think the tanker had much oil left, but it had enough to take care of any of them who survived the strike."

"I'm kind of ashamed to admit I hoped some of the guys off the tanker would make it ashore. I really, really wanted to line them up against the wall. It really hurt to see those big birds unable to avoid the SAMs."

"The drop was a shoestring operation. The C-17's barely had the fuel to make the round trip, even with tankers, and they had to come in low to make the drop, which brought them into SAM range."

"Damn, damn, damn!"

"Yeah, I know. One thought I've had, and it isn't a pleasant one, is there might still be somebody hearing us back home, and he's made a cold-blooded decision *not* to respond. There's an old military maxim that says, 'Don't reinforce failure.' Our efforts here have certainly been a failure."

"But we took out so many! Thirty, fifty times what we lost!"

"But the barbs have the people to lose. We don't. They're still seizing ships and heading here—we've heard some of *those* messages. The animals coming at us may not like or trust each other much, and they may fight each other to the death after they've killed all of us, but they hate us more. Plus, we're the only organized military force left in England. The last of the Brit military went under months ago."

The two digested their unpalatable situation; then McDunn stirred. "You got any more good news, Dancer?"

"Yeah," Sandra said, her teeth flashing in her usual brilliant smile, and McDunn struggled to hide his sudden difficulty in breathing. "The surgeon finally decided the situation's become serious enough she needed to know how to load and fire the rifle the colonel made her carry. After I picked up what little she had for me in the way of med supplies, I gave her some quickie instructions on making sure the pointy part of the cartridge points into the chamber as well as how to change a magazine."

"If the Corpsman MOS hadn't moved over to the Corps, Commander August would be your CO, Dancer."

"She's a good egg—just kind of impractical outside of her surgery."

She turned somber and continued. "She swore to me she'd make sure none of the barbs got their hands on her patients. It was kind of gallant, even if it was rather pathetic. Damn the Iranians! I wish President Davis had hit 'em with nukes when he first became president back in '30!"

"No nukes."

"What?" Sandra said in outrage. "Whaddya mean 'no nukes'?"

"Nuclear weapons don't last forever," McDunn said mildly. "Neither do ICBMs. They both need maintenance and regular testing. After a couple of decades of neglect, the cupboard was full of useless missiles and inoperative warheads."

"I never heard that!"

"It wasn't advertised, but it was an open secret to us grunts before I got out. Davis tried to build things back up. That's why I saw so much combat during my enlistment. We were buying time, keeping the terrorists busy while the government tried to get the economy and the military back up to speed. Restoring our nuclear capability was just one of the things on the list. The president ran out of time. We all did."

There was almost a minute of somber silence; then Sandra shook her shoulders and deliberately tried for a lighter mood to end the conversation.

"So now, I suppose, you'll be returning to your literary classic."

"I could use a little escapism right about now. What about you?"

"I need to make the rounds and make sure everyone has their med kits in the correct BDU[11] pocket. Probably everyone's ship-shape—all the careless

---

11 Battle Dress Uniform

ones haven't made it this far. But it's something to do."

There was nothing really to say after that, so she rose and left. McDunn watched her go, pushing down the approval he felt at watching her graceful, cat-like prowl or the many other attributes he liked just as much.

Then he sternly made himself shove those thoughts back into the box in his mind he'd labeled "wishful thinking." When he had his thoughts about as close to composed as he could achieve, he got out his personal tablet again and opened it.

Maybe I can get through the meeting at Pemberley before the bastards show up.

Tuesday, October 10, 2045
Cornwall, England, 0955 hours

McDunn DIDN'T GET FAR IN HIS READING BEFORE THE BARBS MADE THEIR appearance. He'd known they were getting close from his landline connection to Colonel White, who used his sole remaining RPV drone to scout their advance. But the drone had gone dead a half hour before, even as the lookout posts started filtering back to their lines to report all the barbs in the world were coming at them.

It didn't even take PFC Smith shouting, "Here they come, Gunny!" to alert everyone. Fifteen seconds later, a weird whistling filled the heavens, accompanied by a few shouts of "Incoming!" to alert everyone. But few of the marines left in the battalion had ever heard the dreaded whistling sound of mortars, McDunn instantly realized. Even the vets. The bad guys they'd faced usually didn't have anything heavier than rifles and grenades.

"Mortars! Incoming mortars! Get down, Bravo!" he bellowed.

The term wasn't exactly accurate, since the unit he commanded was the skeletal remains of Second Battalion, but everyone seemed to get the message and hunkered down in their fighting holes.

"Where'd the bastards get mortars, Gunny?" Sandra shouted from the hole next to his. He'd positioned her in the center so she could go either left or right when her services were needed.

"I dunno," he yelled back, as he heard the dull *krruuump* of shells exploding far to their rear. "If you hear 'em, it means they're going over! You likely won't hear the one that's gonna land in the hole with you, so stay down!"

As though he was foretelling the future, the next series of whistling sounds included a smattering of nearby rounds going off before the whistling was heard. It also included a high-pitched call for a corpsman.

"Gotta go, Gunny," Sandra yelled back and immediately was out of her hole and scuttling left. McDunn desperately wanted to tell her to stay under cover until the barrage lifted, but he knew it would be a waste of time. In any case, he had problems of his own since he needed to see where the bad guys were. So he stood up high enough to look over the lip of the barricade in front of his fighting hole, his binoculars to his eyes.

He was thus standing high enough so the next mortar shell, which buried itself in the dirt at the base of the barricade, went off without any whistling sound whatever and blew him backwards through the air. He was unconscious before he hit the ground, grievously wounded but not dead.

Second Battalion had lost its most experienced leader within a minute of the outbreak of battle. Their last battle.

Tuesday, October 10, 2045
Cornwall, England, 1140 hours

IT WAS THE SOUND OF A MAN SCREAMING IN A FRENZY OF PAIN AND TERROR beyond his comprehension that brought McDunn to his senses. He was immediately aware of terrible agony deep in his gut, and he instinctively froze to avoid making his torment worse.

But the scream sounded again, and it wasn't his own cry, so it had to be one of his men. One of his men was hurt. Terribly hurt. He was needed. Duty was a stern taskmistress, and it was duty that forced his eyelids open to witness the horror.

The ground was carpeted with bodies—two, three, and four deep—draped over the lip of the barricade his marines had thrown up to protect their positions. Bodies covered the ground behind the barricade, some in marine camo but most dressed in the weird assortment of rags the barbs favored.

But the horror came from the vision of three people who weren't dead. The screaming came from PFC Smith, who was clearly badly wounded but not yet dead. He was being held by one very alive barb, who looked European, while another one dressed like a jihadi had just begun to saw on Smitty's throat with a long knife. The grievously wounded marine screamed again, trying to jerk his arms free from the barb who held him and laughed at his captive's terror.

It was the laugh—cruel, exultant, and barbarically savage—that cut through McDunn's concern over his own wounds. He was lying on his side, curled up around his belly wound, but his right arm was free. Without thought, he unfastened his shoulder holster and jerked out the HK-Colt 13 mm pistol his parents had given him during his first enlistment. The safety came off with a *click* that made the barb with the knife look up. The dirty-looking jihadi had just silenced Smitty by cutting halfway through his throat, and the sound made him look around in time to take the first round between his eyes. McDunn saw the hole open up, and the man's head snapped back on the initial impact and then forward as the hollow-point round exited the back of his head. He simply dropped to the ground.

McDunn's front sight blade was already on the second barb, who had dropped Smitty and was trying to get his AK-47 off his shoulder. He jerked as the major's second round hit him under the throat.

That's probably a fatal shot, McDunn thought in a weird, preternatural calm, but he took no chances. Three other shots impacted the barb in the torso before he collapsed beside his brother-in-arms and their victim.

McDunn instinctively put on the safety and returned his pistol to its shoulder holster, snapping the strap over it before his calm disappeared. Then there was nothing but the throbbing agony in his gut, and he felt himself spinning downward again.

Tuesday, October 10, 2045
Cornwall, England, 1158 hours

McDunn was wrenched out of the comfort of unconsciousness by stabbing bolts of white-hot agony coursing through his midsection and spreading outward through his torso. At first, he could see nothing other than a darkness shot through with blood-red streaks of lightning, even though he thought his eyes were open. Only gradually did he become aware that he was being moved. It was the bumping about resulting from the movement that was causing him to hurt so badly. There were hands under his armpits, lifting and pulling. Something—or somebody—was moving him bodily and causing his anguish.

A cry was ripped from his lips by an especially hard jolt, and suddenly he was wide-awake and fully conscious of the hideous surge of pain searing through his lower midsection.

A belly wound, he realized, struggling to find his voice. *A belly wound, and*

I didn't even fire a shot. Some warrior to go down like this! Just like Edranger in the first firefight, my luck finally ran out. Someone's pulling me…got me under the arms…it can't be one of the barbs.

"Dancer?" he croaked, hoping it might be his corpsman because the sudden image of the lovely girl being buried under all those bodies he'd seen was excruciating to consider. "Is that you, Dancer?"

"I am not a dancer," a rumbling voice said in strangely accented English. "But I am a friend, Yank. Oh, yes, very much a friend of anyone who fights these murdering butchers."

"Hurts—"

"I know, but you must be strong. I must get you into the cave before more of the swine return, drawn by your shots. You and the others killed almost all of them, but there are still a few."

Despite the pain gripping him, McDunn recognized he was not in a position to reject assistance from someone—anyone—who called himself a friend. He gritted his teeth and forced himself to endure the jolts as his unknown benefactor pulled him over the ground and through the heaps of bodies his foggy vision revealed. He was impressed by the strength of the other man. McDunn wasn't small, and pulling him had to be difficult.

The light of the sun was suddenly blocked, and he saw rock all around him in the dim light filtering through a thick screen of bushes at the mouth of the rock tunnel. Finally, he found himself dragged into a cave lit by many candles.

"Please, Yank," the man behind him said. "You must try to stand. I cannot pull you to your feet without your help."

McDunn opened his eyes fully to see he was sitting on the rock floor of the cave beside a massive rough stone about three feet high and six feet long. With the help of his protector, he managed to struggle to his feet, though he could not stop himself from groaning from the nauseating surge of molten fire flaming through his belly.

"Can you swing your leg over the Siege and sit on it? You have lost much blood, and I may have to send you early, even though you would not go where you are supposed to go."

The words were discernible despite the man's accent, but they made no sense whatsoever. But the man had made his order clear, so McDunn, bracing himself on the rock with his hands, managed to swing one leg over it. The effort wrenched another cry through bloody lips as the man helped to ease him into a sitting position, his buttocks fitting into a rounded depression seemingly designed to fit his hips.

"Good, good, Yank. Now, just sit here and try not to faint while—"

"Friend," McDunn interrupted, "nothing you say makes any sense at all." His words were slow, and he was hard-pressed to form them into a sentence as the stranger helped him place his hands on the stone to hold himself upright. Again, there was the strange sensation that his hands fit naturally into a pair of hollows in just the right location. He knew vaguely that such coincidences shouldn't happen, but his mind was too befuddled to worry about trivialities.

"I know," the man agreed, his voice sympathetic. "The pain must be very bad. Do you have any of those foreign medicines to relieve your distress?"

McDunn pointed to the pouch on the right shin of his BDUs. "In there. In a case. Some morphine syringes."

"Ah yes! I have heard the word 'morphine.'"

McDunn saw the man for the first time as he dropped to a knee beside him. He was tall and massive, just as large as his voice suggested. He wore some kind of long robes, much like a priest would wear except his were deep blue and covered in strange symbols. The man unzipped the shin pocket and removed the hard-shell case, opening it to reveal four long, thin plastic-wrapped packages.

"Hand me one," McDunn said with some effort, and the man extended one of the packages before replacing the case and re-zipping the pocket. McDunn's fingers trembled, but he forced himself to move deliberately as he tore the plastic covering open and took out the disposable syringe. He took the protective caps off and didn't even bother to try to swab a place on his forearm. Considering how badly his belly hurt, an infection was the least of his worries. He jabbed the point through the skin and into the muscle before pushing the injector home.

Relief, while not instantaneous, was quick, and a few minutes later McDunn sighed as the searing pain started to fade. He knew he was mortally wounded, but he needed his wits less muddled if he was going to make any sense of what this stranger was saying.

At last, his eyes opened, and the world, while still suffused with a lower level of misery, was clear enough to think. "Thank you, friend," he managed, turning his head toward the stranger who stood silently beside him. "But I have to ask…who are you?"

"As I said, I am a friend," replied the man who towered over him. "I was aware of your coming, and then of the arrival of the satanic barbarians. I hoped you might defeat them utterly and wipe them from the face of the earth."

"Too many and too few of us. Were there…any other survivors? My corpsman… She's—"

"Ah! One of your female warriors! But I saw only three, and I looked at them closely. Sadly, they were dead. She is—was she—important to you?"

"Yes…yes," McDunn said, the pain in his belly matched by a different kind of pain, one that seemed to clutch his heart at the confirmation of Dancer's death. "She and I…well, we—"

But there was nothing he could say at this final touch of grief, so he buried his chin in his chest and tried not to think of what might have been.

"I am very sorry, Yank," the stranger said, his rumbling voice soft and tinged with clear regret. "I searched when the sound of your guns grew quiet, but all I could find had perished, save only one or two of the savages very far off. They were looking through the dead, so I had to be careful as I searched. But I examined as many as I could before I found you. None of your fellow soldiers were alive."

"Marines. We were *marines*, not soldiers," McDunn corrected automatically, thinking of the men—and the few women—who died in the firefight while he was unconscious. His men. His friends. Dancer. It was the doom all of them had expected for months, but still it hurt to think on it. It hurt so much.

Everyone in my world is dead. Mostly vaporized. Mom and Dad and my sisters in the Parris Island nuke attack. Virtually all of the Corps in Lejeune with so many pulled from Pendleton to beef up the numbers for the Brigade. Everyone from high school since most stayed close to Beaufort. My whole world gone!

"I would have thought you dead if I was not looking for you," the man said, "since I sensed your presence from inside my cave."

"Sensed me?" McDunn asked. "What does 'sensed' mean?"

"I felt you here," the man said, tapping his head. "I can always sense those who are meant for the Siege. So I knew you were alive, especially after I heard the shots break the silence."

McDunn shook his head, wishing the man wouldn't keep talking nonsense. "Thanks. I didn't want to die at the hands of those murderous devils. But…but who are you anyway? My name is McDunn by the way."

"I know," the man said, pointing to the nametag on McDunn's chest. "My people named me Kaswallon in the ancient tongue though it is not the name I used in the outside world. But that world is gone now, and I will be Kaswallon for as long as I remain in this world, which shall not be long. I am descended from a line of priests who marched with Arthur's army almost two millennia ago, and these robes are those of my profession. I have the gift of sensing those of Cornish descent. That is how I knew you were still living."

"All of my family considered ourselves Americans no matter where we might have come from. I suppose I'm part Cornish since my grandmother and grandfather on my mother's side immigrated to America from Cornwall. But I didn't pay it much attention, and neither of them talked about it very often. But who is this Arthur you keep mentioning?"

"I knew you were of Cornish descent when I first sensed you. And Arthur is King Arthur Pendragon, ancient and rightful ruler of these lands. Cornwall is his true home though other districts have laid claim to the title."

"But Arthur is just legend. There never was a Camelot. Or a Round Table, much less a Lancelot or Guinevere. It's just a tale to amuse the kids."

"Ah, there you are wrong, brave McDunn, for you sit on a remnant from Arthur's court—the Siege Perilous, the vacant seat at the Round Table. It was found by Merlin, who proclaimed only the knight who was successful in his quest for the Holy Grail could sit in it without dying. Six of Arthur's knights tried to and died, or so the legend says. But the legend is wrong, as was Merlin, for the knights who disappeared did *not* die. They were sent elsewhere to the world meant for them. Only Sir Percival and Sir Galahad, who together achieved the Grail quest, were able to sit in the Siege without disappearing. Or so said Merlin, wrong as always, because the real reason they remained was they *belonged* to this world, not elsewhere."

"Wait, wait," McDunn protested again. "King Arthur—the legend is just a fairy tale."

"No, it is real. Rather, parts of it are real though you are correct about many of the embellishments. They were invented by the storytellers to make their tale more entertaining. My family knows the true story, for the tale of what happened has been passed down from father to son—as you will learn once it is full dark and the moon rises. Tell me, are you familiar with Stonehenge?"

"Of course. A big tourist attraction. Or used to be before jihadi terrorists blew it up. I've only seen pictures."

"Stonehenge is but one example of stones of great power mentioned in legends. The Stone of Scone was used for the coronation of the kings of Scotland, and later England, for centuries. The same was true for the *Lia Fáil*, where the High Kings of Ireland were crowned.

"But the most powerful was the Siege Perilous, whose ancient home was Cornwall before Merlin took it to Camelot. It was returned to Cornwall upon the death of Arthur and the dispersal of his knights, and it remained in the care of my family down through the centuries. However, as I said, its power is not to destroy the unworthy as Merlin thought. Rather, it has the power, bestowed by God, to judge a man, determine his worth, and then deliver him to his fate."

McDunn was grateful to the strange man who had dragged him away from the abattoir outside the cave, but the guy was clearly not playing with a full deck of cards.

But what did it matter, after all? He wasn't going to live, not with a shit-load of shrapnel in his belly, no aid station, no surgeon, and no antibiotics to prevent peritonitis. When the first dose of morphine started to wear off, he had three more syringes.

That ought to make death painless, at least, rather than lingering for some unknown time in terrible agony—and possibly falling into the hands of the barb bastards.

"I see the doubt in your eyes, friend McDunn," Kaswallon said with a crooked smile. "That is understandable, for you have not lived as I have. I have seen men and women sit in the Siege and disappear. My family was careful who they allowed to be judged by the stone, but there were those who heard the old tales and sought our services—and would pay handsomely. There were those fleeing enemies they could not fight or who were being sought for crimes, real and imagined."

Kaswallon smiled again, but it had no humor in it. "There was a rather urgent demand for our services after the great war of the last century—what you would call World War Two. Many were fleeing the justice of the Allies, and they found an escape by means of the Siege Perilous. But remember, I said the Siege judged the worth of a man and then consigned him to his fate. I think most of those men were not pleased with the world in which they found themselves."

This is getting loonier and loonier, McDunn thought, *but the big man seems harmless enough, despite his ravings.*

But again, it seemed as though Kaswallon was reading his mind since he beamed happily at McDunn and said, "Have you heard of alternate worlds, friend McDunn? The idea of different outcomes flowing from great decisions or events, leading to two different and parallel worlds?"

"I've read stories, but it's just an idea, a fictional device."

"Much like the tales of King Arthur, Merlin, and the Siege Perilous? But never mind. You have heard of the concept. For example, suppose you had not come with your fellow marines to Cornwall. There would be a different world resulting from that decision, and you and your fellow marines would not have fought the butchers today. Thus, you and I would not be in this cave at this moment. Does this make sense?"

"Sure," McDunn said savagely. "Of course, I'd have disappeared in the same nuclear explosion that consumed my parents and my sisters. Some alternative!"

"Not all alternatives lead to good outcomes as both of us know from the catastrophe consuming my country."

"In that case, I would think you would wish to make use of your Siege Perilous yourself to escape this catastrophe. Why haven't you?"

"I will in good time. I have dispatched all in my family and all of our close friends. I, myself, was loath to leave until I saw whether all hope had indeed fled. Remember, the journey through the Siege portal is one-way. Only a few of my family who have been Guardians have used the Siege themselves, and most of them did so because of grief they could not bear in this world—the death of a beloved wife, for example, or even the death of all his family in a fire in the case of my great-great-grandfather."

"Britain's gone, believe me," McDunn said savagely, jerked into alertness by the sudden rage flooding through him. "Their military went down months ago. They waited too long to rebuild, and they were handicapped by all the enemies of civilization inside this country. My country didn't do much better. Our homegrown fanatics tried to remake our country into their vision of Utopia but really only succeeded in destroying everything they touched.

We may have started recovering sooner than you Brits, but we both ran out of time. It was probably some of those fanatics who nuked our government and commercial centers—who left me and my guys stranded over here."

McDunn's lips thinned, and the grimness of his expression made him look momentarily as lethal and dangerous as he likely had been before he was wounded.

"A good man for a friend," Kaswallon whispered under his breath. "A bad man for an enemy."

McDunn knew his mind had started to wander, and he looked up at the tall man, blinking. "Sorry about running off at the mouth. Morphine's good stuff, but it starts to fuzz you up after a while."

"Do not worry. Now, we have a little time before your Gate opens and you go into the world in which your mind and soul will be at home. It is the world for which you unconsciously yearned even if you knew it not. You may then seek your fortune there."

"Yeah, and bleed to death with a belly wound," McDunn said, the doubt clear in his words even if they were starting to slur.

"I think not, friend McDunn. If the lore is correct, the Siege Perilous sends a man to a new existence, and the ills and ailments of this world do not make the transition with him. Did I not say the Siege is an artifact of the Lord, associated with the search for Christ's cup at the Last Supper?"

"Whatever you say." McDunn had no desire to argue religion at a time like this though he was a faithful attendee at Sunday chapel back in the States. Perhaps he wanted to believe the ravings of this madman, or perhaps his strength to offer any objections was fading.

"Now, as I said, we have to wait until the moon rises before your Gate opens."

"Why wait? Why not now? You said this Siege of yours would make me whole, and I'm bleeding to death as I sit here."

"You shall go when the moon rises, for that is when *your* Gate will open. The right one for you. Then you will believe!"

Kaswallon smiled at him beatifically, and McDunn desperately wanted to trust his smile.

"So, there is a bit of time, and you may take a few things with you—but only what is on your body or which you hold in your hands. Is there something I might find for you outside? But I must be quick. There may still be savages left alive."

"Rifle," McDunn said with difficulty. His mind was becoming clouded from the morphine, and he could feel he was on the verge of unconsciousness. "Working rifle. And some ammo if you can find it." Then the dizziness swept over him, and he felt himself falling into welcome unconsciousness.

He had wanted to ask for his pack, which had been in his fighting hole, because of the valuables in it. His computer tablets, pictures of his parents and his sisters, Jill, Teresa, and Megan. His grandfather in his dress blues when he was sergeant major of the whole blessed Marine Corps. His grandmother, who so loved *Pride and Prejudice*. His graduation picture and one of his high school football team. All he had left of his world. The world that was gone.

But he was the one that was gone. Gone into unconsciousness and into relief from the pain.

When McDunn's head dropped to his chest, Kaswallon was alarmed and feared the wounded man had died unexpectedly. But his concern ebbed as he saw the easy rise and fall of the man's breathing.

He seemed stable sitting on the Siege, with his arms holding him up, so mumbling a quick prayer for this stalwart warrior's welfare, Kaswallon left the cave.

MCDUNN CAME PARTIALLY OUT OF HIS STUPOR WHEN HE FELT HANDS ON him, pulling his arms to the side before a heavy weight settled on his shoulders. Another weight went over one shoulder, and other items were tucked up against his belly. He felt his hands being thrust under straps, which were wrapped around his forearms.

He was grateful when the hands stopped jostling him since every movement caused his belly to hurt again. It appeared the morphine was wearing off. Dimly, he thought he heard voices speaking to each other, but that couldn't be. No one was left but him and this strange guy, Kaswallon, the Guardian of the Siege Perilous he had called himself though McDunn was starting to think of him as the Druid.

Then Kaswallon's voice boomed off the walls of the cave, chanting strange words McDunn couldn't understand in a language he'd never heard. Finally, the words were ended, and a sharp *Craaaacckk* resounded through the cave as though a hammer had hit stone.

"Now!" Kaswallon said, his voice thundering through the cave.

There was an indescribable moment in which the whole universe twisted into a pretzel, coupled with one of wrenching, nauseating fire in his gut. But the pain somehow thinned out, and then it disappeared completely. McDunn felt himself thrust into a weightless, timeless nothingness.

In that moment during which time had no meaning, McDunn was finally overwhelmed by everything he had lost: his family, all his friends from school and the Corps, and most of all, the one whose loss hurt the most because she was the love that might have been. He felt himself falling through nothingness...

"Dancer," he groaned, the pain in his heart worse than the pain in his belly. Then he hit hard, and blackness closed in.

Chapter 1

If a coin comes down heads, that means that the possibility of its coming down tails has collapsed. Until that moment the two possibilities were equal. But on another world, it does come down tails. And when that happens, the two worlds split apart.

— Philip Pullman, *The Golden Compass*

Tuesday, October 10, 1809
Pemberley, Derbyshire

"Sir! Sir! Mr. Darcy!"

Fitzwilliam Darcy had been half-dozing as his coach rumbled along on this still-warm autumn day. He was on the final leg of a journey to his Pemberley estate when, startled from his comfortable doze, he sat bolt upright at the call of his driver and the subsequent hard braking of the coach.

"Yes, Wainwright?" he called, looking over at his sister, Georgiana, and his cousin Colonel Richard Fitzwilliam as the vehicle lurched to a stop. "What is it?"

"Over there, sir! A man!"

"A man? Where?"

"In the grass, sir! To your right! A-lyin' in the grass!"

Darcy felt the coach shake as one of the footmen scrambled down from the back of the coach, and he was not surprised when Brown appeared suddenly at the door.

"I will see what it is, sir," he said in a gravelly voice and started to turn away.

"Wait!" When Brown turned around with a surprised look, Darcy continued. "I want to have a look myself."

He opened the door and jumped lightly to the ground without bothering to lower the entry step. Behind him, he heard his cousin descend in the same manner.

"Stay inside the coach, Georgiana," he called without turning his head. He did not have to look to know she had intended to jump to the ground. Her natural curiosity grew by the day.

"But William!" Georgiana said, beginning to protest. It was clear from her expression that past experience told her the uselessness of doing so when her brother spoke in such a tone of voice. "Oh, very well," she said, settling back on her seat.

"Now, where is this man, Wainwright?" Darcy asked. "I cannot see anyone."

"Over there, sir," his driver said, pointing. "He is just there. Maybe dead. I canna tell."

"I should do this, Mr. Darcy," repeated Brown.

"Or I," Fitzwilliam said, stepping up beside Darcy with his hand on his cavalry saber.

"I want to see for myself," Darcy said. Then, seeing the look of distress on his footman's face, he relented. Brown, after all, did have a secondary duty as an armed guard against the possibility of highwaymen on the road. The threat was admittedly rare in recent years, but it remained.

"Very well, then. We shall all investigate."

"Yes, sir," his footman said reluctantly, touching the pistol he had stuck in his waistband. Darcy was careful to conceal his smile at Brown's protectiveness. The man had never had occasion even to withdraw his firearm from under his coat, but he took his duty seriously.

As he and Fitzwilliam walked in the direction his driver had pointed, Brown followed slightly behind and off to the side. Something was clearly pressing down the long grass of the field.

As they got closer, Darcy realized his driver had been right. There was indeed a man lying in the grass, curled up almost into a ball, but he was attired in a most baffling fashion, which added to the mystery of his presence.

His clothing resembled a military uniform since the trousers and jacket were similar in appearance, but the material itself was like no uniform Darcy had ever seen. It had no constant color, being composed of a mottled conglomeration of browns and tans, but the sharp demarcation of the mottling showed it was intentional and not accidental. The man wore a pack of the same material except its mottling was different in pattern.

In addition, the man's clothing and pack were incredibly dirty and deeply stained with mud. This was puzzling since the roads and fields were dry. There had been no recent rains, yet the man's boots, unlike any Darcy had ever seen, were also covered in the same type of mud.

As the men moved closer, Darcy was shocked to realize many of the stains on what he was increasingly certain was a kind of uniform looked more like blood than dirt or mud. Dried blood. A *lot* of blood.

The reddish-brown stains were down the entire front of his uniform. Adding to the mystery was an unfamiliar helmet on the stranger's head, covered in the same brown and tan cloth as his clothing.

Darcy heard a rustle of cloth and a snapping sound behind him, and he knew Brown had just withdrawn his pistol from his waistband, cocked the hammer, and was no doubt turning the pistol sideways slightly to get a few grains of powder into the priming pan. Darcy felt no inclination to reprove him. The unconscious man's presence was enough to justify a degree of caution, especially when coupled with his complete unfamiliarity and the strangeness of his clothing.

A sense of alarm struck Darcy as he saw the item his footman had seen, and he understood why Brown had drawn his pistol. Under the stranger's left armpit was some kind of leather holster, and protruding from it was what appeared to be the butt of a pistol. The butt was significantly smaller than the pistol in Brown's hands, as well as being quite oddly shaped. Regardless, there was a sleek deadliness about the weapon that convinced him of its danger.

A second shock ran through him when he saw a long object lying in the grass just beyond the stranger's out-flung hand. From its length and similar appearance of precision as the pistol, Darcy was certain the long object was also a weapon of some kind. It bore a superficial resemblance to the muskets and shotguns with which he was familiar, but this musket was too short, had strange protrusions in various places, and did not appear to be made of metal. Everything, including the barrel, was colored the same as the man's pack. Perhaps those colors were paint, but he wondered why a musket would be painted.

Darcy stopped about ten feet away and regarded the stranger. He was deeply tanned but unshaven with several weeks of dark beard. He could see the man's clothing was not only dirty and bloody but also badly worn with numerous tears, especially about the knees and elbows. Some type of bulky vest or harness was strapped about his torso, supporting numerous pouches bulging with unknowable contents. There were also pockets everywhere about his clothing—on the sleeves and down his baggy trousers—all of them bulging like those on his vest. He lay quietly on his side, breathing slowly and deeply, and the large pack strapped to his back looked vaguely like the packs worn by soldiers illustrated in the London newspapers. For the first time, Darcy noticed several canvas bags nearby, and he realized the mottled coloring of the bags had made them almost blend in with the vegetation.

He looked over at Fitzwilliam, but his cousin only shrugged his thick shoulders. His military experience apparently did not provide any more answers than Darcy's civilian knowledge.

But caution seemed advisable. The man might look rough and bedraggled, but he was also large and muscular with broad shoulders and large hands, somewhat resembling Fitzwilliam who was a colonel of dragoons and a rather formidable man in his own right. The two shared the same weathered features acquired by a life spent mostly outdoors.

Unable to bear the mystery any longer, Darcy ignored the voice of caution sounding a warning in his mind and stepped forward to nudge the sole of one of the stranger's boots with his cane. It was only a slight touch, but the results were both startling and violent!

With a rapidity that caused the three men to recoil backward in complete surprise, the stranger seemed to explode up from the ground. With astonishing speed, he rolled abruptly to the side while simultaneously whirling about and half-rising. His head whipped about in a blur, quickly scanning the surroundings before fixing on the group of men in front of him. A *click* sounded as he came to a halt on one knee, and Darcy realized that a strange-looking pistol had somehow appeared in his hands. It must be the pistol from beneath the man's armpit, and it was held in a completely unfamiliar manner, supported by both his hands.

The sight of the pistol caused Darcy to freeze, instantly and completely. The stranger's dark eyes were locked on him with a dangerous fixation, and the sound he had heard was made doubly ominous because of its similarity to the earlier sound of Brown cocking his pistol.

"Brown, do nothing!" Darcy barked the command. He instinctively realized he had made a grave error; the strange pistol was not pointed at him but rather at Brown, and the muzzle, while clearly not as large as the pistols with which he was familiar, seemed even more deadly.

No one moved for a long second or two before the stranger spoke.

"He's with you?"

Darcy gave a jerky nod.

"I haven't fired," the stranger continued, "since the muzzle of your man's blunderbuss isn't exactly pointed at me and his finger isn't on the trigger. Please have him lower the pistol and un-cock the hammer. I don't want to kill anyone over a misunderstanding, but I also don't want to die by mistake either. And I won't warn him again."

"Brown!" Darcy said quickly. "Put the pistol away!"

"Yes, sir," Brown said reluctantly, and Darcy heard the sound of the pistol being uncocked and the subsequent rustle of cloth indicating it was being returned to its place.

"And perhaps, if the big man in the red coat might loosen the death grip he has on that large knife he has partway out of its scabbard, I'll holster my pistol."

Out of the corner of his eye, Darcy saw Fitzwilliam reluctantly lower his saber back into its sheath and uncurl his fingers from the hilt. He felt a bit of amusement at the way the stranger referred to his cousin's beloved saber as a big "knife"—though he was not sure Fitzwilliam shared his amusement.

"Better," the stranger said, standing up. "Much better."

He touched something on the small, black pistol. It made the same snapping sound Darcy had heard previously, and he put it back in the holster and buckled a strap over it. Darcy saw he wore a matching holster with a similar pistol beneath his right armpit, and he also had what might be another rifle over his back under his pack. The weapon was covered by a multi-colored canvas sheath with a long belt-like strap across his chest, holding it in place.

Clever idea, all those belts and straps, thought Darcy in wonder. *It would make sure they stay in place when galloping about a battlefield, but how did he unfasten the strap so quickly when he awoke?*

"I did not mean to startle you," Darcy said, but the stranger waved away his apology.

"And I didn't mean to startle you either, but when I felt something touch my boot…well, where I've been lately, you wake up instantly or you might not wake up at all. It tends to make one *twitchy* when startled."

"Ah yes," Darcy said in confusion. "Twitchy. Interesting word."

The stranger looked at Darcy and gave him a crooked smile. "You have no idea what I'm talking about, do you?"

"I have never been so confused in my life, sir," Darcy answered, and his comment seemed to amuse the stranger further since his smile broadened as he looked about him, taking in the attire of Darcy, Fitzwilliam, and Brown as well as the coach and horses.

The stranger waved at Georgiana, who was standing beside the coach in wide-eyed excitement and curiosity.

"I'm sorry if I startled your passenger. I didn't even know she was there until just now."

"My sister." Darcy glared at her. "I had *suggested* she remain in the coach while we investigated."

"I suppose all of us are completely confused, sir. Me, for example. Not only do I have no idea where I might be, I don't even know *when* this is. It's certainly not where I came from."

Brown stood nearby, and Darcy remembered his father's admonition never to discuss serious matters in front of the staff. Turning to his footman, he said, "Please rejoin the coach and keep a sharp eye out. I think we will be safe enough now."

"Aye, sir," Brown said dutifully, but the tone of his voice made it clear he did not fully agree with his employer. Darcy waited until he had mounted the coach again before turning back to the stranger.

"You do not know where you are?" Darcy asked, his surprise evident.

When the unknown man shook his head, it seemed to make him aware of the helmet on his head. He unsnapped the strap and removed it, revealing a mop of dark hair that had not been barbered in quite some time.

"I'm not at all sure how I came to be here," the stranger said slowly with visible uncertainty. "If it would not be too much of an imposition, might you first tell me *where* I am?"

"You are on my land. This is a meadow on my estate, sir," Darcy answered with a trace of irritation in his voice.

"Ah, so I'm a trespasser. Very serious, sir. Very serious, indeed. But since

I wasn't aware I was trespassing, perhaps you might enlighten me as to just *where* I'm trespassing? I assume your estate's in England?"

Darcy openly smiled at the renewed evidence of humor in the stranger's speech as he had consciously modified his speech to match his own.

Except for the use of those contracted words, Darcy thought. *I know they are becoming more fashionable in these modern times, but still…and that accent of his! It is definitely not one with which I am familiar. Nevertheless, this is an educated man. It shows in his speech.*

"Yes," Darcy said with a nod. "Pemberley is indeed in England. In Derbyshire to be exact."

The man flinched momentarily at this information. "Interesting," he mused. "I thought I would be in Cornwall." He shook his head and continued. "The next item to assuage my curiosity is the date—the year to be more specific."

Darcy wrinkled his brow in confusion, looking at the stranger oddly for a moment before he replied slowly, "It is Wednesday, the tenth of October in the year of our Lord, 1809."

The stranger's eyes grew large at the information. "It's 1809!" he murmured. "I thought the stone—"

Whatever else he meant to say went unsaid, and he shook his head again before standing up straighter.

"I do apologize for appearing in your meadow, sir, but I assure you I'm as surprised to be here as you are to find me. But as an intruder and a trespasser on your land, I really should introduce myself. Edward McDunn. I'm American despite my Scots name. Brevet Major and late Gunnery Sergeant of the United States Marine Corps."

Darcy's eyebrows rose just a bit at this bit of information, but he was not completely surprised. "I had surmised you to be American from the manner of your speech."

"My accent, you mean?"

"Indeed. We both speak the same language, but you clearly hail from elsewhere. If I may hazard a guess, I would say one of the southern of our former colonies."

"South Carolina," McDunn confirmed.

Darcy was still confused. What was an American doing in England, much less in Derbyshire? And lying in a Pemberley meadow, especially at this time?

From what his cousin had told him, bad feelings between Britain and the United States of America still lingered from the *Chesapeake-Leopard* affair back in '07. Fitzwilliam worried that the Royal Navy's insistence on stopping ships flying the American flag and impressing seamen from their crews might eventually cause the two countries to stumble into an active state of hostilities.

Have we not enough enemies, he thought sourly, *with Bonaparte and the rest of his coalition?*

He shook his head at his woolgathering and decided this was not the time to stand on propriety. There was certainly no one to introduce the two of them. "I am pleased to make your acquaintance, Major McDunn...or is it, what did you say, Gunnery Sergeant?"

McDunn smiled wryly. "It's *late* Gunnery Sergeant, sir. That rank, as well as my majority and my place in the Marines are—well, it's long off in time and far away. Very much so."

"I see," Darcy said though he did not see at all. "My name is Fitzwilliam Darcy, and as I said, I own Pemberley. And may I present my cousin Colonel Fitzwilliam of His Majesty's Sixth Regiment of Dragoons."

Darcy's hesitation was due to his decision to include his Christian name as the American had done. It was not usual, but he supposed Americans had different customs.

Both men gave the stranger a quick bow, but both Darcy and his cousin were taken aback by McDunn's reaction. His mouth had dropped open slightly, and he was staring at Darcy as though he had seen a ghost.

FITZWILLIAM DARCY? MCDUNN THOUGHT, SO STAGGERED BY THE MAN'S name that he questioned his sanity.

The name "Pemberley" he had put down as coincidence, but it could not be a coincidence that the man who owned Pemberley in this alternate world also claimed the name of Austen's hero in *Pride and Prejudice*.

What in the seven levels of hell is going on here? Darcy! And Colonel Fitzwilliam! And that has to be Georgiana by the coach! Has that Siege stone sent me to a world of fictional characters? Characters created in the imagination of an unmarried author of old-time novels? But this man, this Darcy, said this is his estate! Pemberley in Derbyshire! I know Kaswallon said there were an infinite number of alternate possible worlds, but still—! This is not bordering on the ridiculous; it is so far beyond such boundaries, it's ludicrous!

Why would this be the world where I belonged? I would have thought it would be fighting Nazis or maybe the Japanese in World War II! At least, in that war, I always thought it would be easy to figure out who were the good guys and who were the bad guys. You didn't have to protect yourself against men who weren't wearing uniforms unless you found out they were spies, in which case you just stood 'em against a wall, shot 'em, and moved on!

His realization put a different complexion on what he could or should tell this man to answer his questions. If Kaswallon's rock had just sent him to an earlier time in his own world—the concept referred to as time travel—he would have worried about changing the future by something he did in the here and now. Not that such a course would be a bad idea, seeing how things turned out! But because *this* world, this world of Pemberley and Darcy, never existed, he did not have to worry about such eventualities. This world was a *fictional* construct, for God's sake! It meant he could tell whatever seemed prudent without worrying about changing the future of the world he came from.

McDunn knew complete honesty would not work. Not only that, but it would be dangerous. If Darcy was who he appeared to be, it placed limits on certain parts of his explanation. The idea of this world being modeled after Austen's England was one he simply couldn't reveal—not just to this man but to *anyone* in this world. *Ever!* He simply couldn't chance being judged insane by telling someone that the world they lived in was similar to a novel he had read in a far-away parallel world!

How could this man ever believe such a fanciful tale? That the world in which he lives ought never to have existed at all, save in the fertile imagination of one Jane Austen who actually did exist? Yet this world is real! It exists! Unless I am off my rocker! I'll have to exercise careful control over my mouth!

McDunn realized he had been thinking for long moments while the other men looked at him with a mixture of surprise and…was that disapproval?

"Sorry," McDunn said. "Somehow, everything that's happened to me hit me all at once. Pleased to meet you, Mr. Darcy, Colonel Fitzwilliam. Very pleased indeed."

McDunn stepped forward and extended his hand.

"Ah yes, I understand. You Americans shake hands," Darcy said, taking the proffered hand, his expression showing his bemusement.

McDunn was careful to control his strength as the two men shook hands. Darcy's handshake was not weak, not at all, but he had not lived as McDunn had for much of his adult life.

However, he was somewhat taken aback when he shook Fitzwilliam's hand. He was used to moderating his own handshake since he was usually much stronger than other men, but he instantly realized that Darcy's cousin was doing the same. In fact, he did not think he had ever before felt a harder grip, and a quick glance at the other man's wrist above his gloved hand revealed a wrist thicker than he'd ever imagined a man of his size might have. Clearly, it was the result of a lifetime's constant use of a sword, and since his left wrist was as large as his right, he must practice with both hands. With a wry thought, he vowed to refrain from a contest of strength with the good colonel!

"But the question remains," Darcy said, his brows furrowed, "if you are an American, how do you come to be on my estate?"

McDunn looked pensive for a few moments, musing over his alternatives while staring intently at Darcy's coach and the two men before him.

Finally, he shrugged somewhat helplessly. "That's a long story, and it's likely to leave you even more confused than you are now. That's if you believe me at all."

Darcy thought for a few moments. "Then, rather than continue this discussion in an open field, Major, perhaps it would be best if we repaired to my home. I hope you will not consider it impolitic when I say you look as though you might welcome a bath. And some clean clothing."

"Far from being impolitic, Mr. Darcy," McDunn said fervently, running his hands over his bearded cheeks, "I cannot think of anything I would appreciate more than to scrub off this dirt and get this fuzz off my face—unless it's to get out of these BDUs."

"BDUs?" Darcy asked in confusion.

"Battle Dress Uniform. It's what we call it," McDunn said rather absently, running his hand over his clothes. He suddenly froze as his fingers found a score of rips in the abdomen of his jacket just below the chest plate of his body armor. A strange look came over his face, and he pressed his hands against his stomach, gingerly at first and then more firmly. He unsnapped several straps before dropping his pack to the ground and laid the canvas-enclosed rifle more carefully beside it. His bulky vest came next, but he made no attempt at delicacy, simply dropping it to the ground with a heavy thump. He felt all over his torn and blood-marked tunic, pressing inward with a look of wonderment on his face and even lifting the bottom edge up to examine an even more heavily stained and rent undergarment.

"Excuse me, sir," he said finally with a rather sheepish look on his face. He had presented a rather strange and comical spectacle by examining himself in front of these proper English gentlemen. "I just suddenly realized—" He left the sentence unfinished.

"Is something wrong?" Colonel Fitzwilliam asked carefully.

"Actually, no—everything's all right. Yet, that's what's wrong since I shouldn't be all right. Before I woke up in your field, I was wounded in battle. I had a belly wound, a bad one—a mortal wound, in fact, since all our medical staff was dead, and their medical supplies were exhausted anyway. Even if our surgeon had survived, which she didn't, poor woman, she couldn't have saved me. You can see from the bloodstains how much blood I lost."

He waved at his clothing and continued. "But now, not only am I *not* mortally wounded, there isn't any tenderness. I wonder if I'll even have scars. And I was wounded in Cornwall, but I woke up in a field in Derbyshire. Very strange, don't you think?"

"Cornwall!" Fitzwilliam said. "I have heard of no violence or unrest in Cornwall."

"It was not *your* Cornwall, sir," McDunn said softly. "Another topic for which I am not sure I have an answer."

"Ah yes," Fitzwilliam said doubtfully.

"You two are really showing remarkable steadiness in the face of such mysterious happenings. I couldn't blame either of you for wondering if this strange man who babbled such nonsense wasn't just a little bit crazy."

Darcy thought over this comment for a minute before looking at his cousin, who slowly shook his head. Then Darcy nodded in agreement.

"Perhaps I ought to think so, Major McDunn, and I freely admit to being both confused and mystified. Yet, neither Richard nor I think you are deranged, possibly because you freely admit to being as confused as we are. In any case, I believe you are telling me what you know and what you believe. I would very much like to hear more of your tale and possibly, if I can, assist you in resolving some of the mysteries you represent."

Very much like the Darcy Austen imagined, McDunn thought. *Fair in his dealing with his peers, respected for his opinions, and judged to be honorable and honest. Damn it! I like this man already whether he's a fictional character or not. And you can't doubt everyone. Sometimes you just have to take a chance on your judgment and trust* someone.

"Fair answer," McDunn said at length, "and a generous one. Very well, I'll respond in kind. I'll tell you my tale, at least as much of it as I know for certain."

Except for the fact that you shouldn't exist! he thought sardonically.

"And I pledge to meet fairness equally and share what I can with you," McDunn said, continuing his thought. "But I have to warn you: I'm quite confused myself about many parts of my story."

A mischievous twinkle came to his eyes. "As an American, I suppose I'm not what you English would consider a gentleman. So I won't mind in the least if you put me up in the stables. After sleeping in a hole in the ground for months, I would find a stable to actually be quite comfortable."

Darcy smiled, and he looked more relaxed. "I believe we can do better than a bed of straw in the stable, Major. And you look to be of similar size to my cousin. Some of the clothing he keeps in his rooms might be suitable for you."

"I do appreciate your hospitality, sir," McDunn said, giving Darcy a quick bow.

"And your generosity, sir," he said, giving Fitzwilliam a bow of his own.

He started to pick up his pack, and Darcy looked back at his coach. "Please help Major McDunn with his…ah, baggage," he called, and two of the three men quickly descended.

McDunn smiled at Darcy's footman when he came up. "I do apologize for threatening to shoot you, Brown. I was a little startled."

"Quite all right, sir," Brown said, returning the smile. "All's well that ends well as my mum used to say. You did give us a fright when you spun about like that."

McDunn picked up the rifle and the canvas-enclosed item he'd had slung under his pack, giving them to Brown before handing the pack and harness with his body armor to the other footman. But when he started to pick up the three canvas bags by their carrying straps, he gave a startled grunt and quickly released them. He knelt and opened one of the bags.

After a single look inside, he settled back on his haunches and whistled. "Well, what do you know?" he said, his question a rhetorical one. Quickly, he looked inside each of the other two bags and whistled again.

"What is it, Major?" Darcy asked, a bit concerned. "Is something wrong?"

"No, sir, nothing's wrong. But it's just one more surprise I'm not sure I can explain," he said, closing the bags. "But it's the nice kind of surprise." He looked up at Darcy and Fitzwilliam. "I'll tell you more when we get to your house. I think we need some privacy for this. Do you think you could place one of these bags inside the coach, Colonel?"

Fitzwilliam gave a nod as he started to pick up one of the multi-colored canvas bags. He gave McDunn a look of surprise as he lifted it and turned toward the coach. McDunn picked up the other two bags, grunting from the effort, and followed the colonel to the coach. Fitzwilliam slid his bag inside under the front seat then accepted each of the other bags and did the same.

Darcy gave a chuckle as he looked fondly at his sister, who shifted uncomfortably in her seat due in equal measure to curiosity and irritation at being excluded from whatever the three men had discussed.

"Georgiana, may I introduce Major Edward McDunn of the American Corps of Marines? Major, my sister, Miss Darcy."

Unable to curtsey, Georgiana contented herself with a nod while McDunn, who had not a clue how one responded in this society, tried his best to mimic the bows Darcy and Fitzwilliam had given him.

"I hope I didn't startle you when your brother woke me up, Miss Darcy," McDunn said, entering the coach at Darcy's gesture.

"Oh no, sir!" the young girl said enthusiastically, her worry for her brother and her cousin evaporating at her brother's introduction. "Your discovery was most exciting! What kept you men in such intense conversation?"

"We will discuss that more a bit later, Georgiana," Darcy said. "The Major expressed an interest in mortgaging his soul to the Devil in return for a bath and a shave."

"And a haircut if it can be managed," the American said, running his hand through his ragged mop of hair with a look of distaste. "As well as a bite to eat if I might further impose on your hospitality. Then we can make a start on answering questions on all sides."

"All ready up here, sir!" Brown called. He and his companion had finished securing McDunn's belongings to the top of the coach.

The driver immediately started the coach in motion, and McDunn pointed to the three canvas bags under the seat where he sat beside Colonel Fitzwilliam.

"I think I ought to keep these within reach," he said. "You'll see why a bit later."

"One might think you had discovered gold in your belongings," Darcy said with a smile. To his surprise, McDunn cocked his head at him with a sober look.

"Keep that thought until we can talk."

Darcy only nodded at this oblique response. It gave him much to think about during the short ride to his home. He could only hope he might soon find at least a few answers to his multitude of questions.

Chapter 2

///

After Vizzini cuts the rope being climbed by the
Dread Pirate Roberts—
Vizzini: *He didn't fall? Inconceivable!*
Inigo Montoya: *You keep using that word. I do not think it means*
what you think it means.

— *The Princess Bride*,
William Goldman, author

\\\

Tuesday, October 10, 1809
Pemberley, Derbyshire

At his first glimpse of Pemberley across the valley, McDunn was greatly impressed despite himself. He had not been at all sure what he was going to see when they reached Darcy's estate since he had no idea how closely the similarities would extend in this world for it and for so many other things. But there was no word to describe Pemberley other than magnificent—in both its size and architecture.

Already, there've been enough similarities to astonish me, he thought. *Even after what Kaswallon said about alternate worlds, to find one resembling a work of fiction seems impossible. An author wouldn't even try to write this stuff! I wish I'd been able to pay more attention to what the priest told me in the cave, but the morphine was hitting me too hard. Still, nothing other than an alternate world makes sense. Nothing! Nevertheless, it's just so...so bizarre!*

Then he had another thought and stifled a smile. *Whatever the explanation might be, it's a whole lot better than being dead! Or being alive when the barbs found me!*

He turned back to find Darcy's eyes on him. "That's a very impressive house, sir, and very attractive. My compliments."

Darcy nodded in acknowledgement, but McDunn thought he could detect a hint of appreciation in his otherwise inscrutable expression.

"He is very proud of it, Major," Georgiana said. "He often tells me how fortunate we are to live there."

"And he even quarters his less wealthy relatives," added Fitzwilliam beside McDunn, who could hear the warmhearted teasing in his tone. "Where else could I get such inexpensive lodging and board while this leg heals? Though it could be worse. At least I am not stuck on half-pay."

"I do wish you would be a bit more circumspect about bringing up family affairs in front of strangers, Richard," Darcy said, his face deadpan.

"Stop it, you two!" Georgiana said, trying to suppress a giggle. "They do this all the time, Major. It is usually in the privacy of the family, however."

"Nonsense, Georgiana," Fitzwilliam said, his teeth flashing in a broad smile. "The major is a military man. He understands completely!"

MCDUNN LOOKED ABOUT HIM WITH INTEREST WHEN HE WAS ESCORTED to a bedroom by one of the male servants. What he had seen since arriving at Pemberley had been quite elegant in his less-than-expert opinion, and this bedroom was no exception. It looked quite comfortable in size and furnishings though it was not nearly as gaudy as he had expected.

"Good evening, sir," came a voice behind him, and he turned to find a tall, thin man in his middle years, dressed similarly to Darcy. "My name is Jennings, and I am Mr. Darcy's personal valet. He asked me to look after you until he can select a suitable valet for you."

McDunn's eyebrows rose at the implication that he was due the hospitality accorded to Darcy's own class. He had rather expected something different, remembering the class-consciousness inherent in Austen's works.

"That is very gracious of Mr. Darcy," he said in response.

"Mr. Darcy is a very thoughtful employer, sir," Jennings said. He looked him up and down before continuing. "I suspect you will want to bathe first before getting shaved. May I ask whether those stains on your clothing are blood?"

"They are," McDunn said, looking down and fingering the holes in his BDU tunic again. "And they're kind of ripped up and worn."

"I shall inform the staff, sir. They can usually remove such stains as well as mend the…uh, tears. I take it the clothing is meaningful, and you do not wish to dispose of it."

"I'd prefer not to if it can be helped. And there's some other clothing in my pack over there. But I need to warn you: we were in the field for six months without a break. Everything may be infested with critters as well as dirt."

"I understand, sir. It can be managed. Now, if you would simply leave your washable items in the dressing room, the hot water should be brought up directly."

As McDunn sat in the barbering chair while Jennings clipped his hair, it felt exceedingly strange to be waited on. He had never known anything like it. But it had felt so wonderful to stand in the copper tub, lathering time after time while a servant poured buckets of blessedly clean, hot water over him to rinse off the suds and dirt. When most of the grime was gone, the calf-deep water in the tub was filthy with dirt, powder smoke, and other unnamed contaminants. Some of the dirt was ground so deeply into his skin, especially on his hands and knuckles, that it would take more than one bath to get rid of it.

"I believe you should step out of the bathtub so it can be emptied, sir," Jennings had said judiciously. "Then you can do one final lathering and rinse with new water."

Well washed for the first time in months, McDunn felt gratifyingly fresh even though it had been difficult to fit his frame in the copper bathtub when he sat down to wash his head and hair. And Darcy's valet seemed to know what he was doing with his scissors though it had taken some convincing to make him understand McDunn really did want his hair as short as he described.

"But it is not at all fashionable, sir," Jennings said, looking quite distressed. "Gentlemen wear their hair short but not nearly as short as you wish."

"Ah, but remember: I'm an American, Jennings."

That seemed, for the first time, to alter the man's calm expression, and his lips twitched upward the slightest bit.

"As you say, sir," he replied and proceeded with the haircut.

THE TWO DARCY SIBLINGS AND THEIR COUSIN TURNED AS THE BUTLER announced, "Major McDunn, sir."

"Thank you, Hamilton. Please show him in."

The enigmatic man strode in, looking taller and even larger than he had on their first meeting. At the same time, his martial erectness and almost dangerous appearance had been softened by the fashionable attire Colonel Fitzwilliam had loaned him.

McDunn laughed softly at the looks on his hosts' faces and did a slow turn, showing that the borrowed clothing fit him tolerably well. Since he was taller than the colonel, his trousers showed evidence of hasty tailoring. But his shoulders and chest were comparable in size to Colonel Fitzwilliam's, so his shirt and frock coat fit well. In fact, except for his moustache and his close-cropped hair, he looked as though he might be just another visitor to Pemberley and nothing at all like the mysterious stranger they had found lying in the meadow.

"I had to keep my boots, though one of your people did an excellent job of cleaning them up," McDunn said. "My feet are larger than your cousin's. And I would still be struggling to dress myself if you hadn't provided the assistance of your valet, for which I thank you, Mr. Darcy. It was difficult enough trying to figure out the fastenings, and I won't even mention my mystification at watching Jennings tie this thing he called a cravat. But I understand your surprise at my appearance. I was a bit stunned when I took a look in the mirror. It was almost as though I belonged here."

"Well, I think you look very handsome, Major," Georgiana said.

"Especially in those fine clothes," Fitzwilliam said with a teasing smile.

"Except for the major's hair and moustache, of course." Darcy said, smiling. "But please, have a seat. I know you must be hungry."

"I thought beards and long hair were in fashion about now. And yes, I am famished."

"Not so," Darcy said, as he held the chair for Georgiana. "Beards and long hair started disappearing about ten or twelve years ago. Most men of my age are clean shaven and favor shorter, more natural hair."

McDunn grinned and took the seat Darcy indicated at the small, square table. He ran his hand appreciatively over the short stubble of hair on his head. Unfashionable or not, he had wanted his hair short again. He was used to it after spending years as a marine. He had even kept up the same standard of grooming when he attended college as had so many other returned veterans.

At first, he had been rather anxious to have another person shave him. McDunn had always done it himself just as everyone did in the Corps, and he hated having such a wickedly sharp straight razor in the hands of a stranger. But being shaved by Darcy's valet turned out to be quite pleasant. In fact, the sharp razor had made short work of his several weeks of beard, guided by a hand much more expert than his own. The man was a magician with his tools and made no argument about his moustache, merely trimming it as McDunn desired.

"It's what I'm used to as a marine—*my* marines, that is, not yours. It's short by tradition these days—*my* days—though it originally was implemented to curtail pests. That problem went away some time back, but short hair remained."

"I believe that is one of a thousand questions I might wish to ask," Darcy said. "But I think we ought to postpone all our questions until after we dine." He glanced almost imperceptibly at the servants bringing in the dishes, and McDunn nodded in understanding.

During the meal, McDunn watched the others closely to pick up what he could of the etiquette of the day.

Mom would be beside herself with glee if she could see me having to observe proper table manners, he thought. But his contemplation was tinged with the same melancholy he always tried to suppress when thinking of his murdered family. It had been four and a half months since the Memorial Day Massacre, but it was only now that he might be able to start dealing with all he had lost. Before this, the Expeditionary Force had their hands full with fanatical opponents who seemed to care nothing for their own lives if they could take one or more Americans with them into darkness.

McDunn rigidly forced himself to dismiss these morbid thoughts and turned his attention to Darcy's sister. She was more lively and curious than he would have expected from Austen's portrayal, but perhaps she might turn meek at barely being saved from an elopement by her brother's eleventh-hour rescue.

Good old Jane and her many, "nick of time" coincidences! he thought. *I couldn't help noticing that much, though I'm no Regency scholar, no matter what Dancer thinks.*

His thoughts came to a screeching halt by another savage stab of grief, this one piercing him particularly deeply when an image sprang into his consciousness of Dancer's lithe, graceful body lying dead and twisted on an unknown hillside.

Everyone, he thought bleakly. *Everyone I ever knew, as well as the country I served, is gone.*

He forced himself to shove his grief into a corner until he had some time for solitary contemplation and, instead, fixed his mind on Jane Austen.

Maybe I'm being a bit harsh on good old Jane because I really enjoyed her books. I've read them many times over the years though not since heading off to the university. But I made sure I had e-copies on my tablet before we came over here.

But how long can my tablet last, even if it re-charges from sunlight? There sure won't be any replacing it when it croaks! I'd better get busy backing it up to my other two tablets and use them instead. My personal tablet will probably last far longer that way. It was made to be really rugged, after all, even if it's a civilian model, and I know it cost Mom and Dad too much. But I couldn't refuse the gift! They were so glad I made it home from the Marines and was heading off to the university.

His attention was drawn back to Darcy's sister, who was having fun teasing her much older brother and cousin.

What should I do if I see any of Miss Austen's crucial coincidences? Should I make sure Georgiana isn't ruined by George Wickham? Or should I simply stand back and allow events to occur?

After all, he thought, *everything turned out for the best, even though most everyone—Darcy, Elizabeth, Jane, even Georgiana—had to endure a considerable amount of—what's the word? Yeah, angst. I remember one girl at my high school found out I had read* Pride and Prejudice, *and she made the interesting point that one of the biggest reasons for the enduring popularity of the book was angst. "It was the angst that made Darcy and Elizabeth's love deep enough to bridge the social gap separating them," she'd said.*

So it might be better if I just observe. I'd probably just make things worse if I tried to stick my oar in anyway. I may be worrying for nothing since the events in this world might not follow Austen's storyline at all. And there's no guarantee I'd even have a chance to see anything significant from the novel. Darcy might put me off his land as a lunatic after hearing even a sanitized version of how I got here!

Nevertheless, these people are real, living, flesh-and-blood persons with all the foibles and inconsistencies that go with it. They aren't puppets dancing to the tune of an author lost in an endless variety of possible worlds. They could be hurt.

None of what he had seen thus far, other than the similarity of certain names, had been mentioned in Austen's novel, which left unanswered the question of why the Siege Perilous had sent him to this world. Because of his own religious beliefs, McDunn was convinced the Siege Perilous could only exist as an artifact of divine inspiration. Nothing else made sense to him, especially if one rejected, as he did, the premise of the universe simply being a cosmic accident. He had always believed in a universe created by a divine Creator, but now he wondered why the Lord who created a universe of suns and planets might have decided an infinity of parallel universes was needed to make his Creation complete.

Talk about twisting my mind into pretzels and getting sucked into areas of thought with no way to reach a conclusion! he thought before a more mundane question occurred to him. *Is there a Jane Austen alive in this world of her creation? If so, she surely wouldn't be writing and publishing anything like P&P, would she? Talk about inconceivable!*

AT LENGTH THE MEAL WAS COMPLETE, THOUGH WITH LITTLE CONVERSA-tion given Darcy's unspoken decree that serious subjects should be held in abeyance. Actually, that was quite agreeable to McDunn since it allowed him to concentrate on eating, which quickly became a near full-time occupation diverted only slightly by the many questions running through his mind. He had heard English food described as bland and relatively simple, but the fare at Darcy's table, even though centered on meat and potatoes, was exactly what he wanted.

And needed. The regiment had been on half-rations for a couple of months before the last battle. All their provisions were long gone, and they'd barely been able to purchase enough to keep the regiment going. It wasn't that the populace was unwilling, even though they were terribly submissive and lacking in any sort of fighting spirit, but food supplies were dangerously short, and winter was coming. All the disasters had resurrected an adversity that had almost disappeared in modern times: famine.

At length, Darcy said, "It appears you approve of the efforts of our cook, Major McDunn." His face was composed, but McDunn was pretty sure he was being teased. After all, he had eaten an amazing amount of food!

"It was quite excellent, sir," he said, "and I was even hungrier than I'd realized. But I do apologize for extending the meal for everyone else."

Darcy nodded in agreement, but he now showed the ghost of a smile, confirming McDunn's guess at being teased. McDunn also saw something else—the mingling of curiosity and determination on Miss Darcy's face.

That girl is going to want some answers to her questions, he thought. *This isn't Austen's shy, submissive young lady, at least not now, though perhaps Ramsgate might shatter her confidence. If we don't include her in our after-dinner discussions, she's going to start seeking some answers on her own—maybe listening at keyholes. I'd best ask Darcy if she can be relied on to keep confidences. I don't want to be fitted into one of those shirts with the long sleeves and buckles. Uh, that's if straitjackets have been invented. I could check the history database on my tablet.*

His last thought caused him to wonder whether his twenty-first century electronics would work in this universe. Hopefully so, but it needed to be checked. In any event, he would try to bring up the query about Miss Darcy before the question-and-answer session started.

Chapter 3

//

Be not astonished at new ideas; for it is well known to you that a thing does not therefore cease to be true because it is not accepted by many.

— Baruch Spinoza, Dutch philosopher,
exponent of Rationalism

\\

Tuesday, October 10, 1809
Pemberley, Derbyshire

After dinner, Darcy led the way to his comfortable study, but before anyone else could speak, Fitzwilliam said, "Before we get started, Darcy, have you considered whether Georgiana should remain? She is but thirteen, after all."

"I would like to see you try to send me to my room with a nanny to tuck me into bed, Richard!" Georgiana said furiously.

"Hush, sweetling," Darcy said soothingly. "Richard was only trying to do his duty as one of your guardians. We would be failing in our responsibility if we did not at least consider whether we ought to put you into a situation with unknown dangers."

"But—"

Darcy held up his hand. "Please be patient, Georgiana. I can see Major McDunn wishes to say something."

McDunn picked his words carefully. "I realize I have no part in deciding this matter, but I thought I ought to mention that I have—or rather, *had*—three very inquisitive sisters of my own. I think it's likely Miss Darcy will have to learn how I came to be here sometime, so perhaps now would be better. The question of whether I'm a lunatic and should be confined to Bedlam will have to be answered. I don't think there's any danger to anyone but me, so my thought is, if she can keep a confidence, you might consider swearing her to secrecy now rather than keeping her in the dark."

"Although I raised the topic, I find myself inclined to agree with the major," Fitzwilliam said, looking at Darcy. "It might be best to take his suggestion and include Georgiana."

After a moment's reflection, Darcy reluctantly nodded. "I trust you understand the seriousness of these matters, Georgiana. Everything we discuss tonight has to be considered a family secret between us and Major McDunn."

"I understand, William," she said in a voice much smaller than she had used previously.

Darcy nodded and said to McDunn, "With that settled, might I offer you something to drink, Major? Wine or brandy? Perhaps ale?"

McDunn frowned slightly. "I'm not too familiar with wine or brandy. Actually, I have no idea what types of spirits are even available."

"I have a number of different types of wine, though French wines are scarce these days and only available from smugglers."

"The war, you see, Major," Fitzwilliam said.

"Ah! That explains it!" McDunn said wryly.

"But, though the coast of France is *supposed* to be completely blockaded by our navy," Darcy replied with equal dryness, "it somehow seems most smugglers find their way through. So, French wines are scarce but still available. For something stronger, there is brandy, and though the French brandies also are smuggled, I have a number of bottles."

"Do you have any Scotch?" Seeing the confused look on the faces of both cousins, McDunn explained. "You might call it Scotch whiskey rather than simply Scotch."

Darcy nodded his head. "I see. I have a bottle of whisky distilled in Scotland that may be the drink of which you are speaking. It is almost full. I sampled it once but found it too harsh for my taste."

"Well, it sounds like it's worth a try. Thank you."

"Just to assuage your curiosity," Darcy said, locating the bottle in question and holding it up, "this bottle was smuggled out of Scotland. It is a little misshapen. I think the size and shape of each bottle depends on the power of the glassblower's lungs. In any case, all whiskey available in England is smuggled from either Scotland or Ireland. The taxes are so high, there is no legal trade in whisky."

"Interesting," McDunn said, accepting the glass of dark-colored liquid while Darcy and Fitzwilliam selected brandy and Georgiana contented herself with a glass of watered wine. After a moment's somber introspection, McDunn held up his glass.

"If I may, I would like to propose a toast. It comes from my world. On occasions when we raised a glass together, my comrades and I would toast friends who were no longer with us. Thus, I give you, gentlemen and Miss Darcy—absent friends."

"To absent friends," Darcy replied though he looked somewhat confused.

"Absent friends," echoed Fitzwilliam with more understanding though his eyes seemed focused on something far away. Georgiana said nothing but took a small sip of her wine.

McDunn tasted the dark liquid and closed his eyes as the fiery stuff burned its way down his throat and warmed his stomach.

"Oh my, that *is* raw, just as you said. But after a long abstinence, it tastes mighty good. It's certainly much better than no whiskey at all, even if it's not like the Scotch I'm used to."

McDunn put his glass down after a single sip, and his eyes met those of the other three in turn. He had no intention of imbibing a full glass of courage. This conversation would be difficult enough without endangering its success with a strange beverage of unknown potency.

"I promised to be forthright about how I came to be in your meadow, and I intend to do so," McDunn said. "But I'll warn you all that what I have to say will be exceedingly strange to your ears. Almost inconceivable, in fact. I won't take it amiss if you have difficulty accepting the truth of my words. I wouldn't even try to explain if I couldn't provide certain pieces of what I hope will be incontrovertible evidence to bolster my account."

He paused for another sip of Scotch—a small one—before continuing. "I'll keep what I'm going to say tonight as simple as possible. We can discuss the details later if you don't decide to bundle me off directly to Bedlam.

"So, let's start with what we do know. You discovered me on your property, a stranger with an even stranger appearance, and you likely expect my story will also be strange. I can guarantee you that. Many parts of my story will be difficult to reconcile with what you know about the world—your world of Great Britain today. Clearly, I come from somewhere else. And…well, there's no other way to say this than to just say it. I come from another time than yours." He looked directly at the men. "I'm sure you thought it odd when I asked you the date."

It was a statement of fact, but McDunn waited for the two men's nod before continuing.

"Then I'll start by telling you of my time, the time I come from—the future. I was wounded while a member of a United States military force sent to repel an invasion of your country in the year of our Lord 2045."

McDunn leaned forward, looking at each of the three intently before he said softly, "More than two hundred years in your future."

McDunn thought Darcy did an admirable job of controlling his expression, but his eyes did widen slightly and his eyebrows twitched. Fitzwilliam was not as successful at disguise, and his expression was frankly incredulous. Georgiana simply nodded, perhaps because she had not lived as long as the others and had not developed the skepticism that might make her instantly dismiss his words. In any event, none of them jumped up to exclaim they were being lied to, so McDunn continued.

"As partial evidence that I'm not blatantly fabricating my facts, let me first show you these as part of the evidence I mentioned just a while ago."

He reached into one of the interior pockets of his frock coat, extracted a number of coins, and laid them on Darcy's desk. All three family members leaned forward to get a better look.

"These are some gold coins our regiment was given before we were sent to the England of our time," McDunn said. "They were meant to be used in case of emergencies, such as buying supplies when our own ran out. These are called Krugerrands, and they were coined in the country of South Africa, which lies at the tip of the African continent."

When the three others looked at him blankly, McDunn said, "The country doesn't exist at the moment and won't for a while."

"Actually, I think you refer to what we call the Cape of Good Hope, which we annexed some years ago to keep it out of French hands," Fitzwilliam said.

"It was an independent country in my day, and the Krugerrand was the most popular gold coin in the world. Everyone accepted it, no matter what type of currency or coinage they used."

Which made it the obvious choice to take with us since we already knew Britain was even more chaotic than the US, he thought.

"Note the date of minting," he said, indicating the coin Darcy was examining, and Darcy gave a visible start of surprise.

"It says 2039," Darcy said with wonder in his voice as he passed the coin to Fitzwilliam. "And it has the name you mentioned—Krugerrand."

"Here are some coins and some paper currency we used in my time and in my country," he said, taking money from another pocket and placing everything on the desk. "You can see the dates on the coins as well as the dates on the paper money showing when they were printed."

While Georgiana was still examining the currency intently, McDunn reached inside his frock coat and withdrew his pistol from his waistband, and keeping the muzzle pointed away from everyone, carefully laid it on the desk. Both Darcy and Fitzwilliam looked at it with even greater interest than they had the coins and bills.

"This is a Hekkler-Koch-Colt semi-automatic pistol, caliber 13 millimeters, with an internal magazine holding nineteen cartridges," McDunn intoned in the monotone of an oration repeated innumerable times. He hit the magazine release and caught it as it dropped free, handing it to Fitzwilliam. He then worked the slide, letting the long, fat cartridge fall onto the desk before handing it to Georgiana and handing the newly unloaded pistol to Darcy. Fitzwilliam stood on one side of Darcy to look more closely while Georgiana did the same on the other side.

"Since I normally carry my pistol with a round in the chamber and with nineteen in the magazine, I can fire twenty rounds as fast as I pull the trigger. Then I can eject the magazine as I just did, load another with nineteen rounds, and fire nineteen more times. I can repeat this until I run out of ammo. It's a powerful pistol, and it kicks like a mule. It's no fun whatsoever to fire, but it's guaranteed to knock an enemy combatant off his feet and put a hole as big as your fist through him. It'll even punch through the kind of body armor I was wearing in my harness. It was a gift from my parents at the recommendation of my grandpa during my enlistment. That was, what?—yeah, seven years ago. He wanted me to have some serious protection if I had to use it. And I bought another when I was called back into the Corps before being sent over to England."

The eyes of all three of the Darcy family had grown wider during his brisk, matter-of-fact explanation.

Darcy looked at the black pistol in his hand in wonder. "What you have said is almost unimaginable, yet I have the evidence of these coins and this almost magical pistol in my hands. I have never seen anything like it."

"There *is* nothing like it, Darcy, nothing at all," Fitzwilliam said. "I would dearly love to see you demonstrate your pistol, Major. Not that I disbelieve you, for I do not. What you have shown us is indeed, in the words you used, incontrovertible evidence. It is just that, as a soldier, as a cavalryman, such a pistol in battle would be unbelievably useful, and I would dearly like to see it fired—and to fire it myself if it might be possible."

"I believe it can be arranged," McDunn said with an understanding smile. As military men, they had the same affinity for weapons that seemed to puzzle civilians, but he and Fitzwilliam understood each other.

"We need to conserve my meager supply of ammunition, so any test firings will be short."

Darcy gave a nod of acknowledgement, and McDunn continued. "I also have my two rifles upstairs as well as a number of other items in my pack you'll find just as strange and, as you say, *magical*. In fact, it's interesting you chose that specific word, Mr. Darcy. I remember reading one of our... ah, speculative fiction writers who made the statement that any sufficiently advanced technology will seem like magic when shown to an indigenous native. The steam engines of your Mr. Watt, newly invented as they are, as well as your military cannon and muskets, would be just as magical if demonstrated to Julius Caesar. I assure you the items I'm speaking of are in common use in my time and aren't reserved for some kind of upper class or priesthood."

"I believe you, Major," Darcy said. "Any trouble I am having in accepting what you have related is only because it is so new. I assure you, I do not doubt either your veracity or your sanity. Who could with such examples as these?"

"So, with that out of the way, let me begin my story. I was born in the state of South Carolina in the year 2022. My parents were schoolteachers in Beaufort, and my earliest memories were of intense social turmoil and economic hard times. Our country had been basically hijacked from the legitimate government by a political faction that hated our Constitution, our economic system, and much of our population. Once they were firmly established in power, they attempted to institute a complete redesign of our country along radical, extremist lines into their vision of political utopia. Of course, it didn't work, and as the economy crashed, the population grew more and more rebellious. Finally, the citizens of the country had had a gutful. There was a near rebellion and the subsequent election of a new president and a new Congress that set out to try to unravel the unbelievable clusterfu—"

McDunn stopped suddenly and looked at Georgiana in embarrassment. "I apologize, Miss Darcy, but the language of marines in my day was laced with profanity, and as I said, I'm no gentleman. Anyway, everything in my country was truly messed up, and the new government set about trying to fix what was broken. The process was only partway complete when a disastrous war broke out in the area I believe you refer to as Judea and Egypt. It started with…"

"AND THIS STONE, THIS SIEGE PERILOUS, IS SUPPOSED TO SEND A MAN TO the world where his mind and soul are intended?" Darcy asked.

"That's one of those areas where I hate to speculate, but it's what the man Kaswallon told me, and now I find myself in your world. Those are simple facts. Whether this Siege Perilous was actually a seat at Arthur's Round Table or a man named Arthur Pendragon even existed are questions I can't answer. But what else makes any sense? I was mortally wounded, and today I woke up in your meadow with a torn and bloody uniform and unmarked skin. In fact, I'm not even certain the Siege sends a man to the world he's meant for. I can't remember having any particular interest in the Britain of your time other than some casual reading. Considering my background as a marine, I would have thought I'd be sent to fight in some kind of war, like the Civil War or World War II. I had an interest in history, and I read about those events in my grandfather's books."

"Civil War? Do you mean the Wars of the Three Kingdoms? Cromwell and the Parliamentarians against the Royalists? I thought you knew little of English history."

"Actually, I may have been a little imprecise when I said I didn't have a particular interest in your England," McDunn said. "I actually was interested in the Napoleonic Wars, but my reading focused on the battles on the continent and at sea rather than England itself. I was speaking of the *American* Civil War. It won't take place until the years 1861 to 1865 to be specific, and it was primarily fought over slavery."

"Ah. We ended slavery in England a few years ago, thank goodness."

"Thank goodness indeed since the American Civil War was really a vicious war, as all civil wars are. We had more than six hundred thousand dead before it was over."

"So many?" Darcy said, looking shocked to his core. "And you thought that was the world where you might belong?"

"Who knows? As I said, much of what's happened to me is as mysterious to me as it is to you."

It looks like treating my appearance here as though it were simple time travel is the best choice, McDunn thought. *The two-century jump is true, and it explains everything completely without trying to explain the fanciful concept of a world where fictional characters live and breathe. I still wonder if the rest of Austen's cast of characters are here and will make their appearance.*

"There's one additional point I want to reemphasize, and that's the impossibility of explaining how I came here as some type of magic or sorcery. I'm an engineer. I simply do not believe in magic. But I am also a life-long Christian, and I'm convinced that any inexplicable events in the real world are either the working of advanced technology, as I explained earlier, or of Divine influence. Divine work is how the priest, Kaswallon, explained the working of the Siege. I may have been a bit fogged out by the morphine I took for my pain, but I clearly remember him explicitly saying that the Siege was the work of the Divinity—a tool of God. It was a relic from the time of Arthur Pendragon when all of Camelot had been Christian in belief as inherited from the Romans who had colonized and then abandoned Britain. Remember, many of the Roman legionnaires took their retirement in Britain rather than return to the Empire. They considered Roman Britain their home, and their descendants were to be found among the knights and soldiers of Arthur."

McDunn paused and then said forcefully, "It's the only thing that can explain the unexplainable."

He paused again, looking at each of the three who stared at him silently. "I think I've given you enough information to overwhelm you. I know it is since it's overwhelming to me, and I lived through it! And since I also know intellectual jolts this staggering take some time to digest, I think it would be best to leave these matters as they are for the moment and let you think over what I've told you. We can pick up the conversation later, and we might even have a shooting demonstration tomorrow."

"Please!" Fitzwilliam said eagerly, returning McDunn's pistol along with the magazine and the loose cartridge.

"I have other things to show you that will also be interesting—and explanatory."

Perhaps emboldened by being involved in such an adult conversation, Georgiana turned to McDunn. "Does your name imply your family came from Scotland, Major?"

"I have no idea, Miss Darcy. No one in my family talked much about where we came from. When Kaswallon said I was of Cornish descent, all I really knew was something my grandmother once said about her and my grandfather being Cornish. But that's all I know. Ancestry wasn't of much interest in my family. My personal opinion is my ancestors got out of Europe just a hop, skip, and jump ahead of the authorities and the gallows."

Georgiana giggled again. "Oh, I see you enjoy a good jest, Major!"

"Well, we do know where Major McDunn hails from, Georgiana," Darcy said, his face deadpan. "Though our accents are similar, I detect the characteristics of his southern climes in the speech of our formerly colonial cousin."

"Do not make sport of your guest, William," Georgiana said in McDunn's defense. "I think his accent is most charming."

"You have to be patient while waiting for a South Carolinian to finish his sentences, sir," McDunn said, giving Darcy a grin. "Yes, I know that's what the folks up north say of us, but I'm used to it. I take no offence at your brother making sport. At least he has a sense of humor—even if it is a common one."

Georgiana laughed aloud and clapped her hands. "At last, a friend as quick-witted as you, brother! He will be a good companion for both of you! You, William, are used to being much more intelligent than your usual friends. And you, Richard, are used to intimidating others because you are so big and broad. But you cannot overawe the major!"

Fitzwilliam looked up from his intent examination of McDunn's pistol while Darcy only smiled at his sister's teasing. "It is probably time for you to retire, Georgiana. We will talk to the major tomorrow afternoon, I think."

Georgiana clearly didn't wish to go, but Darcy smiled at her gently. "Richard and I are just going to have another brandy before we go upstairs ourselves."

"Oh, very well," she agreed reluctantly.

"And with your permission, I'll accompany her since I'm looking forward to a night's sleep in a bed rather than a hole in the ground," McDunn said. "However, if I may, I'd like a refill of your scotch whiskey before I go."

Darcy was quick to agree, and as his sister and McDunn left the room, Georgiana continued asking him questions. Darcy and Fitzwilliam looked at each other and smiled before refilling their glasses.

When McDunn finally managed to convince Georgiana to allow him to seek his own room, he found Jennings waiting as though some signal had announced his coming. He allowed his temporary valet to assist him in undressing and putting on the knee-length nightshirt that appeared to be fashionable bedtime attire for gentlemen. McDunn thought it scratchy and uncomfortable, but he said nothing until after Jennings informed him to ring when he arose in the morning and departed.

McDunn immediately removed the uncomfortable garment and sat down with his glass to do some thinking. The first thing he did was to retrieve the three tablets from his pack and open them. He still had no idea how his pack had come to be on his shoulders, but he was extremely happy it arrived with him.

Perhaps Kaswallon really is a magician, he thought as he opened his enlisted-issue military tablet and powered it up. It had been months since he'd even had the thing out of his pack, and he was a little worried whether it had enough battery charge to start up. He breathed a sigh of relief as it finished going through its brief startup-check and came to life. He quickly powered it down and verified the other tablets were equally functional before picking up his glass of what passed for Scotch.

As fantastic as all this is, McDunn thought, *I'm unbelievably lucky to be alive and well. And even if this world is some kind of clone derived from Austen, I'm even luckier to find myself rescued by Darcy and his cousin—especially since Darcy has turned out to be even more intelligent and open-minded than Austen portrayed him.*

Most people wouldn't have listened to me no matter what bona fides I was able to present. They'd have simply dug in their heels and reacted with their emotions rather than their intelligence. I'm unbelievably fortunate that Darcy granted me—provisionally at least—a status more or less equivalent to that of a gentleman. Adjusting to this class-conscious society is going to take time and flexibility on my part, however.

He remembered Austen's description of Darcy's obtuseness with respect to Elizabeth Bennet—from not realizing how he had offended her to his disastrous proposal, driven by his wildly mistaken belief that she had discerned his interest and was waiting for him to express it openly.

Yet, the Darcy I met today made a rather quick decision to trust me, at least enough to listen to me, which gave me the opportunity to show him evidence to back up my story. I have no idea how things are going to turn out, but whatever happens, things should be both more interesting as well as more pleasant. At least nobody's shooting at me. That's gotta be worth something!

Chapter 4

The next time you check your moves in the mirror and reflect on how special you are, consider that somewhere in this universe or in another parallel universe, your double might be doing the same. This would be the ultimate Copernican Revolution. Not only are we not special, we could be infinitely ordinary.

—Seth Shostak, American astronomer

Wednesday, October 11, 1809
Pemberley, Derbyshire

When Darcy came down to the breakfast room the following morning, he found McDunn and Fitzwilliam drinking coffee while Georgiana had just begun her meal. McDunn started to rise, but Darcy waved him back to his seat.

"Despite our manners being different than in your country," Darcy said mildly, "it is not necessary to rise when your host comes down for a simple family breakfast. Look at Richard, for example."

"It is this leg, you see," Fitzwilliam said, slapping his right thigh.

"I thought it was your other leg that needed healing!" Georgiana said.

"That too," Fitzwilliam said, raising his cup. "The cavalry is quite dangerous, you know."

Georgiana could not restrain a smile at her cousin's usual imperturbability before she turned to her brother. "Perhaps the major is just being cautious. At school, they are very strict about proper manners at all times, even in informal family situations."

Darcy gave a sniff of derision as he sat down. "I am beginning to wonder about that school. Too fashionable," he said, and Georgiana smiled again as she resumed eating.

"I hope standards of dress might be relaxed for unexpected visitors," McDunn said, gesturing at his newly washed and mended marine battledress. "My wardrobe is a bit limited at the moment, especially since I preferred to dress myself this morning—though I did allow Jennings to wield his razor again. He's a wizard with his blade."

"Major McDunn has told me about his home and how different things are there," Georgiana said. "Did you know that women's fashions are quite different in his country? He would not describe them in detail, but he said I would find them quite scandalous!"

Darcy looked at his guest quizzically, and McDunn shrugged. "We didn't discuss anything significant and nothing at all when the servants were present. Your sister and the colonel both made sure of that."

Darcy gave a nod at hearing this. "Our staff are faithful and very loyal, but servants do talk among themselves. Many families ignore their presence during private discussions and then wonder how scandal comes to embroil them."

"And you would not believe the size of the breakfast Major McDunn ate, William!" Georgiana said. "Richard said it was more than twice the size of his, and the major even had more!"

"Even after last night's dinner, I was simply ravenous," McDunn said in explanation. "Your cook is excellent, as is your coffee. I haven't had coffee—real coffee—for months."

Georgiana lowered her face toward her plate to keep her raging curiosity from showing. She had so many questions! And most of them could not be discussed at the breakfast table. She had to be patient, but it was difficult. She was wildly curious about this extraordinary stranger and his breathtaking tale. And he had promised further explanations that she was sure would lead to even more thrilling accounts!

She glanced at her brother as she ate, surprised but pleased at his ease with the mysterious major. Georgiana was used to her brother's reserve with people outside the family, but he seemed to have set it aside on this occasion for reasons she could not discern. Perhaps it was something only men could know, and if so, she wondered whether even *they* could explain it.

Her mind kept returning to the vague references the major had made. *Just what does he mean about the scandalous nature of women's fashions?* she thought. *I would definitely like to know more.*

Since her eyes were lowered, Georgiana had no idea that the men read her barely suppressed inquisitiveness with the knowledgeable eyes of older brothers and exchanged smiles of amused tolerance at the foibles of female siblings.

"...AFTERWARDS, RICHARD AND I SHALL BE TAKING A RIDE," DARCY SAID in the privacy of his study. "Would you care to join us?"

McDunn looked blankly at him for a brief moment before comprehension bloomed in his eyes. "On a horse, you mean," he said, and Darcy gave a nod.

"Sorry, but you caught me by surprise," McDunn said. "It's just that there were very few horses in my home town, and they cost a fortune to maintain. So, I've never even been on a horse, much less learned how to ride."

"I would be happy to provide instruction," Fitzwilliam said quickly. "You did mention there were many things you need to learn. Riding is certainly one of the first things, I would think."

"If I may, could I reserve that for another day, Colonel? What I really want is to take a nice, long run and work some of the kinks out of my muscles."

"A run?" Darcy asked blankly. His sister, who had been invited to join them, was equally confused.

"Yeah, about three miles or so if I'm not too out of shape to make it that far."

He smiled at the surprised looks he saw. "That's another difference between my military and yours. Physical training was part of life in the Corps. We learned through bitter experience that if we had to go against a really tough enemy, we had to be just as tough. And that meant we trained, trained, trained."

"That sounds like Richard describing a day in camp," Georgiana said with dawning comprehension. "The officers and men train all day, most of it on horseback."

McDunn nodded, looking at Fitzwilliam. "That sounds about right. Different than how we did it, but the same rationale. If you don't work hard, you die easily."

Seeing the uncomfortable looks on the faces of Darcy and Georgiana, he shrugged. "Sorry to be blunt, but war is so brutal, I may unconsciously say things that will be shockingly inappropriate in a setting like this. Sorry."

"Do not apologize, Major," Fitzwilliam said. "I understand perfectly. I have even been guilty of saying similar things in the past."

"I'll try to watch it, though. I know I'm a bit uncivilized at the moment, but I'll work on it."

As Darcy and Fitzwilliam discussed where to ride, McDunn regarded Georgiana in a more troubled manner.

It's going to be difficult to remain an impartial observer when I already like everyone so much, especially this young girl. After just one day, I don't think I could stand aside and let Wickham talk her into eloping from Ramsgate. I'm already invested here. Damn!

DARCY AND FITZWILLIAM'S HORSES CANTERED UP TO THE STABLES JUST AS McDunn made the last turn toward the same destination, his run a rapid, ground-eating stride. Darcy was more than a little surprised to see Georgiana waiting for him along with several of his household staff. All of them were staring in frank astonishment at Darcy's guest who wore his marine trousers, boots, and a simple green shirt. The morning was cool and brisk, so he was not sweating as profusely as he would on a summer day. Still, parts of his shirt were dark with moisture, and drops of sweat rolled down his face. But he was breathing easily as he slowed to a trot and then a walk.

"I hadn't planned to do my exercising to an audience," McDunn said as the two men dismounted.

He looked closer at the horses as a pair of stable boys took the reins. "Speaking as a city-raised guy, those look like beautiful horses, Mr. Darcy. Of course, I know little of them, but they seem impressive to my eyes."

"Marlborough is a fine animal, possibly the best horse I have ever owned. Quite spirited, though. He seems to respond well only to me."

"Unfortunately, I had to pick from what was left," Fitzwilliam said, "but what else can a poor, younger son expect?"

"You are simply making excuses for not overtaking me on that last turn for home," Darcy said. "But come. Let us get away from the *audience* as you called them. I can see my sister has a thousand questions she can barely contain."

"Are you well, Major McDunn?" Georgiana asked as soon as the four of them were out of earshot of the others. Concern was plain to see on her forthright face.

"Certainly, Miss Darcy. Why do you ask? Do I look unwell?"

"But you are so…so…"

"I've been sweating, you mean," McDunn said with a smile. "It's what happens when you run. It's how we kept ourselves prepared. If the bad guys were tough, we had to be tougher. It's like what you said about a day in Colonel Fitzwilliam's camp. The only difference is that I was a ground-pounder, so we didn't ride. We ran."

Seeing the looks of confusion, McDunn realized what he had said and smiled ruefully. "A 'ground-pounder' is an infantryman, Miss Darcy. We walked instead of rode, which is why you find me with damp clothing. I intended to have one of your brother's men dump a bucket or two of water over me before I changed into my borrowed clothing, but everyone arrived before that happened."

McDunn had a twinkle in his eye as he said to Georgiana, "Despite the fact that your brother is treating me like a gentleman, you must always remember I'm a mere colonial."

"Now stop that!" Georgiana said. "I think you *are* a gentleman, sir, at least in the qualities that matter. You look so…so dangerous—almost sinister in fact. Yet, I feel very safe in your presence, and I am convinced that, somehow, you would protect me to your dying breath!"

McDunn stopped abruptly, looking at Georgiana intently before shifting his eyes to her brother. His voice had a tender quality when he finally spoke.

"I…I'm honored by your sentiment, Miss Darcy, and that is the God's honest truth. My own sisters—may God rest their innocent souls—were dead months before our last battle, but I believe they are nodding their approval in Heaven because you have paid me such a profound compliment."

He resumed walking. "Though I hope you'll forgive me for wishing I do not have to prove my devotion anytime soon!"

"You and Fitzwilliam are much the same in that regard, Major," Darcy said quietly. "Despite his polite demeanor, I often see more than a hint of danger in him."

"I suppose that means I must spend more time refining my manners," Fitzwilliam said. "It may also explain why no young ladies of large fortune and astonishing pulchritude have rushed to throw themselves into my arms and take me away from my dangerous occupation."

McDunn took note of Georgiana's expression, and he could tell she did not find Fitzwilliam's last comment particularly humorous.

If I had to guess, I'd think Darcy's sister has some plans for her cousin, even if she's a mere girl, he thought. *I guess a union is feasible if Britain allows first cousins to marry. But is she really thinking of marriage so soon? Girls of this time have to be careful, especially those with a substantial inheritance. They can't divorce a cad and continue the search if they make a mistake!*

McDunn was trying to think of something to say when Georgiana turned to her cousin. "How long will you be remaining at Pemberley, Richard? You have been absent far too often these past few years."

"I am not completely sure," he said uncomfortably.

"It will be some weeks," Darcy said. "His regiment must be recruited back to full strength, and he was ordered to rest and heal, so he came to stay with us. And you are his favorite cousin—after me."

"Hmmmph! That is not true! Richard told me I was his favorite before he departed for Spain."

"But you did not write him as often as he thought you should."

"I wrote him every week, just as I promised!" She looked to Fitzwilliam for confirmation before she saw the mischief dancing in her brother's eyes.

"You are teasing me again, William!"

"Of course. That is what older brothers are supposed to do."

Georgiana rounded on McDunn. "I thought you said you would be my defender, sir! Are you going to allow my brother to tease me this way?"

"I learned a long time ago not to intervene between squabbling brothers and sisters," McDunn said mildly. "Far too dangerous."

"In any case, my dear," Darcy said, "I have a task for you. Since the major needs clothing of his own, I sent for a tailor from Lambton, and I would appreciate you working with him to make sure everything Major McDunn needs is put on order."

"It would be my pleasure," Georgiana said, looking at McDunn and his rather disreputable attire. "Of course, some of what he needs will have to be ordered from town."

"Explain it all to the tailor so the necessary measurements are taken. And winter is almost upon us, so include suitable clothing."

"Uh, look, Mr. Darcy," McDunn said, then lowered his voice. "That sounds expensive, and you've already been most hospitable. I can't ask you to buy my clothing, especially since I can pay for whatever I need. Remember my gold coins?"

Darcy waved a hand in dismissal. "I think a single one of those coins will take care of everything. Do not concern yourself."

McDunn nodded thoughtfully and then gestured to his BDUs. "In that case, I'd like to add some items similar to what I'm wearing. Exercising in the dress clothing both you and the colonel wear would be…well, kind of uncomfortable."

"I daresay," Fitzwilliam said with a dry chuckle.

"And hopefully, everyone here will get used to the *mad American*, so I won't draw an audience every time I go for a run."

Darcy nodded. "I believe the tailor can devise something similar to your trousers and jacket for this disgusting exercise you seem to find so necessary."

Fitzwilliam gave a bark of laughter and clapped McDunn on the back, almost staggering him. "I think my cousin likes you, Major. I know he likes me, and this is how he deals with me."

"I suppose so," McDunn said, turning his torso back and forth experimentally. "I suppose you like me too, which is why you just broke two of my ribs."

"Of course!" Fitzwilliam said cheerfully. "Besides, you should not worry about intruding on my cousin's hospitality. Do you not realize you are like a mystery puzzle that will keep all of us intrigued for weeks and weeks? Do you think Darcy would dare turn you out, penniless and forlorn, until we had drained all your secrets? Do you think Georgiana and I would let him?"

"You are perfectly welcome to remain at Pemberley for as long as you wish while you get your sea legs in our British world, Major," Darcy said, "and to accompany our party to London before we get snowed in."

McDunn looked at Darcy for several moments before nodding. "You're very gracious. In fact, I almost feel…"

He stopped talking, but Darcy's curiosity was obviously piqued. "Yes? What is it you feel, Major?"

McDunn looked directly at Darcy for a moment and then quietly said, "Your assistance has been so valuable, sir, and so freely given that I…well, I almost feel as though I was destined to be found by you."

After a moment's silence, he continued. "Yet, as a rational man, I don't believe in destiny unless inspired by God, and I know for a certainty I'm too small a speck in an infinite cosmos to warrant even the slightest second of the Lord's attention."

"But what about the Siege Perilous my brother described to me?" Georgiana said. "Did you not say you thought it was of Divine origin?"

"I did and I do. Still, everything seems too good to be true."

"It was not so for your comrades who perished in your world. Your survival is solely due to this man Kaswallon finding you and sending you on to our time before you bled to death."

"I remember asking myself if he was a Druid when he was explaining everything, but that can't be since he said he was a Christian. Anyway, I thought Druids painted themselves blue, and Kaswallon certainly wasn't blue—though he did wear a costume that looked as though it was designed for the theatre."

"I think the Druids were more prevalent in Wales than in Cornwall," Darcy said thoughtfully. "And it was the wild Celtic warriors who painted themselves blue when battling the Romans. Not much is known about the Druids though you are right about them not being Christian."

"But this is still so thrilling," Georgiana said, her eyes gleaming with excitement. "His family having charge of the Siege stone for all those centuries—sending people to those other dimensions! Why, the mere thought is fascinating!"

"Which reminds me, Mr. Darcy," McDunn said. "I figured parallel dimensions would be rather difficult for you to accept, but it didn't seem to jar you very much. I'd expected the concept to pose a problem since it was a fictional concept in my time in books and some…uh, theatrical productions. I remember tossing around the idea with other students at college when we were taking a break from studying, but it was really casual and fanciful. We usually dwelt on more trivial topics like whether the Tarheels could really take the Wolfpack after six straight seasons of disappointment."

"Tarheels?" Fitzwilliam asked.

"The nickname for our university sports team. The Wolfpack was the nickname for our main rival who had beaten us badly for six years in a row. It seemed so important back then, but now it seems trivial."

"It does not sound trivial to me," Georgiana said. "Those details you call trivialities are some of the things that make everything you tell us so believable. You are not inventing a story to tell us but are simply remembering your other life."

"True. I had not put the thought into words, but Georgiana has expressed it perfectly," Darcy said. "It was one of the reasons I accepted what you told me and decided to be of assistance to you."

"My brother is glad to help you, Major. He truly is! Oh, everything is so exciting! I cannot wait to see what marvels you are going to reveal! And I thought life at Pemberley, even with Richard visiting, would be so dull!"

"But we must remember to keep this a family secret as we agreed," Darcy said, his voice gentle but firm, the voice of a guardian instructing his ward.

"Oh, certainly, William. I understand completely. But I wonder—shall we include Mr. Bingley when he comes to visit?"

Darcy and Fitzwilliam glanced at each other; then Darcy said slowly, "Bingley is a good friend, and I enjoy his company exceedingly. But I think not. Unlike Richard, he really does not have anything to contribute."

"And the more people you bring into a secret, the more likely it is to be compromised," McDunn said. "I've got a number of things to discuss with you, not the least of which is the kind of work I can do to produce income. I can't live off the gold coins that so fortuitously arrived with me. Even if we melt them down, using too many might make people suspicious, and they won't last forever. After thinking it over last night, I plan to use my knowledge from the future to produce and sell new products. But all my knowledge is academic—not real-life experience. So I need to pick your brains as much as you want to pick mine."

"He has hundreds of these sayings!" Fitzwilliam exclaimed. "'Pick our brains!' We need to keep this man around just to listen to him speak, Darcy!"

"Your firearms alone are so amazing in their precision that they would be priceless to the military," Darcy said.

McDunn shrugged. "Unfortunately, I think something like that would be a bit too ambitious as a first effort."

"Which brings us to the demonstration of your pistol you mentioned," Fitzwilliam said eagerly.

"Indeed it does, and I'll get it from the stables where I left your fine clothes, Colonel."

McDunn left at a trot and returned a few minutes later with a cloth-wrapped bundle.

"This thing is really loud, and the projectile has a lot of energy," McDunn said. "I think we'd better get a lot farther away from the house."

Darcy nodded and led everyone about a half-mile along one of the paths to a cleft in the hillside behind the house.

McDunn looked around and nodded then knelt and unwrapped his holstered pistol as well as some triangles of wood one of the stable-hands had found for him. He took these about fifteen paces into the cleft and rammed the point of each into the turf so they stood upright. On his way back, he found a branch that he laid on the ground before them.

"Those will be your targets," he told Darcy and Fitzwilliam, indicating the wooden triangles while removing his pistol from the holster, instinctively keeping the muzzle pointing away from everyone. "And this branch will be the firing line."

Pointing into the cleft, he said, "That direction is downrange. When you have a pistol in your hand, it must always be pointing downrange."

He looked intently at each of the men. "Remember, gentlemen, your pistol always points downrange. Always!"

Both men as well as Georgiana nodded seriously at McDunn's stern instructions.

"Spoken like a man who has commanded troops and is used to having his orders obeyed," Richard said. "Listen well, cousins. He knows what he is about."

McDunn continued with both men, showing them how to load the pistol, take their stance, aim, and fire it. But before starting the demonstration, he pulled a handful of small cloth rectangles from his pocket then demonstrated how to roll them into a cylinder and insert them into their ears to protect their hearing against the loud muzzle blast.

"Remember to slowly squeeze the trigger…like this," McDunn said, and a loud click sounded as the internal hammer hit the firing pin. "I want you to fire three rounds, but do it slowly, releasing the trigger and taking aim as I instructed." He paused and said, "Any questions?"

When there were none, he said, "Then I think we're ready. You first, Mr. Darcy. Take your position at the firing line."

McDunn handed Darcy the pistol after he was in position and coached him through inserting the magazine and racking the slide to insert a cartridge. Then, just as he had been instructed, Darcy held the pistol with both hands and took careful aim. He began to squeeze the trigger slowly, slowly…

Unexpectedly, there was an immense roar, and the pistol kicked back as the muzzle rose into the air.

"My word!" Fitzwilliam said breathlessly.

"Did I hit the target?" Darcy asked plaintively, seeing all six wooden triangles still in place.

"You were just over the one on the left," McDunn said. "Your form wasn't bad. Try again."

Darcy fired two more times, neither one coming as close to his target as his first shot, and McDunn took the pistol and removed the magazine and the round from the chamber.

"I told you it would be loud," McDunn said, motioning Fitzwilliam into position before handing him the pistol and magazine.

"And you were correct that it would kick like a mule!" Darcy said fervently, working the fingers of his right hand. "I have shot a pistol many times, but never like this! And I could not hit a single target."

"A couple of your shots would at least have hit a man-sized target," McDunn said. "And it takes some training to shoot a pistol accurately. Now, let's see how the good colonel does."

A few moments later, there was another roar, followed by two others. Fitzwilliam had managed to hit the target once, causing the wood to fly to pieces.

"Well, that is disappointing!" Fitzwilliam said. "I expected to hit three times, and I only hit once. I suppose I ought to depend on my sword arm."

"Like I said, it takes training to shoot a pistol accurately. I simply don't have enough cartridges to train you."

"Major," Georgiana said timidly as McDunn unloaded the pistol and started to put it in its holster. "Could you please demonstrate the pistol yourself?"

McDunn looked at her in surprise, then Fitzwilliam chimed in. "Yes, please, Major! I would dearly love to see how it is supposed to be fired."

Darcy nodded his agreement, and McDunn thought for a few moments before giving a shrug.

"Very well, but only a few shots."

Stepping back to the branch on the ground, he reloaded the pistol and took a firing position.

BAAAAMMMM! BAAAAMMMM! BAAAAMMMM! BAAAAMMMM! BAAAAMMMM!

With each loud detonation, a wood triangle disintegrated, and each shot followed on the previous one by less than a second.

"The oak at the end of the cleft. See the lowest branch to the left of the trunk?"

Again he assumed a firing position but aimed more carefully. When the front and rear sights came into line, he began to squeeze the trigger.

BAAAAMMMM!

The sound of the explosion as well as the kick of his brute of a pistol came as a surprise to McDunn, just as it always did when it was done right. The branch thrashed about and a number of leaves fell off.

"That is amazing, sir," Fitzwilliam whispered in astonishment. "Simply amazing."

"The result of long training and thousands of practice rounds," McDunn said mildly, unloading and holstering the pistol before flexing his fingers as Darcy had done. "And now you see why it's no fun to fire. It's really powerful, and it's made for one thing only—and that's war."

Fitzwilliam paused then asked, "Is there any possibility of making similar firearms for our army?"

McDunn shook his head sadly. "As I mentioned, it's a bit too ambitious at the present time. I'm not yet familiar with the state of things here in Britain, but I know your—what's the word—ah, mechanical arts simply aren't up to the challenge. I knew you were going to ask the question, so I gave the matter some thought. I'm afraid it will be years before even a single-shot pistol could be produced. For one thing, the steel has to be much stronger than you can make right now."

"I wish I could fire your pistol," Georgiana said sadly, taking the rolled up shreds of cloth from her ears. "But I know I am not nearly strong enough."

"I am not sure *I* am strong enough!" her brother said, patting her fondly on the shoulder.

"True words, Darcy," Fitzwilliam said with a nod. "But did you see how fast Major McDunn hit those targets? Five shots, five hits! In only a few seconds!"

"In my time, it took a full two weeks and hundreds of rounds to train a marine to shoot the pistol adequately," McDunn said. "But now, I believe I need a bath before the noon meal. I'm famished!"

"You are always famished, Major," Fitzwilliam said cheerfully. But this time McDunn managed to dodge the gargantuan clap aimed for his shoulder.

As the party returned to the house, Georgiana glanced at Fitzwilliam, savoring the sight of him as she always did. She spared a quick glance at the taller man beside him.

Richard may not be as strong and as powerful looking as you, Major McDunn, she thought contentedly, *but he is the man with whom I am going to spend my life. I might have been tempted by your dark, dangerous figure if I had not already decided Richard would be my husband.*

Enjoy yourself for the moment, cousin. I do not believe you have any idea of my plans for you!

With that thought, Georgiana lengthened her stride to join her brother and Fitzwilliam.

"It is very good to have you returned from Spain safe, Richard. Despite what my brother tried to say, I know I really am your favorite cousin."

Fitzwilliam showed pleased surprise at hearing this. "How could there be any other opinion on the subject?"

Chapter 5

If I get a parking ticket, there is always a parallel universe where I didn't. On the other hand, there is yet another universe where my car was stolen.

—Max Tegmark, Swedish-American physicist and cosmologist

Wednesday, October 11, 1809
Pemberley, Derbyshire

The two Darcy siblings and their cousin called on McDunn about two hours later and found him sitting at a small table he had pulled over to a window for better light. A thick piece of canvas was draped over the table, obviously to protect the polished wood surface, and a collection of metal items of varying sizes were spread over it. McDunn was holding one of them in one hand while he held a small brush of some kind in the other, and he stood to greet his visitors.

After the three came over to the table, Fitzwilliam said in surprise, "It's your pistol! Or rather, the parts to it."

"Almost," McDunn said. "To be exact, it's the parts to *both* my pistols. I'm giving them a good cleaning." He sat down and resumed brushing the small metal piece for a few moments, examining it carefully and nodding in satisfaction before putting it in a pile of parts to the side.

"What do you mean when you say you are cleaning your pistols, Major?" Georgiana asked, indicating the parts spread over the table.

"I haven't been able to clean any of my firearms for some time, maybe a month, Miss Darcy. Normally, marines in combat would disassemble their weapons and give them a good cleaning whenever they had a stand-down. Having a clean weapon was almost sacred writ in the Corps, and I thought I'd better get my firearms clean before I packed everything away."

He looked up and grinned at Georgiana. "It feels pretty strange to actually feel safe. And I won't be firing any of them for practice or fun. Limited ammunition, you know, though I'll keep one pistol for myself."

"But how will you be able to get everything back together?" Fitzwilliam asked with concern in his voice.

"I've got most of the parts for both pistols cleaned and oiled. Want to see how I can reassemble one pistol?"

When Fitzwilliam nodded, McDunn smoothed out the pile of cleaned parts so he could see everything. Then his fingers started flying as he fitted part after part into place, usually with a loud clicking sound as it was pressed home, and the assembly was swiftly completed.

"Voila!" McDunn said proudly, holding up the pistol.

"That took about a half-minute," Fitzwilliam said, impressed.

"During training, we had to assemble our rifle and our pistol blindfolded, and woe to the poor recruit who didn't complete both of them within ninety seconds—or worse, came up a part short! Bad things happened then!"

"I daresay," Fitzwilliam said with a smile. "It seems some parts of training have not changed very much in two centuries."

"'Train hard in peace or die uselessly in war' was our mantra," McDunn said. "But now, having impressed you with my speed in reassembling my pistol, I'm sure you came with questions."

"Indeed we have," Darcy said. "But first, I want to make clear that our questions indicate no disbelief in what you told us. But we are exceedingly curious, and you indicated you had other things to show us."

"That I do, Mr. Darcy. Do you have any particular questions you'd like to ask first?"

"Perhaps we might start with what you just said—'Mr. Darcy.' Our customs have to be different from yours, so I thought I would mention what we would consider proper forms of address."

McDunn nodded, and Darcy continued. "As a casual acquaintance, I would address you as Major McDunn or perhaps Major, and you would call me Mr. Darcy. Friends, however, usually refer to each other by their surnames, to wit: McDunn and Darcy. I would say we are well past mere acquaintances, even in the span of barely a day, so while I might call you 'Major' on occasion, I do not think of you as Major McDunn any longer."

"It works for me. As someone said in my world, 'When in Rome, do as the Romans do.' Is that current here?"

"Oh, yes. I have heard it many times."

"Interesting."

"And I, of course, am Fitzwilliam," the colonel said.

"And I am Georgiana!" Darcy's sister said eagerly.

But McDunn only shook his head and smiled. "No, you're Miss Darcy, and I'm your protector, not your brother."

Darcy laughed at the anger on Georgiana's face and touched her hand. "I think it would be best to acquiesce. Remember, you yourself described him as dangerous."

"Yes, but—" Georgiana started to protest before conceding unwillingly. "Oh, very well, William. But I warn you. I *am* growing up!"

"My sister is very dear to me," Darcy said, "especially since we have lost both our parents."

"I'm very sorry to hear that," McDunn responded, hoping his face showed no hint that this was not news to him.

"My dear mother died giving birth to Georgiana, and we lost our father almost five years ago. Richard and I have had the care of her since then in accordance with Father's will. Though the task does, at times, intrude on our affections."

"It must be a weighty task for both of you."

"It is one I shoulder willingly. She and I are all that are left of the Darcy family, and I am torn between keeping her at my side as much as possible or setting up an establishment for her in a few years so she can manage and order her own friends and associations. It would be more pleasant to have her accompany me, of course, but I have to think of her welfare."

"Judging by the expression on Miss Darcy's face at the moment," McDunn said thoughtfully, "I think she might prefer to accompany you rather than stay home." He stopped abruptly, aghast at how thoughtlessly the words had popped out of his mouth.

I've just been thinking I shouldn't interfere in things! he thought, chastising himself for his stupidity. *Then I open my big yap and immediately do just the opposite! Idiot!*

Darcy appeared not to notice and merely glanced at him.

"It was impertinent of me to say anything at all after such a brief acquaintance," McDunn said carefully, "and I apologize most profoundly. The words were out of my mouth before I realized it. I will only offer this. As you know, I had three younger sisters at home, and I remember how they always wanted to follow me everywhere. It really didn't stop until I went off to the Marines when I was sixteen. When I saw Miss Darcy's reluctance just now, I remembered my sisters and thought the best stability for your sister might be to have her travel with you. It might be more preferable than having the two of you separated, even for the best of reasons."

"Hear, hear!" Fitzwilliam said. "Out of the mouths of strangers!"

Darcy nodded thoughtfully. "It is a point I had not considered, and as you just heard, Richard is in agreement. Perhaps further thought is needed."

"Again, I apologize for speaking when I—"

"Dismiss it from your mind, McDunn," Darcy said, waving his hand. "I asked, and you responded forthrightly."

"So," McDunn said, "back to your questions."

"I think my first one is about these Krugerrands you have. Do you have any idea what one of those coins was worth in your time?"

"I haven't a clue," McDunn said, retrieving the coins from a drawer and placing them on the table. "My colonel said Krugerrands never had a face value because they weren't circulated. Their value was the gold they contained—one troy ounce of almost pure gold. More than ninety percent pure, he said."

Fitzwilliam looked at a coin. "Interesting. But one of these is clearly very valuable. How many do you have?"

McDunn shrugged. "I don't really know, but it's easy enough to find out."

He retrieved two heavy canvas bags from the closet, setting them down carefully. "I've only glanced into these," he said, unzipping both of them and pulling them open wide.

"Oh, my!" Georgiana whispered in surprise and amazement while Darcy and Fitzwilliam simply looked at the paper-wrapped cylinders filling each bag.

"And all those...packages contain these, ah, Krugerrands," Fitzwilliam said slowly.

"I assume so. I've only made a cursory check as I pulled out these coins, but it seems to be the case."

"Why, the bag I carried to the coach must have weighed…oh, eight stone[12] or more!"

Darcy blinked in surprise. "More than eight stone in each bag?"

McDunn nodded. "That was why I mentioned I could pay for the clothing I need. I seem to have brought some resources with me though I simply cannot explain how I came to have them. Remember, when Kaswallon asked me what I wanted, I said a rifle and some ammo. Nothing else. Now I have my personal field pack with a bunch of additional stuff in it and even an extra rifle as well as these coins. All these extras are as amazing to me as to you."

"Oh, this is so exciting!" Georgiana said, jumping up and down in her chair as she clapped her hands. "A dark, mysterious stranger with all kinds of arcane knowledge and a fortune in gold! I never would have forgiven you, William, if you had tried to keep this secret from me!"

"Just remember—"

"It is a family secret. Yes, I know," she said firmly.

"I never had time to count everything after I inherited command of the battalion and the colonel distributed the gold between himself and the two battalion commanders. I do know it made my pack a real beast to hump with an extra fifty kilos. Where the other bag came from is a mystery to me, as is the third bag filled with ammunition."

"Kaswallon," Fitzwilliam said firmly. "You said there could be no one else."

"It had to be, but how could he know about my pack, much less these three bags?"

"Because he was a Druid!" Georgiana said. "Oh, I will help you count everything, Major! Please let me help!"

"Well, I'm certainly not going to turn down an eager volunteer, Miss Darcy. You've just got yourself a job."

Darcy rolled his eyes in good humor at his sister engaged in the throes of girlish excitement, but McDunn only smiled.

"I expect you shall have to melt down your coins," Darcy said, his brow creased in thought. "Otherwise—"

"Absolutely," McDunn said with a nod. "Otherwise, questions might well be asked about strange coins with exceedingly strange coinage dates. Needless to say, I want to avoid any undue attention."

---

12 Eight stone is more than one hundred pounds.

"To be sure. Though I am ignorant of the exact price of gold, I suspect your coins will bring a tidy sum."

"Thousands of pounds, certainly," Fitzwilliam said.

"Which I inherited by virtue of being the last man standing," McDunn said morosely. "I can't help feeling a bit guilty about it. 'Survivor's guilt' is what we called it."

McDunn was silent for a few moments, remembering the depression that had afflicted them all, especially the commanders, in the days leading up to the last battle. He was walking dark paths only he could see. Finally, his distant stare faded and he continued.

"In any case, we all knew the score, and the colonel ordered us to make a try for the open sea if we got the chance. He didn't suggest it; he made it an order because marines don't abandon other marines—usually, at least. He said this was an exception since there was no chance we were going to defeat the barbs. We didn't have enough ammo to kill them all. Too many of them, and more were arriving."

"There was a chance to make for the open sea?" Darcy asked. "Were there ships available?"

"Perhaps, but if there were, they were hidden. The rotted-out wrecks I did see weren't going to get far at sea, and they wouldn't have held more than four or five men."

"But some of you might have escaped, I would think."

"Sure, but none of us were going to obey the colonel's order. Marines don't leave other marines behind. We usually don't leave our dead behind either, but we had no choice during the retreat. Usually, there wasn't even time to dig graves before we had to pull out to avoid being flanked and surrounded."

"I see," Darcy said rather tentatively, but he still looked confused.

Fitzwilliam, on the other hand, understood everything McDunn had said as though he could visualize it, and he nodded grimly.

McDunn smiled at the confused look on Darcy's face. "We'll be here all night if I try to tell you what it was like to be a marine in my world, Darcy—an American marine, though I understand there were some similarities in the Royal Marines. Suffice it to say the Marines were part of a number of things—some military, some economic, and some cultural—that led the United States to play a dominant role in world affairs for more than a half-century—before we committed societal suicide."

Seeing the confused look again from all three of his guests, McDunn thought over what he had said and concluded he had used unfamiliar terms again.

"Was it my use of the term 'societal suicide' that's causing the looks on your faces?" he asked. "Or perhaps the term 'economic'?"

"Both," Darcy replied. "Though I have heard the word economy a time or two—"

"I have not," Fitzwilliam said.

"—but the men who used it seemed to speak some kind of strange, unknown language."

"I had the same thought when I used to read what economists had to say back in my world," McDunn said, nodding. "And economics was a standard course of studies in universities for more than a century. I think you had to be inducted into their secret cabal to really understand them."

"But I do have an inkling of what you meant by 'societal suicide.' History contains a number of cases of a country making a wrong turn and leading itself to ruin."

"Ancient Athens and their strange idea about democracy," Fitzwilliam said forcefully. "Remember how the citizenry voted to execute all their generals because the war was not going well?"

"I do," Darcy said with a nod. "Needless to say, the results were disastrous."

"I remember my grandfather using the same example," McDunn said. "He wasn't an officer, but he was a student of history, especially military history. As he told it, the voters at the time were little more than a mob, and they acted with herd stupidly. In my world, there were factions in the United States who chose a foolhardy path. Worse, they *knew* the path they proposed was self-destructive, and they chose it anyway. So, societal suicide rather than stupidity."

"But why would they do that?" Fitzwilliam asked, his brow furrowed.

"You've seen the results of the French Revolution, haven't you?" McDunn asked. At a nod from both men, he continued though Georgiana still looked completely lost.

"So, you're aware certain factions among the French revolutionaries were willing to do anything to bring down the existing aristocracy, no matter how many innocents were hurt. Our case was similar since the factions who eventually gained control of the country used revolution as a tactic to bring down the existing establishment and replace it with one of their choosing. The result was more than fifteen years of absolute disaster. We were trying to dig out of the mess we inherited when the whole world blew up in our faces."

"An understandable explanation though it is difficult to believe intelligent people could act in such a way."

"Most of the individuals involved were highly educated and considered intellectuals, Darcy," McDunn said morosely. "As an elite group, they considered themselves superior to the ordinary citizen who they believed needed to be controlled and guided for their own good. By the elite, of course. There was a wise man who once said there are some ideas so stupid that only intellectuals will believe them."

Fitzwilliam pounded the arm of his chair. "That is a wonderful saying, McDunn! Some ideas so stupid—did you say that?"

"Actually, no. It was said by someone more than a hundred years from now. But no one has said it exactly that way now, so feel free to use it when it fits."

"Oh, I shall, friend McDunn! I certainly shall!"

"William, may I start counting the gold?" Georgiana asked. "I want to do something useful."

"I understand," Darcy said. "Go ahead, sweetling. I understand these are unfamiliar topics to you. Your schooling concentrated on making you a proper young lady, knowledgeable in all manner of fashionable things, but it did not prepare you to be a part of this enterprise. Accordingly, I have just decided I need to make some changes. Instead of returning you to your school, I think you need a different kind of education. I am going to get some proper tutors to teach you more of the world, including some of the things Richard and I learned."

"That sounds exciting, William!"

"But it is something I shall need to address when we return to town. For now, you can be of assistance by counting the major's gold."

As Georgiana began to pull paper cylinders from the canvas bags, Darcy said, "And returning to the topic of money and your gold coins, McDunn, I seem to recall hearing gold was worth approximately £10 per ounce. If you have about three thousands of those Krugerrands, they might be worth about thirty thousand pounds. You should not have to worry about a roof over your head with so much to invest in the Funds."

"I'll likely need every pound before I'm through," McDunn said, and for the first time, there was something akin to excitement in his eyes.

"As I mentioned, I was trained in the sciences of my time," McDunn said. "I had just completed my bachelor's degree and had started graduate school when the whole world went crazy and I was called back to the Marines. So I have a lot of knowledge about things that will be invented in your future, like steam locomotives. I think I can put my knowledge to work, but it'll require money to get things fabricated so they can be sold. Based on my memory of history, I'm afraid the economy of England is going to change dramatically over the next fifteen years or so. I think it will change even faster with some of the inventions I can devise."

"I have read of steam engines, but I thought them little more than a novelty," Darcy said.

McDunn nodded eagerly and rose, pacing about the room and waving his hands as he spoke. "They may be novelties now, but they'll be improved and made more practical. I know in about forty years there will be railroads crisscrossing England."

Everyone, including Georgiana, looked at him in amazement.

"It's going to happen whether I do anything about steam locomotives or not. The important thing is that I have knowledge others don't, so I can produce workable versions in less time. But I have to be careful with my funds to avoid spending them on inventions that'll require more money than I have. Some careful thought is needed before I go charging off to make my fortune. For one thing, some inventions will have to wait until I have the tools to make a practical version. In my world, it was standard to produce parts that were identical, down to the nearest thousandth of an inch. It allowed for mass production since all the parts were interchangeable as you've seen in my pistol. That can't be done in today's England."

"So, does that mean you have the intention to journey to your homeland? To America?"

"Not at all!" McDunn's denial was instant and forceful. "I said today. What history will someday call the Industrial Revolution will take root and grow to maturity here in England and, to a lesser degree, in continental Europe. England is where I must develop my inventions because the tools here will be many years ahead of anything that could be made currently in the United States."

He stopped suddenly and gave everyone a broad grin. "Besides, the Siege

Perilous sent me to this England of the past rather than some other world. There has to be a reason I didn't wind up in America—why I woke up on your property. For the first time, I have a hunch that the world in which I would fit is one where I can do meaningful work and produce tools and mechanisms to make the life of everyone much easier and safer. It will allow individuals to do more than they have ever done before."

He looked at Darcy closely, wondering how to phrase what he wanted to say, but forthrightness seemed the best approach.

"I'm afraid it's going to result in a scarcity of servants as they take employment that pays more. It will bring about a dramatic change in the way things are and the life you and your family lead. Sorry about that, but it's going to happen anyway."

Darcy waved his hand, dismissing the apology. "In fact, it is already happening, for some of the sons of the staff have decided to look for factory jobs in London rather than stay at Pemberley. We shall find ways to make do just as we always have."

He was silent for a few moments, thinking hard until he came to a decision. "If you are correct about needing every pound, then perhaps I can provide at least some assistance and make Pemberley available to you as a place where you can stay and make your plans. I have a house in town for your use when you have to make arrangements with artisans and mechanics. It will save you the trouble of having to set up an establishment of your own, and we have plenty of room, both here and in London."

McDunn was stunned by the generosity of this unexpected offer, especially considering the usual reserve of the Darcy that Austen described.

"I am honored beyond words to have you offer such hospitality to a stranger with all the wild stories I've related about the world I come from. It is most generous, sir. Most generous. I shall repay you in the future. I pledge I will do so."

"Nonsense, McDunn! You have whetted my appetite and stimulated my curiosity to a level I did not know possible! I *have* to see how your endeavors will work out, and the best way is to have you close at hand! You are a wildly different man than I, but it is often said opposites attract!"

"Thank you again from the bottom of my heart. Your kind offer will remove many of the difficulties I would have otherwise had in…*acclimating* is the word I would use, but the word may not be in use yet. It means to become accustomed to new conditions, and this world of 1809 is much different than mine."

"I wish it were possible for you to make more of your pistols for myself and my troops, but you have explained all too clearly why it is not possible," Fitzwilliam said wistfully.

"For your sake, Colonel, I wish I could, but your war with Napoleon will be over in a few years, and England is going to drastically cut back any kind of military spending. It would be impossible to produce the pistols before then."

"Now that we have come to an agreement, perhaps we ought to sample some of Darcy's excellent brandy."

McDunn stood and went to the sideboard, returning with four glasses. He handed two glasses of brandy to the two gentlemen and a glass of wine to Georgiana before holding up his own glass of Scotch in a toast.

"Here's to the future, gentlemen and lady! Some of what I have predicted may vary considerably in the test of time. It seems as though things never work out in the future quite like even the most knowledgeable planners forecast."

McDunn took a healthy drink from his glass and then looked at the depleted bottle on the sideboard. "Um…might we convert one or two of those Krugerrands into some more of this smuggled whisky? For some reason, it's tasting better and better."

"I daresay it is," Darcy said, rising to his feet and clinking his brandy glass with McDunn's. "I shall have Hamilton ask about procuring some. If anyone knows how to get a new supply, it would be him."

"Filthy stuff," Fitzwilliam said, clinking his glass also. "Only an American could drink it."

Chapter 6

These findings illustrate an interesting trend. In the past, a nation's competitive power was determined by its geographical size and population. Beginning in the eighteenth century, however, the industrial revolution changed the balance of power among nations, and today even a small nation can achieve affluence and economic strength through its industrial achievement.

—Hajime Karatsu, Japanese business educator and author

Mid-October 1809
Pemberley, Derbyshire

L ife at Pemberley soon settled into a routine as curiosities moderated under a barrage of questions asked and resolved. McDunn continued to rise early to exercise, and interest waned among the servants about the eccentric habits of their master's new American friend.

In a few days, the Lambton tailor brought the first products of his labors. McDunn was pleased with the first delivery of a pair of simple cotton trousers and a T-shirt for exercising, allowing him to retire his worn and mended BDUs to an upper shelf in his closet. He kept his boots since the first delivery from the boot maker had not arrived.

McDunn continued to work his way carefully through the contents of his pack while Georgiana soon completed her inventory of his gold. She was careful and thorough, documenting more than thirty-four hundred Kruger-rands along with a smattering of other gold coins. All the precious metals were now secured in the massive locking strongbox in her brother's study.

During his ponderings about what he might be able to accomplish in this new world, McDunn usually had the assistance or at least the company of one or more of his new helpers. After only a few days, they had started to feel as though they were members of a secret coterie, especially since their many gatherings had to be held in private where they could ask the myriad of questions that still bubbled up.

But some of the things his new friends found truly interesting surprised him because they were things McDunn had taken for granted for so long, he barely thought about them anymore. For example, when Georgiana was examining his wallet, she gave a sharp cry of surprise.

"What is the matter, dear?" Darcy asked, crossing to her side.

"Look!" she said, pointing to McDunn's Marine identification card. When McDunn and Fitzwilliam joined them, McDunn realized none of them had ever seen a photograph before, only paintings and drawings.

He pulled the card from his wallet and handed it to Georgiana, who looked from the card to him and back to the card.

"This is magic, Major! It is not a portrait at all! It is you to the life!"

"True," McDunn agreed then found his driver's license and handed it to her. The photograph was in full color, which drew more expressions of amazement.

He explained early photographs and the ability to capture an image on specially treated paper inside a box called a camera, and he pointed out that this was one of many discoveries soon to be made. He also showed them his family photographs, which proved a much more painful process.

Georgiana gasped as she came upon a photograph of his three sisters at the swimming pool, wearing two-piece swimming suits. The suits were pretty restrained, especially since the girls ranged in age from eight to thirteen years. Then he realized Georgiana never would have seen so much exposed skin in her life, either male or female, and probably would not until she married.

And perhaps not even then from what I remember about marital customs during the Regency, McDunn thought. But his amusement was tempered by the familiar pang of grief, and when he thought he had his voice under control, he said, "Well, I did say you'd find women's fashions rather scandalous, Miss Darcy. Those are my sisters, and I can tell you their swimsuits were considered quite modest by the standards of our society."

Inspired by the small photos, McDunn looked deeper into his pack and found a padded manila envelope from which he removed about a dozen color photographs. Handling them by the edges, he spread them out on the top of the desk.

"This is my Mom and Dad," he said with tenderness and suppressed grief in his voice. "They were schoolteachers back in Beaufort, South Carolina. They never made a whole lot of money, but they raised us four kids and never complained. Not once.

"And these are my sisters. Jill's the oldest, and Megan is next. Teresa's the baby of the family—she's only in the ninth grade." His face went stony, and he whispered, "*Was* in the ninth grade."

"And they were all killed in those explosions you described?" Darcy asked softly.

"Nuke. Yeah. Memorial Day Massacre."

He was silent for a moment then quickly pointed to the other pictures. "This is my grandfather. He was in the Corps well before I joined, and he did thirty-four years. He deliberately turned down a chance for an officer's commission so he could marry my grandmother. They lived about a half-mile from us and must have died with the rest of the family."

He quickly went through the other pictures, showing them the house where he grew up, the family automobile, their dogs and cats, the picture of his high school football team, and his other memorabilia. At the end, he returned the photos to the protective envelope with the same care with which he had removed them.

"I'd like to find a way to display them, but I don't dare. There's nothing like these photos in this world."

"True, true," Darcy said. "Perhaps you might be able to do so if you introduce this camera you described. But you are right about the present time. It would be best to keep them hidden away."

"Along with the other stuff that won't be useful right away. I hesitate to dispose of anything until I'm absolutely certain it won't prove useful."

THE MOST ASTOUNDING ITEMS MCDUNN SHOWED HIS FRIENDS—BAR none—were his computer tablets. After watching over his shoulder as he demonstrated their various capabilities, he locked them so nothing could be altered, and handed one to each of them with a minimum of instructions, letting them experiment. It was more than a half-hour before any of the three looked up. They simply stared at the tablets in their hands and then at him in wonder, trying to comprehend what they had just observed.

"This is—I cannot think of a way to describe it other than to use Georgiana's word. It is magical," Darcy said slowly. "The pictures…the documents…I have no words to describe what I am seeing."

"This alone"—Fitzwilliam motioned toward his tablet—"would be sufficient to validate everything you have told us. If you were just describing what I am seeing without the evidence of my eyes, I could do nothing other than dismiss it as the ravings of a madman. Yet I cannot deny what is in front of me. These computer tablets are real—almost frighteningly so."

"They are wonderful, William!" Georgiana exclaimed in awe as she scrolled with increasing rapidity through the different screens on McDunn's personal tablet. "They are not at all frightening! There is so much to learn! And the pictures are so beautiful!"

One thing is definitely the same between my more advanced world and this one, McDunn thought, *and it's the way the young seem to pick up the important elements of computer tools faster than their elders. Give this girl a month, and she'll know my tablet as well as I do and likely be just as good at pulling information out of the files.*

"It's not magical, I assure you," McDunn said. "Such tools—for they are tools for learning—were the products of two centuries of science and technology that started with your emerging Industrial Revolution. And they weren't only for the rich. Mom and Dad weren't wealthy at all, but we always had computers in our house. And my parents were able to buy my personal tablet for me as a gift when I left for the university, including the extensive technology package I showed you. The detailed information in the package is critical to what I hope to do here since so many of the things I learned at the university won't translate to what's feasible at this time. They'll be invaluable in helping me choose things doable in the here and now, at least for my first projects, because I don't have the resources to build whole industries. I have to find a worthwhile project that will generate enough profits so I can think larger."

He looked over at Georgiana. "How are the error-checking test routines coming, Miss Darcy?"

Georgiana reluctantly ceased her explorations and tapped the icons

McDunn had shown her when he started the test. "It says all tests were successfully passed complete, Major."

"Excellent. It's what I expected, but it's a relief all the same. But I'm afraid I have to ask you to stop now. It's time to put them all on recharge and start backing up my personal tablet to the other two."

"Why is that, McDunn," Darcy asked while Georgiana reluctantly closed the cover on the tablet and handed it to McDunn.

"It's usual to make backup copies of important files on a regular basis to avoid losing data. I have to use my other tablets for that since I don't have any other types of backup devices. We were sent over here to fight the invaders after all, and preserving the data in our tablets was quite a ways down our list of important things to stuff in our packs. Ammo and clean socks were more important."

McDunn placed all the tablets in their cases and set them on a table with their solar cells positioned for maximum sunlight and their infrared data ports facing each other. He pointed toward the dark squares embedded in the case cover behind protective plastic shields.

"These are solar cells. They use the energy in the light from the sun to recharge the batteries in the tablets. If the batteries get too low, the computers shut down."

"*Energy* in the sunlight?" Georgiana asked in confusion. "Sunlight is just…well, light, is it not?"

"But sunlight does contain energy, Miss Darcy. Your skin gets warm in direct sunlight, right?"

"Well, yes, I suppose it does."

"That's energy. Heat energy. The solar cells convert sun energy into electrical current for the batteries."

"Ah," she said a bit hesitantly. "I think I see…at least a little."

"It's a lot to take in, I know. And you're hearing it for the first time. Just as before, think it over for a few days, and we can always discuss it in more detail."

Georgiana nodded as did the other two gentlemen. McDunn knew all three could hardly contain their curiosity, and only politeness kept them from asking questions from morning until night.

"When the backups are done, which may take the rest of the day," McDunn explained, "I can get started on my technical research. I'll use my enlisted

Corps tablet first since it's not as adapted for hard use as the other two. I'll put them aside until the first one starts to fail before switching to one of the more ruggedized tablets. I figure it's the best way to make all three of them last as long as possible. When they die, it'll be the end. I need to have as many of my plans as possible converted to paper before then."

"How long will these magical tablets last, do you think?" Fitzwilliam asked.

"Hard to say. My experience is that devices like this either go bad very quickly or they last quite a while. Probably the weakest component is the battery, but I figure I might still be able to use them if I work where sunlight can fall on the solar cells and provide voltage to the electronics."

"Uh, Darcy," Fitzwilliam asked, "did you understand a single word the man just said?"

"Not one, cousin. Not one. But perhaps it will become clearer if we pay closer attention."

"Unlikely," Fitzwilliam muttered.

McDunn laughed sympathetically. "After the battery, it's just a matter of chance about what'll fail next. As I said, all the tablets are ruggedized to some degree, but none of them are going to last forever. I hope to get at least twenty, maybe twenty-five years out of them, but I'll be astonished if any of them are still working longer than that no matter how little I use them."

McDunn opened the cases and lifted the covers of both tablets to inspect the status indicators on their screens.

"Ah! Copying has started, and it wouldn't be doing so if the system hadn't found enough storage on the two tablets for what I'm backing up. I had to delete a bunch of garbage files from those tablets to free up enough space."

Darcy and Fitzwilliam looked at each other before Darcy shrugged and shook his head. "Again, I recognize your words, my friend, but I am afraid I do not understand their meaning."

"Not surprising. Think of it this way. If you have a single bookcase in which to store books, and you buy a bunch of new books, you must remove enough books from your bookcase to allow you to put your new books on the shelf. The storage in the tablets is similar. I had to get rid of—delete— enough useless books to make room for my new books. Is that any clearer?"

Again, Darcy and Fitzwilliam looked at each other, but this time they nodded.

"More or less, McDunn," Darcy said. "So, electronic books instead of leather-bound books. I am not sure I am altogether comfortable with not having a book in my hand."

"I feel the same way, but electronic data is all I have to work with right now."

"And these useless books you got rid of were no longer needed?" Fitzwilliam asked.

"Not in the slightest. Most of it was military information like regulations, manuals on how to clean our rifles and similar stuff we already knew. It was a bunch of junk that bureaucrats who'd never worn a uniform thought we had to have. Uh—does the word 'bureaucrat' mean anything to you?"

"Oh yes," Fitzwilliam said emphatically.

"I wish it were possible to keep the breed from appearing in your world, but I suspect it's already too late. Likely, they're already burrowed deep into the foundations of your government."

"I am afraid you are quite correct, especially in the government," Darcy said. "Clerks and such. Richard has a special dislike for them and has said so more than once. His wording was somewhat excited, and he made sure Georgiana could not hear before he shared it with me."

Since Georgiana's head was bowed as she raised the cover of one tablet to check on the status of the download, none of the gentlemen saw her small smile of triumph.

Richard was not nearly as thorough as he thought he was in making sure I was not within earshot! I shall definitely ensure he minds his language once we are safely married!

AMONG SEVERAL SURPRISES McDUNN DISCOVERED IN HIS PACK WAS A partially used package of ballpoint pens in one of the many pouches.

"Ballpoint pens," he said as he demonstrated how the pens worked and handed one to each of the others. "I think I can get some use out of these, at least, unlike a bunch of the other rubbish I put aside."

"Another marvel!" exclaimed Darcy, inspecting the fine, precise lines of his signature using McDunn's ballpoint pen.

"But only of transitory use for us since the ink in them won't last forever. I doubt it'll be possible to manufacture anything like them very soon."

McDunn picked up a quill pen from a nearby writing desk and inspected it critically. "It's going to be a pain to have to learn to write with one of these, though."

"There are metal nib pens available. I purchased one in London, but it seemed to clog too often," Darcy commented. "I think it might be due to the ink, but determining such things is your skill rather than mine."

"I'll take a look at it," McDunn said, putting the pens in a drawer of the desk Darcy had directed be moved into his room. "I might figure out something better, but it's doubtful a new writing implement would be initially profitable. Perhaps later, but feel free to use these when you're in this room. We might as well get some use out of them before the ink dries up, but we'd best keep their existence private."

Pulling a pad of paper from his pack, McDunn handed it to Darcy. "Here's something else I had forgotten about. I'd like to figure out how to make paper like this eventually, but I think it'll have to wait for a while. Maybe I'll look at it when I try to develop a better ink pen."

Darcy and Fitzwilliam inspected the pad of paper. The sheets were thin and dense compared to the rather porous paper they used. Georgiana showed no interest. Her letter writing had been limited since Fitzwilliam returned from Spain.

When McDunn had gone through everything in his pack, the only things remaining were his rifles and the canvas bag of ammunition. Georgiana's curiosity again seemed boundless, and she was quite interested.

"William described your rifles to me, but I have not seen them closely. May I examine them, Major?"

McDunn glanced at her brother who only shrugged and said nothing. Fitzwilliam, on the other hand, openly chuckled.

"Very well, then," McDunn said. "Let me take everything out."

He retrieved his battle rifle first and laid it on the table, first pulling the bolt open to ensure it was unloaded. "This is the main weapon most of us in the Brigade used. The M-36 rifle. It's not mine, but it was the one on my shoulder when the Siege sent me through the portal. It really doesn't matter, though, since all of these rifles were exactly alike, just like my pistols."

"That is not at all like our muskets and pistols," Fitzwilliam said. "My pistols were hand-made by a master artificer, and I would not dare try to change a single part from one pistol to another."

McDunn nodded and, the tone of his voice like a chant, said, "This is a United States Rifle, M-36, a gas-fed, rotating bolt, semi- or full-automatic shoulder weapon with a detachable thirty-round box magazine. It fires the

7.62-by-51 millimeter NATO cartridge at a maximum rate of fire of seven hundred fifty rounds per minute, a muzzle velocity of eight hundred fifty meters per second, and a maximum range of five hundred meters with iron sights and eight hundred meters with an optical sight."

Life came back into his face and he smiled. "We had to memorize this description during recruit training, and woe to the recruit who couldn't spit it back to the drill instructor whenever he demanded it! I expect to go to my grave with the recitation on my lips."

"What is this *meter* you mentioned?" Darcy asked. "And *millimeter.* Those are French measurements, are they not?"

"Yup. In the Corps, everything was metric as was almost everything in engineering. Those maniacs who ran the country for a decade and a half tried to ram the metric system down the throats of the populace. It was about the only thing they did I could agree with, but it never caught on completely. The metric system makes sense from a logical point of view."

He handed the unloaded rifle to Fitzwilliam, who inspected it with intense interest. His cousins stood at his elbow and watched.

"Thirty cartridges in one magazine, you say?" Fitzwilliam asked in awe.

"Right. With the rifle set on semi-automatic, a marine could fire one round every time he pulled the trigger, just like my pistol."

"And seven hundred rounds a minute."

"That's a theoretical maximum on full automatic, but we never used full-auto. It used up ammo too quickly, and we didn't have any to spare. 'One round, one bad guy down,' was our motto."

"Ah," Fitzwilliam said, his expression almost ferociously intent as he listened to details he could understand better than the others

"Now, this is a standard thirty-round box magazine," McDunn said, pointing it out on the table. "It slides into the recess on the bottom and doesn't require the marine to stand up to insert it or to change it, unlike your infantry when reloading their musket."

"It would be a great advantage to the British soldier," Fitzwilliam said. "I wish it were one of the inventions you are considering."

"Not in the foreseeable future, at least, for reasons we talked about earlier. I'm not sure the proper strength steel can be made today. And even if it could, there's the difficulty of machining parts to the proper dimensions and tolerances."

Fitzwilliam nodded, his unhappiness quite apparent, and handed the rifle to Darcy, who examined it without his cousin's insight. And Georgiana had to be content with simply holding the rifle in her lap. It was too heavy for her to handle as her cousin and her brother had done.

"As I've mentioned, you'll defeat Napoleon in four or five years. Afterwards, Britain will cut back its armed forces dramatically, especially the army. There simply won't be any money for even simple improvements to their muskets. The army might think it's a good idea, but they won't have the funds to buy it in any numbers."

"Too bad," Darcy said, "but you say England does put paid to the Corsican?"

"In the end. I remember Napoleon was exiled to some island off the coast of Italy, but he came back, and the French nation flocked to his flag. The British and their allies had to fight him all over again. The second time they sent him far away to an island called St. Helena, I think, and he died there."

McDunn stood and retrieved the brown-and-green sheath that had been across his back when he was first discovered. He opened it and pulled out a rifle similar to his M-36 but with a few obvious differences.

"This is an M-40, one of the regiment's sniper rifles. We used it to pick off barbs at really long ranges. It uses the same cartridge as M-36 but it has a thicker, more accurately machined barrel and a highly machined trigger assembly. But the real secret is the optical sights."

He pointed to a black, cylindrical device mounted to the top of the rifle and moved a switch on the top of the scope to turn on the electronics.

"Put it to your shoulder and look through the sights out the window, Colonel," McDunn said.

Fitzwilliam did so and then exclaimed, "Good Lord!"

He took the rifle from his shoulder, looked at it in astonishment, and then looked again. "Do you mean to tell me I can hit anything I can see in this…this—"

"Optical sight. And not exactly. It's zeroed in at eight hundred meters. If a marine sniper calculates range and wind adjustments accurately, he could put a round within a few inches of where the crosshairs lie."

"Astonishing!" Fitzwilliam said, and handed the rifle to Darcy. "With rifles like these, how could your marines lose to those—what did you call them—'barbs'?"

"Because there were always at least twenty or thirty *barbarians* for every one of us," McDunn said bitterly. "We sometimes couldn't kill them quickly enough before we had to bug out to keep them from turning our flank."

McDunn paused at the looks on their faces and thought back to what he'd said. "Uh, 'bug out' is slang for retreating. Fast. The barbs didn't seem to mind dying, you see. Suicide fighters. 'Berserkers' might be a term you're more familiar with. We called them kamikazes, as well as less polite terms."

"I want to see!" Georgiana said. "I want to see!"

But when her brother handed her the rifle, she couldn't lift it to look through the sights.

"Here, let me help, Miss Darcy," McDunn said. "Hand me the rifle and sit in the chair."

By leaning back and supporting the rifle on his chest, McDunn was able to allow Georgiana to look through the telescopic sight. Her exclamations of amazement were on a par with the gentlemen.

McDunn looked over at her brother and cocked one eyebrow. "Blood-thirsty sister you've got, friend Darcy."

"I was thinking the very same thing," Darcy said in response, but he could not fully restrain his smile.

"Be quiet, you two!" Georgiana said, moving the rifle slightly, experimenting with letting the crosshairs move across the landscape.

"We are indeed fortunate your rifle is too heavy for her, Major," Fitzwilliam said dryly. "Otherwise, she would pester you for cartridges so she could deplete Darcy's groves of his deer!"

"There shall be no jests at my expense from you either, Richard!" she said forcefully.

McDunn recognized the tone in her voice, and he glanced aside at Fitzwilliam, who seemed to have noticed nothing.

There was a note of possession in that young lady's voice just now, he thought. *I wonder if Fitzwilliam knows his days as a carefree young bachelor are numbered.*

The only unexamined item remaining was the ammunition, and McDunn started by pulling it out of his pack and stacking it in groups on the table.

"I remember asking Kaswallon to find some ammo," McDunn said, shaking his head in amazement, "but the man stuffed rounds into every little pocket and pouch. There was even some in the pockets of my BDUs. Where'd he find it all?"

When McDunn added the ammunition from the canvas bag, he regarded the piles in a mixture of wonder tinged with frustration.

"It's not quite enough to fight a war, but it's a lot of ammo!" McDunn said to the others. "I'm really amazed. From what I saw when Kaswallon was dragging me to the cave, it looked as though it was hand-to-hand fighting on both sides. That usually doesn't happen until both sides have empty weapons."

He sorted the ammunition into classifications. When he was through, he looked at the stacks a bit less cheerfully.

"I'm disappointed the rifle ammo isn't all the same. Only about two-thirds of it is even ours."

"I am sorry," Georgiana said, looking at the cartridge McDunn was holding up, "but I do not understand."

"This is our ammo, what we called 7.62 mm NATO," McDunn said. "It's actually rather old and was considered obsolete, but there was a lot of it stuffed away in the back of our old ammo dumps. Because the British army used this cartridge longer than we did, we figured we might find a bunch of it in some of the British army dumps. And we did, but not as much as we'd hoped."

He held up a different, smaller cartridge. "This is the ammo the bad guys used for their AK-47s. It's shorter and lighter than ours, and it won't fit our rifles. Without an AK, it's useless. But at least there are a couple of dozen loaded magazines for my pistols."

The other three fell silent. Since McDunn was mystified, they seemed even more so.

"This is more ammo than I originally thought," McDunn said, "but I'm still irked, and I shouldn't be. Maybe that's it. I've had so much good luck, I'm reacting childishly to some bad luck. Whatever the case, I think I'll have a drink. Anyone care to join me?"

Darcy nodded his assent, and his cousin said, "Capital idea! In fact, I believe I will have a glass of your disgusting whisky since I know my cousin sent you another bottle."

McDunn gave a sharp laugh and returned with glasses for everyone, including two glasses filled with the dark liquor.

"Absent comrades," he said, holding up his glass.

"Absent comrades," all three said, and there was now a world of understanding and friendship in their toast. McDunn and Fitzwilliam had understood each other from the first, but the past few days had given the others a deeper meaning of it.

Chapter 7

A friend is a person with whom I may be sincere. Before him, I may think aloud.

— Ralph Waldo Emerson (1803-1882)
US poet, essayist, and lecturer

Late October 1809
Pemberley, Derbyshire

After going through all of the items he'd carried through the portal, as well as the contents of his pack and his canvas bags, McDunn turned his attention to the software and technical data in his tablets, spending hours sorting through the files for information relevant to his new world.

One afternoon while he was deeply immersed in his investigations, his three friends interrupted him, and the twinkle in their eyes informed him this was something more than a casual visit.

"I have some interesting news," Darcy said.

"May I assume it's good news, given that you're not even trying to maintain your usual dour expression?"

"You may," Darcy said, laughing aloud, which was even more unusual. "You remember Georgiana did a definitive accounting of your gold?"

"I do. More than thirty-four hundred Krugerrands."

"Three thousand, four hundred, and forty-four Krugerrands," Georgiana said firmly, "along with one hundred fifty-seven Canadian gold maple leaf coins and thirty-two Britannia bullion coins."

McDunn's eyebrows rose, and she smiled slightly. "I looked up the other coins in the encyclopedia on your tablet, Major."

"Ah! Very enterprising, Miss Darcy."

"And she also weighed your coins using a jeweler's scale I had sent up from town," Darcy said. "All of them."

"Almost all the Krugerrands were heavier than a troy ounce, and they varied quite a bit," Georgiana said. "The other coins did the same."

"We will most likely get some variation when we melt down the coins and take the nuggets to a gold dealer in town, since only a precious metal dealer can truly assess the purity of the gold," Darcy said.

"And I've been doing a little snooping of my own," McDunn said. "If we can find a way to send the blacksmith and the stable-hands somewhere for an afternoon, I believe the three of us—"

"—and me!" said Georgiana.

"I stand corrected. The *four* of us can use the blacksmith forge to melt down the coins without involving anyone else."

"In any case," Darcy said, "using the figure of ninety percent pure for the Krugerrands, I believe we can now put an approximate value on your fortune. You should be able to put more than twenty-four thousand pounds into the Funds when we sell all the gold."

McDunn was tempted to nod knowledgeably at this, but it seemed better to be truthful. "I think I need to admit my ignorance here, Darcy, but from your expression, I assume it's quite a bit of money."

Fitzwilliam gave a bark of laughter at this, and even Darcy smiled. But it was Georgiana who said gently, "That is more than twice my brother's yearly income, Major. Twice."

Of course! McDunn thought in embarrassment. *Austen said Darcy had an immense fortune of ten thousand a year! What an idiot I am!*

He looked at his tablet and did a search, after which he leaned back and whistled appreciatively. "I'm not totally certain about these conversions, but that amount seems to be more than twenty million in 2045 US dollars."

He looked at the others with a serious expression. "So, it appears I'll be a wealthy man, which is certainly a good deal better than being penniless. But I'm still worried about being able to fund what I want to do. When I figure out what that *is*, of course. I just don't have any experience in business matters. All my training was in technology, not in monetary affairs."

"I have been thinking on that topic, Major," Darcy said carefully. "When all of your gold is converted to pounds and invested in the Funds, it will prove somewhat difficult to move money in and out. It would be better for me to make the purchases from my own income. Then you can reimburse me when the total becomes large enough to make a withdrawal worthwhile. I am so interested in your projects, I would like to be a part of them. In fact, I think I would like to share the risk with you in equal measure."

McDunn regarded Darcy silently for some moments, his mind racing as he digested what his friend had just offered and its possibilities. Finally, he said, slowly and carefully, "Let me make sure I understand you correctly. You've already offered your estate as a location for my investigations and even some experiments when I get to that point. Now you're offering to participate in my projects by advancing the funds needed for purchases to be paid back later. In addition, you offer to share the risk with me. Would that be a correct summary?"

"Of course," Darcy said with a smile. "But you phrase it so formally when your usual mode of expression is quite informal."

"It's because I'm in uncharted territory. My training is in science, but I never had a chance to gain any practical experience. But I do know this: I cannot simply accept your proposal without offering anything in return. I believe you should benefit from whatever we do together."

"I see," Darcy said though clearly he, in fact, did not see at all.

"Yes. If I accept your generous offer, my plans can't be just *my* plans anymore. They have to be *our* plans. And you need to have a voice and a vote in how we do things as well as benefit from our successes. It cannot just be an Edward McDunn endeavor. It must become a *joint* endeavor."

McDunn turned suddenly and looked at Fitzwilliam, who had only been listening politely.

"In fact, we also need to include your cousin since the time will come when we need his help with the military. In short, my friends, I'm afraid you *both* must enter the world of trade. We must form a partnership."

Darcy looked taken aback. "A partnership?"

"Yes, indeed. Darcy, Fitzwilliam, and McDunn, Limited or something similar. I'm a bit hazy about how corporations work at this time. In fact, I read something on my tablet indicating England outlawed anything other than individual liability for debts. It may leave you holding the bag liability-wise, Darcy, if things go very wrong, and we can't have that."

"Holding the bag?" Fitzwilliam said. "Liability-wise? The first must be one of your Americanisms, of which you seem to have an unlimited number."

"Possibly so," McDunn said, smiling broadly. "My point is, we'll need some legal advice, which I hope Darcy can arrange. We'll also need assistance with things like bookkeeping, and I'm certain there are legal forms we'll have to generate and submit. But if you're going to support my work financially, Darcy, you must have a say in what we do and also benefit from whatever financial benefit we accrue. The same is true for you, Fitzwilliam, though I hope you'll not take it amiss when I say your share will necessarily be less than that of your cousin and me."

"Of course," Fitzwilliam said, "but I have to say I am rather enthralled by how fast events are moving this afternoon, especially since I only accompanied Darcy today to be polite. We all know I cannot contribute what the two of you can, so I shall be more than happy to trust in whatever you decide."

"Good man," McDunn said, clapping Fitzwilliam on the shoulder. "But don't worry. We'll figure out something equitable."

Turning back to Darcy, McDunn said, "We'll have to do everything with a handshake at first while we have someone check on the legalities. And we don't want to do anything that might enable a creditor to go after your personal fortune, which means no borrowing for now. If we can't do what we want with the cash you or I have, we won't do it. We don't want to put Pemberley at risk in case events turn sour."

"No, I do not," Darcy said slowly. "I have to admit, I was a bit surprised you did not welcome my offer wholeheartedly, but that is not the case at all, is it? Instead, you are trying to make sure the Darcy family is protected."

"Exactly. But I'm an amateur when it comes to business, and I still have so much to learn about such matters in your times. We need to find some good people and employ them to give us a hand, but we want to do so without giving them any way of taking control of our partnership. I've read about how sharp operators and outright thieves have done similar things in my time, but I haven't a clue how we can protect ourselves today."

"I see." After a moment, Darcy smiled and extended his hand. "About that handshake—"

McDunn seized his hand and pumped it forcefully, with a broad smile of his own, and then did the same to Fitzwilliam. "Welcome, partners!"

Georgiana, who had been listening with wide eyes, could no longer contain herself. "Oh, this is so exciting! What shall be my role in this partnership?"

McDunn and her brother stared at her in silence for a moment while she beamed happily at them.

"Well, she makes an apt point," Darcy said resignedly.

"True, true. And now we can bind her to secrecy legally. But what should we put her to work doing?"

"Perhaps keeping records and accounts?"

McDunn nodded thoughtfully. "She can become the Chief Financial Officer."

"I was very good at my sums at school! And my penmanship is excellent," Georgiana said happily.

"The work will be very boring," McDunn said, his face deadpan but his eyes full of mischief. "And your hand will cramp from writing down all the figures. Perhaps we should think of another task."

"Nonsense!" she said, with a disdainful sniff. "I know all of you too well by now. If I do not keep the records correctly, you will never be able to figure out what has been done and who is owed money."

A thought struck her, and she spoke with a bit less certainty. "Though it might be a good idea to find someone to assist me. Someone with some experience…"

Her voice trailed off though her eyes lingered on Fitzwilliam, who clapped McDunn on the shoulder. "That seals it, Major! You have a volunteer who is both eager and willing to learn, and all she needs is a bit of assistance from an older and wiser head, which fits me perfectly! What could be better?"

And perhaps, Georgiana thought, *I will not have to be presented at court, come out into society, and have my Season.* As she did not voice it aloud, none of the others knew her secret.

Chapter 8

///

Far better is it to dare mighty things, to win glorious triumphs, even though checked by failure...than to rank with those poor spirits who neither enjoy much nor suffer much, because they live in a gray twilight that knows not victory nor defeat.

— Theodore Roosevelt, American adventurer,
war hero, and twentieth US president

\\

Friday, November 3, 1809
Pemberley, Derbyshire

I'm still not sure this is a good idea," McDunn said, staring doubtfully at the large, dark-brown horse Darcy and Fitzwilliam called a "hunter" that was being saddled in preparation for his first riding lesson. "I know I agreed, but it was in a moment of weakness. I kind of hoped you'd forgotten about it."

"Nonsense, Major," Fitzwilliam said. "Every gentleman needs to know how to ride."

"But I'm not a gentleman, and this thing is immense. I'm going to break something if I fall off—something I'm going to need."

"There is nothing to fear, old stick!" Fitzwilliam said, showing all of his teeth in a fierce grin. "Why, Pollux is so gentle, Georgiana could ride him! And he is barely fourteen and a half hands! My own Pennington is a full hand higher."

"Whatever," responded McDunn, clearly less than convinced, and both his tone and another of his Americanisms brought a laugh from the other three.

"You will make a splendid rider once I get through with you," Fitzwilliam said cheerfully. "His Majesty's cavalry has developed excellent techniques to teach recruits to ride. Officers, being gentlemen, are assumed to know already and have to bring their own mounts. But the other ranks usually have no experience and need instruction."

"Excellent techniques, is it?" Darcy said teasingly. "What, pray, are these excellent methods?"

"We do it by a set of rules, you know," Colonel Fitzwilliam said. "Rule number one: when you fall off your horse, immediately rise and get back on—after you catch him, of course."

"And rule number two?" McDunn asked suspiciously.

"Follow rule number one," Fitzwilliam said, cracking not even a hint of a smile. Darcy gave a bark of laughter, but McDunn's response was a groan.

"Come, come, McDunn!" Fitzwilliam said, now grinning openly. "Would you not prefer to ride to battle than to walk? It is not only more gentlemanly but far less work."

"I regard sitting up on top of one of those massive beasts while galloping about the battlefield primarily as a way to provide an excellent target for the bad guys. My skin crawls at the very thought of it, and my hard-earned survival instincts tell me I should get down flat on the ground and behind some solid cover so I can shoot with a lot more safety. Even better would be a fighting hole so I wouldn't be so vulnerable to artillery."

"Ha! Artillery is frightening, I admit, but musketry, especially French musketry, is pathetic. We lose a few troopers to musketry but not many."

"That's now. Smoothbore muskets are wildly inaccurate except at very short range, but it's going to change in the not-too-distant future.

Fitzwilliam mulled over this unpleasant comment. "From what you have told me, warfare in the future sounds exceedingly unpleasant."

"I've seen it, and I hate it even more than you," McDunn said forcefully. "The only reason I was a marine was because someone needed to defend civilization against the bad guys. Anyway, I think we've had more than enough morbid conversation. Let's talk about something more pleasant."

"Excellent suggestion. Now, the first thing you should note is the saddle. When I was first learning to ride, my grandfather's horse master made me saddle my horse repeatedly until I had blisters on all my fingers and could do it in my sleep. I thought it best to pass over that particular task."

"And a good thing you did, Fitzwilliam, else I'd have instantly forgotten my agreement to learn to ride and would be striding manfully back to the house."

"But you should at least note the following about this particular saddle, which is the type my regiment uses. It is derived from the kind made famous by the Hungarians though some are starting to call it the English saddle."

McDunn's eyes glazed over as Fitzwilliam pointed out the various parts of the saddle, and he stifled a yawn when Fitzwilliam moved on to other salient points such as mounting, correct posture astride the horse, use of the reins, starting and stopping the animal, and dismounting. The cavalryman was just warming to other less critical topics when McDunn held up his hand.

"For Heaven's sake, Fitzwilliam, stop! How am I supposed to remember everything? Nothing more, please! I agreed to learn to ride, so let's get to it."

"But do you not find the topic interesting?" Fitzwilliam asked in genuine surprise.

"Not nearly as engrossing as you do."

"Very well," Fitzwilliam said. Then, unable to hold back any longer, he pointed at the clothes McDunn wore and burst out laughing.

"I know, I know," McDunn said as he looked down at his grey imitation-BDU trousers and his grayish-white T-shirt, both still damp from his morning exercise. "I'm dressed most unfashionably, but I wanted to get my run completed before trying to ride this monster. Since I may well be paralyzed after this morning's adventure, I wanted to be able to remember I could once run for three miles without even breathing hard."

"Oh, Major, you are so amusing!" Georgiana said lightly.

"I'll have nothing out of you, young lady," McDunn said, trying to adopt the firmness of an older brother. "I remember the part you played in talking me into this hazardous enterprise!"

Somehow, this just made all three—especially Georgiana—laugh harder. At last, when the merriment subsided, McDunn pointed to his feet.

"All of you comedians will note I did change from my running boots to my newly delivered riding boots. And I brought my gloves. I realize I'm not nearly the splendiferous example of sartorial elegance you and other members of the gentry usually display, but you must remember I'm—"

"—an American," all three finished for him in unison.

"What, pray, is that on your head, sir?" Darcy asked.

McDunn took off his camouflaged USMC soft hat, which bore a certain resemblance to the caps used by baseball teams in his time. He had found it among the items in his pack when he did his inventory.

"It's just my regulation utility cover."

"Cover?" Georgiana asked in confusion. "Why on earth do you call it a *cover*? It is just a hat, is it not?"

"A *cover* is what we marines called our headgear no matter what type it was, whether full dress or utility dress like this one," he said, feigning infinite patience. "As for why it's called a cover, I haven't a clue. Why do you call the vest you're wearing a *wes-kit*, Darcy? I happen to know it's spelled like waistcoat."

"I have not a clue," Darcy said, attempting to control his expression but having to forsake the effort as the other three laughed.

"But see here?" McDunn said, pointing to an insignia inked on the front of his cap above the bill. "This is the famous Marine Corps eagle, globe, and anchor that you've all seen before on my stuff. And I even pinned my gunnery sergeant chevrons on my cover. I thought it looked pretty spiffy when I checked myself in the mirror. If I'm not to survive this morning, you see, I wish to be buried in suitable attire."

"I am sure you will do well today!" Georgiana said with certainty.

"So you've said before. But you have to admit, Miss Darcy, I'm a lot more comfortably dressed than your brother or your cousin. If I do take a fall, I'd rather be free to tuck and roll without having to worry about splitting a seam like your menfolk would."

Fitzwilliam drew himself up into a haughty pose. "I do not plan to fall."

"Of course, you don't. Now, how do we get this show on the road?"

"Pardon me?" Fitzwilliam asked and then at once perceived the sense of the saying. "Ah. I see. Getting the show on the road. That is a good one, Major! Mind if I steal it?"

"Not in the slightest. I didn't invent it."

"Thank you. Now, use the step to mount your horse. It is possible to do so with the stirrup, but it is easier with a step. Ah, very good. Yes, boots in the stirrups and the toes pointed up as I told you. Excellent."

"Fitzwilliam, this is a lot higher off the ground than I thought it would be."

"You will become accustomed to it. All new riders do. Now, let me examine your posture. Back upright and straight, good. Shoulders up a bit…good. Now, bring your legs forward. You want to have a straight line from your ear through your shoulders and hips down to your heels, your legs in a solid position to support you as you move from a walk through a trot and canter. Galloping will come later. We shall start at a walk today and move to a trot. But we will not spend too much time trotting. Beastly uncomfortable. A canter is much more comfortable. Now, after Darcy and I mount, we can be off."

McDunn was surprised at how much more he could see. He was so used to seeing everything from the vantage of an infantryman that the different aspect from the back of the horse made him understand why officers in the armies of 1809 always wanted to view the ground while mounted.

And though the motion of his horse was initially disconcerting as the three of them left the stables, it was not as disturbing as he had anticipated. Later on, he found Fitzwilliam had been correct about a trotting horse. A trot felt like someone was pounding a hammer up the line of his spine. He was relieved when Fitzwilliam told him to kick his horse up to a canter. That was much better, though they only maintained the pace for a minute or so before dropping back to a walk.

The lesson continued for another hour, moving through various elements of riding, before they turned for the house.

For McDunn, the biggest surprise came when he dismounted.

"Ow!" McDunn exclaimed. "My back hurts low down. And the fronts and insides of my legs are killing me. But how can that be? I'm in good shape, and I was warmed up and loose."

"I am not surprised," Fitzwilliam informed him. "I have seen you run, and riding uses different muscles. It will pass as you get more practice."

"I hope so," McDunn said, trying to stretch out those muscles that hurt but quickly giving up the effort since stretching just made the pain worse.

"You did very well," Georgiana said. "I thought you looked very natural—except for your outlandish attire, of course, but I shall soon put that aright."

"Whatever you say, Miss Darcy. Right now, all I want to do is soak in a hot tub of water, as hot as I can stand."

"It will pass," Fitzwilliam said. "What is the saying you taught me from your Corps of Marines? Pain is only—"

"Pain is only weakness leaving the body," McDunn groaned, hobbling a bit as he and Fitzwilliam returned to the house. "You've far too good a memory, partner. I'm going to have to be more careful about what I say to you."

Fitzwilliam only nodded and smiled.

Wednesday, November 15, 1809
Pemberley, Derbyshire

At the noon meal, McDunn was enjoying a second cup of Darcy's excellent coffee with the other gentlemen when Georgiana finally made her appearance. He waited until her food had been set before her and the servant had left before he spoke. "I would like to suggest a gathering in my sitting room after this for a council of war."

The others looked at him with interest since he had spent the last several days deep in research.

Darcy was the first to speak. "I take it you have decided how best to proceed?"

"I have, but I reiterate I will only be making a suggestion, not a command decision. I need the agreement of my partners.

"What is this council of war, Major?" Georgiana asked with concern. "What *war* are you speaking of?"

"He means a meeting where all of us try to agree on a course of action, Georgiana," Fitzwilliam said. "It is different from the command decision he mentioned where he would simply make the decision without asking our opinions."

Georgiana nodded, though the nod seemed a bit dubious.

McDunn rose from his chair. "Then I'll see you all shortly."

Darcy and his sister found McDunn's door already open and both McDunn and Fitzwilliam holding glasses half-filled with Scotch. Darcy shuddered at the thought that not only had his cousin been corrupted into trying it, but he was beginning to show a real preference for the drink. Darcy could only shake his head in bemusement.

He said as much aloud, and both McDunn and Fitzwilliam chuckled.

"The colonel is a fine fellow, Darcy," McDunn said cheerfully. "A credit to your family. Not only does he show an admirable liberality in associating with a mere sergeant—although it is well known throughout the entire

US Marine Corps that sergeants actually run things—but he's developed a taste for this imitation Scotch your butler supplies."

"I would like to propose a toast to sergeants," Fitzwilliam said with a laugh. "Fine fellows even if we have more sense than to let them run things."

"You only think they don't, Fitz," McDunn said.

"Something leads me to believe this is not the first glass of this swill you two have sampled," Darcy said, pouring himself a glass of port and handing Georgiana a glass of watered wine. "And the sun has barely passed its zenith."

"Swill?" Fitzwilliam challenged, taking another sip. "I used to say the same, but I have learned otherwise. It is the perfect drink for a penniless younger son."

"I understand George Washington owned a distillery, and he pretty much gave you Brits everything you could handle a few decades back," McDunn said.

"And yet another vulgarity!" Fitzwilliam declared with a flashing of white teeth in his tanned face. "Brits!"

"Short for the people of Great Britain. Though you wouldn't suspect it right now, what with the Revolutionary War being relatively recent and with tensions increasing with the US, but both countries will become firm friends and allies in the not too distant future. For almost a century and a half in my world. Two world wars, two minor wars, and a host of smaller conflicts. Yeah, we call you Brits, and you call us Yanks."

"Well, only proper, after all, since we share a common language."

"One of your future statesmen once said the United States and Great Britain were two countries *separated* by a common language!"

"He did, did he?" Fitzwilliam said, pounding a knee. "Sounds like a stalwart fellow! And you know I am going to steal that one too!"

"Of course," McDunn said, thinking Winston Churchill would have been appalled to see his country reduced to what it had been in 2045.

"Well, that Washington fellow was rather stalwart too, even if he did own a distillery," Fitzwilliam said.

"I still cannot believe he did not become King George the First of North America," Darcy opined. "All the dons at Cambridge spoke of it. Everyone, literally everyone, seemed to believe he would. They did not so much as question it."

"Interesting man, Washington. Fine president. We needed more like him. Our President Davis might have gone down in history as very much like him—if the fanatics hadn't killed him and the rest of our government leaders in the Massacre."

Setting his glass on the table, McDunn sighed. "Time to get down to brass tacks."

"Uh, Major?" Georgiana said.

"You don't say that now? Well, it means getting down to essential stuff. I have no idea where it came from, but it looks as though it's sometime in the future."

"American sayings," Fitzwilliam said. "As I said, he must have an unlimited supply."

"As you know, I've been busy these past weeks, especially the last few days. We've talked several times about the possibilities I was considering, but I'm now fairly certain what our first project should be."

"The telegraph?" Darcy said.

"Exactly. I think it has the best possibilities for becoming profitable, and the expenditures to build a working prototype shouldn't be nearly as extensive as something like the steam locomotive."

"I had been holding out hope for the breech-loading rifle," Fitzwilliam said sadly. "Or those revolver pistols you mentioned. My men could use those, but I always knew they were low on your list."

"The dynamite you spoke of was intriguing," Darcy said, "but you are probably correct it would be more valuable in the United States than in Britain. More land there—more construction needed."

"Especially since McDunn says there is going to be a war between our two countries in a few years," Fitzwilliam said morosely. "As though we did not have enough troubles! Those idiots in the government!"

"Well, the US has more than a few idiots of its own, Fitz."

"I do not understand how you can be so casual about a war," Georgiana said, rather anxiously.

"I came from the year 2045, not 1812, Miss Darcy," McDunn said with a shrug. "I have no real feeling of allegiance to the United States of this coming war with your country. It'll be a stupid war with plenty of fault on both sides, but at least it'll be a small war compared to your war with France."

Georgiana nodded, then she turned rather pink before she said timidly, "I liked your ideas about…plumbing."

"Me, too," McDunn grinned. "I miss proper plumbing. But there are too many problems associated with making it work, especially in the cities. However, while I'm working on the telegraph, which I hope to sell to your government for lots of money, I'm planning a side project here at Pemberley with working toilets and water flowing through pipes inside the house. Pemberley has lots of land for the waste handling possible with a septic system. It may not be very cost efficient, but it'll work."

He nodded to Darcy. "Consider it partial payment for not throwing me off your land or having me trundled off to Bethlem Royal Hospital."

"Nonsense. You have successfully convinced me all of us are going to make a great deal of money," Darcy said. "You may be a lunatic American, but you are *my* lunatic American."

McDunn looked at him in stunned silence for a moment. "That sounds very much like an American saying."

"It does?" Darcy said, clearly pleased. "Well, great minds and all that."

"That did, too!" McDunn said before turning to Georgiana. "Your brother is associating with entirely the wrong class of people, Miss Darcy. You must do something."

"Now stop it!" she said, her hand over her mouth. "You were going to speak of the telegraph, brother!"

"Ah yes, the telegraph. The idea appears to have obsessed you to the point that you skipped several days of the physical punishment you laughingly call exercise."

"Well, it is getting rather cold in the morning. And I wanted all of us to consider my suggestions before heading to London. I thought we needed to reach agreement before we left. And I've convinced myself, so I wanted to present my ideas to you. It's always a good idea to have other people comment on your thinking so you don't out-clever yourself."

"Is that a word, William?" Georgiana asked. "*Out-clever*? I have certainly never heard it before."

"No, Miss Darcy," McDunn said. "I very much doubt it's a real word either in your time or in mine. It just came to mind as a description of someone falling in love with his own clever ideas. My research has shown it's happened with distressing regularity throughout history."

"I suppose the word does capture the essence, my dear," her brother said. "Now, I believe it would be best to let the major proceed."

McDunn nodded cheerfully. "One of the best reasons for choosing the telegraph is that it can be done in the here-and-now, and the time is right. Some people are already looking at ways of sending messages electrically, but none of those ideas are anything close to workable and won't be for a number of years. We can produce a better product in a shorter period of time—less than a year, hopefully—since we can avoid the mistakes and the false leads other inventors pursued."

He went on to explain how the telegraph system he envisioned would work. It would use only a single copper wire with a telegraph key sending pulses by means of a simple but effective battery that historically would not be invented until 1860. It would also use electromagnets—not invented until 1824—at the receiving end to produce clicks an operator could hear. He also described how the clicks could be formed into a code for the letters and numbers.

"That's where I think we ought to bring you in, Fitz. I plan to call the telegraph system itself the Darcy-Fitzwilliam Telegraph, and the code I plan to use is going to be called the Fitzwilliam Code. You're going to have to learn the theory of this code by heart until you can explain the ins and outs of it and the advantages it gives. I don't think you'll need to actually learn to operate the telegraph key, but you'll need to learn the theory of the code thoroughly."

"Do you understand any of this, Darcy?" Fitzwilliam asked.

"A word here and there."

"But this madman is saying I have to learn some kind of code! I can ride anything with four legs, and I am an excellent swordsman and a passable shot—but codes!"

"McDunn has obviously spent a prodigious amount of time and effort studying this, and I am sure he has good reasons for his suggestions. We owe him our full attention."

"Be patient, Richard," urged Georgiana.

"It'll all work out," McDunn said. "Trust me. You need to be a full member of this partnership, and if you take ownership of the code, it'll be a weight off my shoulders."

"Ownership!" groaned Fitzwilliam. "*Another* word I do not understand! Will there ever be an end to them?"

"Never, Fitz, never!" McDunn said cheerfully. "I think the version of the code that was the international standard for decades would be best. To tell the truth, I really haven't given it the careful thought I gave the rest of the system, and I'd appreciate another viewpoint on how to make it better."

He paused for a moment then said, "One more thing, Fitz. Being the go-to guy for the code—"

Fitzwilliam groaned at this, so McDunn only grinned before continuing.

"—it'll give you a presence before the government and military people we have to convince to buy this thing. That may come in handy for you in future years."

"*Whatever*," Fitzwilliam said with a depth of feeling that had everyone laughing.

McDunn clapped him firmly on the shoulder and said, "Now, here are some of the sketches and drawings I've made—"

After everything was explained, questioned, answered, and a consensus reached, Georgiana held up her hand.

"There is one thing I find somewhat troubling, Major," she said, and it seemed as though she had a hard time meeting his gaze. "It seems…that is… should we be worried about the people who are working on this problem now? Is it unfair?"

McDunn was not offended. "Progress has always been a cutthroat business, Miss Darcy, and competition always has losers as well as winners. But none of the present versions of electrical transmission of messages is going to work. And when it finally does, the people working on it now won't be the ones who benefit. We'll just be stepping in and producing a workable product right away. I'm going to compete ferociously. We *have* to succeed at this. I will *not* waste your brother's money by failing. No way."

Georgiana still did not look completely satisfied, but McDunn was glad to see her brows unknit as she gave him a sheepish smile.

"Perhaps you could clap *her* on the shoulder, Yank," Fitzwilliam said, only to have to leap from his chair as Georgiana flew after him. Luckily, he was able to get the door open before she could catch him, but she was still in hot pursuit, and the sound of their running feet receded down the hallway.

"Ah," McDunn said, leaning back and sipping his drink, "to quote a movie my grandfather loved and I watched with him a number of times, they'll make a fine, boisterous couple once they're safely married."

Darcy was so startled by the comment he forgot to ask what a "movie" was. He looked at McDunn intently for several moments since he had actually mused a time or two that McDunn himself might make a good match for his sister. At last, he relaxed and leaned back in his chair, looking at McDunn thoughtfully.

"Perhaps they will, Major Edward McDunn," he said slowly. "Perhaps they will."

Chapter 9

Thursday, December 21, 1809
Darcy Townhouse, London

C ome!" called McDunn.

One of the servants opened his door to announce that Mr. Darcy wished him to come downstairs.

"Please inform Mr. Darcy I shall be down directly," he said, turning back to his drawing and adding just one more detail before standing up. He looked at it wistfully, wishing to continue just a bit longer, but he knew himself too well. When he became immersed in a task, he might look up to find an hour or two had passed.

As McDunn rose and donned his coat, he reflected on having grown used to the fashionable attire Georgiana had so gleefully arranged for him. It was much like wearing a military uniform, and he had certainly worn uniforms much more uncomfortable.

Like Marine dress blues, he thought sadly, remembering the only set he had ever owned. They had been presented to him by his regiment when he was promoted to gunnery sergeant, the youngest gunny in the Corps at the time. He left them hanging in his closet at home when he was recalled to duty, and he supposed they were atomized dust floating over the ruins of Beaufort along with everything from his previous life.

Since leaving Pemberley for London the previous month, he had been immersed in the details of preparing to produce their telegraph. The task had been his alone since Fitzwilliam had been called back to his regiment.

The colonel had been uncomfortable when he first began working on the telegraph code, but he had studied the historical records on McDunn's computer tablet and gradually learned what he had to know. From Fitzwilliam's last letter, he had decided on the version of International Morse Code best suited to their plans with the addition of a few extra punctuation symbols—a period, a comma, a question mark, and an exclamation mark.

McDunn had left it in Fitzwilliam's hands, reminding him of the KISS principal—Keep It Simple, Stupid. They did not want to make the code too complicated right from the start.

Fitzwilliam had only nodded and tucked his papers into a pocket of his red coat before leaving. He might have been a bit unhappy at his assignment, but he had understood the necessity and had done his best.

The remaining partners' first task had been finding a suitable workshop in which to hand-craft the components of their telegraph, a venture made difficult by McDunn's total ignorance of London and by Darcy's knowledge being confined to the more fashionable parts of town.

But the task had been completed thanks to assistance from several of Darcy's friends and acquaintances. They had also located and hired a quartet of artisans skilled at working with metal and wood. Even with McDunn's assistance, the four of them struggled to assemble and test the battery and the parts of the telegraph key that would send electrical pulses over the copper wires.

Learning about the less fashionable—and less safe—districts of London had been required for both of them because it was in those areas that most business and trade was conducted. It was where they had found their workshop and workers. Additional employees were going to be required after the parts of the first components of the Darcy-Fitzwilliam telegraph system were crafted by file, chisel, and saw. Once the concept was tested and working, additional units would need to be produced for the demonstration he envisioned.

As a result, he had spent many hours in the dark and narrow alleys of East London. From the first day, it had been clear that traveling to the east side by coach would not work. Neither Darcy's coach nor his carriage could easily maneuver those narrow, twisting streets, so they traveled on horseback.

The problem remained that a pair of fashionably dressed gentlemen were far too attractive to some of the more nefarious denizens of the area. Darcy had insisted, even on their first visit, on a pair of armed footmen accompanying them, and Brown, the footman he had almost shot the previous September, had volunteered quickly and forcefully to be one of the pair.

"I'll not allow any harm to come to ye, Major," he had said.

While that seemed reasonable to McDunn, he nevertheless tucked his own pistol and a pair of spare magazines in a shoulder holster under his fashionable outer coat.

Brown had seen its outline and nodded in approval. "Best safe than otherwise, sir."

ARRIVING DOWNSTAIRS, McDUNN FOUND DARCY SPEAKING WITH A YOUNG man and an attractive young woman.

Bingley, I'll bet, thought McDunn as all of them rose when he entered. *And that's probably the infamous Caroline Bingley, she of the supercilious smile. I believe his other sister is older and married.*

Darcy motioned to McDunn as he walked in. "Bingley, may I present my friend, Major McDunn?"

"Honored, sir," Bingley said.

"The honor is mine."

"And this is his sister, Miss Bingley. Miss Bingley, Major McDunn."

"Honored, Miss Bingley," McDunn said, bowing. Darcy's eyebrows furrowed as Caroline's only response was the merest nod of her head.

McDunn saw the same thing, but he was amused rather than offended. *It was predictable that Miss Bingley and I would never have a friendly relationship. A cool, distant relationship is about the best I could hope for, and even that seems unlikely after her greeting.*

Bingley, seemingly unaware of the cut, turned to Darcy with a smile. "I have good news. Louisa is engaged to be married."

Ah, she's not yet married, McDunn thought.

"That is wonderful news, Bingley. Give her my best wishes."

"She would have come, but she came down with a splitting headache and remained in bed."

"How unfortunate!" Darcy said, though McDunn thought his friend seemed unsurprised.

"Once Louisa is married to Mr. Hurst, Caroline will assume the task of managing my household. I am still interested in finding a suitable residence, hopefully in the country."

"As I have told you before, you must not become discouraged. Finding a suitable estate can be a lengthy endeavor and requires careful investigation. Far too many families in financial straits try to dispose of an estate for more than it is worth. Be patient and keep looking, but be careful."

"Just as a point of information, Darcy," McDunn said, "do I assume this is not a proper time to shake hands? Your English stiff bows seem so lacking in warmth to me."

"As I mentioned, despite our handshake on first meeting, shaking hands is rare in society."

Turning to Bingley, Darcy explained. "The major is an American, you see, and Americans seem to be mad about shaking hands."

"It's what I'm used to," McDunn said with a shrug. "Bowing seems so sterile."

"A colonial!" cried Bingley. "You are the first of my acquaintance, Major. We must, by all means, shake hands."

He thrust out his hand, and McDunn judged his grip to be quite adequate, though by no means as robust as either Darcy or Fitzwilliam.

"What brings you to London, Major?" Bingley asked with an enthusiasm McDunn recognized from Austen's depiction. "Are you visiting?"

"It's more in the nature of a permanent relocation."

"Wonderful! Let us have a seat and you can tell me about yourself. May I interest you in a glass of Darcy's excellent brandy?"

McDunn found Bingley an entertaining and warmhearted fellow, and Bingley's interest appeared stimulated when he learned of the business association between him and Darcy. McDunn had to choose his words carefully as he described what he hoped to accomplish since Darcy had understandably decided not to include Bingley in their secrets. Now that he had met him, McDunn had to agree. He thought the man would be an excellent dinner guest and a good friend, but keeping secrets would never be one of his strong suits.

At one point before Bingley and his sister departed, McDunn overheard Caroline urgently whispering to Darcy.

"He cannot be a gentleman," she said, almost hissing. "I am certain of it, not with his atrocious speech."

"That is merely the accent of his home country," Darcy said with seeming composure, but the hairs on the back of McDunn's head stood up as he recognized Darcy's displeasure.

"And he is completely ignorant of the proper conduct demanded of a gentleman!" she continued, seemingly heedless of the effect she was having. "Look at him! Wanting to shake hands instead of exchanging a proper bow!"

Darcy said nothing but listened as Caroline went on to say she had been informed of this strange guest of Darcy's almost as soon as she returned from the north.

"It is going to be a scandal if you do not banish him from your house, Mr. Darcy. I tell you this because of my brother's regard for you, and I—"

"Major McDunn is my friend," Darcy said icily. "A *good* friend. And he is a guest in my house for as long as he wishes to remain."

Clearly, Caroline was taken aback by the tone of Darcy's voice, but she continued nevertheless. "I was only thinking of your benefit, having been informed that some *tradesman* had infringed on your good nature to—"

"Miss Bingley, I repeat that Major McDunn is my friend. And if he has committed the unforgivable offense of being a tradesman, then I too must be in trade since he and I are partners in our business enterprises. So you have my leave to consider us *both* beneath your station even though trade was the profession of your father, the reason for your family's fortune, and the basis of your present status."

With the merest bow, he came over to sit with Bingley—who had heard none of this—and McDunn, who had heard every word.

Ouch! That had to hurt! McDunn thought, and soon after this most interesting incident, he made his excuses and returned to his room and his drawings.

Wednesday, January 24, 1810
Darcy Townhouse, London

IN ACCORDANCE WITH HIS DECISION AT PEMBERLEY TO FIND A COMPANION and tutor for Georgiana, Darcy had spent more than a month in search of an appropriate lady to oversee Georgiana's wider education. In light of her involvement in McDunn's ventures, he had decided to provide her with an education similar to that of a gentleman at university. While he had made sure Georgiana met each lady, he kept his counsel until he had finally made his choice.

It was then that he sent for Georgiana to meet her new companion and decided to include McDunn in the invitation. While he would not allow Georgiana's support of McDunn's work to overrule her education, he needed to make all parties aware of the need for occasional accommodations.

When McDunn arrived, Darcy said cordially, "Ah, I am pleased you had not already left for the day."

As soon as McDunn saw the tall, handsome lady of middle years sitting beside Georgiana, Darcy made the introductions.

"As you have likely surmised, Mrs. Sturdivant will be assisting Georgiana with her more extensive studies. She will also act as her companion when you and I are absent."

McDunn nodded his understanding, and Darcy continued. "She is the widow of a naval captain with two sons who also serve. And she has a quite unusual spread of knowledge since her father was a professor of natural philosophy at Cambridge. He had a special interest in mathematics, and he instructed one of my classes in that subject as well."

"He still remembers you, Mr. Darcy," Mrs. Sturdivant said. "He informed me of it in his letter after I learned of your interest in securing a tutor. He said you were an excellent student."

"Unfortunately, I did not have an affinity for the subject he taught," Darcy said dryly.

"Still, he did say you studied hard, and my father is rather chary with his compliments." Looking at McDunn, she continued. "As Mr. Darcy knows, my husband was captain of a frigate and evidently a brave and skillful one as his fellow captains attested in their letters of condolence after he died. But he was not a lucky officer, and he made little prize money. A widow's pension was not sufficient to provide anything to my two boys, so I was pleased to learn of this opportunity and delighted to secure it."

She looked intently at McDunn. "Mr. Darcy explained that Miss Darcy often aids you in your work, Major. I thought your rank meant you were a military man, but he said you were also an *engineer*, as he termed it. He went on to say you and he were involved in some kind of business, but I confess I am not familiar with the term 'engineer.'"

"It's a course of study from my country, the United States, where I went to university. It's a bit different from someone like your Sir Isaac Newton, who was what we would call a *scientist*. Rather, it refers to someone like the Scotsman, James Watt, who had so much to do with the steam engine you may have read of."

"Ah, I see," Mrs. Sturdivant said. "I have indeed read of his steam engine. And my father taught me mathematics, including the calculus invented by Mr. Newton."

"Does Darcy want you to teach Miss Darcy calculus?" McDunn asked in both surprise and interest.

"No, no, McDunn," Darcy said quickly. "Not at first, at least, unless she shows a special interest in the subject. No, Mrs. Sturdivant will give instruction in history and the basics of natural philosophy as well as mathematics. Georgiana will also study languages. Mrs. Sturdivant speaks three fluently and several others with a bit less facility."

"I learned languages while I was at home at Cambridge," Mrs. Sturdivant said. "They seem to come naturally to me."

"But I will still be able to help the major, will I not?" Georgiana asked with concern in her voice.

"You will, but you must also learn what Mrs. Sturdivant has to teach you. I encourage all three of you to try to accommodate your needs and interests."

"No problem, Darcy," McDunn said, nodding cheerfully to Georgiana's new tutor.

"I warn you, Major, I am a very forthright woman, and I shall make sure Miss Darcy pays due attention to her studies."

"That forthrightness is one of the reasons I engaged her," Darcy said dryly. "I have no doubt she will not hesitate to stand up to even a stubborn fellow like you.

"On the other hand, Mrs. Sturdivant, what the major is doing is important, and it was my sister's wish to work with him that convinced me to seek a tutor for her instead of continuing a drawing room education. We all need to cooperate."

"Hey, I said no problem, and I meant it," McDunn said. "I'm used to having to balance various tasks. But that means we'll have to talk to each other. Right, Mrs. Sturdivant?"

The new tutor looked at him closely, but eventually her determined look faded, and she nodded back.

Chapter 10

///

Do not confuse motion and progress. A rocking horse keeps moving but does not make any progress.

— Alfred A. Montapert, American author

\\

Wednesday, September 5, 1810
Pemberley Estate, Derbyshire

Edward McDunn, one-time officer of Marines from a far-distant time and place, firmly ordered the butterflies in his stomach to stop performing their Olympic-level gymnastics.

Everything's ready, he told himself. *Virtually nothing went as planned, but I suppose that's to be expected when you hand-make all the components. Still, everything's built, tested, and installed, and we're ready! So there's no reason for these butterflies! Stop!*

The butterflies, as usual, refused to obey.

"How can you be so blasted calm, McDunn," Darcy hissed at his side. "I am ready to bolt for the woods and rid myself of that poisonous breakfast weighing on my innards, and you stand there in perfect serenity."

"What could possibly make you think I'm calm?" McDunn said out of the side of his mouth.

Where they stood, they watched the caravan of coaches approaching the large tent in a meadow near the entrance to Pemberley. The tent sheltered the various components of one end of their telegraph system. The other end was twenty miles away—and the coaches were delivering a contingent of gentlemen from the military and government to both ends to see a full field demonstration of their telegraph.

"I expected perhaps two or three officials and maybe a pair of military or naval officers," Darcy said, the unusual anxiety in his voice quite clear. "But I never expected this horde!"

"Nor did I, but it's actually a good sign. If there were no interest, they wouldn't be here. If it helps, remember we've been passing messages over these lines for two months."

"And fixing those same lines daily as the wires broke in the wind."

"Only in the beginning. It's the price we paid for saving money by stringing the lines through the woods instead of on poles as I first planned. But we've found all the weak points and fixed them. We haven't had a break in almost a month now. And we had the demonstration to the admiralty. You'll have to admit that went off perfectly."

"True, true," Darcy said with a sigh. "You are most likely right, and I should not be so worried. But there were a lot more difficulties than I expected."

"That was my fault, Darcy. Book learning versus real-life experience. It's like Murphy's Law as I explained—"

"Do not remind me. My life was so much easier before we discovered you in my field."

"But a lot less exciting, I'll bet."

"Your presence provides all the excitement I can tolerate."

"I hope your cousin is holding up well with all these high-ranking officers and bureaucrats," McDunn said. "I've never seen so many different and splendiferous uniforms in my life."

Darcy groaned and McDunn knew it was because of his choice of word. He hadn't intended to say it—the word just popped out of his mouth instead of splendid.

But there was no more time to do anything else because the first coach had come to a stop, and Fitzwilliam bounded from it, his face displaying a broad smile.

Then the attendees entered the tent, and it was time to begin the demonstration.

IT WAS MID-MORNING OF THE FOLLOWING DAY BEFORE THE LAST OF THE attendees returned to town. As soon as the dust of the last coach settled to the ground, the three gentlemen lost no time in adjourning to McDunn's room where Georgiana awaited them.

"I'm glad that's over!" McDunn said.

"Now to wait for Parliament to vote their approval," Darcy said softly, to which the others only nodded silently.

"After which the *real* work can begin!" McDunn said. "While it's good to have this ordeal completed, it's even better to have it *successfully* completed."

"From what I overheard, it certainly sounded as though everything went well!" Georgiana said. She had rather grumpily stayed behind at the house despite wanting to be a part of the demonstration, but it would be most unseemly for a girl of her youth to be present among all of those male officers and officials.

"You are eminently correct, Miss Darcy. Everything went perfectly."

"I want to know all the details!"

"The demonstration went as our tests have, and you were present for those. Rather boring, actually, but sometimes boredom is a good thing. And your cousin, the good colonel, was magnificent. He was in complete command of all the technical aspects, and his answers to the blizzard of questions popped out of his mouth without the slightest hesitation. If you ask me, the man has a future in politics."

"Truly?" Georgiana asked, though they had all heard Fitzwilliam practicing his presentation before the test.

"Do not say such things, even in jest, McDunn!" Fitzwilliam said firmly, suppressing a shudder.

"Why not? Field Martial Wellesley was in politics before his successes in the Peninsular War. And he'll go back into politics afterwards and will even become prime minister for a couple of years. Why not you?"

Fitzwilliam regarded McDunn dubiously, but his friend only grinned crookedly.

"I looked it up, Fitz. Trust me."

"Trusting a Yank is not without risk, especially one as clever as you."

"But tell me more!" Georgiana pleaded. "I stayed here in the house just as you asked, did I not? I want to know everything!"

McDunn looked at both Darcy and Fitzwilliam for help. When neither of them offered any, he sighed.

"I was really nervous as I watched all those coaches heading for our tent, but your brother and your cousin were both as cool as cucumbers, and..."

McDunn was not even perturbed by Darcy's groan and continued cheerfully.

"And that's just about how everything happened, Miss Darcy," McDunn said in conclusion. "It was my first experience with something like this, and everything, from beginning to end, was quite a learning experience. I'm sure we'll have similar problems when we start fabricating our steam locomotive."

"I am still not comfortable representing all of this work as my own," Darcy said from his chair. "Most of those men yesterday looked at me as though I had invented this Darcy-Fitzwilliam Telegraph and just instructed Richard on how it worked."

"That's how it needs to be, Darcy. You're well known, and people will believe you're head of our enterprise with the aid of some skilled mechanics to do the dirty work. I need to stay in the background as one of those handymen."

"It still makes me feel ill at ease."

"You deserve it, man!" McDunn said firmly, pounding his fist into his hand for emphasis. "The way you accepted my ridiculous story and didn't have me sent to the loony bin is the act of an unbelievably insightful man! And generous! Virtually all the money we've spent so far has been yours, right?"

"Yes, but—"

"But me no buts, friend Darcy—not today of all times. Remember, at some point, possibly within our lifetimes, some inquisitive types might start asking about this *McDunn* fellow. The possibility will be a certainty if I become too prominent. My story just can't stand much investigation."

"He is right," Fitzwilliam said. "And I certainly cannot act as though I am anything more than a well-rehearsed salesman. We have to make this *your* product. You *will* have to be famous, I am afraid. Bear it like a man!"

Darcy looked at his cousin unhappily, but he could not disagree with a single word. With a sad nod, he accepted his destiny even if the mantle was going to be most uncomfortable."

After finally retiring for the evening, with the success of the project he had worked on so hard and for so long completed at last, McDunn's sleep was anything but peaceful. Instead, he was deeply embedded in a most unpleasant dream, one in which young people whom he somehow knew to be his distant descendants played a central part. As he looked on in horror, his relations struggled against a nightmarish future bearing all too much resemblance to the world he had escaped.

He was impotent to offer either support or advice to these young boys and girls. The boys appeared to be no older than teenagers, and he thought they appeared identical to his memories of himself in high school. Worse, one of the young girls bore an uncanny resemblance to his lost Dancer, and it wrenched at his heart. All of them were enmeshed in a struggle against their own society, which appeared to be breaking down just as his own had. Violence and terrorism lurked around every corner, and all his descendants' efforts to cope with the dangers confronting them came to nothing.

But McDunn grew conscious he was in a dream, and with deliberate willpower, he ordered himself to wake up. It was a struggle to do so, but he jerked himself awake just as enemies of all descriptions were closing in on those young people who pulled so strongly at his paternal emotions.

He sat up in his bed, and his heart pounded, sweat pouring off his face and soaking his nightshirt despite the cool September air.

He threw back the bedclothes and got up, taking off his nightshirt and using it to dry himself before casting it aside and donning a warm dressing gown hanging from a hook by his bed.

Thankfully, the details of his nightmare, which had been terrifying because he was so helpless to stop the impending dangers, faded from his consciousness as he became more awake. Still, it took some time and the calming effect of a drink before he was able to return to his bed.

Chapter 11

Manners are more important than laws, and upon them, to a great deal, the law depends.

— George Bernard Shaw, Irish literary
critic, playwright, and essayist

Thursday, September 5, 1811
Darcy Townhouse, London

M r. Bingley has come to call, sir," Darcy's butler announced after knocking at the door to his study.

Darcy was rather surprised since Bingley usually sent a note first, despite his impetuous and even forgetful temperament. He raised his eyebrows at McDunn, who just smiled. Since first meeting Darcy's friend, he had become accustomed to Bingley's ways.

The break in their activities was fortuitous since he and Darcy had just finished their discussion of the financial aspects of their projects, especially their telegraph system. That initial venture was growing even faster than they had dreamed. The first sale of a few critical telegraph lines to the government was followed rapidly by an expansion to provide the same service to the public.

"Show him in, Sanderson," Darcy said, and Bingley quickly strode into the room and greeted the two men. Then, as he almost always did, he advanced on McDunn with his hand outthrust for their customary handshake.

"If you do not cease this manner of greeting, Bingley, people will soon start to think you an American like the major."

"Doubtful, Darcy, doubtful. Bingley knows who his parents were while I, like most Americans, was raised by wolves."

Bingley cheerfully took the seat Darcy indicated, not at all put off by McDunn's irreverence.

"I believe you have something momentous to announce," Darcy said, "given the bounce in your step and the smile on your face."

"I found what I was looking for!" Bingley said excitedly.

"A young lady to be the companion of your declining years?"

"Nothing like that! Not at all."

"Then, pray tell, what have you found?"

"A suitable estate and it is located less than thirty miles from this very house! You will—"

Darcy smiled and raised a hand. "Pause a moment, Bingley. I know you are excited, but it would likely be best if you accepted a glass of this excellent claret and started from the beginning—when you abruptly left town so mysteriously a week ago. Your note to me was not particularly forthcoming as to the reason." Darcy dug into a drawer and held out a small square of paper.

Bingley smiled somewhat sheepishly. "It was to investigate a manor house a friend recommended as I said in my note."

He stopped speaking at Darcy's slow smile and shake of his head. He snatched up the note and quickly perused it. His face fell when he saw Darcy was correct.

"I thought I told you why I was leaving," Bingley said plaintively.

"I am afraid not. As you can see, it only says you have received some news and had to depart."

"Well, I received a letter from Henderson, a friend from Cambridge, and after informing me of the home he has taken in town, he mentioned a house in the country he had decided not to take—a manor called Netherfield Park in Hertfordshire. His description interested me, and since you and Georgiana were visiting friends, I decided to examine it myself."

Darcy nodded solemnly. "Very good, Bingley. Now, since we know why you departed, what are the particulars of this suitable estate you wish to purchase?"

"Only let, not purchase, Darcy. At least at this time. The house is goodly sized, with enough bedrooms to entertain quite comfortably. And the land looks excellent for the shooting season."

"I wonder you have never mentioned the place to me before, which I find a bit worrisome."

"I spoke with the new owner and raised that very question. He informed me the house has been vacant for several years, the previous owner having gambled away the family fortune. Netherfield was one of several estates he owned, and there was considerable contention within the family about the ownership of the various properties when he died. The legalities have only recently been resolved so the new owner could make it available for lease."

"A house vacant for several years? Such things can be a problem."

"I inquired about that, but the owner assured me a small staff has been in residence while the house was vacant. There will be some repairs needed, of course, but the owner has agreed to address them directly."

Darcy nodded. He was not fully convinced the house would meet his standards, but at least Bingley had made enquiries.

"The owner showed me about the place, and I was more than pleased with the way the house is situated as well as the elegance of the principal rooms. Everything he said in praise of the manor was justified by what I saw, and I resolved immediately to take it."

"You examined it in detail, I hope."

"Of course, Darcy. Or, rather, as much as I could in a half hour. I had to leave in order to reach London and inform my solicitor of my decision. He is negotiating with the owner's solicitor at the moment, and if everything is satisfactory, I plan to lease the estate."

Darcy gave Bingley a nod as he tried to conceal his disappointment at such an impulsive decision. He consoled himself with the knowledge that Bingley had benefited to some extent from past advice since he had applied more scrutiny than would have been the case in the past.

"So, what are the conditions of this lease?" Darcy asked.

"We agreed to a period of two years with an option to buy in a year. I will be responsible for maintaining the house and servants. The owner will deal with the tenants and collect the rents though I will have full rights to hunt the land."

"That sounds reasonable."

"My sisters were somewhat disappointed I did not purchase an estate of my own, but Caroline has agreed to preside at my table. And both Louisa and her husband agreed to join her, at least for a time."

Darcy nodded again though he was not enthused by the news. He was not particularly fond of either sister, especially the younger who he knew wished to preside at *his* table at Pemberley. He considered them the cross he had to bear because of his friendship with their brother. As for Mr. Hurst… well, he could be a fourth at whist.

"When do you plan to take possession of Netherfield?" Darcy asked.

"Sometime in October, I believe, as soon as my solicitor has verified the completion of repairs. I shall keep you abreast of the developments, and I would hope you and your sister—and you also, Major—might join me for an extended visit."

"I am sure Georgiana will wish to visit, and she can continue her lessons anywhere. What say you, McDunn?"

"I am busy, of course, but like Miss Darcy, much of my work can be done anywhere, and Bingley's estate appears to be reasonably close to town, so I can return quickly if I find it necessary."

"So he is hard at work on another task for you, Darcy?" Bingley asked, and Darcy gave a somewhat uncomfortable nod. "You have been rather closemouthed about your plans."

"There is no mystery about it, Bingley. The success of our telegraph has given us sufficient profits to expand into other areas. One is our bicycle, which I know I have mentioned. And our new steam engine is already providing power to our own factories."

"Most impressive. I am all amazement. I never suspected you had such capabilities!"

Neither did Darcy, thought McDunn in amusement, seeing again how his friend had to hide his discomfort. *He's still not happy at becoming known as the man responsible for the new telegraph.*

"So your whole party will join me at Netherfield? Excellent, excellent! Well, I must be on my way." With a quick bow to both, the young man left as energetically as he had arrived.

Of course, I'm interested in seeing Netherfield, thought McDunn, *but I can't tell either of them why! I suspect, given the timing, that the events Austen described are about to get rolling, and I wouldn't miss them for the world! If things continue as Austen wrote them, the coming months promise to be quite interesting.*

Sunday, October 20, 1811
Netherfield, Hertfordshire

"WELCOME, DARCY!" CALLED BINGLEY AS HE BOUNDED DOWN THE STAIRS of the handsome manor house. "I am very pleased to see you. Your note made me fear you would be delayed! This is wonderful!"

"I only said I *might* be delayed by business, but the problems were easier to resolve than I anticipated," Darcy said cautiously, stepping down from his coach.

"You are just in time for a ball to which I have been invited tomorrow evening. The gentlemen of the neighborhood were quick to call as soon as I took up residence, and they informed me of a dance at their assembly hall in the nearby town."

"That was quick work to be invited to a dance after being in residence less than two weeks. But then it is customary in these country neighborhoods to wish to add new members to their limited society."

"Yes. The gentlemen have been exceedingly polite and gracious. They were eager to have me attend their dance, and I was quick to accept. And my sisters and Mr. Hurst also wish to accompany me."

Darcy nodded his head in understanding as McDunn assisted his sister and Mrs. Sturdivant from the coach, saying nothing more as his party climbed the steps since he was a bit doubtful of the *eagerness* of any of Bingley's relatives to attend.

"From what I was told, there are a number of lovely young ladies who will be in attendance," Bingley said, beaming. "I know you are not terribly fond of dances, but it would be splendid if all of you attended."

"Georgiana cannot do so since she is not yet out. She will have to remain at your house with Mrs. Sturdivant."

"I suppose you are right," Bingley said in disappointment before his good humor reappeared. "But I hope you can attend, Major McDunn! As you are an American, it would be a wonderful opportunity to see more of our British society."

"If you don't think my complete inability to dance would be disqualifying, it would be my honor, sir." McDunn's face gave no indication wild horses could not have kept him away from the assembly once Bingley mentioned it. He had often wondered whether he might have the opportunity to personally witness any of the pivotal moments in Austen's tale, and he was determined not to miss the opportunity.

I anticipate considerable diversion from the evening's activities. I love that word, diversion. It's so very British. I'm growing quite accustomed to it.

"Excellent, excellent! I am looking forward to tomorrow, and I am sure you will have an enjoyable time even if you only stand and watch as Darcy often does. Now, let us go in. My sisters are eager to become reacquainted with you, Miss Darcy. And with you, Major, though you have already met Caroline. But I want to introduce you to my elder sister and her husband, Mr. Hurst."

Over his shoulder as he led them into the house, Bingley continued. "Everyone is very interested in these business enterprises of yours, Darcy. Your new telegraph is much talked of, and they want to hear all the details."

I'll just bet it caught their interest, thought McDunn scornfully though his face showed no reaction. *Actually, I expect to find them mostly interested in getting and remaining as far from me as possible, especially since they likely suspect I was the one who ensnared their Mr. Darcy into trade.*

McDunn's introduction to Bingley's elder sister and her dumpy husband unfolded exactly as he had expected. Mr. Hurst greeted him politely enough as he would have expected from Austen's description of him looking the gentleman without possessing the attributes. But his wife responded to her brother's introduction almost exactly as her younger sister had with words expressing her pleasure at meeting him but with an expression of disdain she made little effort to conceal.

Do they know how they're giving themselves away, or do they simply not care? Not that it really matters. Already, Caroline has latched herself onto both Darcy and Georgiana, and she appears to be hanging on their every word. Her objective is unmistakable though I'm not altogether certain of her motives. She doesn't need to marry for money, not with a dowry of twenty thousand pounds. It must be for the social status such a marriage would give her. It would finally put to rest the disadvantage of not fitting into the highest levels of London society as Miss Bingley. She imagines she'll do much better as Mrs. Darcy.

As McDunn looked at Darcy absently responding to Caroline, he knew there was no need for concern about his friend allowing himself to be trapped by her. Though Darcy often mentioned Bingley in conversation, he seldom said much about his relatives. There was only that one time, late at night after a full day of getting prepared for their demonstration at Pemberley, when he confided he mostly endured the attentions of Bingley's relations in silence.

But I remember the way his face lit up when he confessed rather shamefacedly that he occasionally provoked them for amusement, much as one might tease a caged animal!

Sunday, October 20, 1811
Longbourn, Hertfordshire

THE ESTATE WHERE ELIZABETH BENNET LIVED WITH HER PARENTS AND her four sisters was only three miles from Netherfield Park. The family lived a comfortable existence though with significantly less affluence than either Bingley or Darcy. Their father's income was a mere two thousand a year, less than half of Mr. Bingley's. Furthermore, because her husband's estate was entailed away to a cousin, Elizabeth's mother considered the finding of husbands for her daughters to be her most important task. If none of them married well—or at all—there would be little money on which she or the girls might live after her husband passed away. Her fortune of five thousand pounds would provide barely two hundred a year while she lived, and barely forty or fifty pounds a year for each girl after her death. That would likely necessitate the girls seeking employment of some kind.

None of the sisters was thinking as far ahead as their mother, of course, since they were in the bloom of their youth and beauty. The eldest, Jane, was barely two-and-twenty while her sister Elizabeth would not turn twenty for a month. So their excitement this day was totally focused on the upcoming assembly ball, and their interest matched and likely exceeded that of certain parties at Netherfield.

The sisters had been quite surprised to learn their father had been among the first to call on Mr. Bingley, especially since he had previously declared his firm opposition to doing so. Before he visited, there had been some worry about being introduced to the newcomer since it required a third party who knew both the Bennet ladies and Mr. Bingley. The introduction would now be less difficult but would still require an intercessor such as Mrs. Long or Sir William Lucas since they knew their father would never attend the assembly.

Another pressing topic was whether Mr. Bingley would be in attendance; he had declined an invitation to dine at Longbourn because he was required in town. Their fears on that point had been assuaged, however, by Lady

Lucas's informing them Mr. Bingley was gone in order to bring back a large party for the ball.

Elizabeth, however, was rather skeptical of the reliability of the information. Even if Lady Lucas was correct, the size of his "large party" was another complete unknown. But ignorance of the truth had not kept speculations among the Bennet and Lucas sisters from estimates as high as twelve ladies and seven gentlemen.

"It would be better if it was the reverse," grumbled Lydia, a sentiment to which her older sister Kitty quickly agreed.

Elizabeth urged caution. "Lady Lucas said only a large party. These latest speculations hardly qualify as guesses. Mrs. Goulding's husband did not call on Mr. Bingley, so how reliable is her information?"

"Mrs. Long told my mother that Mr. Bingley is bringing a party of six—his five sisters and a cousin," Jane said. "And she was introduced to Mr. Bingley when he visited Mr. Long, so she, at least, might have more trustworthy information."

"Only one gentleman?" wailed Kitty. "Surely, that must be wrong!"

To this comment, Mary only sniffed in derision since she was more interested in her books than in eligible young gentlemen. She was irritated by her younger sisters talking of little else than the handsome newcomer to their neighborhood and his anticipated attendance at the assembly.

Elizabeth tried to calm her younger sisters. "As I said before, we will learn soon. You are wasting your time planning dances with Mr. Bingley and his friends, Lydia. And you also, Kitty. Restrain your wild gossiping. It is most unseemly."

Both girls reluctantly desisted. They were more than a little afraid of Elizabeth because she so often spoke with the same firmness as their father. In Elizabeth's opinion, it was most unfortunate that he seldom spoke in that manner since it might have alleviated the lack of decorum of his two youngest daughters.

Those daughters had no such fear of their mother, however, for they managed her with an experience gained and perfected during their short lifetimes. Thus, when she joined her daughters in the parlor, they felt emboldened to continue their speculations, enjoying the discomfiture of their sister who, out of filial duty, usually declined to directly confront her mother.

Chapter 12

The consequences of things are not always proportionate to the apparent magnitude of those events that have produced them. Thus the American Revolution, from which little was expected, produced much; but the French Revolution, from which much was expected, produced little.

— Charles Caleb Colton, English cleric, writer and collector, well known for his eccentricities

Monday, October 21, 1811
Assembly Hall
Meryton, Hertfordshire

Elizabeth Bennet stood with her four sisters, engaged in quiet conversation with her best friend, Charlotte Lucas, when Lydia said excitedly, "Look, there is Mr. Bingley!"

Elizabeth turned to see a party had indeed entered the hall. "It appears Mr. Bingley's group is not as large as rumored," she said in wry amusement. "I can only see a party of six—Mr. Bingley with two young ladies and three gentlemen."

"My mother said Mr. Bingley had gone to London to bring back a large party," Charlotte said. "She was not aware of its size. As usual, rumor has little to do with reality."

Charlotte stood close beside Elizabeth, her dearest friend despite the disparity in their ages. Charlotte was twenty-seven compared to Elizabeth's nineteen years, and they both shared the same amusement at nonsense and inconsistencies.

"I did not get a very good look at Mr. Bingley when he visited," Jane offered in her soft voice. "But he looks very gentlemanly. And handsome as well."

"And rich!" Kitty said in a loud voice. "Imagine! He has five thousand a year! Come, Lydia! Let us find out more."

Elizabeth had just opened her mouth to tell them to rejoin their mother when both of her youngest sisters disappeared into the crowd, moving in the direction of Bingley's party.

"Those two!" she said softly to Charlotte, but it spoke a lifetime's irritation at the girls' continued propensity for impropriety.

Neither of them should even be here tonight! Elizabeth thought, in renewed exasperation at her mother's lack of judgment in allowing them out into society. *They are too young and act even younger than their age.*

And, though this thought pained her, she also had to condemn her father's fondness for the tranquility of his study and the consequent neglect of his paternal duties.

"The two ladies must be Mr. Bingley's sisters," Charlotte Lucas said calmly, nudging Elizabeth, whose irritation still smoldered. "My father visited Mr. Bingley this morning, after he returned from town. I believe the somewhat portly gentleman must be Mr. Hurst, the husband of Mr. Bingley's elder sister. My father described him as being a man of substance, from which I inferred he carried an extra bit of weight. He also mentioned the younger sister is still unmarried."

"Both of Mr. Bingley's sisters are certainly very fashionable," Jane said, with her usual good-natured inclination to see everyone in the best possible light.

Elizabeth said nothing, but her own thoughts were not quite as charitable. She thought the manner in which the two ladies looked about them implied condescension rather than modesty, but she restrained the temptation to say as much.

"Who are the other two men, I wonder?" she said instead though somewhat rhetorically.

"My father mentioned Mr. Bingley was bringing a close friend, a Mr. Darcy," Charlotte said. "I suppose he is one of the two men though I have no idea which one he might be."

"We know neither of them is Mr. Hurst at least. Both of them are tall and not at all portly."

"The taller gentleman is much darker and looks almost…well, like a pirate, what with his size and his mustache. In any event, I suspect he is not Mr. Darcy."

"No, he is not!" Lydia said, having mysteriously reappeared. "His name is McDunn. How odd he looks with that short hair! If his hair was not so dark, one might think he was bald! And he is certainly not handsome! Not like Mr. Darcy!"

"That is quite enough, Lydia," Elizabeth said sternly. "And speak more softly. Sir William seems to be leading Mr. Bingley and his party about the room. Come, we should join my mother."

As the sisters and Charlotte walked over to Mrs. Bennet, Elizabeth had to give Lydia credit for being at least partially right. Even if the taller of the two gentlemen was not particularly handsome, the same could *not* be said of Mr. Darcy.

McDunn looked about the room with interest as Sir William Lucas led Bingley and the others around, introducing them to the principal people in attendance. Bingley had especially asked for this civility, and McDunn watched the introductions closely. He was still learning the intricacies of how one was introduced, but he knew it depended on the relative social standing of each party. Though he found it confusing, it seemed almost instinctively recognized by everyone in this class-conscious society.

But McDunn could easily figure out who was at the bottom of the social echelon—himself! He was used to it and found it more amusing than irksome. He was too thoroughly an American and too much a democrat to be offended though he was learning to navigate the different strata of English society.

He made no attempt to remember the names of those he met, contenting himself with a small bow. There was only one group in whom he had any particular interest. He thought he had already spotted them a short distance away in the direction Sir William seemed to be taking his charges.

The group of ladies watched their approach though they tried, with varying degrees of success, to disguise their interest. Six of the ladies were quite young, and they stood about a handsome, middle-aged woman who still showed signs of her younger beauty. Her eyes, however, revealed more of cleverness than either intelligence or common sense.

Mrs. Bennet—or I'll be a monkey's uncle, thought McDunn, easily maintaining the poker face that had helped him augment his military pay over the years. *And I'm certain which girls are Lydia and Kitty. I see what Austen meant when she portrayed them as juveniles, too young to be allowed out and about on their own.*

This evening was crucial in Austen's story. Much of the angst had its origin in Darcy snubbing Elizabeth as well as everyone else in the room, and McDunn anticipated an interesting time.

But only as an observer, he reminded himself. *Remember, everything's supposed to turn out okay in the end. Assuming Darcy and Elizabeth really do strike up a lasting love, who's to say their attraction wasn't enhanced by the hard times they endured?*

His suspicions were soon confirmed as Sir William stopped in front of the woman McDunn had pegged as Mrs. Bennet and began the introductions, starting with Darcy.

Actually, McDunn was rather surprised at Darcy's still being with Bingley's party since he seemed to remember him avoiding this introduction in the text.

I think I like Darcy more than I've ever liked another man, McDunn thought, *but he's certainly not perfect, especially to my egalitarian American sensibilities. So I'm surprised. I'd have expected him to avoid people who possessed, as the author phrased it, "little beauty and no fashion."*

He had to wonder whether his mere presence had affected Darcy's reaction, perhaps because his friend preferred not to exhibit his social imperfections in front of him. That was an uncomfortable thought! But there was no way to know, and there was equally nothing to be done about it.

The introduction of Mr. Bingley and his relatives followed along with the introduction of each of the younger ladies.

McDunn was surprised by the beauty of the elder sisters. He'd anticipated they would be pretty since they had been so described by Austen. But these young ladies, without the aid of any makeup he could discern, were simply drop-dead gorgeous. It was especially true of the eldest, who was more of a classic beauty than her sister, but the difference was slight enough to be debatable.

Then it was his turn as Sir William waved him forward. "Mrs. Bennet, ladies, may I present Major McDunn?"

McDunn gave a bow to Mrs. Bennet first and then to the younger girls who responded with graceful curtsies.

They do that so well! he thought admiringly. *They perform their curtsies with such grace! Do they practice? It cannot be easy to make a curtsey look effortless, but every one of them brings it off charmingly.*

After meeting Mrs. Bennet, McDunn was surprised to find himself feeling a degree of sympathy for her. She seemed exactly as described in the novel—a mother dedicated to finding suitable husbands for her girls, and he could no longer be totally disdainful of her. In his world, he had thought her a foolish and uninformed woman of illiberal views. After living in this new world for more than two years, he realized her quandary. With her husband's estate entailed away to a cousin, there was absolutely no safety net for her family, even if they were of the gentry. If none of the Bennet sisters married well, they would have only a miniscule income on which to live after the death of their father. McDunn was sure Mrs. Bennet would turn out just as foolish as he had heretofore assumed, but he now felt a modicum of sympathy for her.

WHEN ELIZABETH BENNET ROSE FROM MAKING HER CURTSEY TO DARCY and looked into his dark eyes, the strangest, most extraordinary, and unique quiver shot through her. It was something between a thrill and a shudder, but she had no word for it as it seemed to blossom in her chest before traveling down her spine.

The mere fact that this tall man might inspire *any* type of reaction was shocking enough. She had instantly perceived his reserve as he was conducted around the room, and such haughty aloofness was not at all to her taste. She admired openness and amiability far more.

Then why this mysterious reaction? she wondered in frantic confusion. In Darcy's eyes, she could see no similar response—nothing at all. But she had never felt so unsettled and confused in her life.

In the midst of her befuddlement, which she hoped to conceal as she had her innermost thoughts and feelings, she could not believe she heard the man asking whether he might have the honor of the next two dances!

Is the whole world coming unhinged? she thought wildly, trying to bring her feelings under control as he led her to the dance floor.

She did not even remember accepting his request!

McDunn hadn't been surprised when Bingley requested a set from Charlotte Lucas and the next two after that from Jane Bennet. He was, however, stunned to hear Darcy make a similar request of Elizabeth Bennet!

This wasn't supposed to happen! Darcy was supposed to snub all the young ladies in attendance and dance only with either Caroline Bingley or Mrs. Hurst before committing the final insult by dismissing Elizabeth Bennet as "not handsome enough" to tempt him!

Can this be due to my presence here? McDunn's logical turn of mind quickly answered his own question. *It's unlikely to make any difference at all. Darcy's entirely a man of his society with much to convince him of his superiority. He'll probably manage to offend everyone soon, including Elizabeth Bennet, just as Austen described.*

"And how do you find our assembly, Major McDunn?" Mrs. Bennet said, and McDunn could hear the cunning in her voice as she continued. "Are there not an abundance of available dance partners?"

"You are indeed correct, madam," McDunn said, absolutely deadpan, "which would be most fortunate if I danced. But, you see, I do not dance. I never learned."

"But every gentleman can dance!" Mrs. Bennet exclaimed, looking as scandalized as though she had just seen a cockroach scamper across the dinner table.

"Ah, there's the trouble, Mrs. Bennet," he said, taking a certain delightful pleasure in teasing her. "You see, I'm an American, not a gentleman."

"But…you are a major!" Lydia said.

"A major of American Marines, Miss Lydia."

"Then you are not a real major at all!" Mrs. Bennet said, and McDunn felt himself go cold inside. The woman might be a fool, but there were limits to his forbearance.

"I may no longer be a serving officer, madam," he said icily, "but I've waded through enough blood to have earned my rank the hard way. However, it appears you find my presence unpleasant, so I beg your leave to withdraw."

He gave her a barely perceptible bow and strode away, still fuming but determined to find a suitable vantage point from which to observe the rest of the evening's activities.

I probably shouldn't have said what I did, but the woman is really an idiot. How could she insult me as she did? I know Austen described her as vulgar, and I was ready to cut her some slack, but Jiminy Christmas!

As McDunn watched Darcy and Elizabeth, his temper gradually cooled, and he began to wonder what had possessed his friend to ask her to dance. McDunn had been fully prepared to see Darcy act in the disdainful manner he had expected, but he had acted wildly differently. What did it mean? He knew he should not expect these people to behave as though they were actors, giving performances from a script written by a long-dead writer. But it was clear that he'd subconsciously expected just that.

He remembered reading that Austen had written a significantly longer version of her novel before editing it down to its published length, but it was difficult to believe she had ever written a version in which Darcy asked Elizabeth to dance at the assembly. Having Darcy snub Elizabeth was too central to her theme of the problems caused by pride and mistaken assumptions.

Whatever the reason for this deviation, he found it more than interesting, and it renewed his curiosity about why he had been sent to this mystifying alternate world by the Siege. Certainly, despite the similarities to what Austen wrote, events might not transpire in the same manner.

From what McDunn could observe, Darcy's dance with Elizabeth Bennet seemed to go well. They certainly seemed to part civilly, after which Darcy danced with Caroline Bingley and her sister as he had expected.

It was during those dances that McDunn started to see a change in Darcy's temperament. For much of the ball, McDunn had heard whispers about Darcy's splendid fortune. While there was only one reference to "ten thousand a year," the whispers were bandied about with such a lack of caution that Darcy could not help but hear them. McDunn recognized as much when Darcy's eyes narrowed and his lips thinned while he danced with Mrs. Hurst.

Uh-oh, McDunn thought. *Though he seldom loses it, Darcy has a fiery temper. He's a proud man, especially of his family, and he's occasionally mentioned how crowds make him uncomfortable on the best of occasions. And he absolutely hates being placed under a social microscope by those he considers below his station. Obsession with social standing has been out of favor in America since the*

Revolutionary War, but that's the way it is in England at this time.

After he finished his dance with Bingley's sister, Darcy was stone-faced as he stalked over to join McDunn. The major made no attempt at conversation and simply stood silently beside him. Darcy looked straight ahead while McDunn watched other people, something he always enjoyed, but Darcy's stern, erect posture discouraged any attempt at social interaction.

Darcy's self-isolation did not sit well with Meryton society, especially among those mothers with eligible daughters. Virtually all of them had longed to see a daughter asked to dance by this most impressive visitor, just as Elizabeth Bennet had. With Darcy's anger keeping him silent and uninterested in further society, those deeply desired invitations were not forthcoming.

Thus, it was not long before McDunn heard the whispered remarks about Darcy turn from admiring to critical and disparaging. Those making the comments increasingly made little attempt to conceal what they said, and he heard Darcy affirmed to be arrogant and prideful.

Bingley, however, with his easy manners and open personality, was judged to be far superior to his friend, who evidently considered himself too good to consort with his social inferiors. Bingley, for example, danced every dance and engaged all he met in a most friendly manner while Darcy now stood apart and regarded all in the room with a baleful glare. Despite his wealth, Darcy was quickly—and with near-universal unanimity—judged to be completely disagreeable, and everyone hoped he would not come again.

I guess I was right about Darcy managing to offend everyone, McDunn thought sadly. *Perhaps my opinion of Darcy is influenced by our friendship, so I can understand why he has no wish for further intercourse with Meryton society. On the other hand, disappointed mothers would vastly prefer to lay the blame on Darcy's disdainful manner and his unpleasant nature rather than their own barely concealed gossiping.*

Bingley seemed to detect the increasing disapproval of Darcy, though without understanding its reason. Thus, he left the dance for a few moments to press Darcy to rejoin it.

"Come, Darcy, I must have you dance. I know you and Major McDunn always have much to discuss, but this is not the time. You will enjoy yourself much better if you dance."

"I certainly shall not dance," Darcy replied, more than a little coldly. "You know how I detest it unless I am particularly acquainted with my partner. In any case, I have already danced with your sisters and with Miss Bennet's sister, which is more than sufficient participation at an assembly such as this." He looked as though he would have said more, but instead he pressed his lips together and stood silently.

McDunn easily understood that Darcy was trying to conceal his displeasure at being urged to do something he did not want to do, even by such a close friend.

Bingley's such a complete extrovert, he hasn't a clue he's irritating Darcy, he thought. *And as I expected, Darcy's proving to be just as reserved and even unpleasant when he's in company. Despite being such a good friend to Bingley and having been so generous with me, he remains a very reserved and private person. He'd make a really lousy used car salesman. Or politician.*

With a start, McDunn realized the exchange had an unanticipated eavesdropper since Elizabeth Bennet was nearby, obliged to sit—as in the book—due to the scarcity of gentlemen. He would have thought she was out of earshot, but the expression on her face indicated she was able to overhear and understand the gentlemen's words.

"If everyone was as reluctant as you, Darcy," Bingley continued, "no one would ever find a wife! Upon my honor, I never met with so many pretty girls in my life as I have this evening!"

"You are dancing with the most handsome girl in the room," Darcy said without emotion.

"She is indeed the most beautiful creature I ever beheld! But Miss Elizabeth is every iota as beautiful and is even sitting down at the moment. You seemed to enjoy dancing with her. Why not hazard another dance?"

Darcy glanced around quickly, catching sight of Elizabeth. But her eyes were not on him at the moment, so he was ignorant of her previous observation. Turning back to Bingley, he said, rather uncharitably, "She is agreeable enough, but I have already danced once with her. A second set would lead to unwarranted assumptions that I would prefer to avoid."

"Nonsense, Darcy! I am dancing with her sister for a second time!"

"Exactly." Darcy returned to his silent viewing.

Bingley looked at him for a moment before giving a shrug and returning to the dance.

McDunn glanced at Darcy just as Elizabeth Bennet arose and walked over to her mother. Darcy looked for a moment as though he might say something. But whatever it was went unsaid, and the two men returned to their perusal of the dance floor.

An interesting evening, all in all, thought McDunn. *And except for my set-to with Mrs. Bennet, I was just an observer. Just how the night's surprises will affect events is still to be seen, but I guess it won't change much. Certainly, the Meryton attendees have formed a very negative opinion of Darcy, and there's still Wickham!*

He had one final disturbing thought, however. *Will Wickham even make an appearance? And will Elizabeth unload on Darcy as she did in the novel? It should provide interesting viewing…but from a distance!*

"How did you find the assembly, William?" Georgiana asked after everyone returned to Netherfield Park.

"I believe Bingley found it quite pleasant," Darcy replied. "For myself, it was less so."

"You are too critical, Darcy," Bingley chided. "Everyone was exceedingly pleasant, you must agree. They welcomed us openly without the formality and reserve so often found. I was quite charmed by everyone I met."

"Perhaps you found them so, but they were of little interest to me. They appeared quite mercenary based on the way they hardly bothered to lower their voices as the news of my fortune went about the room. I felt as though I was being stared at by a menagerie of reptiles with their greedy eyes fixed on me."

"Oh, William!" Georgiana said. "How unfortunate!"

Darcy shrugged. "I should be used to it by now after being pursued so assiduously in town by avaricious mothers and daughters. But I confess I cannot stand it."

Out of the corner of his eye, McDunn caught Caroline Bingley and Mrs. Hurst share a triumphant glance. He knew of Caroline's desires, but he also knew Darcy was quite aware of her ambitions. It was rather amusing to watch him easily and deftly thwart her efforts without seeming to do so overtly.

"You appeared quite taken with Miss Bennet," McDunn said to Bingley, carefully considering his words. He did not deem this interference since Bingley's interest in the eldest of the Bennet sisters had been quite obvious.

"Oh, she is a veritable angel, Major! Her beauty is unmatched, and her temperament is so sweet and constant. She is both an excellent dance partner and a superb conversationalist."

"That is because she said little and allowed you to do all the talking, Charles," Mrs. Hurst said. "Yet, I will agree she is a sweet girl."

"She smiles too much," Darcy said.

"In that I agree, Mr. Darcy," Caroline said. "Though I also agree I should not mind meeting her again."

"I am sure you shall, Miss Bingley," Darcy said casually. "Now that you have been introduced to Mrs. Bennet and her daughters, I believe the ladies of Longbourn will soon be calling."

"You did not seem to find one of the Bennet sisters too objectionable, Darcy," Bingley said slyly. "You danced with Miss Elizabeth."

McDunn saw a quick look of irritation flash over Caroline's face, and he suddenly realized Bingley was as well aware of his sister's fixation as Darcy was.

And he's baiting her! That's something never mentioned by Austen! Certainly not explicitly. I'd have thought he was too dense to notice Caroline's pursuit. That's either another change or careless reading on my part. Certainly, Bingley isn't Darcy's equal in intelligence, but he's apparently capable of recognizing the obvious.

"She was agreeable enough. An excellent dancer even if she does attempt to converse while dancing. As I said when you tried to convince me to repeat the invitation, she was not exceptional enough to warrant such attention."

McDunn saw a quick and hastily concealed look of satisfaction flash over Caroline's face. He felt sure Bingley's attractive sister considered Darcy's remark to her advantage and was marking it up as such in her internal tally book.

"In any case, Bingley," Darcy said, continuing his thought, "the entire assembly struck me as a collection of undistinguished personages of little beauty and no fashion."

Aha! thought McDunn with amusement. *There it is!*

"Speaking only for myself, for you clearly have a differing opinion, the evening was a waste of time, and I would have preferred to stay at home and read."

McDUNN SAT IN HIS ROOM, GOING OVER THE STATUS OF HIS PROJECT TO install running water and toilets at Pemberley, when his reverie was interrupted by a knock at the door. He was pleased with the progress so far in his private endeavor, especially the trenching and installation of clay pipe for the septic system. He was eager to bring Darcy's estate up to a more modern standing in partial recompense for his host's generosity. Reluctantly, he pushed back from his desk and called, "Come!"

He was unsurprised to see Darcy enter, holding a dusty bottle.

"I found this among the items in Bingley's sideboard," Darcy said, raising the bottle.

"Dare I hope it might be something Bingley acquired…ah, a bit illicitly?" McDunn asked hopefully, accepting the bottle.

"Perhaps. There is no bottle ticket on it as you can see, so I hazarded a quick smell. A single cautious sniff was enough to make me suspect it might be something you would like."

"Now, now, Darcy," McDunn said, removing the cork. "You know I can't help my unsophisticated colonial roots. I take it you didn't taste it?"

"That would be highly dangerous, I believe," Darcy said with a straight face. "I thought it best to leave such hazardous experimentations to you."

McDunn took a sniff and nodded appreciatively at the faint woody smell accompanying the more prominent smell of malt. "This does smell interesting—much like the bottles your butler has been procuring for me. Thank you."

"You are most welcome, though I sometimes feel guilty at not convincing you to confine yourself to more civilized libations."

"I got tired of brandy and port after only a single day, but I knew I had to drink something other than water. I'm too experienced a campaigner to fall into the trap of drinking the water unless it's been boiled. But now, as for this interesting bottle you discovered, there's only one way to really judge the quality: the taste test."

He poured an inch of the dark amber liquid into a glass and took a cautious sip. "Not bad," he said thoughtfully. "Not bad at all." He filled his glass and then pulled out a chair at his table for Darcy.

"I thought I would solicit your opinion on the evening's entertainment," Darcy said as he took his seat. "I am sure it was quite unlike similar entertainment in your time."

"Actually, I don't have much to compare with it. The most exciting part was probably my set-to with Mrs. Bennet when I told her I didn't dance."

Darcy raised his eyebrows in question, and McDunn quickly described the incident.

"She appears even more vulgar than I thought her to be," Darcy said with a shake of his head.

"I don't blame her for husband-hunting for her daughters, but I really shouldn't have gotten so angry when she said I wasn't a legitimate major."

"Nonsense, McDunn. Adequate provocation and all that. Think nothing of it."

"I never learned to dance at all, even the dances of my own time, such as they were. My parents and my grandparents told me they danced when they were young, but by the time I was growing up, dancing had all but been driven out of society during the bad years. The fanatics had done much the same with all popular music, and you can't dance without music."

"Quite unfortunate."

"It was. During the bad years, everything—absolutely everything—was politicized, including music, until the people had enough and threw the fanatics out. But music was only one of many things that hadn't fully recovered before everything started coming apart—"

He shook himself and drained his glass. "Enough of that. To get back to your question, I enjoyed much of the ball. I enjoy just watching people. Observing the crowd of people and their varying foibles tonight compensated quite well for not being able to join in the festivities. But now I have a question. Did you really find the assembly so objectionable?"

Darcy was silent for a time before he finally looked up at McDunn.

"Perhaps I was too blunt, though I do not feel comfortable in gatherings where I do not know the people. I find it difficult to enjoy myself among strangers."

"Especially when you keep hearing everyone speculating on your fortune?"

Darcy looked sharply at McDunn and nodded sourly. "So you heard that also."

"And saw how you reacted. Not that I don't understand, but I would have thought you'd be used to it by this time."

"I do not know how the information spread. I am completely new to this county, and I specifically asked Bingley not to speak of my wealth."

"We used to say rumors move faster than the speed of light." McDunn took a sip from his refilled glass. "I'll bet people connected your name with the telegraph. It's no secret we're making money hand over fist with our telegraph service. The message count keeps going up and up, and I'd bet the sending of letters by the post is dropping dramatically."

"It makes me wish I had never allowed you to put my name on it," Darcy said fervently. "I feel an imposter when I hear myself named as the one responsible for bringing this marvel to the country."

"You know the reasons for it. I need to stay in the background, though I thought having my name included in the title of the corporation was innocuous enough. I was really disappointed to have your solicitor tell us that such things as corporations were made illegal in the last century. Only individuals can own property and have liabilities. I still feel uncomfortable about you personally being so much at hazard. And we have to wait until the mid-1820s before the law gets changed if history proves accurate."

"It is not a subject to worry about," Darcy said. His tone was filled with acid as he continued. "I did hear one reference to 'ten thousand a year' tonight, which is hard to explain."

"I heard it too, and it made me wonder."

"Bingley has an idea of my income, I am sure. But it is a mystery how those at the assembly learned of it."

McDunn nodded in commiseration, knowing how painful it was for such a private person as Darcy to have such information bandied about a room of strangers. He was trying to think of a way to change the subject when Darcy chose to change it himself.

"Perhaps I should not have been so dismissive of Miss Bennet's sister. She was an amiable partner when I danced with her even if she was not nearly as handsome as her older sister."

McDunn had to clamp his lips shut since his opinion was that both of the two eldest Bennet sisters were as beautiful as movie stars from his own time—slender and womanly with flawless complexions and expressive faces. The elder was more serene than her sister, who was the livelier of the two. And Elizabeth showed a grace in movement that was quite marked when compared to the other Meryton daughters. McDunn was still rather unsettled to hear Darcy dismiss her so blithely.

"Still, I should have been more gracious when Bingley tried to convince me to dance with her a second time."

McDunn knew he had not guarded his features sufficiently when Darcy leaned forward intently. "It appears I prompted some kind of reaction there."

McDunn considered trying to plead innocence, but he wasn't sure he could pull it off, and he didn't want to lie to Darcy even if it was for his own good. He sighed unhappily. "I think Elizabeth Bennet overheard what you said."

"Surely not!" exclaimed Darcy. "She was well out of hearing, I am sure."

"I thought so, but I saw the expression on her face. She must have unnaturally keen hearing, or perhaps she reads lips. Either way, I'm afraid she heard you. Though what you actually said wasn't too objectionable, just that you preferred not to raise expectations by asking for a second dance. Is that too awful in this time? I'm not sure."

Darcy looked pained and remorseful. "It was not truly ill-mannered, perhaps, but it was…impolitic at the very least. I regret being so thoughtless. Are you certain?"

"I'm afraid so."

"It probably should not matter, but my father advised me against offending others needlessly. One should not make enemies accidentally, he told me, and after seeing how those at the assembly responded tonight, I fear I did not follow his advice."

McDunn could think of nothing to add to this, and he might have already said too much. Certainly, he had said more than he intended.

At the sound of a soft knock on the door, both of them looked at each other. "Perhaps it is Miss Bingley."

"Oh, goodie," McDunn said, which drew a quick smile from Darcy. "Courage, my friend."

McDunn nodded then called, "Come!"

By the time Georgiana opened the door, spied her brother, and quickly slipped inside, both men were already standing.

"Pray, there is no need," she said. "Sit, sit!"

"Only after you, Miss Darcy," McDunn replied, pulling out a chair for her. "I'm finding the manners of everyone I've met so far to be surprisingly pleasing. In my world, there was very little formality, and I've decided the complete absence of manners is not healthy. In fact, I remember my grandmother saying good manners are the grease that makes society function smoothly. I was too young and foolish to give proper credence to her advice at the time, but I've come to appreciate it more and more. So, Miss Darcy,

I shall continue to rise to my feet when you enter the room no matter how nicely you ask me to stop."

He shared a warm smile with Darcy, who said, "Your grandmother seems to have been a fount of considerable wisdom."

"She was a very traditional lady, which you would understand more easily if you met the man she married. Sergeant Major Calvin McDunn III was the top enlisted man in the entire Marine Corps. Ramrod straight both physically and mentally, he never deviated from a course once he decided on something. But that's neither here nor there. Miss Darcy, would I be correct in assuming you had something to ask of your brother?"

Georgiana didn't say anything at first; then she looked up at her brother through her lashes.

Uh-oh, McDunn thought in amusement. *She wants something!*

"I would like to know about the assembly, William," she said earnestly. "I know you prefer not to speak about such things, especially since you did not wish to attend and only did so because it made Mr. Bingley happy."

Darcy looked helplessly at McDunn, who only smiled broadly at him.

"I could never deny my sisters anything when they asked like that, Darcy. They learned how to manipulate me very early in life."

Darcy threw up his hands in defeat. "Very well, Georgiana," he said with a sigh. "But then you must promise to retire to your bed."

"Of course, William," she said with a demureness that did not fool McDunn in the slightest.

It likely did not fool her brother either, but he had no choice but to begin.

Mrs. Bennet had much to relate when she returned to Longbourn, having seen her eldest daughter so much admired by Mr. Bingley and his sisters with the added dividend of her next-eldest daughter being asked to dance by the famous—and wealthy—Mr. Darcy. The evening had been, as she related to her husband, a triumph in all respects.

"Mr. Bingley danced with Jane not once but twice!" she told her husband with even more than her usual enthusiasm. "And Lizzy heard Mr. Bingley say that Jane was the most beautiful creature he had ever beheld. And Lizzy herself, Mr. Bennet—Mr. Darcy asked her for a set though he danced with no other ladies except for Mr. Bingley's sisters. Oh, it was a marvelous evening!"

Her husband listened closely at first. His curiosity had been stimulated by the heightened expectations at having such a wealthy newcomer to their neighborhood in attendance at the assembly. In fact, he had rather hoped his wife's expectations of this young man would have been disappointed, but such had clearly not been the case.

But he had heard all he desired to hear, and as his wife's descriptions continued, his patience rapidly dissipated. He had no interest whatever in hearing how Mary was described to Bingley's sisters as being the most accomplished young lady in the neighborhood nor how marvelous it was that Kitty and Lydia were never without a partner. But when Mrs. Bennet, completely oblivious to her husband's displeasure, moved on to a description of the gowns worn by Mr. Bingley's sisters, Mr. Bennet raised his hand.

"I will hear no descriptions of finery, Mrs. Bennet!" he declared, interrupting her in mid-sentence. His displeasure was so great that he would not even listen when she attempted to change the subject and give details of Elizabeth—alone among all the young ladies in attendance—being asked for a set of dances by Mr. Darcy.

"Enough!" Mr. Bennet said firmly, ushering his wife from his library and closing the door behind her.

ONLY WHEN THE TWO ELDEST SISTERS WERE UPSTAIRS COULD JANE SPEAK more freely. While she felt pleasure similar to her mother's at the attention of Mr. Bingley, she felt it in a quieter way and had been significantly more subdued in her praise of him earlier. Now that she and Elizabeth were finally alone, she could be more forthright in her admiration.

"He is just what a young man ought to be. Sensible, good humored, lively, and with such happy manners. So easy, so well-bred—"

"And so handsome and so possessed of an admirable fortune," interjected Elizabeth. "He has everything a young man ought to have, and you have sketched his character completely. As I have said, such a young man must be in need of a wife."

"Oh piffle, Lizzy. You have to admit Mr. Darcy is even more handsome than Mr. Bingley, and he clearly admired you enough to solicit a set, which is more than he did with anyone else."

Elizabeth suppressed a shiver as she remembered the dizzying effect Mr. Darcy incited within her when she first saw him and even more when they danced. But she made herself smile wryly.

"But Mr. Bingley asked you for a second pair of dances, which Mr. Darcy most explicitly did not. He said he was afraid of raising any expectations on my part."

"I was disappointed when you mentioned that, though it seemed to amuse you more than anything else. But I must admit I was flattered when Mr. Bingley asked me to dance again. I did not expect such a compliment."

"It did not surprise me at all. You are always surprised by compliments, never expecting them. But what could be more natural, Jane? He could easily perceive no other young lady was close to being as pretty as you."

"But what did you think of Mr. Darcy, Lizzy? Were you not surprised at his invitation?"

"Yes, I have to admit I was," Elizabeth said, careful to portray an expression of thoughtfulness since she was not at all sure what she thought of Darcy. "At first, I did not realize he was the Darcy we had read of—the one who is building the telegraph lines throughout the country, and I only realized it when I overheard a comment from Lady Lucas. I would have liked to discuss it with him, but he was not at all interested in further discussion after we danced. He is a very reserved, taciturn man, Jane. Not cold exactly but very controlled in his emotions and his expressions."

"Oh, Lizzy! You are very particular!"

"And I am afraid you are a great deal too apt to like people in general. You never see a fault in anyone! You think of everyone you meet as good and agreeable, and I doubt I have ever heard you speak ill of anybody."

"I do not wish to censure anyone unfairly, and I say what I think. I am not being deceitful."

"I know, Jane. It is that very fact which makes you so remarkable. I know you to have good sense, yet you can simultaneously be blind to the follies, nonsense, and deceits of others! Why, you even think well of Mr. Bingley's sisters, yet they have not a fraction of his excellent manners and amiability!"

"I was uncertain of my opinion of them at first, I must admit. However, upon further conversation, I found them both quite pleasing. Miss Bingley is to remain at Netherfield and keep his house as she did in town. I believe we shall find her a very charming neighbor."

Elizabeth did not disagree openly, but she was not of the same estimation since she was less inclined to deceive herself than Jane. Bolstering her opinion was the fact that both sisters had not gone out of their way to make themselves agreeable to anyone except Jane and had openly boasted of their substantial fortunes and their education at a fine establishment in town. In fact, she had heard enough to conclude they were in the habit of associating with people of rank and, therefore, were entitled to think well of themselves.

It had long been her judgment, even at her tender age of nineteen, that people who held themselves in such high regard often thought meanly of others, and Mr. Bingley's sisters had done nothing to change her opinion.

IT WAS ONLY WHEN ELIZABETH SAID GOOD NIGHT TO HER SISTER AND returned to her room that she had an opportunity to think more on the bewildering Mr. Darcy and the extraordinary effect he had had on her.

It was not simply when I looked at him the first time, either, she thought, perplexed by her inability to explain what happened. *When our fingers touched, even through the gloves we both wore, I felt something similar.*

What disturbed her most was that her reaction to Darcy was solely physical. It was not accompanied by any approval of his character—not at all. She was still convinced the man was as haughty, reserved, and disagreeable as she had first thought.

She did not believe in love at first sight, despite its new popularity in literature. She was certain this was nothing similar.

Yet, with real concern, she remembered the tingling sensation on her skin and the wild, forbidden thoughts it evoked. She gave a moan as she imagined the touch of his hand on her bare skin. She threw herself onto her bed and pulled the covers up to her chin in reaction but gave another moan as an inexplicable vision of his warm fingers moving along her thigh entered her mind.

She squeezed her eyes shut in an attempt to dismiss the images, but that was worse. It was then she saw Darcy's handsome, cold face lowering toward hers from above until his lips finally touched hers...

From whence are such depraved thoughts coming? Am I being possessed by demons?

Elizabeth Bennet knew only what any other inexperienced woman of her time could know. Thus, the merest hint of feeling any sort of passion for a man would have been considered an abomination in her naïve view of the world. Her mother had always said the physical act of procreation between a husband and wife was a duty, and one should simply let it happen, after which her husband would leave her alone for a while.

But a mother's advice was useless to Elizabeth as she wrestled with trying to find some resolution between the never-before-suspected desires of her body and the more sober needs of a young lady who had to be careful in any involvement with the opposite sex.

Sleep was long in coming, and she gained little rest, having been asleep only an hour when she was suddenly awakened by a disturbing dream she could barely remember other than the rapidly dissipating but intense rush of mysterious pleasure surging throughout her body.

It had been years since Elizabeth had last cried, but she sobbed uncontrollably that night. The sun was well above the horizon before her sobs diminished and she was able to return to a fitful slumber.

Chapter 13

Thou and I are too wise to woo peaceably.

— William Shakespeare, *Much Ado about Nothing*

Tuesday, October 22, 1811
Longbourn, Hertfordshire

With the events of the previous evening so much a topic of conversation, and with Lucas Lodge within such an easy walking distance of Longbourn, it was natural to find the Lucas sisters calling there the following morning.

After the appropriate greetings were exchanged, Mrs. Bennet said, "You began the evening well, Charlotte. You were Mr. Bingley's first choice."

"Yes, but he seemed to like his second better."

"Oh, you mean Jane, I suppose," Mrs. Bennet said, feigning ignorance, "because he danced with her twice. Yes, it did seem he admired her."

Elizabeth winced at her mother's inability to refrain from gloating, but Charlotte, as usual, gave no sign she had heard.

"More than simple admiration, I would say. I told Eliza about overhearing Mr. Bingley say the eldest Miss Bennet was the prettiest girl in the room. He said there could not be two opinions on that point."

Jane blushed scarlet and lowered her eyes at hearing such a compliment.

"And you had the good fortune to secure Mr. Darcy as a dance partner, Eliza," Charlotte said. "There was considerable whispering throughout the hall when he led you to the floor."

"Especially when he asked no other young lady!" Mrs. Bennet said immediately. "It was very noteworthy."

"It did not appear so as the evening went on, Mama. It was not long before I heard many criticisms of his haughty pride, saying he was the most disagreeable of men."

Charlotte nodded in agreement. "I heard the same. It was not very surprising with so many mothers wishing desperately for their daughters to be as lucky as you. Imagine what would have been said if Mr. Darcy had asked you to dance a second set!"

"Such an event would have been insupportable, Charlotte," Elizabeth said gaily. "My own opinion of the man is rather conflicted, but I tend to think his disagreeable inclinations overwhelm any compliment he might have given me by his invitation."

"Do not speak such nonsense, Lizzy!" her mother cried. "How can you be so foolish? Why, he is very wealthy and quite famous!"

"Would it make him a suitable person with whom to spend my life, Mama? I think not. And remember he specifically avoided asking for a second set since it might give rise to 'unwarranted assumptions.'"

"Oh, silly girl! Here you are very fortunate, and you do nothing but chatter absurdities!"

"Everyone says he is truly disagreeable, Charlotte," Kitty said in eager agreement. "Mrs. Long said she sat close to him for a full half-hour without him ever saying a word. And the two of them had already been introduced."

"That cannot be the case," Jane said, rising to his defense. "I saw Mr. Darcy talking with her."

"Only because Mrs. Long asked him how he liked Netherfield Park, and he could not help answering her."

"Miss Bingley told me he never speaks much unless among his intimate acquaintances. With them, he is remarkably agreeable," Jane said.

"What do you think of Mr. Darcy's friend, Major McDunn, Eliza?" Charlotte asked. "I found out he really *is* a soldier, as I suspected."

"An American, who freely admitted he was not a gentleman and never learned to dance," Mrs. Bennet said, giving a sniff of disdain. "He should not have been allowed inside the assembly hall!"

"And he does not even wear regimentals!" Lydia said. "Imagine!"

"Mr. Bingley said he is no longer a serving officer," Jane said. "He was in the American Corps of Marines some years ago."

"A hard, tough man, I would judge," Elizabeth said.

"*That* man has nothing to be proud of," Mrs. Bennet said forcefully. "Not like Mr. Darcy, certainly."

"Mr. Darcy's pride does not offend me as much as pride often does," Charlotte said. "There is an excuse for it in his case. He is a very handsome and wealthy young man with a growing reputation from his accomplishments. If I may so express it, he has a right to be proud."

"Perhaps you are correct, Charlotte, but he remains very reserved, taciturn, and more than a little disagreeable," Elizabeth said in response.

"Pride," Mary said, "is a very common failing, and human nature is particularly prone to it. Most people seem to cherish a feeling of self-complacency on some quality or other, real or imaginary."

Elizabeth looked at Charlotte in merriment since they both took great delight in ridiculous statements, which Mary quite often supplied.

"If I were as rich as Mr. Darcy," cried a young Lucas lad, who had come with his sisters, "I should not care how proud I was! I would keep a pack of foxhounds and drink a bottle of wine every day!"

"Then you would drink a great deal more than you ought," Mrs. Bennet said, "and if I were to see you at it, I should take away your bottle directly."

The boy protested she should not, while Mrs. Bennet maintained she would. The argument ended only with the visit when he had to accompany his sisters back to Lucas Lodge.

Wednesday, October 23–24, 1811
Hertfordshire

THE LADIES OF LONGBOURN HESITATED ONLY A DAY BEFORE WAITING ON those of Netherfield, and the visit was returned in due course. McDunn had been present when Mrs. Bennet and her daughters called, and while he soon left to ride with the other men, he remained long enough to observe Caroline Bingley and her sister show a distinct, if rather supercilious, preference for Jane's company.

They had done their best to ignore the other sisters, and though it was not possible to do the same with Mrs. Bennet, they had spoken to her as seldom as was possible, doing so in such a subtle and fashionable manner, the poor woman did not perceive she was being snubbed.

Jane received these attentions with pleasure since she did not perceive their condescending treatment of everyone, even herself, as her sister did. Elizabeth still could not like them, and not even their expressed admiration of her dearest sister was enough to repair their defects in her eyes. She knew their attentions were motivated by their brother's admiration and not real friendship.

In the following days, Bingley was invited to most engagements because of his general approval about the neighborhood. The Bennet family—or at least Mrs. Bennet and her daughters—were also included in those invitations. Such events gave Bingley and Jane many opportunities to see each other, and Elizabeth was pleased to see Bingley's admiration for her sister continue. She was also pleased by Jane confiding to her that her good opinion of the young man was increasing.

Because of his friendship with Bingley, Darcy was included in these invitations despite the general disapprobation in which he was regarded. Such engagements necessarily threw him and Elizabeth into company though not with a similarly favorable mutual regard. Elizabeth could not determine Darcy's opinion of her, but it did not matter since she had no intention of trying to win his admiration.

But his physical effect on her continued to be so intensely disturbing, she wavered back and forth between staying as far away from him as possible and being drawn to him as a moth to the flame that would consume it. Only her love for Jane kept her from pleading one excuse or another to remain at Longbourn.

McDunn saw little of this since he was seldom included in those invitations and Darcy was not inclined to discuss such social events.

That Jane was well on the way to being in love with Bingley was clear to Elizabeth, and she was certain it was equally clear to Bingley until she happened to mention the matter to Charlotte one afternoon where a large party had been invited.

"And you are certain of her feelings, Eliza?" her friend asked.

"Unquestionably."

"Perhaps you are seeing with eyes more closely attuned to Jane than mine are, but I cannot detect evidences of a special regard on her part."

"But such is Jane's nature. She is so distinguished by her calm composure and her universal cheerfulness that the world might not detect her feelings.

But they are there, I assure you. We speak of it every night."

"Which gives you an insight others lack, Eliza. I am well aware of Jane's serenity and composure, but it can sometimes be a disadvantage to be so very guarded. If a woman conceals her affection from the object of it with skill, she may lose the opportunity of fixing him. It would then be poor consolation to her that she kept the rest of the world in the dark also."

Elizabeth had to laugh at this. "Jane is not one to engage in schemes to fix a young man, Charlotte. You know her too well to believe such a thing."

"I do, but any attachment contains many feelings, some of which can pull the two together and others that can push them apart. A slight preference for another might be sufficient at first, but there are very few of us who have heart enough to be in love without encouragement.

Elizabeth felt a pang at this statement since her unexplained attraction to Darcy was certainly not marked by any encouragement.

And I am not *in love with that man, either!* she thought fiercely.

But Charlotte continued. "In nine cases out of ten, a woman had better show more affection than she feels. Bingley undoubtedly likes your sister, but he may never do more than like her if she does not help him on."

"But she does, as much as her nature will allow. If *I* can perceive her regard for him, he must be a simpleton, indeed, not to discern it."

"Mr. Bingley does not know Jane's disposition as you do."

"But if a woman is partial to a man and does not take pains to conceal it, he must find it out."

"Perhaps he must if he sees enough of her. Though Bingley and Jane meet tolerably often, it is never for many hours together, nor are they alone. They always see each other in large, mixed parties that make it impossible for them to converse only with each other. Jane should make the most of every moment in which she can command his attention and thus secure him."

"Your plan is a good one where nothing is in question but the desire of being well married, especially to a rich man. If I were determined to get such a husband, I daresay I should adopt it. But Jane's nature is different. She does not act by design. She is still trying to ascertain her feelings since they have only known each other a fortnight. Four dances and four dinners in company are not quite enough to make her certain of his character."

"Perhaps not, but four such evenings may do a great deal in acquainting them."

"Yes," Elizabeth said with a laugh, "these four evenings have enabled them to ascertain they both like Vingt-un better than Commerce. I am not certain how much else has been unfolded."

"Well, I wish Jane success with all my heart, and if she were to be married to Mr. Bingley, I should think she would have as good a chance of happiness as she would if she had a twelvemonth to study his character. Happiness in marriage is entirely a matter of chance, you know. Even those who begin their life together with a confluence of traits will still grow sufficiently unlike afterwards to have their share of vexation. It is better to know as little as possible beforehand of the defects of the person with whom you are to pass your life."

"You make me laugh, Charlotte," Elizabeth said gaily. "But it is not sound! You know it is not sound! You would never act in such a way yourself."

DARCY STOOD WITH McDUNN AT THE SAME PARTY AT LUCAS LODGE, observing Elizabeth speaking with Charlotte Lucas across the room. This was one of the rare occasions when McDunn had been included in the invitation, likely because of the excessive civility of their host, Sir William Lucas. Darcy thought Sir William made a rather ludicrous figure on most occasions, but he could not fault him today since it allowed his friend to also attend. Sir William simply did not seem to detect the distinctions in status the rest of the neighborhood found so natural.

In his present position with McDunn against the wall, Darcy was too far away to overhear Elizabeth's conversation, but he could easily detect it animated her in that lively, captivating manner he found increasingly charming. Almost without conscious thought, Darcy began to move across the room in order to be close to her. He knew McDunn, who was engaged in his usual occupation of watching people, could not help noticing the change in his usual inclination to remain aloof from the others, but it could not be helped. He knew he could not disguise his interest in Elizabeth since he could hardly look away from her. He had not so much as mentioned her in any of his conversations with McDunn to this point, but the display of his interest had now become a moot point.

Darcy remembered with discomfort his original dismissive opinion of Elizabeth's beauty, comparing her unfavorably to her eldest sister.

Since that first evening, however, his opinions had been undergoing a peculiar kind of metamorphosis. The result was a gradual but rather complete change in virtually everything he had judged on first sight. As one change followed another, Darcy had squirmed in mortification at having been so much in error. He was aware of his critical eye, but he had believed he could compensate for it by applying his opinions dispassionately and logically. That, however, had not been the case regarding Elizabeth Bennet.

He was struck first by her dark eyes, which he soon found so enticing it was difficult for him to tear his own away from hers. And his assessment of her face having little of distinction was brought low by his realization that the lovely expression in those fine eyes lent a beauty to her entire face.

Though he had thought he detected more than one failure of perfect symmetry in her form, he now considered her figure to be light, pleasing, and to his utter surprise, womanly. He remembered her grace on the dance floor as though through a different lens, and he now thought her appearance rendered her, in fact, quite lovely—and desirable.

He found he had formed an equal misconception when it came to her manners, which he had put down at first as not at all sophisticated. He now acknowledged that, even if her manners were not those of the fashionable world, they were marked by an easy, playful nature and an honesty that he now found more appealing. Her mouth seemed made to smile and laugh, which she did often but not at all in the disparaging and disdainful manner of Bingley's sisters.

She was bewitching, and it was only the inferiority of her connections that allowed him to observe her with some equanimity, relatively immune to the danger of falling in love. It was the mark of his character that he equally well did not feel any compulsion to attempt enticing her into the kind of improprieties to which Wickham had proven so adept. He frowned in remembrance, glad he was unlikely ever to encounter *that* man again.

OF ALL THIS, ELIZABETH WAS PERFECTLY UNAWARE. TO HER, HE WAS ONLY the man who disturbed her in such an unnatural manner and who also made himself agreeable nowhere. She had reluctantly acquitted him of his dismissal of dancing with her a second time at the assembly. Bingley had bestowed such a compliment on Jane, with the resulting estimation of all in the neighborhood that Jane might soon displace Miss Bingley as the mistress of Netherfield. Since there had been a smattering of such comments regarding herself after her single set with Darcy, a second invitation would have resulted in the same whispers hailing her as the next mistress of his estate in Derbyshire. She knew this could never be; there was too great a gulf between the two of them. It was just as well since Mr. Darcy had not proven himself to be anything other than a cold and disagreeable man, making it impossible even to contemplate spending one's life with him.

At least he did not dismiss me as not being handsome enough to dance with! she thought with a measure of humor.

Then she had had to suppress her shudder as she asked herself why this man affected her so disturbingly. Why had he asked her to dance even once?

The possibility that he found her bewitching, even if the differences in their station precluded any deeper attachment, never crossed her mind.

In his compulsion to know more of Elizabeth and to speak with her, Darcy drew closer to her and Miss Lucas as they spoke with the colonel of the militia regiment. Elizabeth seemed unaware of Darcy's proximity, and she surely would have moved away if she had become aware of it. But Charlotte was more alert, and after Colonel Forster took his leave, she alerted her friend.

"It seems Mr. Darcy is staring at you, Eliza."

"What?" Elizabeth was startled enough to glance around, and she indeed found Darcy's eyes on her. She was quick to turn away.

"What does he mean by standing there like an avenging angel?" she asked in a whisper, almost hissing the words.

Charlotte looked at her friend, startled by the vehemence in her voice. "Why, I am sure I do not know. But he was listening closely to your conversation with Colonel Forster. Perhaps he wishes to solicit a dance."

"You jest, Charlotte," Elizabeth said more calmly. "Besides, there is no music."

"Ah, but the lack of music is easily rectified since my father has a fine instrument, and I would much prefer for you to exhibit rather than your sister."

"Mary is much more accomplished than I," protested Elizabeth loyally.

"And not half so pleasurable to listen to, as you well know. Look, Mr. Darcy is coming this way. Now is the time to exercise your usual impertinence and ask him what he is about."

"I shall do nothing of the kind. I believe it is better to ignore Mr. Darcy at all times unless absolutely necessary."

But the occasion quickly arose as Darcy approached close. Charlotte seized the chance and turned to him.

"Do you not think my friend expressed herself well just now, Mr. Darcy, when she was teasing Colonel Forster about hosting a ball at Meryton?"

Somewhat startled, Darcy stopped and, after a moment, replied, "She did so with great energy, Miss Lucas, but as to her success, I cannot comment. But dancing is a subject that always makes a lady energetic."

Charlotte laughed lightly, but Elizabeth was not pleased by either Charlotte's impudence or Darcy's answer.

"You are severe on us, sir," Elizabeth said with some asperity. But Darcy only gave one of his rare smiles and shrugged, apparently not at all offended.

"You will forgive my friend her brashness, sir, since she knows it will soon be her turn to be teased. As I just told her, my father has a fine instrument, and I am about to lead her thither. You know what follows, Eliza."

"You are a very strange creature by way of a friend!" Elizabeth cried. "If my vanity had led me in a musical direction, you would have been invaluable, but I would prefer to avoid displaying my meager talents before an audience used to better performances."

"You are the one being severe on yourself. I have often told you so since your talents are by no means meager. Come, take my arm."

Elizabeth was reluctant, but she was also wild to get away from Darcy. The man seemed to exude some sort of magnetism that was far too disturbing to be tolerated, especially in company. Accordingly, she acceded to Charlotte's urging and moved to the pianoforte, and after searching through the sheets, began to play.

Darcy found Elizabeth's performance was pleasing to both the audience and to himself, though he dispassionately judged it to fall short of being capital. After Elizabeth played another tune and was replaced at the bench by her sister Mary, he quickly had cause to re-assess his opinion.

Mary was always eager to display skills sharpened by long practice but unfortunately had neither genius nor taste to match her superior fingering and had not the same feel for the music. Elizabeth, easy and unaffected, had been listened to with much more pleasure though not playing half so well, and Mary, at the end of a long concerto, received only desultory applause.

Her younger sisters requested she play Scot and Irish airs and lost no time in fostering dancing at one end of the room along with some of the

Lucases and several officers.

Darcy lost no time in returning to stand silently near McDunn, his mood one of silent indignation at the juvenile impertinence of the younger Bennet sisters in instigating such a mode of passing the evening to the exclusion of all conversation.

He was too engrossed in such thoughts to realize Sir William Lucas had come to stand beside him until his host attempted a conversation.

Sir William's topic was dancing, and to his boring and trivial questions, Darcy made his answers as short and unresponsive as possible, hoping the man would go away. But Sir William was engaged in his favorite pastime—that of being civil to everyone—and never noticed Darcy's disinterest.

He had only paused in his unsuccessful efforts when Elizabeth and Charlotte passed close by. Sir William was instantly struck with the notion of performing a gallantry and called out to the young ladies.

"My dear Miss Eliza, why are you not dancing? Mr. Darcy, you must allow me to present this young lady to you as a very desirable partner. You cannot refuse to dance, I am sure, when so much beauty is before you."

And, taking her hand, he presented it to Darcy, who though extremely surprised, was not at all unwilling to receive it.

ELIZABETH INSTANTLY DREW BACK WITH THE INTENTION OF REFUSING THE offer. Her mouth opened to say something, but in the flood of confusing and contradictory emotions and feelings surging through her, she could only remain silent.

Her next awareness was of being led toward the dance that was taking place at the end of the room, leaving behind her a triumphant Charlotte Lucas and a rather bemused Edward McDunn.

Sir William beamed happily at the success of his gallantry and soon departed to bestow his attentions to others.

Despite the whirl of her thoughts and the proximity of Darcy's presence, Elizabeth was easily able to execute the dance steps seamlessly. While Elizabeth had to educate herself in other matters, her mother had overseen the tutoring of her daughters in all the dances usual in their part of England.

Nevertheless, because of Darcy's closeness, Elizabeth was exhausted when the dance finally concluded. Though she had in no way planned for it, she believed she had handled her raging emotions better than previously.

After thanking Elizabeth for the dance, which he had enjoyed despite his misgivings, Darcy intended to return to McDunn's side, but he was intercepted by Miss Bingley. The lady seemed almost frantic with alarm at seeing Darcy dance again with this insufferable Bennet sister and reverted to her usual mode of mocking the country neighborhood in general and the attendees at this plebeian gathering in particular.

"I can guess the subject of your reverie," she said with an arch of one fine eyebrow.

"I should imagine not," Darcy replied with evident disinterest.

"You are considering how insupportable it would be to pass many evenings in this manner and in such society. Indeed, I am quite of your opinion. The insipidity, the noise, the self-importance of these people! I am sure your own strictures on them would match mine!"

"Your conjecture is totally wrong, I assure you. My mind was more agreeably engaged in meditating on the pleasure bestowed by a pair of fine eyes in the face of a pretty woman."

Miss Bingley's alarm now reached frightening proportions. "I am all amazement, Mr. Darcy. I beg you to tell me what lady has inspired such reflections. I know it cannot be Miss Elizabeth Bennet, though you did just dance with her."

"The very same."

"I am all astonishment!" cried Miss Bingley, trying to control her voice. "I was not aware she was such a favorite. When, pray tell, am I to wish you joy?"

"Which is exactly the question I expected. A lady's imagination is very rapid, jumping from admiration to love and from love to matrimony. I knew you would be wishing me joy as soon as I mentioned it."

"Nay, if you are so serious about it, I shall consider the matter as absolutely settled. You will have a charming mother-in-law, indeed. And, of course, she will always be at Pemberley with you."

Darcy could only listen to her, feigning perfect indifference, while she chose to entertain herself in this manner even after he moved back to stand beside McDunn. She could not help herself, Darcy knew. She was distraught at the possible frustration of her desires, never imagining that neither she nor Miss Elizabeth would ever be mistress of Pemberley, but his composure eventually convinced her all was safe.

Interesting, McDunn thought in amusement. *Very interesting.*

LATER THE SAME EVENING, ELIZABETH FELT AS THOUGH SHE HAD BEEN taken up in a nightmare, one she could not end by waking up.

After the disturbing experience of her dance with Darcy, she had been wild to get away from Lucas Lodge and had begged her mother for the use of the carriage to return to Longbourn, saying she had a blinding headache.

But her mother had refused, wanting Elizabeth to remain. She was near to gloating at Bingley's attentions to Jane, and the occasion of Darcy again dancing with Lizzy added to her glee. She was convinced both her eldest daughters would soon be comfortably settled at magnificent estates.

But Elizabeth did not follow her mother's command with her usual filial obedience. Instead, she retrieved her shawl, coat, and bonnet and walked home. It was a short walk, but her slippers had been little designed for the activity and were ruined. It was also unlikely her dress could ever be washed clean of the mud and dirt along the hem.

She cared for nothing but being safely ensconced in her room, where she later rejected all messages sent by her mother to come downstairs and explain why she had so suddenly left Lucas Lodge. Equally, she had rejected the summons to the evening meal and had not even been able to talk to Jane, who was quite worried about her. She sat curled up on the window seat in her room with two blankets wrapped around her for warmth against the chill air just beyond the glass and felt absolutely wretched.

She and Jane had shared their most intimate secrets all of their lives, but Elizabeth simply could not share what she had learned about herself today. Not yet, at least. Perhaps, not ever. For she now knew that the reason for her reaction to Mr. Darcy was nothing less than the indisputable fact that she was a fallen woman—as good as a harlot.

And that handsome man from Derbyshire is the one responsible for my fall! she thought miserably. *Or, rather, I am the one responsible for my fall, and he is just the lure that tempted me to succumb. Has not our parson warned of the sin of fornication and the many evils attendant on being tempted by that sin?*

Imagining she knew the reason for the inexplicable urges afflicting her since the first night she met the man did not, however, alleviate her distress. Worse had been the unbidden urge that came into her mind after her dance when she wished to feel his hand on her skin. On her bare skin!

It was unthinkable! Decent, well-brought-up young ladies simply did not have such thoughts! They did not think of such things as giving them pleasure, as she most certainly had been doing!

On at least four occasions since the first night at the assembly, Elizabeth had awakened with those memories of intense, forbidden pleasure surging through her body.

It was at last understandable that, despite having heretofore been an example of a pure, chaste, and virginal young lady, the daughter of a gentleman and thus the equal of Mr. Darcy of Derbyshire, she was instead nothing more than a common tart, a strumpet, a woman of licentious desires.

I do not even LIKE the man! Mr. Darcy is not at all amiable or likable! But I can delude myself no longer. I want him to touch me! As a man touches a woman! As a husband touches a wife!

She winced at the thought because she knew such a connection was impossible. Certain of her fallen state, utterly dismayed at the mere thought of having been subject to such forbidden longings, she threw herself into her bed. She sobbed as she had never sobbed before, sobbed for all she had lost because of her desire for this horrid, objectionable man. Sleep eluded her for eons, but exhaustion of spirit finally brought a surcease to her anguish.

No dreams disturbed her deep sleep during the night, and she did not hear Jane's knock at her door to summon her to breakfast. Nor was she aware of Jane looking into her room at her motionless form and only departing in relief after seeing the slow rise and fall of her sister's breathing.

Chapter 14

For as men in battle are continually in the way of shot, so we, in this world, are ever within the reach of Temptation.

— William Penn, English nobleman, writer, early Quaker, and founder of the colony of Pennsylvania

Monday, November 11, 1811
Netherfield, Hertfordshire

McDunn took another sip of his brandy, lamenting his empty bottle of smuggled Scotch whisky. Brandy was better than nothing, but it just wasn't his style.

He had just finished reviewing the paperwork sent from town on the construction of his prototype steam locomotive, and a glow of satisfaction added to the warmth of the brandy. There had been a litany of the usual problems associated with doing things for the first time, but he had been able to determine the problem and detail a solution for all of them. He would probably go to town in a day or two to check things over, but all seemed to be going as well as could be expected.

In the midst of his self-satisfaction, a diffident knock came at the door.

"Come!" he called, and a female servant opened the door, curtseying with her eyes downcast.

Do I scare the servants so much? he wondered idly. *They all seem to regard me with a measure of fright, but I cannot think of anything I've done to warrant it.*

"Beg pardon, sir, but Miss Bingley asks whether you might come downstairs. It seems a guest has taken ill."

McDunn's eyebrows went up in reflex. Caroline gave as little notice of him as she could, consistent with at least a modicum of courtesy. But what was this about wishing his presence because someone was sick? But there was only one way to find the answer, and he stood immediately.

"Tell Miss Bingley I shall come down directly," he said, receiving another timid curtsey as the girl all but fled.

Shaking his head in disbelief, McDunn got his first-aid packet and slipped it in his pocket. In more than two years, he hadn't used any of its limited supplies except for a couple of touches of the antibiotic ointment. He had seldom allowed anyone other than Darcy to see it though the canvas packet was outwardly innocuous.

But the Velcro fastenings aren't, he thought, *and I'm not in the mood to answer questions from either of the Bingley sisters. But I might need an aspirin, so I'll bring it and make sure they don't get a good look at it.*

The servant awaited him at the bottom of the stairs and led him to the parlor where the two Bingley sisters stood, looking down at a sofa.

Mrs. Hurst was wringing her hands as she looked up. "Major McDunn, do you know anything about sicknesses?" Her anxiety was plain to discern, and McDunn gave her a nod.

"A bit. One picks up a little knowledge here and there in the military."

"That is what I told Caroline. Might you see to Miss Bennet?"

By now, McDunn had reached the sofa and had seen that the eldest Bennet sister lay on her back with a small pillow under her head. Her eyes were closed, and she indeed did not look well.

McDunn knelt by the sofa, not even noticing Caroline hastily moving out of the way.

"Miss Bennet?" he asked gently, and the girl opened her eyes partway.

"Yes?" she said, rather weakly.

"I'm told you're not feeling well."

"I shall—it is just a moment of dizziness."

"Uh-huh." McDunn smiled slightly with the tolerant amusement of an older brother who had heard the same from sisters trying to stay out of bed while their mother looked for a remedy from her medicine cabinet.

"With your permission, may I see if you have a fever?"

When she nodded, he put the back of his hand against her forehead for just a moment.

"—and you have. At least a couple of degrees. Tell me your symptoms, Miss Bennet. That is, have you been shivering?"

Somewhat unwillingly, Jane nodded.

"Sore throat?" Jane shook her head in the negative.

"Headache?"

"Only a slight one."

"How long have you been feeling ill?"

"It was after dinner when she first mentioned it," Caroline said. "The gentlemen are dining with the officers, and we invited Miss Bennet to dine with us."

"She came on horseback through the rain," Mrs. Hurst said.

"Oh, great!" McDunn exclaimed. "I was returning from my ride when the rain started, and it was a *cold* rain!"

"Miss Bennet arrived later than you did, Major McDunn," Caroline said uncomfortably. "Nearly an hour later, in fact."

"And didn't get out of her wet clothing and under some warm blankets, I imagine."

Caroline was forced to admit the truth of that.

"Well, it's most likely just a cold. When is your brother supposed to return?"

"I am not certain," Mrs. Hurst said. "Since it is the officers the gentlemen are dining with, it is likely—" Her voice went quiet.

"—that they stayed to have a few snifters of brandy," McDunn said, finishing her sentence before continuing. "It's too late to send her home, especially on horseback or even in a drafty coach. It's still raining steadily."

To this, the two Bingley sisters quickly, almost eagerly, nodded.

"I suggest getting her upstairs, out of her wet clothing, and into bed under some warm blankets," he said, ticking off points on his fingers. "Miss Bennet needs a warm nightgown, a foot-warmer at her feet if possible, and a fire in the fireplace."

Putting his hands in his pockets and looking down at the sick girl, he continued. "It's likely all that can be done tonight. Tomorrow, Bingley can send for—"

He stopped and looked at the two fashionable sisters. "What is it you English call your doctors? I know you have several different people in the medical trades while we Americans would just send for the doctor."

"Possibly you mean the apothecary," Mrs. Hurst said. "They dispense potions while surgeons see to things like broken bones. And physicians—"

McDunn threw up his hands and turned for the door. "Three people, as I said! Then I suggest sending for the *apothecary* in the morning. And I'll take a look-see myself. Have the servants call me immediately if her fever rises. Otherwise, I'll look in on her before breakfast. Good night."

With a nod, McDunn turned and strode briskly out of the room, leaving two highly genteel, refined, and fashionable ladies somewhat speechless. They had asked for help and got it, but this American was nothing like the gentlemen they were used to. He seemed supremely confident and was not at all submissive, which they considered more appropriate to his station.

Tuesday, November 12, 1811
Longbourn, Hertfordshire

THE NEWS OF JANE'S ILLNESS WAS DELIVERED TO LONGBOURN THE FOLlowing morning, relating her illness and the forthcoming arrival of an apothecary.

Reading the missive, Elizabeth could only shake her head at her mother's machinations. After Jane had received a note from her new Netherfield friends the previous day, inviting her to spend the day and dine with them, her mother had forced Jane to go to Netherfield on horseback rather than her father's carriage, even though—or perhaps especially because—it looked like rain.

And rain had come, cold and hard, necessitating her remaining overnight, which her mother knew would throw her into the company of Mr. Bingley. But now Jane had taken ill, and her friends insisted she stay until she was better.

Mr. Bennet was most philosophical on the matter. "I am awestruck, my dear, at your skill in managing the chase for a suitable husband for your eldest daughter. In the event she dies of her illness, it should be a comfort to both you and her that her demise was in pursuit of Mr. Bingley and under your direction."

"How can you be so tiresome, Mr. Bennet? Healthy young girls do not die of trifling colds, especially if they are properly cared for. So Jane should stay at Netherfield as long as may be. I should go see her, if I might have the carriage."

Then a cunning light came into her eyes. "On further thought, it would be better to send Lizzy since she and Jane are so close. Even better, Jane will undoubtedly insist Lizzy should stay, which means *she* would be in company with Mr. Darcy!"

Elizabeth looked up sharply. She had entertained the idea of accompanying her mother because of her concern over Jane. Since it still rained, she had known her mother would be able to obtain the carriage from her father, which would make the trip more pleasant.

However, after her mother's proposal that Elizabeth go in her place and remain with Jane, the impropriety of her even visiting Netherfield, much less remaining with Jane, became apparent. Despite the neighbors' aversion to Mr. Darcy, due to his neglect of their own daughters, they were still abuzz at his having shown such an attraction to her. If she went to Netherfield—or worse, stayed there to take care of Jane—it would be instantly known in the mysterious manner in which supposedly private happenings became the gist of neighborhood gossip. The whispers would label her as a blatant fortune hunter pursuing one of the most eligible and wealthy bachelors in the land.

And there was the disturbing desire she felt for the gentleman, of which only she was cognizant. Even if Elizabeth now knew why Mr. Darcy disturbed her so, she was still trying to reconcile the fact of those dreadful revelations. She had to force herself not to glance down at her fingers when she remembered the disturbing surge whenever their fingers touched.

Even through her gloves!

"No, Mother, I shall not go," she said, suddenly declaring her resolution firmly. "It would be regarded as highly unseemly if I did so, as though I was throwing myself at Mr. Darcy. Jane will be well taken care of."

"Lizzy, how can you be so silly?" cried her mother. "None of our friends will think such a foolish thing! Your attachment to your sister is known everywhere! Now, go to your room and dress. I wish to leave in a quarter-hour."

"I said I shall not go, and that is an end of it. It would not be proper."

"Disobedient girl! You will do as I say! And order the maid to pack a trunk for you."

"I shall not go!"

"Mr. Bennet!" cried her mother. "You must make her go! Make her obey!"

"I shall not go, Father! I shall stay in my room and read!"

"Mr. Bennet!"

"What should *I* do, Mrs. Bennet?" that worthy gentleman said, throwing his hands up. "I see the sense in what Lizzy says, and it does not seem as though it is a matter on which to gainsay her. She is likely correct in the inferences that would be drawn by the neighbors."

He rose from the breakfast table even as his favorite daughter did the same. "I shall be in my library," he said, "not to be disturbed."

"And I shall be in my room," Elizabeth said. "Take my other sisters with you if you must."

"Mr. Bennet! Lizzy!" wailed Mrs. Bennet.

But she was alone, listening to the sound of receding footsteps.

Tuesday, November 12ᵗʰ, 1811
Netherfield, Hertfordshire

"You are entirely correct in your estimation, Major McDunn," the apothecary said. Mr. Jones stood with Bingley's party at the foot of the stairs, relating what he had found during his examination. "Miss Bennet does indeed appear to have a cold, acquired certainly from her exposure to yesterday's cold rain."

"I've seen it many times with troops in the field," McDunn said with a nod. "They seem to forget—or never to have known—that most times the only way to get dry when it rains is not to get wet in the first place. I assume she still has a fever."

"Indeed, but it is not worrisome at the moment."

"Then it's much the same as last night. That's good."

"Indeed, Major. The real danger in illnesses like this is an unchecked fever. In addition, she now has a headache, her throat is sore, and her back aches. This last symptom might suggest it was the more serious *la grippe*,[13] to use the French term. But that illness does not usually come on so quickly after exposure. I still think it is simply a violent cold. I advised her to remain in bed and get what rest she can. I shall have some draughts delivered."

And I'll sacrifice a few of my small store of aspirin if her fever gets worse, thought McDunn. *I'm not going to be foolish when a girl's life might be in the balance. In these days before they even knew about germs, people often died unbelievably quickly from simple illnesses that would be treated with over-the-counter drugs in my time.*

---

13 Influenza.

"Miss Bennet shall stay here at Netherfield as long as necessary," Bingley said, concern clear in his voice. "A note was sent to her home this morning, and I shall send another with the particulars of your observations, Mr. Jones."

And either Elizabeth by herself or her mother and perhaps all her sisters will be arriving shortly! McDunn thought, glancing aside at Darcy. *Assuming Miss Bennet doesn't sicken further, the next few days should be very interesting with Elizabeth remaining in this house.*

But in this expectation, McDunn was to be disappointed for no one arrived from Longbourn. When prodded by his wife, Mr. Bennet had been unwilling to release the horses from the farm, so Mrs. Bennet and three of her daughters were unable to make the journey.

So, all McDunn could do was scratch his head and wonder about yet another perplexing deviation from Austen's novel.

But at least he had his work, and both Georgiana and Darcy had expressed an interest in being apprised of the progress on the steam locomotive and preparations for laying metal tracks near the Wylam colliery for a demonstration.

Wednesday, November 13, 1811
Netherfield, Hertfordshire

Mrs. Bennet was more successful in obtaining the carriage the next day, and she arrived in good time soon after breakfast with all her daughters, including Elizabeth, who simply had not been able to stay away.

Elizabeth quickly assessed that Jane was in no danger. Her ailment had indeed been a cold, and the pain from her sore throat was reduced, as was her fever. Jane had even pressed to return to Longbourn, to which Elizabeth agreed, thinking Jane would be more comfortable in her own bed.

But her mother was not at all of the same opinion. Once she had satisfied herself that Jane's illness was not alarming, Mrs. Bennet had no intention of having her quit Netherfield since it would remove her from any contact with Mr. Bingley. Despite Jane's wish to return home, Mrs. Bennet stated firmly that Jane was still too ill to be moved. In this, she was supported by Mr. Jones, who had also called at Netherfield.

"I think it advisable that Miss Bennet remain indoors and in bed rather than hazarding a journey by carriage, with the attendant drafts, just when she is regaining her health," he told Bingley when he and the party from

Longbourn adjourned to the breakfast parlor where Bingley waited with his sisters and guests.

"Then we shall surely follow your advice," Bingley said immediately. "Miss Bennet is most welcome to stay as long as necessary."

"Oh, thank you, sir," Mrs. Bennet said. "That is most gracious and is just what I would expect of a young man with your gentlemanly manner. It is this mother's opinion that she is much too ill to be moved, just as Mr. Jones says. I am afraid we must trespass a little longer on your kindness."

McDunn was not sure whether he agreed, but he had no intention of contradicting this conservative approach. It certainly would not do the young lady's health any harm to remain for a day or two longer.

"You must not worry about it, Mrs. Bennet!" Bingley exclaimed. "Moving your daughter must not be considered. Neither of my sisters could support such a suggestion, I am sure."

"You may depend upon it, madam," Caroline said. "Miss Bennet shall receive every possible attention while she remains with us."

McDunn could not help but note that Caroline made her remark civilly but with no real warmth. Mrs. Bennet, however, did not seem to notice and was profuse in her acknowledgment.

"I am sure," Mrs. Bennet said, "I would not know what would become of Jane if it were not for such good friends for she is very ill indeed. But she suffers with the greatest patience in the world, which is always the way with her for she has, without exception, the sweetest temper I have ever seen. But she especially wishes her dear sister Elizabeth might remain with her, to assist with her care and provide cheer during her affliction."

Elizabeth looked sharply at her mother. Jane had indeed made such a request in her room, but Elizabeth had firmly opposed it as being an imposition. In any event, she had just been introduced to Darcy's sister for the first time, and Jane had attested to the many hours Miss Darcy had sat with her in conversation and reading to her.

"It can be easily accomplished, Mrs. Bennet," Bingley said. "The room next to Miss Bennet's is unoccupied, and Miss Elizabeth could stay there."

Elizabeth saw her mother look down to hide her smile of triumph at outwitting her, and then she could not prevent a quick glance at Darcy. His eyes were on her, and she thought she discerned a modicum of interest in his gaze, though deciphering *that* man's thoughts was not an easy task. But the mere thought of there being *any* interest whatever was enough to send a surge of warmth up and down her spine. She looked about desperately for some way of evading her mother's deft ploy.

In her unsettled state, she could think of no way to do so except to tell an outright lie. She hated to do it, but another quick and furtive glance at Darcy convinced her of the danger if she remained in this house with him.

Despite his effect on her peace of mind and the realization of this disruption's carnal nature, she also had conflicted feelings about him otherwise. Elizabeth knew of his elevated status, of course, and she also knew he could have no possible attraction to a young lady whose father only had two thousand a year and whose estate was entailed away to a male cousin when he died.

But the unlikelihood of a connection between her and Darcy was actually the least by far of her concerns. She was, in fact, dearly terrified of what might happen if she remained at Netherfield. If he were, in fact, a man without honor and made a subtle invitation for her to enter his room, what would she do? She did not know! Might she succumb to such a man?

Of course, she had no indication that any such dishonorable intentions might be part of his nature. From Bingley's information to Jane, the truth seemed the complete opposite.

In essence, it was not Mr. Darcy's nature that most concerned her, but her own! If he opened his bedroom door, would she go inside willingly?

She stiffened her resolve and looked directly at her mother. "I do not think it would be advisable, Mama. As I already told Jane, I am not feeling well myself. I think I should not care for my sister when she is recovering her health."

Mrs. Bennet opened her mouth to make an instant rejection but then closed it without saying anything. From her expression, Elizabeth knew how unhappy her mother was at having her least favorite daughter thwart her wishes, but what could she say?

However, she was surprised when her mother summoned the self-control to accept defeat with as much grace as she could summon. Mrs. Bennet changed the subject to compliment Bingley on the many fine attributes of his new estate. She also, of course, included as many compliments for her own daughters into her conversation as she could manage.

Elizabeth was certain her mother believed herself to be quite cosmopolitan in the way she made her comments, but she could not help being loud, unsophisticated, and plebeian. She hoped she was successfully controlling her expression, because she shuddered at each faux pas. And Miss Bingley all but sneered in triumph. Even Darcy had to struggle not to show his disdain for Mrs. Bennet's lack of breeding.

In particular was one of her attempts to praise Jane's beauty when she made reference to one of her brother's acquaintances in London who showed a marked partiality for her.

"It was when she was only fifteen, and a gentleman so admired her that my sister-in-law was certain he would make her an offer before we departed. Perhaps he thought her too young, for he did not do so. But he did write her some verses, and very pretty they were."

Elizabeth was mortified, and her words were out of her mouth before she could stop them. "And so ended his affection," she said, wishing she could leave the house and wait in their carriage. "I fancy there has been many an attraction ended in just that way. I wonder who first discovered the efficacy of poetry in driving away love."

"I have been used to consider poetry as the food of love," Darcy said, smiling at her witticism, and Elizabeth felt herself compelled to make some sort of response.

"Of a fine, stout, healthy love it may," she said carefully. "Everything nourishes what is strong already. But if it be only a slight, thin sort of inclination, I am convinced one good sonnet will starve it entirely away."

Darcy smiled at this, and McDunn chuckled outright. He had forgotten the passage, and hearing it spoken by a real person once again, he thought himself an on-stage spectator at a performance of Austen's signature work.

With differences, though! he thought, realizing again that the events he witnessed bore only a general similarity to the published scenes.

In the pause that ensued, Elizabeth trembled in dread of her mother's embarrassing herself again, but Mrs. Bennet only repeated her thanks to Mr. Bingley for his kindness to Jane. But Elizabeth's fears were more than answered by the improprieties of her two youngest sisters, who had been whispering together during the whole visit. It was now Lydia who stepped forward.

"Mr. Bingley, I remember you saying, when you first came into the neighborhood, that you would soon give a ball at Netherfield."

Lydia was a tall, well-developed girl who had just turned fifteen years of age, about the same age as Georgiana but without any semblance of Miss Darcy's composure and intelligence. She did, however, possess a fine complexion and a lively, good-humored manner. She was a great favorite of her mother, who had possessed many of the same attributes in her youth.

She instantly proved herself just as ready to express herself thoughtlessly as was her mother. "All of us have been depending upon your word, and it would be the most shameful thing in the world if you did not keep it."

Bingley seemed little affected by what Jane's sister said and pledged himself perfectly ready to keep his engagement and even to allow Lydia to name the day as long as she waited until her sister was recovered.

Both Lydia and Kitty pronounced themselves more than satisfied at this promise and even declared it would give them an opportunity to inform Colonel Forster and some of his officers of the event.

When the party finally departed the house, Elizabeth was the first in the carriage, exceedingly anxious to return home. She intended to immediately go to her room and move a set of drawers in front of the door so no one could enter.

I shall not come out until dinner! she thought angrily. *Is it possible to die of mortification? My mother seems determined to find out whether such is possible!*

Then the memory of Darcy's handsome face and tall figure flashed into her mind, and she hugged herself reflexively as her family climbed into the carriage.

What in the world is happening to me? she wondered miserably. *I must drive this man from my mind! It is useless to remember him even if I am now seized with urges more like those of a tart than a proper lady. There is no possibility of a connection between two people of such different character and station.*

Saturday, November 16, 1811
Netherfield, Hertfordshire

McDUNN LEANED BACK IN HIS CHAIR AFTER TAKING A SIP OF HIS WHISKY and gave a contented sigh. He had just returned from town after inspecting the progress on his steam locomotive and had journeyed the extra miles to Darcy's townhouse to retrieve a pair of dusty bottles from Darcy's butler.

"This," he said, holding up his glass, "is immeasurably better than brandy, which I will remind you is produced by the French."

"*Whatever,*" Darcy said, smiling as Georgiana stifled a giggle. "Your whisky is smuggled, you know."

"Well, so is your brandy. And we're at war with the French."

"You said 'we,' Major," Georgiana said seriously. "I cannot remember you ever saying it that way before."

"Did I?" McDunn said with a frown. "Well, Miss Darcy, I can't go home, as we all know. This country of yours is now my home for better or worse. And I would much rather live in Great Britain than in any other country I can think of. Especially one ruled by the mad corporal."[14]

"The Tyrant is how I prefer to think of him," Darcy said firmly.

"He is that," McDunn said agreeably, taking another healthy sip. "I'm becoming so fond of this stuff, I can't really remember how smooth Chevis Regal was. Oh well. Home, as I said."

"How much longer will it be before you are ready for your new demonstration, Major?" Georgiana asked.

"I would imagine it will be early next summer before we're completely prepared. We can't even start laying the rails until the ground dries out in the spring, and there are still problems with the rails and the ties the rails will be laid on that have to be solved. I really need to find a way to make steel production much less expensive. The demo's got to be perfect since there's already competition. But the most promising of them was designed by Mr. Stephenson, and history tells me it was hardly less expensive at hauling coal than doing it with horses. Ours is going to be better and more powerful, though it'll be a bit larger."

"Competition again will push another competitor aside, eh?" Darcy said, and McDunn nodded.

"As I said, progress is relatively heartless at times. And it's not as though steam locomotives, even the one we're fabricating, will be a perfect end product. But we need a working locomotive right away so we can get track laid and start making money from transporting freight and passengers."

Turning to Georgiana, he continued. "I want to compliment you on helping comfort Miss Bennet. The servants tell me she looks forward to the time you spend with her."

"She is very amiable," Georgiana said, pleased at the compliment. "It was no trouble at all."

Darcy muttered something under his breath, and McDunn thought he heard the words "Miss Bingley." He gave his friend a sharp glance, but

---

14 Napoleon Bonaparte.

Darcy only gazed back innocently, never giving an indication he had made a derogative comparison between the true sympathies of Bingley's sisters compared to his own.

"And Miss Elizabeth is very agreeable also," Georgiana said. "I wish she had been able to stay with her sister, though she did come to sit with her for a short time today. She is very witty and amusing."

She looked at her brother. "If Mr. Bingley marries Miss Bennet as everyone is saying, then you ought to marry Miss Elizabeth, William."

To his dying day, McDunn considered this particular moment—and his silent acceptance of Georgiana's suggestion—as his best demonstration of what he liked to think was his rather excellent self-control. His reaction was exemplary compared to Darcy, who had taken a sip of brandy at that exact moment.

McDunn was quick to assist his friend in alleviating a sudden coughing attack, pounding Darcy on the back until the gentleman could breathe again.

"This smuggled brandy is nasty stuff when it goes down the wrong pipe," McDunn said solicitously, which earned him a glare from Darcy as he wiped his lips with his handkerchief.

Turning to his sister, Darcy finally managed to say, "Why would you make such a suggestion, Georgiana? Miss Elizabeth is an amiable young lady, to be sure, and she would certainly be a suitable friend for you, but you know the inferiority of her connections in comparison to our own. Attention must be paid to the value of each partner in the marriage union, you know."

"Yes, I do know, William, but I am thinking of your happiness not whether our family fortune is increased by what everyone calls a splendid marriage. A young lady like Miss Elizabeth could bring you far more contentment than would someone like—"

She stopped. She was too properly bred a young lady to say the words. But McDunn, possibly emboldened by his beloved Scotch, was easily able to do so.

"Like Miss Bingley, you mean?" he said, and Georgiana nodded her head vigorously, though her eyes turned to Darcy's in apprehension.

Darcy looked at her silently for a few moments. "Is there any possibility this heightened spirit of my sister might be in any way attributable to the time we have both spent with you and your unique viewpoints, McDunn?"

"Possibly, but I suspect your sister lives in terror you'll marry Caroline. She's not yet able to read your emotions well enough to know you'd cut your throat before you did that to her. Or to yourself."

Georgiana laughed aloud and exclaimed, "I love your delightful American sayings, Major McDunn! 'Cut your throat!' It is so wonderfully different from the usual way everyone else converses!"

McDunn gave her a quick, abbreviated bow. "Always glad to bring a little amusement into your otherwise drab, uneventful life, ma'am."

"You must stop! I have something I want to say," she said through her muffled giggles. She looked at her brother worriedly, but he remained silent, so she plunged ahead. "William has been a wonderful older brother, and I value everything he has tried to teach me. And one topic he has spoken of many times is how our parents emphasized it was his duty to uphold the Darcy family name and fortune. It has him all…all confused between what *he* might want to do and what our *parents* would want him to do. But I love him dearly, and I want him to be happy."

"Georgiana," Darcy said, "I have no plans whatsoever to marry Miss Bingley—no matter how much she schemes and plots."

"I am very glad to hear it. I was worried because you tolerated so much from her, and you had never shown any signs of attraction to any other woman, despite all who pursued you."

"How could I?" Darcy said with a snort. "Had I given even the slightest hint of interest, I would have been deluged."

"By fortune seekers," Georgiana said. "It is what comes of a concern only for status and wealth in seeking a wife. Pursuit of a gentleman with a fortune is a…"

"A socially approved trait?" suggested McDunn, which brought rueful laughter from both Darcys.

Darcy shook his head. "What you *should* do, Georgiana, is play match-maker for my friend here. He will need a suitable wife to manage the fine estate he will one day purchase. Perhaps Miss Elizabeth Bennet would make *him* a fine wife."

Darcy immediately wished he had bitten his tongue because he saw an all-too-familiar expression come over McDunn's face. It was the one his friend wore when some particularly grief-laden memory of his lost world came to mind.

What did I say to provoke that reaction?

Chapter 15

///

The young man went to India, where he was drowned. As there is no mystery in this matter, it may as well be stated here that young Heaton ultimately returned to England, as drowned men have ever been in the habit of doing, when their return will mightily inconvenience innocent persons who have taken their places. It is a disputed question whether the sudden disappearance of a man, or his reappearance after a lapse of years, is the more annoying.

— Robert Barr, Scottish-Canadian
short story writer and novelist

\\\

Monday, November 18, 1811
Longbourn, Hertfordshire

Shortly before four o'clock on the day following Jane's return from Netherfield Park, the whole of the Bennet family was outside Longbourn to greet a certain Mr. Collins, who had presumed to invite himself for a visit of seven days. The surprise visitor had explained the reason for his presumption in a letter to Mr. Bennet, who at breakfast had acquainted his family with the arriving guest and the reason for his visit.

"Our guest is a gentleman and a stranger, and is, in addition, a person whom I never saw in the whole course of my life. To be clear, it is my cousin, Mr. Collins."

Elizabeth had stopped with her fork halfway to her mouth. "Papa, is that not the man—"

"—who may turn you all out of this house after I am dead. Yes, Lizzy, it is the very man, my nearest male relative, the beneficiary of the entailment of my house and property. This latest letter"—he waved the letter in the air—"informs me of his arrival at, he estimates, four o'clock today."

More pertinent to the fortune of the Bennet family was that, as Mr. Bennet's nearest male relative and because of a curious facet of British law known as an entail, he was to inherit Longbourn and all its property upon Mr. Bennet's quitting this mortal sphere. Mr. Bennet provided this and additional information by reading aloud his latest letter in which Mr. Collins stated he had been recently ordained and had the good fortune to be the recipient of an adequate living at the behest of a member of a noble family. The new clergyman stated his intention to visit and his further intention to attempt to heal the breach between his father and his cousin, for the two men had cordially loathed each other their entire lives. Mr. Collins expressed, but did not explain, his intention of making amends to the Bennet family, especially their daughters.

Jane could not discern how this unknown relative might make atonement but, with her usual sweet disposition, thought the offer was much to Mr. Collins's credit. Elizabeth, on the other hand, was struck more by the man's extraordinary deference to his patroness and his kind intention to demean himself by carrying out his clerical rites and ceremonies.

"He appears quite an oddity, I think. I cannot make him out," Elizabeth said to her father after listening to the letter. "Can he be a sensible man?"

Mr. Bennet considered the possibility to be unlikely, and for that reason, considered it probable this servile and self-important young man would provide him considerable amusement. He was, after all, a critical observer, and Elizabeth's nature tended to the same occupation.

Mary was of a different opinion. She did not consider the letter defective and believed Mr. Collins had expressed himself well. To Lydia and Kitty, of course, there could be no possible interest in a clergyman since their enthusiasm was only for officers of the regiment.

As for their mother, Mrs. Bennet had been attentive to the offer in Mr. Collins's letter to make amends for the entail. Alone among her family, she correctly inferred that this unknown visitor proposed to marry one of her daughters, thus providing a home for the other Bennet females after the demise of their protector. To her, the words in the letter could have no other interpretation.

In the manner of finding husbands for her daughters, Mrs. Bennet possessed a degree of cleverness more akin to the supernatural than to any form of logic, and this capability was not at all matched by the more intelligent members of her family.

MR. COLLINS ARRIVED QUITE PUNCTUALLY, AND HE WAS RECEIVED POLITELY by the whole family, save Mr. Bennet, who said little. This was not an impediment, since Mrs. Bennet and her eldest daughter were ready enough to converse with him.

The tall, heavy-looking young man, on the order of five-and-twenty years, was not at all inclined to silence and spoke freely, though in a grave and stately manner.

He quickly demonstrated his propensity to both compliment and apologize. His gallantries toward the five sisters were not fully appreciated by the subjects of his praise, but Mrs. Bennet was not inclined to quarrel with any compliments to her daughters and received such in good humor, except she took the opportunity to complain of the entail. Mr. Collins was cautious on that subject, however, and he would say no more.

His proficiency at apologizing was equally well demonstrated during dinner when he complimented the excellence of the meal but then thoughtlessly inquired as to which of her daughters had prepared it. This raised Mrs. Bennet's ire, and she was quick to state, with some asperity, that she kept a good cook and her daughters had nothing to do in the kitchen. Mr. Collins was quick to beg her pardon, and though she declared herself not offended, he continued to apologize for a quarter-hour.

WHILE HE HAD SPOKEN SELDOM DURING DINNER, MR. BENNET HAD LIStened closely and afterwards took the opportunity to give his cousin a chance to exhibit and hopefully provide some diversion. His guest was more than equal to the challenge, especially when Mr. Bennet first observed that Mr. Collins seemed favored in his patroness, Lady Catherine de Bourgh, and her consideration for his comfort appeared very remarkable.

"Oh yes, I could scarcely wish for a more fortunate situation," Mr. Collins said enthusiastically since the subject inspired him to more than usual eloquence of praise. "I have never in my life witnessed such behavior in a person of rank as that displayed by Lady Catherine toward me. Such affability and condescension! She was pleased by both discourses I gave so far and has even asked me to dine at Rosings twice. I have heard she is reckoned proud by some, but I have never seen anything but affability in her, and she has always spoken to me as she would to any other gentleman. She even condescended to advise me to marry as soon as I could, provided I chose with discretion. She also toured my humble parsonage to observe my alterations and even went so far as to suggest some shelves be added to the closets upstairs."

Mr. Collins went on to say more, and all of it was most laudatory to Lady Catherine and her daughter, who had the misfortune to be rather sickly and thus required to stay at home.

"Has she been presented?" Mrs. Bennet asked. "I do not remember her name among the ladies at court."

"Her indifferent state of health unhappily prevents her being in town, and as I told Lady Catherine, her daughter's misfortune has deprived the British court of its brightest ornament since she was clearly born to be a duchess. These are the kind of little things which please her ladyship, and it is a sort of attention which I take care to pay."

"It is a happy situation that you possess the talent of flattering with delicacy," Mr. Bennet said slyly. "May I ask whether these pleasing attentions proceed from the impulse of the moment or whether they are the result of previous study?"

"They arise chiefly from what is passing at the time, though I do sometimes arrange little elegant compliments. But I always try to give these as unstudied an air as possible."

Mr. Bennet's expectations were fully answered. His cousin was as absurd as he had hoped, and he listened to him with the keenest enjoyment. He maintained at the same time the most resolute composure of countenance— save only for his occasional glances at Elizabeth, who seemed as amused as her father.

All too soon, the dose had been enough, and Mr. Bennet was glad to take his guest into the drawing room for tea. When it was over, he sought to distance himself from the man by suggesting he read aloud to the ladies. Unfortunately, when Mr. Collins chose to read from *Fordyce's Sermons*, the younger ladies, especially Lydia, would not listen. Rather piqued at such disinterest, Mr. Collins offered himself to Mr. Bennet as an opponent at backgammon.

Tuesday, November 19, 1811
Longbourn, Hertfordshire

MR. COLLINS, BEING NOW IN POSSESSION OF A GOOD HOUSE AND A SUF-
ficient income, had journeyed to Longbourn with the intention of choosing
a wife from among one of the daughters if he found them as handsome and
amiable as they were represented by common report. Since he possessed little
in the way of common sense, he thought this an excellent plan, especially
after being introduced to them.

Thus, during a tête-à-tête with Mrs. Bennet the following morning before
breakfast, he opened the conversation by describing his parsonage house and
the adequacies of his income before going on to relate his hope of finding
a mistress for it at Longbourn.

"My thought was preference should naturally be given to the eldest of
your daughters, and meeting them only confirmed to me the correctness
of my intention."

Mrs. Bennet was full of complaisant smiles and general encouragement
since this was in accord with her fondest wishes. However, she struck a
note of caution.

"I feel compelled to mention to you that my eldest, Jane, is likely to be
engaged very soon. And the same is true for my next youngest, Elizabeth."

Seeing the dismay on his face, she was quick to continue. "However, the
same is not true for my younger daughters. I might take the opportunity
to mention my next eldest, Mary, who is often spoken of as being the most
accomplished young lady in the neighborhood. In addition, she has read
from *Fordyce's Sermons for Young Ladies*, which I notice was your choice
last night, had it not been for the rudeness of my youngest daughter, who
is sometimes too lively."

"Think nothing of it, madam. I understand completely."

Thus, it was quickly done, with Mr. Collins's interest switched from the
two eldest to the middle daughter. Mrs. Bennet stirred the fire and treasured
the thought of soon having three daughters married.

And the man, whom she originally could not bear to speak of just the
day before, was now high in her good graces.

"LOOK!" BINGLEY SAID WITH ANIMATION. "THERE IS MISS BENNET AND
her sisters."

Both Darcy and McDunn followed Bingley's finger to see he was right. The gentlemen were riding through Meryton on their way to Longbourn to inquire about the health of Miss Bennet.

"She appears in good health," Darcy said as they headed for the group standing by the side of the road. "She and her sisters have clearly walked from their home."

Lydia had originally made the suggestion of walking to Meryton, and her sisters were not opposed. Their father had been quick to encourage Mr. Collins to accompany them since he was desirous of having his library to himself. He had been unable to rid himself of his cousin since breakfast, and this seemed an excellent way to do so. Mr. Collins had no opposition to the plan since he was really much better fitted for walking than reading.

Mary had originally intended to stay home, but Mrs. Bennet urged her to go with her sisters. So, rather unwillingly, Mary accompanied them, only to find herself the target of conversation by her father's cousin during the walk. Mary was not well acquainted with social discourse, but she had early discovered that merely listening could not get her in much trouble. It served her well on this occasion since Mr. Collins required little encouragement to talk.

Tuesday, November 19, 1811
Meryton, Hertfordshire

UPON ENTERING MERYTON, THE YOUNGER TWO SISTERS LOOKED UP AND down the street in search of officers, with immediate results in the form of Lieutenant Denny on the other side of the road with a young man they had not seen before. His presence was most interesting to all the young ladies and theirs to the young men, so after some maneuvering, a meeting was accomplished.

After an exchange of greetings, Lieutenant Denny said, "If I might, ladies, I would beg your permission to introduce my friend Mr. Wickham. I have just returned from town as you know, and I enticed my friend to accompany me and, I am happy to say, to accept a commission in our corps."

Lydia and Kitty were highly pleased to hear such of this young man who presented a most gentlemanlike appearance and only wanted regimentals to make him completely charming. All the ladies found his appearance to be greatly in his favor, combining the best part of beauty, a fine countenance, and a good figure. He possessed, in addition, a pleasing and gentlemanly address and quickly showed an ease and command of amiable conversation.

The whole party was talking together agreeably when the sound of horses drew their notice. They looked up to see Bingley and his two guests riding down the street and obviously headed their way.

"Ah, Miss Bennet, ladies!" Bingley exclaimed, removing his hat with a sweep of his arm and bowing from the saddle. "We were riding to Long-bourn to enquire after your health, Miss Bennet, but I am pleased to see you are in fine spirits."

"Thank you, sir," Jane said, returning his bow with a curtsey, as did her sisters. She was about to make introductions when Darcy's eyes were arrested suddenly by the sight of the new friend of Lieutenant Denny.

Mr. Wickham immediately touched the brim of his hat and said simply, "Darcy."

Despite his surprise—a most unwelcome one—Darcy said in reply, "Wickham," giving a nod and touching his brim. "I thought you remained in town," he said, and would have said more if not for Lydia's interruption.

"Lieutenant Denny just told us Mr. Wickham accompanied him from town and is going to accept a commission in the regiment!" she said breathlessly.

"I see," was Darcy's only comment, and Jane then proceeded to complete all introductions.

Bingley and his friends stayed for only a few minutes of conversation before making their farewells and continuing their ride. The party resumed speaking with Denny and Wickham quite amiably, but Elizabeth idly wondered how Darcy and Wickham knew each other.

They do not seem as though they are particularly acquainted, she thought. *They must hail from similar backgrounds. Perhaps they met at Cambridge.*

For herself, she did not know whether she was sorry or relieved Darcy had not spoken to her.

Once beyond Meryton, McDunn turned to Darcy. "I got the distinct impression of a certain coolness between you and this Wickham."

Darcy nodded. "In truth, I have known George Wickham since we were boys, McDunn. His father was a fine man who had the stewardship of Pemberley during my own father's life. He was quite taken with young Wickham, who was his godson, and even supported him at school and later at Cambridge, neither of which Wickham's own father could have afforded."

McDunn digested that for a bit, looking over at Bingley, who also listened. Finally, McDunn said, "Stop me if this is none of my business, but was I correct that you weren't particularly pleased to see him today?"

Darcy gave an immediate nod. "You are indeed correct, and such is an understatement. At one time, Wickham and I were fast friends, playing together and fishing and hunting all over Pemberley. But he changed as he got older, and not to my liking. He began to show a preference for the most improper, indeed licentious, behavior, especially at Cambridge and afterwards. My father, however, never discerned any of this for he could not see what I saw, and Wickham remained high in his esteem until Father died. He even wished Wickham might find a place in the church, planning to provide for him in it and even saying as much in his will. I was not at all pleased since I knew the church was no place for a man like Wickham, and I could only accede to the wishes of my father with reluctance."

"It doesn't appear he joined the church, not if he took a commission in the militia."

"No, it does not, and I wonder about his commission. I am not sure you know this, but officers in the militia are not paid. They usually come from the noble or gentry classes, and are assumed to have money, either themselves or from their families. I believe they even provide their own horses and uniforms. That makes no sense with Wickham since I do not think he has any money."

"No money?" Bingley asked. "The cut of his clothes bespeaks a gentleman. I assumed he had at least *some* money."

"None at all," Darcy replied. "He received a bequest from my father's will of a thousand pounds, but he came to me within half a year, pleading to be given a cash award rather than waiting for the living of our family parsonage to become vacant. I assumed he had exhausted his bequest, so we made a bargain in which I gave him three thousand pounds, and he resigned all claim to assistance in the church. I was glad to do so since, as I said, I believed Wickham should not be a clergyman. It was the last I saw of him for some three years, when the living at our parsonage became vacant. Then who should appear but Wickham, asking for the presentation of the living to which he had resigned all claim. It seems he spent all his money in less than four years."

"Four thousand pounds in such a short time?" Bingley said in shock. "How did a single young man spend so much so fast?"

"I assume on wine, women, and song," Darcy said dismissively. "I already thought so ill of him that I would not admit his acquaintance in town or invite him to Pemberley. So I had him thrown off Pemberley land with a warning not to return, and I have not seen him since. In fact, I thought him gone from my life completely."

"As they say, a bad penny always seems to turn up," Bingley said, which drew a bitter laugh from Darcy.

"Exactly, Bingley, exactly."

To all of this, McDunn could only give silent thanks that Darcy had decided against an establishment for his sister, especially since the summer just passed had been the time during which Wickham's attempted seduction was supposed to have occurred.

A deviation from the novel I would have prevented had it proved necessary, McDunn thought. *And I wouldn't have felt the slightest tinge of guilt, even if I'd had to invent a sudden desire to visit that seaside town and deal with the handsome Mr. George Wickham personally. With extreme prejudice.*

Wednesday, November 20, 1811
Meryton, Hertfordshire

On the following afternoon, Mr. Bennet's carriage conveyed his five daughters and his cousin to their engagement at their aunt's home. Mrs. Philips, Mrs. Bennet's sister, was married to a solicitor in Meryton, and she had been glad to see her nieces when they had called on her the previous day. She had been particularly happy to see Jane since she had not known of her recovery from her illness and her return to Longbourn.

Mr. Collins had been introduced when they arrived, and Mrs. Philips received him with her best civility, which he returned with many apologies for not having any previous acquaintance with her. She informed all of them of her plan to have a party, including a few of the officers, at her house the following day for games and a bit of hot supper afterward. She graciously included Mr. Collins, and after hearing of the new arrival in Meryton who was to have a commission in the militia, she promised to have her husband call on the regiment and extend him an invitation.

As a result, when the girls now entered their aunt's drawing room, they had the pleasure of hearing that Wickham was even then in the house.

Elizabeth's first sight of him confirmed her favorable impression from the previous day. The officers of the regiment were, in general, a creditable and gentlemanly group, and the best of them were at the present party. But Mr. Wickham easily outshone them all in his person, his countenance, and even his walk. Every feminine eye was cast in his direction, and Elizabeth felt the compliment of being the lady by whom he chose to sit.

The easy and agreeable manner in which he began their conversation—though the subject was only a trivial one related to it being wet weather—was a perfect example of an amiable conversationalist and was much to her liking. She was easily able to add her own comments, and his manner of listening to her when she spoke flattered her vanity.

It is his eyes, she thought, *the way he looks into mine when I am talking that I find so appealing. It informs me my words are of interest. He is, in short, everything Mr. Darcy is not.*

They were forced to interrupt their conversation when the card tables were set up. Elizabeth was indifferent to whist and was happy enough to see Mr. Collins sit down to the game, hiding her smile when the foolish clergyman openly admitted he knew nothing of it. She was more pleased when Mr. Wickham sat beside her at the lottery tickets table, though she was unhappy at Lydia taking the place on the other side of him. Her sister was a most determined talker, and Elizabeth at first feared her sister might engross Mr. Wickham with her conversation.

As it happened, Lydia became the one engrossed as she got more and more involved in the game, leaving Elizabeth and Mr. Wickham at leisure to talk since both of them gave the game only a passing thought.

But the conversation now veered in a direction other than Elizabeth wished. She desired to continue the light, easy topics they had enjoyed before sitting down to cards. Wickham, however, raised a different topic.

"How far, I wonder, is Netherfield Park from Meryton," he asked unexpectedly.

"It is about two miles, I believe," answered Elizabeth casually. "My home of Longbourn is about a mile from Meryton but in the other direction."

She noticed Wickham hesitating slightly before he said, "I understand Mr. Darcy has been staying at Netherfield. Do you know how long he has been there?"

"About a month," Elizabeth replied, her brow furrowed. Considering her history with Fitzwilliam Darcy, she had no wish to discuss the man. He disturbed her quietude when she even thought of him, so she was rigid in her determination to avoid discussing the man entirely.

"His family has a noble estate in Derbyshire, which Mr. Darcy inherited. I am quite familiar with his family for I have been connected with them in a particular manner since my infancy."

Elizabeth made no response to this statement, and Wickham's surprise at her lack of interest was easy to discern from his expression. However, his face quickly cleared, and at length he said, "Are you much acquainted with Mr. Darcy?"

"Somewhat," Elizabeth said with a dismissive shrug. "Though I have danced with him, I cannot say I know much of his character."

Wickham paused a moment then moved the subject to music and the theater in London, which Elizabeth found significantly more interesting. Since he had just come from town, she was eager to know what he could relate from personal knowledge.

"All I know is what my father and I read in *The Times*," she said, "and we often think more goes unwritten than appears in the pages."

"Given that the editors pay by the word and are known to be rather parsimonious, it is to be expected that they want to keep payments as low as possible," Wickham said with a warm laugh much more in keeping with his previous manner.

As the conversation continued, Elizabeth derived much amusement and pleasure from Wickham, and she soon considered him one of the most pleasant and amiable young men she knew.

GEORGE WICKHAM HAD WISHED TO DISCUSS THE DARCY FAMILY AND HIS own grievances against the present head when he sat down with Elizabeth Bennet. To find some way of revenging himself on his one-time boyhood companion was a constant desire. He considered he had been badly used by the Darcy family, especially Fitzwilliam Darcy.

I should have had that living! he thought viciously. *I needed it!*

It never crossed his mind that the events he spoke of so freely and convincingly had many falsehoods and deceits. By this time, he had related his ill-treatment so many times that he had actually come to believe the story he told was true.

Perhaps I can find interested listeners among those families who malign Darcy's name, but Miss Elizabeth Bennet is a right delicious chit and no mistake there! A bit of tupping with her would suit me quite nicely indeed!

But the prudent side of him raised a warning. *Considering the position of her family in the community, any illicit doings with her or any of her sisters might not only be difficult but also dangerous to my position with the regiment. I need a place here in Hertfordshire. The collectors were close on my heels in town when I came upon Lieutenant Denny and managed to vanish. I must take care.*

The whist party broke up soon afterwards, and the players gathered round the lottery ticket table. Mr. Collins took his station near his cousin Mary but within a distance to converse with Mrs. Philips easily. When asked about his success at whist, Mr. Collins confessed he had lost every point. But when Mrs. Philips began to express her concern, he was quick to reassure her.

"The money is a mere trifle, madam," he said. "I know very well that when a person sits down at a card-table, they must take their chances. Happily, my circumstances are such that a five-shilling loss poses no difficulty, thanks to the generosity of Lady Catherine de Bourgh. I beg you not to make yourself uneasy on my account."

Wickham's attention was caught by this comment, and he said to Elizabeth in a low voice, "Mr. Collins was introduced as your cousin. It leads me to wonder whether your relations are very intimately acquainted with the family of de Bourgh."

"Lady Catherine de Bourgh has very lately given him a living. I hardly know how Mr. Collins was first introduced to her notice, but he certainly has not known her long." She appeared quite willing to give this information about her foolish cousin.

"You know, of course, that Lady Catherine de Bourgh and Lady Anne Darcy, the present Mr. Darcy's mother, were sisters. Consequently, Lady Catherine is aunt to Mr. Darcy."

"I knew nothing of Lady Catherine's connections until this moment," Elizabeth said flatly.

Wickham's usual sense of perception failed him with her as he completely missed her aversion to the subject and continued on. "Her daughter, Miss de Bourgh, will have a very large fortune when her mother dies, and she is betrothed to Mr. Darcy. Their marriage will unite the two estates."

Elizabeth made no immediate response to this, but when Wickham opened his mouth to go on, she said, "I fear I have a sudden headache, Mr. Wickham. I think I shall ask my aunt if I might return to Longbourn and send the carriage back for my sisters."

Wickham realized the statement was merely a social practice, and since he had seen no indication she found his company tiresome, he came to realize she had no desire to speak of anything related to the present master of Pemberley.

Believing Miss Elizabeth more vexed with Darcy than he first believed, Wickham urged her to move her seat beside the window where she might get a breath of fresh air. Elizabeth was not opposed, so she took his proffered arm and left the table for the indicated chair. They continued talking together with mutual satisfaction on other topics until supper put an end to cards, which gave the other ladies a chance at Wickham's attentions.

CONVERSATION WAS NEARLY IMPOSSIBLE IN THE NOISE OF MRS. PHILIPS'S supper party, but Wickham's manners recommended him to everybody. Whatever he said was said well, and whatever he did, he did gracefully. Elizabeth went away with the highest regard for him, and she would have asked Jane her opinion, except she was not able to mention his name in the carriage since neither Lydia nor Mr. Collins was once silent. Lydia talked incessantly of lottery tickets, of her wins and losses while Mr. Collins continued to protest that he did not in the least regret his losses at whist.

Elizabeth rolled her eyes at Jane as their foolish cousin continued by enumerating all the dishes at supper and repeatedly apologizing for crowding his cousins. He had far more to say than he could manage before the carriage stopped at Longbourn.

Chapter 16

//

The sun's gone dim, and
The moon's turned black;
For I loved him, and
He didn't love back.

— Dorothy Parker, American poet, writer, critic, and satirist

\\\

Tuesday, November 26, 1811
Netherfield, Hertfordshire

Finally, the day of the long-expected ball at Netherfield arrived, and it could not have come too soon for the younger Miss Bennets. Forced to remain at Longbourn due to the incessant rains, they were kept from their usual distraction of walking to Meryton in search of officers or scandal. Neither Lydia nor Kitty could tolerate such enforced inactivity with any grace whatever, and their spirits had been in a pitiable state since Bingley and his sisters delivered the invitations.

Elizabeth alone had not looked forward to the occasion. Her sleep had been troubled repeatedly by dreams of a tall visitor to her bedroom. He had not been identifiable since his face was a vague blur, as was much of his body as he disrobed and climbed into her bed. But she had no doubt that her forbidden desires had manufactured dreams of Darcy.

As the day of the ball approached, she dreaded the thought of Darcy again asking her to dance. She had toyed with the idea of a refusal even though it would end any hope of dancing with another, for a refusal of one meant a refusal of all, and she held out hope of at least a pair of dances with Mr. Wickham. She remembered his manners and air with pleasure though the rains had precluded any opportunity for renewing their acquaintance.

Even Mary had come to the opinion there might be occasion for diversion at the ball, especially after Mr. Collins solicited the first set and announced his intention of remaining by her side the entire evening.

"I think it no sacrifice to join in evening engagements occasionally," she said pontifically. "Society has claims on us all, and I deem that intervals of recreation and amusement are desirable for everybody."

Elizabeth's observations of her mother and Mr. Collins had provided the first hint of an agreement regarding the making of amends for the entailment of her father's estate. Whether such an agreement had been formal or not, she could not know. But she guessed it had been both informal and unspoken, given what she knew of both personages.

Oh, I do hope you are ready for what is going to befall you, Mary, she had thought, her opinion divided between worry for her sister and hope that it might give Mary an opportunity she otherwise would have missed. *Mr. Collins as husband and Lady Catherine as his patroness! I hope you find some comfort in being the mistress of Hunsford Parsonage and of helping form a quadrille table in the absence of more eligible visitors.*

The Bennet party was greeted by Mr. Bingley and his sisters in the entry of Netherfield Park. Jane in particular was received with considerable animation by all three while the Bingley sisters paid as little attention to the rest of the family as possible.

When she entered the drawing room, Elizabeth looked for Mr. Wickham among the cluster of red coats. Instead, her eyes discerned the tall figure of Mr. Darcy moving toward her, and a sudden anxiety clutched at her heart. She had dressed with more than her usual care tonight, but it had been for the purpose of meeting Mr. Wickham.

Her fears were confirmed as Mr. Darcy asked, with considerable politeness, whether he might solicit the honor of the dances just before supper. Despite her misgivings, which were marked at the moment by a chorus of jangled nerves demanding her attention, Elizabeth had no choice but to accept.

He will escort me to supper after those dances, she thought apprehensively. *If he had asked for any others, I would only have to endure two meaningless dances and a little conversation. Instead, I may be afflicted with him for an hour or more!*

As soon as Darcy gave her a bow and passed on, Wickham emerged from the crowd of officers and approached her most cordially, his face already showing his marvelous smile.

"I hope you are not already engaged for the first two dances, Miss Elizabeth," he asked. "If not, dare I hope for the honor of your hand for that set?"

Elizabeth, highly gratified by this invitation, was quick to assure him she was not engaged and accepted with pleasure. She was also delighted when Wickham stayed to converse though the pair was interrupted by another officer asking for a dance.

MCDUNN WATCHED THIS WITH INTEREST THOUGH HE INTENDED TO OBserve the festivities from a balcony with Georgiana and Mrs. Sturdivant. Darcy had been unwilling to allow his sister down on the floor because of her youth, but he had no aversion to her viewing the event.

At the moment, McDunn had Bingley in tow since he had specifically asked for an introduction to Mr. Bennet. He had met all the other members of the family and wanted to see whether Austen's description of the man held true.

Mrs. Bennet stood with her husband as Bingley came up to them. "Mr. Bennet, allow me to present my friend, Major McDunn. Major, Mr. Bennet."

Bingley excused himself and departed quickly for his duties as host continued to engage him, and McDunn turned to the elder Bennet.

"I asked Mr. Bingley for the introduction, sir. I've already made the acquaintance of the rest of your family, but I'd not before been introduced to you."

Mr. Bennet gazed at the tall, dark man reflectively. "I am pleased to make your acquaintance, Major. I am always pleased to meet a friend of Mr. Bingley."

"I'm more Mr. Darcy's friend than his though we have formed a friendship over the last month as Bingley's guests. Darcy and I have business affairs in common."

"Ah, the telegraph. An amazing device, sir. Simply amazing. What will come next, I wonder?"

"Oh, we have a few ideas, Darcy and I," McDunn said with a smile.

"I hesitate to ask, but I have to wonder about your accent. I cannot place it."

"American, sir. South Carolina to be exact."

"So you are not in the army. I wondered about that since you are not in a red coat."

"'Major' is a courtesy title, Mr. Bennet. I am no longer a serving officer though I was a major in the American Marine Corps."

"Ah. Well, I hope you enjoy yourself tonight."

"I'm highly interested in your English festivities though I did attend a dance in Meryton shortly after I arrived. But I'm only an observer. As I told your wife when we first met, I don't dance."

Turning to Mrs. Bennet, he said slyly, "And I still don't, madam."

McDunn gave both Bennets a bow and departed, thinking as he went away, *I do so enjoy teasing the animals even though it's not particularly smart.*

In his wake, he left Mrs. Bennet sputtering in rage.

"What an uncouth, ungentlemanly man!" she said hotly. "I cannot believe a true gentleman such as Mr. Bingley would invite him to his ball or have him as a guest at his fine estate! And I cannot see why a gentleman like Mr. Darcy would tolerate his presence at all, much less call him friend!"

Meanwhile, McDunn had climbed to the balcony where Georgiana and her companion sat watching events. Georgiana was quite excited even though Mrs. Sturdivant already had a book open.

"This is the first time William has ever allowed me to view one of his social events," Georgiana said enthusiastically. "It is so fortunate Netherfield has such excellent balconies. I can see Miss Elizabeth and her sister, of course. But who is everyone else? Do you know them, Major?"

"I'll do my best, Miss Darcy, but as a mere colonial, the ins and outs of your complex social system often leave me at a loss. Still—"

"You are nothing of the sort. Now, tell me everything!"

"Well, I'll try. First, the two young girls you see darting about among the officers are the youngest two Bennet sisters, Lydia and Catherine, whom they call Kitty. And the young lady over there by the black-coated clergyman is the middle sister…"

ONE SURPRISING DIFFERENCE IN THE EVENTS OF THE EVENING CAUGHT McDunn's attention immediately when Collins danced the first set with Mary rather than Elizabeth. He had wondered why the man was standing by the middle Bennet sister as he pointed out everyone he knew to Georgiana.

It seems he won't be soliciting Elizabeth's hand tomorrow, he thought. *I wonder why? I remember he fixed on Elizabeth because her mother said Jane was soon to be engaged. I'll bet she did the same for Elizabeth because Darcy asked her twice to dance, once at the assembly and once at Lucas Lodge. Another deviation!*

His curiosity aroused, McDunn kept an eye on Mrs. Bennet as she watched Collins dance with Mary. He had to suppress a chuckle as he watched the couple stumble through their steps on the dance floor. The sight also provided amusement for Georgiana as he heard her trying unsuccessfully to muffle her giggles.

When he glanced back at Mrs. Bennet, he saw that her expression of triumph had settled into an expression of deep satisfaction. Clearly, she knew Collins had settled on who would be the mistress of Hunsford Parsonage, thus putting to rest her worries about a secure situation for herself and her daughters.

Different and highly interesting. I know she saw Darcy ask Elizabeth to dance—and for the third time! She must be rubbing her hands in glee as all her carefully laid plans seem to be going along just swimmingly.

Bingley probably *will settle on Jane, and Darcy* might *settle on Elizabeth. But the marriage of Collins and Mary was now a virtual certainty!*

FOR HER PART, ELIZABETH ENJOYED HER DANCE WITH WICKHAM GREATLY, and she would have preferred to continue on with him except she was already engaged for the next set. But then came the moment she had been dreading when she saw Darcy's imposing figure walking in her direction.

She took his offered arm, expecting a repetition of the feelings that greatly disturbed her before. And indeed a profound effect swept through her in a breathtaking rush not at all as she expected.

When she laid her gloved hand on the sleeve of his coat, she anticipated a surge of the same strange warmth. Instead, Elizabeth felt a deep and sublime pleasure of a far different nature. It was as though her hand was where it belonged. And she *wanted* it to be on the arm of this tall, handsome man who once again wished to dance with her.

That was what took her breath away. She *wanted* to touch his arm. She *wanted* to walk with him to the dance floor. She could not explain it, but something—something within her—had changed for reasons as mysterious as her previous feelings of desire!

As the dance started, Elizabeth looked up at the man she said she did not like, and she could not find the antipathy she expected. She knew he was still as proud as he had been...and it no longer mattered. She knew it was a defect...and she accepted it. It was innate within him. She was not happy at the realization...but still, she wanted to dance with this man.

How could everything change so fast and for no logical reason? she wondered wildly since she felt the same acceptance of his other unfavorable attributes—his sense of superiority, his concern for his family name, even his disdain for others and his selfishness. She wished it were not so, but now she would rather be dancing with this most imperfect man than to be anywhere else in the world.

What am I going to do! she thought frantically. *Have I actually fallen in love with such a man? How could I? I know what he is! How could this happen?*

But her memory provided at least a partial answer.

Jane said Bingley considered Mr. Darcy a most admirable man. He is supposed to be quite amiable with his close acquaintances. And I have not heard of anything that betrays him to be unprincipled, unjust, or even hints at irreligious or immoral habits. Bingley said he was esteemed and valued among his own connections. And Miss Darcy, when she and I sat with Jane, esteemed him as the most wonderful brother. How could such an amiable man as Mr. Bingley be such close friends with a man of no worth? What is the truth of the matter?

However, as Elizabeth was guided through the steps of the dance with an increasing sense of contentment and comfort, it did not matter. She could do nothing other than admit she had fallen in love with the man who had awakened forbidden passions within her, passions that upset...and fulfilled her. She had fallen in love with Fitzwilliam Darcy, the man who would never marry her.

She would not allow herself to think about that now. She just wanted to dance with him.

MCDUNN NOTICED NOTHING UNUSUAL WHEN DARCY AND ELIZABETH danced. There certainly had not been the altercation he expected though he knew that by now Wickham must have spun to Elizabeth the tale of his boyhood friend's betrayal. For whatever reason, she had not confronted

Darcy with it. There had been conversation between them as they danced, but it had all seemed light and amiable with smiles on both sides.

When the dances ended and the people started to move toward the dining room, McDunn left the balcony and descended to the main floor. Bingley had specifically told him he would reserve a place for him in the dining room even if he did not dance. Moreover, he had promised to seat him near Mrs. Bennet. Bingley supposed the two had formed a pleasant acquaintance and desired to talk at supper, when the truth of it was different: McDunn was interested in seeing and hearing Mrs. Bennet humiliate herself as Austen described.

It should prove most interesting! Though I definitely need to refrain from baiting her!

Upon entering, he found considerable crowding and confusion as everyone sought their seats, not all of which were marked by placards. When McDunn realized only the gentlemen had placards, it became apparent this had been done intentionally since it would allow each gentleman to be paired with a partner of his choice. He spotted Bingley at the main table with Jane already at his side. Bingley saw him in turn, waved, and pointed to a table not far from his own.

Sure enough, McDunn found a placard with his name on the table near the Bennets, but he was rather surprised to see Darcy and Elizabeth seated several places away from him.

When supper was served, he was not surprised to find the meal up to the same high standards he had grown used to since arriving. Caroline might be an obnoxious twit, but she was a skilled hostess and had brought an established cook from town when Bingley took possession of the estate.

Because of Darcy's attention to Elizabeth, McDunn had expected his friend to be seated other than in the novel. Thus, as Mrs. Bennet opened her conversation with Lady Lucas, McDunn could not find the diversion he had expected because both Darcy and Elizabeth were close enough to hear the exchange.

"It will meet with all my desires when I see Jane comfortably settled at Netherfield and Lizzy equally well disposed in Derbyshire," she said, with an animation and lack of tact that made McDunn wince, though he had fully expected as much.

"It will be such an advantageous match with Netherfield being only three miles away from Longbourn. Mr. Bingley is such a charming young man—I think you would agree—as well as being so rich. And his sisters are so fond of Jane, you know, and they must be as desirous of the connection as Mr. Bennet and myself."

Mrs. Bennet seemed incapable of fatigue as she continued. "And Lizzy's match with Mr. Darcy will be just as splendid, though Derbyshire is so far away. But both connections will be such a promising thing for our other daughters, who cannot help but be thrown in the company of other rich men."

Perhaps realizing, at last, the impropriety of her conversation, Mrs. Bennet began to speak of the advantage of being able to consign her single daughters to the care of their sisters so she might not be obliged to go into company more than she liked.

McDunn could well imagine Lady Lucas must have had to bite her tongue after this remark for she must have known as well as he did that no one was less likely to remain at home than Mrs. Bennet. It had to have been equally hard for the woman to remain silent as Mrs. Bennet concluded with many good wishes for Lady Lucas to soon be equally fortunate, though her lack of belief in such an occurrence and her insincerity in expressing it was clear to see.

McDunn knew both Darcy and Elizabeth could easily overhear her mother, and he saw Elizabeth blush repeatedly at her mother's vulgarity and lack of sense. Her embarrassment was clear, and she did not raise her eyes from her plate as she ate mechanically and with no grace. For his part, Darcy had listened to the beginning of Mrs. Bennet's self-satisfied boasting with an expression of indignant contempt that gradually changed to a composed and steady gravity.

But Mrs. Bennet's proclamations about possible connections were not only a topic of conversation in the dining room. McDunn had heard whisper after whisper speaking of the unbelievable good fortune of the Bennet family as he made his way into the room. The connection between Bingley and Jane was accepted while the new awareness of Darcy's attentions toward Elizabeth trailed somewhat behind due to his elevated status and fortune.

But McDunn had to listen closely to discern those whispers, whereas Mrs. Bennet had broadcast her coup to all those about her. And true to the text, her husband had so little diligence he did nothing to restrain his wife.

Elizabeth had entered the dining room flushed with the unexpected resolution of her previous conflicts. Even though it had been one she never could have expected, it had sprung upon her full-blown without any impingement on her consciousness. It was like nothing she had ever experienced.

Such had been her satisfaction at having her doubts settled that she had done what she had never expected: she followed Charlotte's advice not to conceal her affection from the object of it, impelled by her newfound love for this man. Her happiness shone through, and she made no attempt to conceal it. She laughed, talked, and barely took her eyes off his.

She felt Darcy responding to her in a manner neither he nor she had expected or heretofore experienced. His cold, reserved half-smiles became warmer and more frequent. His words were no longer delivered in his usual stiff and restrained manner.

Then her mother began to speak to Lady Lucas.

As soon as she comprehended what her mother was saying, Elizabeth's eyes were torn from Darcy's to stare at her mother in horror.

This cannot be happening! How could my own mother openly boast of things such as this, especially since Mr. Darcy can hear every mortifying word! Does she think such people as he and Mr. Bingley would want a connection between themselves and a family such as ours? Does she even think at all?

It took only a single glance at Darcy to verify her concerns. Where his face had been softening just minutes before, it was now hardening into lines of contempt. The usual haughtiness and reserve had returned. Improvements she had imagined a short time earlier had disappeared under the avalanche of her mother's boasts and improprieties. Her father sat beside his wife, and yet, he did nothing—*nothing!*—to restrain her wild talk. Was he as lost to civil and mannerly behavior as her mother? Could anyone in her family besides Jane and herself conduct themselves with any decorum at all?

She could not look at Darcy and bent her head to look down at her napkin. She began to eat but could not seem to taste anything. Her belly was twisted into knots, and she could feel bile rise up within her.

Everything is ruined, she thought dully. *My mother's remarks may even destroy any hopes for Jane and Mr. Bingley. When Mr. Darcy informs him of what he heard, he will surely advise him to break off any attachment. And how could I blame him? Our family deserves all the contempt they will attach to us.*

How, oh how can I tell Jane the destruction of her hopes was directly attributable to our own family?

Even now, when my hopes are ashes in my mouth, my traitorous body still longs for him. Perhaps I should simply accept what is clear, that I am ruined utterly and completely, both in hopes and in virtue.

HAS ANY MOTHER EVER SO UTTERLY DISGRACED HER FAMILY AS HAS MRS. BENNET? Fitzwilliam Darcy thought icily. *I thought I was immune to the plotting of fortune-hunting mothers, but it seems the coarseness of this one has had an untoward effect on me.*

Of course, I should perhaps thank her for displaying her inability to know how to act with propriety. Had she been as skilled as some mothers at the art of finding rich husbands, I might not have realized the degree to which I had allowed myself to be bewitched by this daughter of hers.

He looked at Elizabeth seated beside him, remembering how much he had enjoyed their dance and the heightened liveliness she had shown. She had been so clearly pleased by his attentions that he had momentarily thought she might bring him the happiness in marriage Georgiana had so casually suggested. Now, he was shocked to realize he had so forgotten his place in society as to even consider it. He wondered how it had happened because he had thought himself immune to her attractions because of the inferiority of her family and connections. He had let her increasing attractiveness and pleasing manner overwhelm him, it seemed.

It had been a narrow escape, but he did feel a pang of sympathy for her. It was not Elizabeth's fault she had been saddled with a stupid and improper mother, a lazy and indifferent father, and totally unrestrained sisters.

Except for the eldest, he thought. *Miss Bennet is as gracious and proper in behavior and person as is Miss Elizabeth. Somehow, they escaped the influence of their ill-mannered mother as well as their father. But I shall have to talk to Bingley before he leaves for town in the morning. I will have to make sure he realizes the kind of expectation he has inspired in this country neighborhood with his attentions to Miss Bennet. Dancing four times with her tonight! What other conclusions could be drawn?*

HARDLY DARING TO LOOK AT DARCY, WHO NOW SAT GRAVE AND SILENT beside her, Elizabeth looked toward Jane to assess whether she had heard her mother, but she was calmly talking to Bingley, who gave every evidence of enjoying himself greatly. His two sisters bore their usual look of amused, supercilious contempt, and Elizabeth dismissed them from her thoughts, sinking back into the blackness of dejection and regret.

It appeared as though her family had determined to expose themselves as much as they could during the evening. In any case, it would have been impossible for them to play their parts with more spirit or finer success at destroying her personal longings. She was cautiously happy for Jane since it seemed as though Bingley had not noticed anything that impacted her, and it was her opinion his feelings were not of a sort to be overly distressed by the follies of the evening.

Unlike Mr. Darcy! He is more easily affected by such defects in manners and propriety. I have known as much since the first night I met him, and it was only the brief raising of my hopes that allowed me to forget it. The shattering of my hopes, unrealistic as they were, has brought down a gloom I never thought possible. If it were not a sin, I would wish to die this instant.

Her gloom and despair continued to increase until Darcy rose to escort her back to the ballroom. He had perceived Elizabeth's dejection and understood it though he had not a clue as to its extent. In his ignorance, he made an attempt to relieve Elizabeth's unhappiness, intending to tell her he bore her no blame for her mother's improprieties.

But Elizabeth only shook her head, clearly not wishing to talk. He had no idea what to do, and he clumsily attempted to alleviate her gloom by asking whether she had any dances not spoken for. Knowing her affinity for dancing, he thought he might make his sympathy known, even if she was not in the mood for talking.

Only then did he realize her shoulders had started to shake, and now more worried, he moved to see her face.

She is crying! But why? She had no part in her mother's impropriety!

Elizabeth's face now crumpled completely as she was overwhelmed by whatever caused her grief, and she sobbed uncontrollably. Suddenly, hiding her face in her handkerchief, she turned and all but ran through the doors near at hand, ones leading to the garden. As quick as he was, Darcy could not reach the exit before she disappeared through it, though he lost no time in following her.

It was bitterly cold outside, far too cold for a lady wearing slippers made for dancing and without a coat for warmth. Darcy looked around, not able to see her at first in the darkness.

Then he spotted her beside a hedge and moved her way. When he got close, he was unsurprised that her shoulders still heaved and her hands covered her face as she sobbed.

"Miss Elizabeth," he said as gently as he could manage, "is there anything I may do to help you?"

She shook her head fiercely, but Darcy was still alarmed. "Did I offend you in any way? I do not know what I may have done, but I must urge you to return indoors. It is far too cold for you to be out here."

At this, Elizabeth took her hands from her face, and the light shining through Netherfield's windows allowed him to see the tears still streaming down it.

"It is no use," she said, her voice so soft and expressionless, he leaned forward to hear her more clearly.

Her eyes, sparkling with tears, looked directly into his, and he thought them as lifeless as her voice.

"It will never change. Nothing will ever change. There is no hope whatever."

"Of what, Miss Elizabeth? Surely, there must always be hope!"

"There is none," she repeated. "None whatever. There never was. There never will be. There is no chance you even know what I am talking about."

"I have to admit my complete bewilderment, Miss Elizabeth."

In response, she stepped close to him until they were only inches away. "I am sure that is true," she said, and there was an element of anger in her voice to match her grief. "But the simple fact is—for reasons I cannot explain either to you or even to myself—that I love you."

Seeing his reaction, she nodded fiercely and repeated, "That is correct, Mr. Darcy. I love you despite my insignificance. It is my curse to love you."

Reaching down, she took hold of his hand. Taking his wrist, she carefully removed his glove and dropped it on the ground.

Then she stunned him by bringing his palm to her lips and lightly, caressingly, kissed it before moving on and kissing the tip of each finger.

Darcy was dumbfounded by what was happening, and his mouth went dry. Her eyes rose to meet his, and there was no hint of sobbing as she spoke, almost fiercely.

"In addition to loving you, Mr. Darcy, I desire you—fiercely and completely, as a woman desires a man. But this will have to serve as my memory. At least I have kissed you, after a fashion. There is no hope of more. I know and accept it now."

She looked at him with mingled coldness and regret. "I would recommend you find a fashionable woman such as Miss Bingley to marry. Such a lady could give you a proper heir or two. After which, you could both take lovers, as is common among those of your station, so you could both live a life almost completely separate from the other."

Then, releasing his hand, she stepped back and pulled her handkerchief from her sleeve to dry her tears. Her voice was firm as she spoke. "Goodbye, Mr. Darcy. I do not think we should ever meet again."

Then, her back stiffly straight, Elizabeth Bennet marched past him and returned to the Netherfield ballroom, leaving Darcy gaping in complete incomprehension as to what had just transpired.

She has had an attraction to me that I never suspected! I cannot know for how long. And all the time I thought it was my bewitchment for her that was an impediment! How could I have been so blind? There must have been indications, clues of some sort, but I never realized it!

I have hurt her deeply without ever intending to! How could I have known?

But she is correct. There is no hope of anything more. Though she is a gentleman's daughter, our spheres are simply too far apart, and she could bring neither fortune nor status to any connection between us. That would violate the dictates my parents impressed on me when choosing a wife. And most importantly, I simply cannot inflict the improprieties of her family on Georgiana.

With his thoughts settled, Darcy re-entered the ballroom. He did not espy Elizabeth anywhere in the room, nor did he see her for the rest of the evening.

But he did not look for her. She had been correct. They should not meet again.

Chapter 17

//

Thus much and more; and yet thou lov'st me not,
And never wilt! Love dwells not in our will.
Nor can I blame thee, though it be my lot
To strongly, wrongly, vainly love thee still.

> — Lord Byron, British nobleman, poet, peer, politician,
> and leader of the Romantic Movement,
> final verse of "Love and Death"

\\

Wednesday, November 27, 1811
Hertfordshire

The next day was not at all a quiet one, neither at Longbourn nor at Netherfield. At Longbourn, Elizabeth remained ensconced in her room, having gone there immediately after returning from the ball. She refused to come out for breakfast even though her mother twice sent a servant to demand her presence. Thus, she was not downstairs when Mr. Collins made his declaration to Mary.

Mrs. Bennet had met no resistance from Mary when Collins had solicited the honor of a private audience with her shortly after breakfast, and her mother was shameless at listening at the door while their guest made his lengthy offer of marriage and Mary rather off-handedly accepted it.

Mrs. Bennet thereupon entered the breakfast room, congratulated the newly betrothed pair in the warmest of terms, and urged Collins to hasten immediately to her husband for his approval. For her part, Mary bore her mother's exultation with her usual forbearance.

Mr. Bennet issued from his room with Collins in trail and convened his family, not even excepting Elizabeth, who responded to his summons when she had ignored her mother's. Jane was worried when she discerned the redness of Elizabeth's eyes for she well knew her sister never cried.

But her concerns had to be put aside as her father made his announcement of the impending marriage of his middle daughter, which brought renewed celebration from Mrs. Bennet and raised eyebrows from her youngest daughters, who thought their sister had lost her senses to have accepted a man who wore a black coat rather than red.

Mr. Collins, meanwhile, bore the congratulations of the family with a measure of satisfaction that his choice would prove pleasing to Lady Catherine.

For her part, Mary was well satisfied with the match and had no real objection to the man with whom she was to spend her life. She had always assessed Collins's abilities higher than did her sisters, and she did not believe him as silly as her father and Lizzy did. Rather, she thought she detected a certain solidity in his reflections, which was to her liking. And while she knew Collins was not nearly as clever as she was, she had hopes that, if she encouraged him to read and to improve himself by her example, he might, in time, become an agreeable companion.

Mary had never anticipated being married, expecting she would likely remain at Longbourn and attend her mother, who was quite unable to sit alone. The possibility had not been entirely objectionable, but this prospect was by far superior since she would be mistress of her own house. The establishment might be inferior to Longbourn, but at least it would be hers. And when her father died, she would have the management of this house in place of her mother, an expectation she secretly cherished.

At about this time, Charlotte Lucas came to spend the day with them. Elizabeth met her in the vestibule, having seen her friend approaching through the window. She quickly informed Charlotte of what had occurred, but her friend was little surprised since she had seen Collins hovering at Mary's side the previous evening.

Though Charlotte must have wondered at Elizabeth's reddened eyes, since her friend volunteered no information, she did not enquire about it, and they passed into the sitting room. Mrs. Bennet was already preparing to set out in her husband's carriage to inform all the neighborhood of her family's good fortune, and barely had time to accept Charlotte's congratulations before she and Mary departed.

The mood at Netherfield was even more tumultuous. As Bingley had mentioned when bidding the Bennet family adieu the previous evening, he was obliged to go to town for a short time, and he had left early in the morning. He was quite unaware that he left behind two highly agitated sisters concerned by his close attention to Jane Bennet. And they could not but be aware of the whispers about their brother's attachment to the eldest Bennet sister soon achieving a more formal status.

Adding to Caroline's concern, of course, was her awareness of Darcy's interest in Elizabeth, being affronted at his having danced with her again and even escorting her to supper! The existence of a competitor to the position of mistress of Pemberley accentuated her worry about her brother connecting himself to such a common family as the Bennets.

Despite their presumed affection for Jane, most of which was insincere, Caroline and Mrs. Hurst had hoped to advance the family status by encouraging their brother's connection with Darcy's sister and Caroline's marriage to her brother. Such a double marriage would advance all their dearest ideals!

So, in hopes of thwarting their brother's intentions, the two sisters discussed the matter and decided to travel to town and to enlist Darcy in their venture. They both agreed he must be as concerned as they at the intentions of their brother and would undoubtedly take their point and accompany them in their quest. They were not at all sure they could prevail on their brother themselves. Bingley invariably listened to Darcy's suggestions and followed the advice he gave while both sisters were painfully aware of how seldom he took theirs.

Darcy listened to their pleas with what both Caroline and her sister thought was attentive seriousness, but their perception was quite erroneous. Darcy had spent a restless and almost sleepless night, disturbed by his shocking and bewildering encounter in the garden with Elizabeth. Never in his wildest imaginings could he have anticipated what he had learned, and he still struggled to understand and deal with all of it.

He did not, however, have any qualms about the impossibility of a connection between them. Even if Elizabeth still had a hold on him, which seemed likely since he was having the utmost difficulty putting her from his mind, the fact remained she was not a lady whom his parents would have recommended. Accordingly, he told himself he had to force his near bewitchment from his mind. Their futures lay in radically different directions, and that was an end to it. As she had said, they should never meet again.

As distracted and tired as he was, he still concentrated and heard the Bingley sisters' plan to the end. He agreed that Bingley would be connecting himself to a most unseemly family if he acted as they feared. But Darcy also knew that doing so would not present the same problems it would if he did the same with Elizabeth. As for the affections of both parties, he was fairly certain of Bingley's feelings. And while he might have been less certain as to Miss Bennet's sentiments, he recalled Elizabeth's haunted voice affirming her sister's love for his friend.

At length, after thinking on the matter for several minutes while he sipped his coffee, he shook his head.

"I think your endeavor rather ill-advised, ladies. I know you oppose your brother's marriage to Miss Bennet, but it really is his decision to make. If she is the woman he prefers, I do not think it my place to try to convince him otherwise.

"You are likely unaware of this, but I spoke with your brother at some length last night. I made the same points you raised about a marriage to Miss Bennet being disadvantageous to your family's status or fortune, but he was adamant about such matters being of no concern to him. He said he had not fully decided how to proceed, but he was certain of Miss Bennet's affections toward him, which he felt was most important. In short, I believe we must leave the matter in your brother's hands."

Caroline leapt to her feet. "You are infatuated with Eliza Bennet!" she cried in unrestrained fury. "You cannot keep your eyes off her and her fine eyes! That is why you will not help us save Charles from this disastrous marriage! You wish the same connection for yourself!"

From deep within her, Caroline heard a small voice urging restraint, but she ignored it. She was too angry, too mortified, and too desperate to turn back.

"If such was my intention," Darcy said with a gentleness that surprised him, "then such an accusation as you make would be more likely to enhance my intention than otherwise. But you are free to do as you please, Miss Bingley, though I believe you and your sister are wasting your time."

But Caroline's blood was up, and she rushed on heedlessly. "A fine friend you are turning out to be, Mr. Darcy! You are determined to let my brother be drawn into the muddy pit where that idiot of a mother and those improper sisters reside—not to speak of the father! Well, I will have no part of it, and my only hope is to save my brother from utter disaster, despite you who purport to be his friend!"

"Suit yourself, Miss Bingley," Darcy replied icily, and he silently watched the two ladies quit the room.

I believe Bingley is quite satisfied with his new estate. As for me, it is past time to leave Netherfield and put Miss Elizabeth Bennet behind me. I do feel sympathy for Elizabeth's disappointed hopes, but I had no part in inspiring them. She will simply have to deal with her circumstances. I think I shall return to town within a day or two.

Darcy was unaware that Caroline was upstairs composing a note to Jane, informing her of her brother's departure. She stated that she and Louisa planned to follow him to town, giving as their reasons a small amount of truth mixed with outright fabrications. She then sealed the note, addressed it to Jane, and gave it to the butler with instructions to dispatch it to Longbourn the following morning.

Caroline went upstairs to supervise the packing of her things, wishing she did not feel terribly sick at how everything was going so wrong.

Thursday, November 28, 1811
Hurst Townhouse, London

"So, what is the urgent matter that brings the two of you here?" Bingley asked cheerfully, sitting down at the breakfast table with his sisters.

"We had hoped to talk with you last evening, Charles," Caroline said, not inclined to waste any more time.

"As I told you, I had some friends to see. I had intended to be home earlier, but we became so involved with memories of Cambridge, I am afraid I was late to home and to bed." Bingley was not concerned with his sister's ill humor. When in private, his sisters were not nearly as mannerly as when others were present.

"We are greatly concerned for your welfare," Louisa said. "We believe you are on the verge of making a terrible mistake."

"Is that so? I am not aware of anything pending requiring my attention."

"Even in the matter of Miss Jane Bennet?" Caroline said, her lips compressed into lines of disapproval.

Bingley put down his biscuit and looked sharply at his sisters. "What do you mean, Caroline? Miss Bennet is, after all, a good friend to both of you."

"She has no money to bring to a marriage," Louisa said gently, trying to placate her sister, "and we believe you are contemplating making her an offer."

"Her family, Charles!" Caroline said. "I do not know of a family with less to recommend them! They have no connections! None at all!"

"Their father is a mere country gentleman with a tiny estate, and it is entailed away to that Collins fellow we met," added Louisa. "When Mr. Bennet dies, his wife and daughters will have nothing. That is why Mrs. Bennet has schemed to make her daughter seek an attachment with you. It is her only hope of providing for her other daughters."

"So Mrs. Bennet is a fortune hunter? Is that what you are saying?" Bingley was no longer interested in his breakfast, and he looked angrily at his sisters, who gave no answer to his challenge. "And is Miss Bennet also a fortune hunter?"

Caroline and Louisa were silent, and Bingley snapped, "Answer me! You appear to be labeling the sweetest, most gentle young lady I have ever known a fortune hunter, pursuing me for my wealth at the behest of her scheming mother! Is that what you are saying?"

Bingley's anger had taken the sisters aback for they had seldom seen their brother so irate. After a few seconds, Louisa said, "You must think of the future of your family before you rush into—"

"I am not rushing into anything," Bingley said icily. "And it is my decision to make! Darcy said as much before I left!"

"Charles, look at their connections!" Caroline cried. "One uncle is a country solicitor in a small town and the other makes a living in trade! In Cheapside! Are these the type of people you want associated with our family?"

"Our own father made his fortune in trade. You live under this roof and eat at this table based on the fortune he settled on you. Mr. Bennet is a gentleman of more than one generation while we are only the first generation of our family to aspire to that station."

He looked at both his sisters with contempt. "I had thought Miss Bennet was your friend and you would celebrate her happiness if—and I say *if*, for I have not yet made any decision in the matter—I made her an offer of marriage and she did me the honor of accepting it. To find your protestations of friendship were nothing but pretense is disingenuous at the very least! It might be better described as despicable, ladies! Despicable!"

Caroline muttered something under her breath, but Bingley's sharp hearing picked out the name Darcy.

"Darcy!" he said angrily. "What does Darcy have to do with any of this?"

When they again made no answer, he leaned over the breakfast table and commanded, "Tell me! What is Darcy's involvement?"

After his sisters made some attempts at diversion and even deceit, Bingley finally forced them to admit they believed he would have listened to these arguments if Darcy had made them. And when further questions elicited the fact that they had attempted to enlist his aid in their quest and Darcy had declined, Bingley sat back in his chair.

"I think it best," he said finally, "that I take myself off to a hotel for the remainder of my stay in town. When I return to Netherfield, I shall send anything you left behind to you here. And I shall not need you to act as my hostess any longer, Caroline. Now, if you will excuse me, I have an urgent express to send to Darcy."

Thursday, November 28, 1811
Hertfordshire

Mrs. Bennet's joy had begun to decline by the next day since she had already dragged Mary to see most of their friends. Since her two youngest daughters were more than desperate to escape from her presence, they expressed their inclination to walk to Meryton as they so often did in the mornings. Elizabeth was reluctant to go with them, despite her usual zest for exercise and sunshine, but Jane was most urgent in wishing her to come, and Elizabeth reluctantly relented.

Upon reaching the town, the group almost immediately met with Lieutenants Denny and Wickham, who greeted them warmly—or mostly so since Elizabeth noted his greeting to her was terser and less cordial than on previous occasions. However, since she was far more concerned with recovering from her encounter with Darcy, she paid his coolness little attention, especially since she knew he never could have had any intentions toward her because of her lack of money.

At her younger sisters' insistence, Wickham joined their party when they went to their aunt's house. When they arrived, Mrs. Philips was most enthusiastic about Mary's good fortune. She was also cognizant of the events at the ball and slyly complimented both Jane and Elizabeth on their good fortune, even going so far as to wonder whether additional good news might not be forthcoming.

This latter statement was not received well by Wickham, who now carefully looked all about the room at everyone except Elizabeth. He realized why she had been so unresponsive on the first evening they met when he tried to spin his tale of Darcy's malefactions toward himself. However, as a seasoned campaigner in the pursuit of the opposite sex, he put the topic from his mind. There were far more fish in the sea than Miss Elizabeth Bennet, even if she was one of the more delectable ones.

As Wickham and Denny walked back with them to Longbourn, the Netherfield ball remained the prime topic of conversation. Elizabeth noticed that Wickham continued to ignore her, seeming to pay more attention to her youngest sister, who was so flattered by the attention that she invited the two officers inside to introduce them to her father and mother.

Soon after their return, a letter arrived from Netherfield for Jane, who opened it immediately. Elizabeth saw her sister's expression change as she read the sheet of paper covered on both sides with a fair, elegant hand. Though Jane collected herself and tried to join the conversation with her usual cheerfulness, Elizabeth knew her sister too well. She guessed the note came from Caroline Bingley, and her sisterly eye told her it contained news less than pleasant in nature. As soon as possible, even though Wickham and Denny had not yet departed, Elizabeth gave a nod of her head toward the stairs and both sisters went to Jane's room.

There, Jane confirmed her suspicions. "This letter is from Caroline Bingley, and its contents have surprised me a good deal. It was written yesterday, and it says she and her sister have decided to follow their brother to London with none of them intending to return to Netherfield. Caroline does declare her only regret was being thus deprived of the society of me, her dearest friend."

Despite the worries afflicting her, Elizabeth heard these high-flown expressions with her usual distrust of the writer's sincerity. Yet, what she had heard so far did not explain the unhappiness she could see in her sister.

"While it is unlucky you did not have an opportunity to see your friends before they left the neighborhood, their leaving will not prevent Mr. Bingley from returning to Netherfield. In that case, the absence of your friends will be offset later by the greater happiness you will have as sisters."

To this, Jane shook her head. "Caroline decidedly says none of their party will return into Hertfordshire this winter. She says her brother's business in London will take more than the three or four days he imagined, and since he does not plan to return, she and her sister decided to follow him immediately so he would not be left alone without the company of family. She goes on to wish my Christmas in Hertfordshire would be joyous, and I would have so many beaux I would not feel the loss of their presence."

Jane choked back a sob. "Do you not see, Lizzy? Caroline means Mr. Bingley will not come back this winter."

"It is only evident *Miss Bingley* does not mean he should."

"Why do you think so? It must be his decision since he is his own master. But there is more. Let me read you the most painful parts for me. I will keep nothing from you."

Elizabeth could hear the pain in Jane's voice as she read Caroline's words singing the praises of Miss Georgiana Darcy and their hope that the affection she and Louisa held for Georgiana would soon be heightened by the three of them being sisters. She went on to talk of her brother's great admiration for Georgiana, which she expected to deepen into a more serious association.

"Listen to what Caroline says: 'With all these circumstances to favor an attachment, and nothing to prevent it, am I wrong, my dearest Jane, in indulging the hope of an event which will secure the happiness of so many?'

"What think you of this sentence, my dear Lizzy?" Jane said as she finished it. "Is it not clear enough? Does it not expressly declare Caroline neither expects nor wishes me to be her sister? That she is perfectly convinced of her brother's indifference and, suspecting the nature of my feelings for him, means to most kindly put me on my guard? Can there be any other opinion on the subject?"

"Yes, there can, for mine is totally different. Dearest Jane, Miss Bingley knows her brother is in love with you while she and her sister wish him to marry Miss Darcy. As a result, the two of them followed their brother to town in the hope of keeping him there. Then she wrote you this despicable note to persuade you that he does not care about you."

Jane shook her head.

"Indeed, Jane, you ought to believe me," Elizabeth said urgently. "No one who has ever seen you and Mr. Bingley together can doubt his affection. Miss Bingley, I am sure, cannot. She is not such a simpleton. Could she have seen half as much love from Mr. Darcy for herself, she would have already ordered her wedding clothes."

Jane looked doubtful since she had not seen Miss Bingley's attentions to Darcy through the same eyes as Elizabeth.

"We are not rich enough or grand enough for her and her sister's aspirations to rise in society, so Miss Bingley is anxious to attach Miss Darcy to her brother because it will aid in her goal of achieving a similar attachment for herself with Mr. Darcy. There is certainly some ingenuity in her plan since one marriage might well engender another.

"But you must not believe Miss Bingley when she tells you her brother greatly admires Miss Darcy since he never would have shown you the attentions I witnessed on Tuesday were it true. Miss Bingley is possibly mistaken in everything she writes, but it is far more likely she wrote with the object of deceiving you."

"If we thought alike of Miss Bingley," Jane replied, "what you say would make me feel quite easy. But your charges are not just. Caroline is incapable of willfully deceiving anyone. I simply hope she is deceived herself."

"Believe *that* if you will not believe me. Believe her to be deceived, by all means. Now you have cleared your friend of my suspicions and must fret no longer."

"But, my dear sister, can I be happy in accepting a man whose sisters and friends all wish him to marry elsewhere?"

"You must decide for yourself. If you find the misery of disobliging his two sisters too distressing in comparison to the happiness of being his wife, then I advise you to refuse him."

Jane had to smile slightly at this comment. "You know better, Lizzy. I would be grieved at their disapprobation, but I could not hesitate."

"I did not think you would."

"But what if he returns no more this winter? If he does not return until summer? A thousand things may arise in six months!"

Elizabeth heaped scorn on the very idea of his returning no more. It appeared to be yet another of Caroline's wishes. And how could such wishes influence a young man so independent and master of his own house and fortune?

She made this point as forcibly as possible and soon had the pleasure of seeing the growth of hope for Bingley's return to Netherfield, which would answer every wish of Jane's heart.

They were undecided on how much to tell their mother since they knew learning of the departure from Netherfield would alarm her. Since they could reach no decision, they decided simply to wait for further developments if they were to occur.

AT TWILIGHT, JANE AND ELIZABETH'S WORRIES ABOUT WHAT TO TELL THEIR mother were put to rest by the arrival of Mr. Darcy at Longbourn. Elizabeth easily recognized his figure as he turned his horse up the drive, and she quietly left the room and climbed the stairs to her chamber.

Darcy found all the ladies save Elizabeth in the parlor and greeted them in his usual, reserved fashion.

Turning to Jane, he said, "Mr. Bingley sent me a note today, asking me to inform you of his planned return to Netherfield in four or five days, which is longer than he had anticipated. My own party, including my sister and Major McDunn, will be returning to town before then since McDunn and I have business associated with our several enterprises."

Mrs. Bennet received the news with a frown. She had not realized Bingley would be gone so long, but what concerned her more was Darcy's sudden and unexpected departure. How would he make his declarations to Elizabeth if he did not return?

But Darcy saw the relief on Miss Bennet's face, and he knew she had likely received some kind of distressing news, probably from Caroline Bingley.

I was right, Darcy thought to himself. *Bingley's note did not mention it, but it would be just like Caroline to try to throw Miss Bennet into despair by sending a nice, little, vicious note of some kind.*

He was not surprised at Elizabeth's absence. In light of their encounter, he had anticipated she would remove herself rather than meet him. From the intensity of her reaction and the totally unexpected passion she had revealed, there had been a remote possibility she might not truly comprehend the impossibility of a connection between them and could thus engage in a hopeless pursuit embarrassing to all parties.

He turned to Jane. "Please convey to your sister my most sincere felicitations and all hope she will have a joyous Christmas season—as I hope for all of your family. Farewell to you all, ladies."

And so he departed, suddenly and precipitously, leaving Mrs. Bennet with an open mouth. She had been so involved with worrying about Elizabeth, she had not even had time to tell him of Mary's impending marriage.

From the window of her room, Elizabeth watched the tall, handsome man mount his horse, and both her eyes and her heart followed his every movement. The grace and muscular power inherent in his performance of such a familiar action spoke to those parts of her that vainly loved and desired this unattainable man.

She was completely aware she might never see Darcy again, and she tried to memorize his every aspect as though it had to last her a lifetime. As he turned down the drive, she felt a stab of pain at how his head made not even the slightest movement to glance up at her window. It was apparent he was determined to abide by her parting words—that they should not meet again.

Her fingertips went to her cheek, only to find fresh tears there. At the moment, she was only cognizant of the desperate yearning in her heart for what could never be, and her tears became rasping sobs as her shoulders heaved with the grief derived from losing something incredibly dear.

Elizabeth felt a sudden impulse to dispel all propriety, to run down the stairs of Longbourn, and chase Darcy down the drive. Her words echoed in her mind as she called out to him, desperately begging him to pull her up behind him on his horse and carry her away to an unknown future with no regard for consequences.

But Elizabeth Bennet was a woman of her time, and thus, she did nothing. She could only watch as Darcy turned at the end of the drive and disappeared before she threw herself onto her bed and buried her head in her pillow.

What am I going to do? she wondered, her fist in her mouth to quell the sound of her sobs. *How shall I ever get by?*

ELIZABETH WAS THANKFUL IT WAS ALMOST A HALF-HOUR BEFORE SHE HEARD Jane's footsteps in the hall, allowing her the time to get her emotions under regulation and to repair the evidence of her tears.

And Jane's news did much to cheer her when Elizabeth learned the reason for Darcy's visit.

"Did I not say as much, Jane?" Elizabeth said, forcing a laugh she believed to be unaffected. "I said Mr. Bingley would not be kept from Netherfield by his sisters' departure! Do you not see his supposed attraction to Miss Darcy was entirely contrived by Caroline Bingley? I sat with Miss Darcy once when you were sick, and I discerned nothing on her part but polite attentiveness to Mr. Bingley."

"Yes, you must be right. This is very difficult for me to understand, but Caroline must have written her note to deceive me. It is I who was deceived in thinking her a true friend."

"There you see Miss Bingley's skill in her polite and sophisticated ability to slip the knife of deceit into the back of another. No matter how attentive she and her sister were to you, I never trusted them—not at all. But let us not dwell on this! When she sees the failure of her efforts, I have no doubt her supposed friendship will make a sudden reappearance!"

"You are likely correct." Jane was more than a little unhappy at being forced to this admission.

"That is because I love the sweetest and most unaffected sister."

"And I love you, Lizzy," Jane said then suddenly stepped forward and clasped Elizabeth's arms when her sister would have turned away. "But I have to ask why your eyes are so red? Have you been crying on my behalf?"

Elizabeth made no response, and Jane went on. "That is the reason, is it not? You were distressed at the possibility of Bingley not returning to Netherfield, just as you always think of the happiness of others before your own."

Jane did not get the response she expected since her sister would not meet her eyes and instead cast them downward.

"And why did you slip out of the room when Mr. Darcy arrived?" Jane asked slowly, her eyes on her sister. "I wondered that he did not ask for you. Instead, he sent his good wishes, but the words seemed more like a farewell than the usual pleasantry. And now I find you have been crying, and you never cry!"

Elizabeth hugged herself and turned to the window and the darkness beyond, which seemed to mirror the darkness she felt inside. At length, she said, "It *was* a farewell, Jane. I shall not see him again."

"But how can it be?" Jane cried. "I saw the two of you at the ball, and my heart swelled for joy at how at ease both of you seemed, how well you appeared to be getting on. What has happened?"

To this, Elizabeth made no response at first. When she finally turned around, Jane was shocked to see tears flowing down her sister's face.

"Whatever is the matter, Lizzy? What has distressed you so? Oh, now all my joy at Mr. Darcy's news is gone!"

Elizabeth met her sister's eyes. "I love him, Jane."

At these shattering words, Jane simply collapsed onto the bed. "Mr. Darcy?" she said in shock. "You love Mr. Darcy?"

Elizabeth nodded, and her voice broke. "I do, Jane. I think I love him more than life itself."

"How can this be?" Jane said in complete disbelief. "I know he danced with you, and I have heard the whispers our neighbors have made about you, but I never saw any indication of a particular regard!"

Elizabeth came over and sat beside her, taking one of her hands in both of hers and clasping it to her chest. "It just…happened. And I am ashamed to tell you, it did not even seem like love. Not at first. Not from the first night."

"At the assembly?"

Elizabeth nodded. "From the first time I laid eyes on him. I felt a sudden surge of a most shocking and inexplicable attraction. It spread through my whole body. It was…disturbing."

"Not love? I do not understand, Lizzy."

"It was passion, Jane. The passion a woman feels for a man. The passion a wife feels for her wedded husband, which is supposed to be consummated in the marriage bed.

"I did not understand my feelings, at first. They were new and foreign— nothing I ever imagined. I tried to shove them away, pretend they did not exist, but I could not. They went too deep and…and they affected me in ways I could not explain."

Jane could only stare at her dear sister as Elizabeth searched for words.

"Every time I met Mr. Darcy, every time our fingers touched when we danced, I could feel the attraction he had for me, and I was lost. He invaded my dreams—but I did not realize at first that it was Mr. Darcy who came into my bedroom in my dreams. Only slowly did I connect those dreams with him. And I was equally slow to put a name to what I felt—what had taken possession of me."

Elizabeth went silent, staring into the night, until Jane asked softly, "And that was…?"

"It was passion, dear sister—physical passion for a man when I had no intimation such an attraction even existed."

"Nor do I," Jane said slowly.

"It is more than simple passion now, Jane. Much more. I knew it as soon as we danced together. I felt something I never imagined to feel with this man; I felt as though I belonged in his arms. And I am certain he felt something similar—an acceptance of me as a woman."

Elizabeth was silent for a moment before going on. "But make no mistake, Jane. My passion for Mr. Darcy was real—*is* real. Do you remember how our mother warned of the misfortune of the marriage bed? And how we should just lie still since it would soon be over?"

Jane nodded, and Elizabeth continued. "Well, it seems some women—not our mother, I am sure—must take pleasure in the carnal side of marriage. They must desire it. As I desire it."

Jane's lack of understanding was clear to see, but she asked no questions, so Elizabeth could only continue. "Imagine how I felt after the assembly with unaccountable longings plaguing me. I could come to no other conclusion than I was wanton—a harlot in fact. A woman who seeks physical intimacy for her own gratification."

"You cannot be wanton, Lizzy."

"What other conclusion could I reach? I had no one to advise me. I thought once or twice that Aunt Gardiner might be able to help me since she is so much more levelheaded and sensible than our mother. But we see her so seldom."

"But you keep talking about feeling passion for Mr. Darcy—"

Elizabeth nodded. "I wanted to feel his touch. And I wanted to touch him. It is shameful, I know, but I wanted it then, and I want it still."

Elizabeth rose from the bed and went back to look out the window. "But as I said, now there is more. I love Mr. Darcy, as well as desire him, even though we both know I did not like him when I first met him. He had so many disagreeable traits—pride, haughtiness, selfishness, and a disdain for others. He still has those traits. It is the side of himself he shows the world."

Elizabeth began to pace the room. "And with the realization of my feelings, something inside me changed since I saw the side of him you spoke of—how he is pleasant and amiable with those he knows well. He showed that side to me at the ball, and my joy overflowed when we went into supper with the way he smiled and talked easily with me. He wanted to be with me the way I wanted to be with him. He still has those faults I first saw, but he is more than those faults."

Elizabeth stopped and looked out the window for a time before she spoke again. "The simple fact is: I love this very complicated man, and I want more than just passion from him. I want to be with him always. I want to love him and make him feel loved. I want him to make love to me, I want to bear his children and raise them. Most of all, I want to be his companion and grow old with him."

She turned around, and Jane saw her tears had returned. "And it shall never be, Jane. Not ever. I saw everything change in just a few minutes. We were conversing as we never had before, and Mr. Darcy was smiling and laughing with a warmth I had never seen. I am convinced, at that moment, that he was entertaining the possibility I might bring him happiness.

"Then my mother destroyed everything," she said, with flat, cold finality.

"How?"

"As she usually does—by her words. You were too far away to hear, but she crowed aloud about her good fortune. She would soon have one daughter well settled in Derbyshire and another at Netherfield Park. And the other girls would then be in company with other rich men. She did not say these things quietly, but announced them to all about her with Mr. Darcy and me sitting less than ten feet away!"

Jane closed her eyes in shared pain.

"Everything changed. Suddenly, Mr. Darcy was his haughty, prideful self, and all my dreams were less than mist—gone as though they never existed. Mr. Darcy reverted to the man I first met, a man of his class, a man who will choose a wife who can bring fortune or station to the marriage. I can bring nothing."

"But Bingley—"

"—is not Darcy. Those things matter little to him. His fortune was earned in trade by his father. While our own father's fortune may not match his, our family has been part of the gentry for generations. But Darcy is different. That is why he only gave a disguised farewell tonight. We agreed to as much at Netherfield."

Elizabeth could say no more for she could not hold back her sobs any longer. Jane opened her arms to her, embracing her fiercely and pulling her down to the bed beside her while her brave and independent sister wept uncontrollably for a love that could never be.

Jane said nothing, for there was nothing to say. She just held Elizabeth close until her poor sister finally cried herself to sleep.

Chapter 18

//

*'Bereavement is the deepest initiation into the mysteries of human life,
an initiation more searching and profound than even happy love.*

— Dean Inge, Dean of St Paul's, London

\\

Saturday, November 30, 1811
Hertfordshire

M r. Collins was to leave Longbourn on Sunday, and because he was to begin his journey far too early in the morning to see any of the family, the ceremony of leave-taking was performed just before the ladies retired for the night. Mrs. Bennet was effusive in her wishes to see him again soon for she was exceedingly anxious to have Mary safely married to this savior of their family.

"We shall be most delighted to host you again at Longbourn whenever you should be able to come back, but we do hope the occasion will be as soon as may be. I know Mary is waiting on pins and needles for the happy event to follow your return."

Whether this statement was strictly true could not be determined from Mary's expression since there was little to read in it of her mother's enthusiasm. There was, however, no animus to be seen either, so Elizabeth considered her sister was rather content with being married to this man.

"My dear madam," Mr. Collins replied, "I shall return as soon as I have secured the blessing to my marriage of my esteemed patroness, Lady Catherine de Bourgh. We may then finalize all necessary arrangements so I may become the happiest of men. You may be very certain I shall avail myself of your hospitality at that time."

Mr. Bennet had no wish for such a speedy return by this man even if he was to wed his daughter. "Is there any danger of Lady Catherine's disapprobation? You had better delay your return than to run the risk of offending your patroness."

"I am particularly obliged to you for this friendly caution, and you may depend upon my not taking so material a step without her ladyship's concurrence. But she has already commanded me to take a wife, and I have no doubt she will be delighted with my inestimable good fortune."

Mary colored slightly at hearing herself described in such terms, but she was pleased with his method of delivery. She again thought, with her to advise him, that Mr. Collins might eventually make a tolerable companion.

Further exchanges of a similar nature were made before the ladies retired, but Elizabeth missed most of them, seizing a chance to escape when her mother was delighting in the satisfaction of at least one daughter married.

And I hope she will soon have two, thought Elizabeth, remembering the message Darcy had brought from Bingley. *He enabled Jane to find a measure of contentment, but he also made clear he would abide by my parting suggestion.*

With this melancholy thought, she entered her room and undressed in the dark, deigning even to light a candle. She knew Jane would notice the lack of a light at the bottom of her door and would thus refrain from visiting, and she was not up to any further conversation, even with her beloved sister.

Sunday, December 1, 1811
Longbourn, Hertfordshire

TRUE TO HIS PLANS, COLLINS DEPARTED EARLY THE NEXT MORNING, UNSEEN by any of the Bennet family. Any despair at the absence of the clergyman was more than compensated for by the arrival of Mr. Bingley in the afternoon. Lydia had been the first to see him turn up the drive, and she immediately made the announcement in her usual loud voice. Thus, all the sisters learned of their visitor at virtually the same time and were thus waiting in the parlor when he arrived.

"I decided to call for just a few moments before continuing on to Netherfield, Mrs. Bennet. I hope my arrival poses no imposition," he said, and Jane had to lower her eyes when his gaze immediately turned toward her. A rush of optimism filled her heart near to overflowing since she had hardly dared to hope, even after Mr. Darcy's unexpected visit.

"You are always most welcome, sir!" Mrs. Bennet said. "And you must stay far longer than only a few moments. This evening would be the perfect opportunity for you to partake of a family meal at Longbourn! I always keep a very good table, so it will be no trouble at all to set another place."

Bingley was quick to agree since he knew the obliging Mrs. Bennet would ensure he was seated next to Jane. Her covert glances through her lashes were a sure indication she was pleased by his arrival, which made a shambles of the ridiculous arguments Caroline and Louisa had made earlier.

Jane was gratified to find his attentions as they had been at the ball. That thought, however, did bring a pang of pain to her for it reminded her how his sisters had proven themselves so false. Jane would cheerfully have lived her whole life without finding anyone capable of such deceit.

Elizabeth was overjoyed to see her sister so happy, and it was enough to put her own concerns aside for this one night. She was also pleased to hear Bingley casually mention that Caroline was remaining in town and would no longer manage his house and table.

That is most excellent news for Jane, she thought gleefully at this evidence Bingley was aware of his sisters' machinations. *I do not doubt both sisters will return just as soon as Bingley makes his declarations. It is just like them, and I am equally certain they will proclaim their everlasting love and affection for their dearest friend, soon to be their sister! What a pair those two are!*

Rigidly, she forced herself to put aside what she knew to be vindictive thoughts and just enjoy Jane's happiness. Though she was much more of a critical observer than her elder sister, Elizabeth knew such angry thoughts were unlike her, and she could only suppose they were caused by her own unhappiness.

Saturday, December 14, 1811
Longbourn, Netherfield

ELIZABETH WAS ON ONE OF HER WALKS WHEN BINGLEY TOOK THE LONG-anticipated step. Before she opened the front door on her return to Longbourn, she heard her mother in the throes of an ecstatic celebration. When she entered the room, her father was talking quietly with Bingley, who wore the broadest smile she had ever seen on that always-amiable man. At his side stood Jane, who smiled less but looked just as happy.

Elizabeth needed no explanation as to what had occurred—not with her mother all but dancing about the room. Clearly, Bingley had declared his intentions, her father had given his approval, and her mother was overjoyed at her family's good fortune.

That led to the dour thought that, when two daughters were safely married, her mother's thoughts would again turn to Mr. Darcy and her delusion about him desiring a similar connection to Elizabeth. Only she and Jane knew how impossible such an event was although Jane sometimes tried to convince herself it was not as hopeless as her sister knew it to be.

"Ah, Lizzie," her father said, catching sight of her. "I presume you can discern what has just transpired."

"I can indeed, Papa, and I would like to tender my congratulations to all," Elizabeth replied, giving Bingley a curtsey in response to his bow.

"Thank you, Miss Elizabeth, thank you," Bingley said cheerfully, and then he gave his soon-to-be sister a sly smile before he continued. "Of course, Miss Eliza, you will soon inherit the title your sister bears once we are married. Your father and I will be going to your parson to obtain a license presently, which will allow us to make arrangements for the ceremony.

"A special license, sir!" Mrs. Bennet exclaimed thoughtlessly. "You must and shall be married by a special license! Oh, I am so happy for you, Jane!"

Elizabeth saw the sour look her father gave his overly enthusiastic wife since a special license could only be obtained from the archbishop himself. Few other than the nobility or those with great wealth would go to either the trouble or the considerable expense. Her father knew such a license was a frivolous notion, even for Bingley.

Of course, his wife was blithely unaware of her ignorance, and neither he nor Elizabeth was inclined to try the fruitless endeavor of educating her.

Monday, December 23, 1811
Longbourn, Hertfordshire

Mr. Collins had been timely on his return, arriving on the sixteenth as all had expected, and Mr. Bennet had had the bittersweet duty of arranging the marriage of two of his daughters. Eventually, all plans had been completed to the satisfaction of all save Mrs. Bennet, who had stridently wished for more time to engage in these most satisfying endeavors. But Mr.

Bennet had made one of his rare exertions, mandating that both ceremonies would take place soon after the start of the New Year with Collins and Mary scheduled to marry on January 9 while Bingley and Jane's nuptials would follow a week later on the sixteenth.

Accordingly, Mr. Collins had returned to Kent five days later while the Bennet family enjoyed the continual presence of Bingley as he visited Jane. Mrs. Bennet herself was quite busy preparing for the arrival of her brother and his wife, who were coming to spend Christmas at Longbourn, as was their custom.

Mr. Gardiner, the younger brother of Mrs. Bennet, was most unlike her in nature or education, having had the good fortune to earn a scholarship to attend the University of Edinburgh. Unfortunately, he had been able to attend for only two years due to the unexpected death of his father, which required him to take up the reins of the family business. It was due to his education, combined with his own amiable nature, that he had become such a sensible, gentlemanlike man, greatly superior to either of his sisters in both civility and conduct. Caroline Bingley and her sister would have flatly denied that such a man, who lived by trade and within view of his own warehouses, could be so well-bred and agreeable.

His wife was a year older than her husband but several years younger than either Mrs. Bennet or Mrs. Philips. She possessed an amiability and intelligence similar to Mr. Gardiner and was a handsome, elegant woman who was a great favorite with all her Longbourn nieces. She had an especially close relationship with the two eldest, and they had frequently stayed with her in town.

The Gardiners also brought their four children, all of whom were loved by both Jane and Elizabeth. Jane was their particular favorite due to her steady sense and her sweetness of temper, which prepared her for teaching them, playing with them, and loving them.

The first thing Mr. and Mrs. Gardiner did after they arrived on the Monday before Christmas was to issue their congratulations to both Jane and Mary since they had been well informed of all the related events by the correspondence of Elizabeth, the most prolific letter writer in the household. After discharging this first duty, Mrs. Gardiner proceeded to distribute her presents to all her nieces, who received them with exactly the same courtesy one would expect—appreciation by Jane and Elizabeth, politeness by Mary, and a general air of inattentiveness by the younger girls.

Mrs. Bennet, as well as Jane, was eager to hear her describe and demonstrate the newest fashions in town, and it was at this time her sister noticed Elizabeth was not at all interested in a discussion that usually held her attention. Mrs. Gardiner had no explanation at first though this deficit was soon corrected by her next and less active role—listening to Mrs. Bennet.

She nodded in acknowledgement when her sister described the wonderful good fortune of having a daughter soon to be married to Mr. Bennet's cousin, thus breaking the entail that would otherwise have impoverished her and all her daughters. She was even more eloquent in enthusing about the splendid marriage of her most lovely daughter who would soon be well settled at Netherfield.

It was only when Mrs. Bennet turned to her grievances and complaints against Elizabeth, who by this time had slipped out of the room, that Mrs. Gardiner had an inkling of what might be afflicting her niece.

"I do not understand Lizzy's disinterest," Mrs. Bennet bemoaned, "for Mr. Darcy distinguished her when he completely ignored every other young lady he met. He danced with her a number of times while he danced with no one else save Mr. Bingley's sisters, and he even escorted her to dine after the supper dance at the Netherfield ball. But he left the county afterwards and has not returned. I know not what Lizzy might have done to drive him away, and she absolutely refuses to discuss the matter with me. I suppose it is too late now but, Sister—to imagine Lizzy might have become the mistress of his magnificent estate had it not been for her own perverseness! However, I suppose I should cease my grievances regarding an opportunity now gone, so I would be very glad to hear what you can tell us of long sleeves in town."

Mrs. Gardiner had been informed of what her sister related in the first two instances due to Elizabeth's correspondence, but she thought it highly significant that neither Jane nor Elizabeth had said a word regarding Mr. Darcy. She had spent some time in her younger years in a village near the Darcy estate, so she was at least familiar with the family name. But she knew nothing of this latest inheritor of the family fortune, which she knew was quite extensive.

When she had an opportunity to be alone with Jane later in the evening, her aunt was able to speak more on the subject.

"It seems it might have been a desirable match for Lizzy, at least from the aspect of securing her future, so I suppose I am sorry it went off. But, from what I have learned, I cannot see the kind of distinction Mr. Bingley showed to you."

Jane nodded in agreement, but she was uncomfortable discussing her sister. There were many things Elizabeth had confessed to her that she should not share.

"But these things happen so often, Jane! A young man seems to fall in love easily with a pretty girl, only to forget her when accident separates them for a few weeks. This sort of fickleness occurs frequently."

"That is true. And you make a good point about Mr. Darcy's attentions to Lizzy. My mother makes the most of the situation by pointing out he did not do anything similar with any other young lady, but I agree he did not show a distinct preference for Lizzy."

"Still, what does Lizzy feel? Does she suffer much, do you think? I know it is difficult to tell with her since she has kept her own counsel for so long, but a general neglect of civility is often an indication of love concealed."

Jane knew she had to speak carefully because she could not disclose the extent of her sister's despair and hopelessness. But she could not deny her aunt's quick and easy discernment.

"I cannot be sure," she said, speaking only of what she might have observed while keeping her sister's confidences to herself. "But there is one point that convinces me she is not happy at all. She has told me she does not wish to stand up with me."

Mrs. Gardiner's eyebrows rose. "That is quite startling, Jane. Not to stand up with you! That is unmatched for Lizzy even if she is feeling more than she shows."

"In truth, there is more," Jane continued uncomfortably. "She has said she does not wish even to be present. I know it cannot be because of Mr. Bingley since I know she likes him. I have to assume it is because she does not wish to see Mr. Darcy, who will stand up for his friend."

Jane had been unable to find another way to make this point, despite thinking on it for days before her aunt and uncle arrived. She squirmed a bit under her aunt's searching gaze, but Mrs. Gardiner finally seemed to comprehend Jane would not—or, perhaps, could not—say anything more.

"Not even be present!" her aunt said at last. "Yes, such a desire is remarkable for Lizzy. I can see you have not told me everything, but I have to assume you have a reason. But she cannot simply remain in her room. Something more is needed. I wonder—"

Jane nodded quickly, grateful her aunt did not pursue a more explicit answer. She was even more grateful when her aunt went on.

"Do you think Lizzy might agree to accompany us to town when we leave? A change of scene might be helpful to relieve her melancholy, and she might stay with the children when we return for the ceremony. It would make it somewhat easier to explain why she will not be present."

That brought an eager affirmation from Jane, and she said she thought her sister would readily agree to the offer. With a nod, Mrs. Gardiner said she would take the earliest opportunity to broach the subject with Elizabeth.

Knowing the Gardiners planned to stay a week, Mrs. Bennet had taken care to provide for the entertainment of her brother and sister, so there was not a day when they sat down to a family dinner. There were engagements with local families as well as with the officers of the regiment. And when the engagement was at home, some of the officers were always invited. Due to Kitty and Lydia's preference as well as that of her mother, Wickham was always present though it little pleased Elizabeth.

Mrs. Gardiner was quick to notice this indifference—indeed antipathy—for the gentleman when Elizabeth first introduced him, and she had to wonder at it since she would have expected her niece to show more interest in such an amiable and gentlemanly young man. It was just one more piece to be added to the others she tried to fit into the puzzle of Elizabeth's new and altered character.

Elizabeth had been loath to make the introduction, but she knew Wickham had been raised in the same part of Derbyshire where her aunt had spent some dozen years before her marriage. The two of them had, therefore, a number of acquaintances in common. Though Wickham had not lived there since the death of Darcy's father some five years previously, he could provide her aunt with fresher knowledge of her former friends.

Mrs. Gardiner had seen parts of the great estate of Pemberley in passing and had known the previous owner, the late Mr. Darcy, by reputation. Here, consequently, was an inexhaustible subject of discourse for the two of them since her aunt could compare her recollection of Pemberley with the more detailed descriptions Wickham could offer. Since Wickham had been the favorite of the previous owner, she could please him, in turn, by her praise of his benefactor, delighting them both.

Elizabeth was less than pleased, of course, when Wickham made her aunt acquainted with the ill-treatment he had received from the present Mr. Darcy. She had expected it of him, but there was really nothing she could say since she knew she could not argue Wickham's points without the danger of revealing something of her own suppressed emotions.

For her part, Mrs. Gardiner could remember little of the reputation of the present Mr. Darcy when he was a mere lad, though she admitted she had heard him spoken of as a proud, ill-natured boy.

ON THE FOLLOWING DAY, MRS. GARDINER TOOK THE OPPORTUNITY TO broach the subject of Elizabeth returning to London with her family when they departed Longbourn. The two of them had been walking in the Longbourn garden, and Mrs. Gardiner chose her words carefully.

"On the first day I arrived, I could not help noticing you were not in your usual good humor."

Elizabeth glanced aside at her and made no reply. But she also made no denials, so Mrs. Gardiner continued.

"I did not attempt to query you since I know you value your privacy. But I did speak with your sister, and Jane informed me you would prefer not to be present when she is married."

Elizabeth simply nodded in acknowledgement, but she clasped her arms about herself, an indication of her discomfort as her aunt continued.

"So Jane and I thought you might agree to return to London with your uncle and me and remain there until after the wedding."

It was several moments before Elizabeth spoke, and then she simply said, "I think it a very good idea, Aunt Gardiner."

After walking on a bit further, Mrs. Gardiner said gently, "Are you sure there is nothing you wish to discuss with me, Lizzy? You know you can rely on my discretion."

Mrs. Gardiner caught a glimpse of Elizabeth's eyes as she shook her head almost desperately, and she thought she could see fear in them.

"I cannot, Aunt, I…" Elizabeth said tightly, her voice trailing off.

"But you did speak with Jane," Mrs. Gardiner said softly. "You confided in her at least."

Mrs. Gardiner put her arm around Elizabeth's shoulder. "I am not going to enquire further, Lizzy, but I am glad you unburdened yourself to her. It is not good to keep such matters to yourself. We all need a little help sometimes, and you could not pick a better confidante than Jane."

Thus, on the day before the beginning of the New Year, the Gardiners returned to London, taking Elizabeth with them though Mrs. Bennet waxed eloquent in her vituperative complaints on the thoughtlessness of her least favorite daughter. Her father said nothing at the time, having previously met with no success when he enquired about her departure. He knew neither she nor Jane was telling him everything, but it was not in his nature to be overly inquisitive, so he kept his silence.

Mrs. Bennet was even more upset when Jane asked Charlotte Lucas to stand up with her since she was *Elizabeth's* most intimate friend. In fact, her mother demanded Jane change her mind and give the honor to one of her younger sisters. To this, Jane demurred since Elizabeth had carefully coached her before leaving that such a choice belonged to her and her alone. She would soon be leaving Longbourn forever, and it was time she started behaving as she would need to when she was in charge of her own establishment and had to make her own decisions.

So the atmosphere at Longbourn was fraught with hurt feelings until the incipient arrival of Mr. Collins forced her mother to attend to the wedding preparations of her two daughters.

Mr. Collins arrived at Longbourn a few days after the departure of the Gardiner party, and a week later Mary Bennet made him the happiest of men. The following week saw the ceremony solemnizing the nuptials of Jane and Bingley and their departure to Netherfield, leaving Mrs. Bennet more than a little dazed and discomfited by the near desertion of Longbourn with only two of her daughters in occasional attendance when they were not walking to Meryton in search of officers. It was only when the weather prevented such excursions that she had any company whatever.

Mr. Bennet, of course, was overjoyed at having his tranquility so seldom violated since not even his wife dared to interrupt him after being summarily commanded to desist.

Two days after Jane's departure to Netherfield Park brought the return of Elizabeth to Longbourn. She resolutely ignored the remonstrations of her mother over her abandonment of her sister and simply climbed the stairs to her room and closed the door.

With the momentous events of concern to the Longbourn family finished, the early months of the year passed away, sometimes dreary and sometimes cold, with only the walks to Meryton to give diversion to the younger Bennet sisters. On rare occasions, Elizabeth accompanied Lydia and Kitty, but she always returned to Longbourn in a worse humor than when she left.

She was hard-pressed to ramble through the countryside on many days due to the rains and occasional snows. But when she found good weather, she tried to engage herself in long and challenging walks.

All this time, Elizabeth had only one thing to look forward to with any pleasure: the invitation she had received in a letter from her aunt to accompany the Gardiners on a tour to the north during the summer.

Chapter 19

//

We are all born ignorant, but one must work hard to remain stupid.

— Benjamin Franklin, American statesman, scientist,
philosopher, printer, writer, and inventor

\\\

Monday, March 23, 1812
Darcy Townhouse, London

A re you certain you will not change your mind, McDunn?" Darcy
asked as he and Fitzwilliam prepared to leave for their yearly visit
to their aunt.

"No, I think it best to remain here, Darcy. If you remember, your aunt
and I didn't get along all that well last year. She thought I was too young to
be a major and wasn't a true gentleman, neither of which really bothered me
since I have heard as much previously. But she also wanted you to dismiss
me to the stables with the hired help, which did disturb me. I've gotten
used to sleeping in your comfortable beds."

"Well, yes, I remember. Lady Catherine can be a trifle caustic at times."

"At times, Darcy?" Fitzwilliam said with a snort. "Only at times?"

"But I had hoped to repair the bad memories from last year's visit," Darcy
said, ignoring his cousin. "Lady Catherine and my mother were very dear
to each other, and she is the closest relative I have, so I would have liked to
see the two of you achieve a more polite accommodation."

"Perhaps at a later time," McDunn said, his face showing nothing. "Your
sister and I have a lot of work to do. Getting the tracks laid at the Wylam

Colliery for our demonstration also needs my attention. One of the local merchants has provided a ready supply of ties for the rails that are marvelously consistent in their dimensions, but we're not having the same luck with the rails themselves."

"I know, I know," Darcy said with a sigh. "When you and I discussed your plans, this part of it seemed so simple compared to the difficulty of getting the locomotive built."

"That surprised me too, which was an oversight on my part. In engineering school, I was taught that this part of the production process is especially susceptible to Murphy's law: That which can go wrong—"

"—will go wrong!" Fitzwilliam finished. "As it is in battle, you have a plan and then you have to improvise desperately while the air is filled with shot and shell!"

"Nevertheless, your points are valid," Darcy said, "so we shall be on our way. I have told Mrs. Sturdivant to make sure Georgiana maintains her pianoforte practice as well as her lessons, though she would much prefer to be assisting you."

"Despite how helpful your sister can be, Mrs. Sturdivant and I will make sure she doesn't neglect her studies."

"Then we shall see you in about a week. Come, Richard. We had best get on the road."

Monday, March 23, 1812
Rosings, Kent

LADY CATHERINE'S ELDERLY BUTLER REENTERED THE ROOM AND ANnounced in a squeaky and unpleasant voice, "Her ladyship will see you now."

He led the two gentlemen to a room where three women awaited them. Darcy had to repress a smile at the scene, which had clearly been staged to resemble a throne room.

His aunt, Lady Catherine De Bourgh, was a tall, large woman, and she rose to greet her nephews. She had strongly marked features and appeared to have once been handsome, but age and added weight had adversely affected her appearance.

"There you are!" the formidable woman said, in a strong voice that filled the room. "I expected you an hour ago!"

"We were delayed by muddy roads, your ladyship," Darcy said gravely, bowing over his aunt's hand.

"My father sends his felicitations, Aunt," Colonel Fitzwilliam said. He was dressed in formal attire rather than the uniform he preferred, and his greeting mirrored Darcy's.

"You, of course, already know my daughter's companion, Mrs. Jenkinson."

"Of course, your ladyship," chorused both men as they bowed to both Miss de Bourgh and her companion. Lady Catherine's attention now moved from Darcy to her other nephew.

"Fitzwilliam!" she said sharply. "What is the hair on your face?"

"It is a beard, your ladyship."

"It is most ungentlemanly. You should remove it immediately!"

"Beards are very fashionable in the Peninsula Army, Aunt. Many of Wellesley's officers have grown them."

"I remember the man you brought with you last year, Darcy. He had a most disreputable moustache, which is not unexpected, considering his antecedents. I am pleased you had the good sense not to bring him with you."

"McDunn was an officer in the American Corps of Marines," Fitzwilliam said before his cousin could say anything, "and is a most honorable gentleman. Beards were frowned on in his corps, but moustaches were quite popular."

"What is the world coming to? First, allowing such a common fellow to become a major, especially with his moustache and with all his hair cut off, and now you with your beard, Fitzwilliam. Those whiskers are entirely disreputable."

"In Major McDunn's military, they keep their hair very short for the sake of cleanliness in the field," Fitzwilliam said loyally, ignoring his aunt's comment about his beard. Darcy, meanwhile, struggled to keep a straight face on witnessing his aunt's oft-displayed disapproval.

"My word, you seem to have learned impertinence since your last visit, Fitzwilliam," Lady Catherine said grumpily before continuing. "You both will undoubtedly wish to refresh yourselves before dinner. I have invited my parson, Mr. Collins, to have tea with us after dinner along with his most charming wife. She is marvelously accomplished at the pianoforte, and I am sure you will be quite entertained."

Despite having been invited to come in the evening rather than to dine, Mr. Collins was in an enervated state of excitement as he and his wife joined the rest of the party in Lady Catherine's drawing room. They were received civilly, as usual, though Mr. Collins had insufficient discernment to realize his patroness did so with no great enthusiasm, only desiring their company when she could get no one else. Their reception by Darcy and Colonel Fitzwilliam was considerably warmer. Even if Darcy had no particular liking for Mr. Collins, he was far too refined to show it, but he was greatly surprised to discover he already knew the man's wife. Or, at least, he *thought* he did.

He was almost certain she was one of Elizabeth Bennet's sisters, the one who played music at Lucas Lodge. He had been introduced to her casually in Meryton, but his memory of her was not clear.

He resolved to assuage his curiosity before the evening was over. The warmth of Colonel Fitzwilliam's reception was due to his relief at having anyone at all at his aunt's previously untenanted parsonage since anything out of the ordinary was a welcome relief while visiting at Rosings. When his aunt turned her head to say something to her daughter, obviously trying to bring her into the conversation with Darcy, Fitzwilliam took the opportunity to sit beside Mrs. Collins.

His knowledge on a wide variety of topics was enough to finally draw Mrs. Collins from her natural shyness, and their conversation was soon agreeable and lively enough to draw the attention of Lady Catherine.

"What is it you are saying, Fitzwilliam?" she said, her voice loud and carrying. "What is it you are speaking of with Mrs. Collins? Let me hear what it is."

Darcy saw that Fitzwilliam was not at all pleased to be interrupted in such a peremptory manner, but his cousin was unable to avoid a reply.

"We are speaking of music, madam," he said with tolerable control.

"Of music! Then pray speak aloud! It is of all subjects my delight. I must have my share in the conversation if you are speaking of music. There are few people in England, I suppose, who have more true enjoyment of music than myself, or a better natural taste. If I had ever learnt, I should have been a great proficient. And so would Anne if her health had allowed her to apply. I am confident she would have performed delightfully. How does dear Georgiana get on with her music, Darcy?"

Darcy was able to conceal his annoyance with even better skill than his cousin, and moreover, he was always prepared to speak of his sister with affectionate praise.

"She is doing quite well with her pianoforte and her other studies, your ladyship."

"I am very glad to hear it. But what are these other studies you mention, Darcy? A young lady does not need to be educated as a gentleman might. Such is not her place in life. You must focus her effort where it is most needed and ensure she practices her music most diligently and faithfully."

"I assure you, madam, she does not need such advice," Darcy replied tightly, less able to disguise his exasperation this time. "She practices her music very constantly, but both Fitzwilliam and I think she should know more of the world than just the affairs of the drawing room."

"I cannot agree," his aunt said in reply, oblivious to the flush mounting her nephew's cheeks. "She cannot practice her music too much. You must include her practice schedule when next you write, and I shall examine it carefully to ensure she is not neglecting her instrument. I often tell young ladies that no excellence in music is to be acquired without constant practice, and I have encouraged Mrs. Collins, as well as she plays, to feel free to come to Rosings and play on the pianoforte in Mrs. Jenkinson's room. She has been quite attentive to my advice, and she is not in anybody's way in that part of the house."

Darcy's flush was now accentuated by a pair of red spots over his cheekbones since he was both infuriated and ashamed of his aunt's ill breeding. He made no answer to her commands though he was resolved to ignore them, and he endured his aunt's conversation until tea was over.

As soon as Lady Catherine rang to have the tea service removed, she entreated Mrs. Collins to play for them. Mary was never hesitant about exhibiting her talents even if they were not as capital as she imagined them to be. Fitzwilliam was quick to add his encouragement and escorted her to the instrument.

Fitzwilliam drew up a chair beside the splendid pianoforte, and Darcy moved to join them.

While Mrs. Collins shuffled through the available music sheets, Darcy said, somewhat diffidently, "I am sorry to display the defects of my memory, Mrs. Collins, but am I correct in my conjecture that we have already been introduced?"

Mary nodded happily. "You are indeed correct, sir. I am one of five daughters of Mr. and Mrs. Bennet of Longbourn."

"Ah, then my memory did not mislead me. I do hope your family is doing well and all are in good health."

"Indeed, sir, they are," Mary said, greatly pleased at such a polite response. "My parents are most hale and fit, and my eldest sister, Mrs. Bingley, wrote just this week at how delighted she is to settle at Netherfield with her husband."

"And what of your other sisters—if I might enquire?"

"Of my two youngest I know little since they do not often write," Mary admitted somewhat uncomfortably, "but my sister Elizabeth says they are healthy enough, though I am somewhat worried about her own well-being."

Darcy was a bit taken aback by this casual comment, and he quickly asked, "Is Miss Elizabeth ill, do you know?"

"Not ill exactly, I think, but my mother writes she is out of sorts and spends almost all her time either walking about the country, which has always been her delight, or remaining upstairs in her room, which is rather unusual for her."

Damnation! Darcy thought uncomfortably. *I would have expected such a lively girl to move past the distressing events of the Netherfield ball more quickly. After all, it has been more than three months, and she is no more than twenty years of age. That is far too young to still be harboring such dejected feelings!*

Meanwhile, Mary selected a sheet of music and began to play. Darcy was unsurprised to find she was much as she had been at Lucas Lodge, possessing a certain skill at application without having the inspiration of either genius or taste.

When Mary finished, she looked at Colonel Fitzwilliam, who had listened with every indication of appreciation. "Well, sir, what shall I play next? Do you have any particular favorite?"

Fitzwilliam's mouth had opened to respond when Lady Catherine interjected herself, again demanding loudly to know what they were speaking of. Made anxious by such an interruption, Mary immediately selected a sheet and began playing. Lady Catherine was already moving toward the pianoforte and stood listening for a few minutes.

"Does Mrs. Collins not play excellently, Darcy? She has certainly improved since beginning to play on the pianoforte in Mrs. Jenkinson's room though she should have had the advantage of a London master. She has a very good notion of fingering though her taste is not equal to Anne's, of course. Anne would have been a delightful performer had her health allowed her to learn."

Darcy froze his expression to prevent his eyes from rolling at the sheer gaucherie and impudence of his aunt's comment. He was not sure he had concealed his distaste from Fitzwilliam, however, since his cousin had suddenly lowered his head, seemingly fascinated by the crease in his trousers. Mary, however, appeared to notice nothing amiss, her eyes focused on the music in front of her.

Lady Catherine continued her remarks on Mary's performance, mixing with them many instructions on execution and taste, to the detriment of the enjoyment of the rest of the party. Mary received all of her ladyship's comments with the appearance of appreciation, and she, at the request of the gentlemen, remained at the instrument until her ladyship's carriage was ready to take the Hunsford party home.

THE TWO COUSINS GATHERED IN DARCY'S ROOM AFTER THE COLLINS PARTY had departed, delayed by Lady Catherine's one-sided recitation of advice for the two of them. Her counsel covered everything from their attire—*Breeches are much preferred over trousers at all times except the most informal*—to how they should spend their time—*Our library at Rosings is superior even to your library at Pemberley, Darcy. That should be where you gentlemen spend most of your time*—to how Darcy ought to desist from his economic interests—*It is not at all seemly, Darcy, this unhealthy interest of yours in trade. It is not a proper endeavor for a gentleman. Not at all!*

As a result, both of them felt the need for companionable company and considerable liquid encouragement.

"That pig-swill is going to make you go blind," Darcy said, watching his cousin pour a glass half full of dark liquid.

"Nonsense, Darcy," Fitzwilliam retorted mildly, taking an appreciative sip. "McDunn was kind enough to give me two bottles of his Scotch when I was packing. I was afraid of evenings like this."

"Yes," Darcy said sadly, "you know as well as I what our aunt is like."

"True, true," grumbled Fitzwilliam. "But I think she gets worse every year, though my father, for some obscure reason, seems to be quite fond of her and would not understand if I evaded the visit."

"I am glad I was unable to convince McDunn to join us. I doubt her ladyship would have been any more amiable than last year."

"I remember her demanding you send McDunn to sleep with the servants!"

Fitzwilliam said, giving a hoot of amusement. "I had to bolt from the room, or I would have laughed aloud. I thought her ladyship was going to have a paroxysm when you flatly refused to do so. Your uncle would not have been pleased to have her perish in such a manner."

"Probably it would be best to change to a less depressing subject, cousin."

"Excellent suggestion, Darcy," Fitzwilliam said agreeably. "Shall we visit the parsonage tomorrow? Mrs. Collins said her husband is usually far too busy in his office or his garden to spend much time with her. It would be delightful if she was young, pretty, and available, but nevertheless, her company is a distraction to be cherished. I cannot imagine anything more dreadfully boring than trying to find an interesting book in my aunt's library!"

Darcy grimaced as he remembered Mrs. Collins's comments about her sister. Fitzwilliam regarded his reserved cousin questioningly as Darcy stared deeply into his brandy glass. He was familiar with his cousin's sometimes-bleak moods, but this was unusual even for him.

But Darcy seemed to have noticed his cousin's curiosity and now had his emotions under good regulation. "I suppose staying away from Rosings would be wise. Her ladyship seems to have rather upset me as you can see."

Fitzwilliam nodded though he was not sure Darcy had actually named the source of his discontent. But he said nothing and kept the whole conversation for later consideration. He intended to keep his eyes and attention sharp, however, since he might acquire a clue or two regarding what was on his cousin's mind.

Tuesday, March 24, 1812
Rosings Parsonage, Kent

IF THE PARSONAGE HAD BEEN A TOPIC OF CONVERSATION AMONG THE gentlemen, then the gentlemen had been an equally interesting topic for Mary's thoughts. Soon after she first arrived at the parsonage, she had learned Lady Catherine's two nephews would visit soon. She remembered Mr. Darcy slightly from Hertfordshire, but she had been completely unacquainted with her ladyship's other nephew.

She knew from her husband that Mr. Darcy was intended for Lady Catherine's daughter, Miss de Bourgh, so she had been quite surprised to see little conversation between them during the evening. She mentioned the subject to her husband, but he re-affirmed that the match was the determined intention of his patroness. Still, she had to wonder.

The arrival of the younger son of the Earl of Matlock was of even more interest because of his relation to the nobility. Her ladyship had referred to him as a colonel though he did not wear his uniform.

That would be a great disappointment to Kitty and Lydia, she thought in satisfaction. *To meet a colonel who deigned not to wear his red coat would strike them speechless!*

Mr. Collins had disappeared toward Rosings early in the morning, promising to bring back information regarding when the visitors might call on them. So she was quite surprised to look out the window and see her husband approaching with the gentlemen at his side.

She immediately went downstairs to the dining parlor, which was a larger room with a more pleasant aspect, and thus had a clear view as Mr. Collins scurried ahead to open the gate for the visitors. Immediately afterward, the door chimes signaled their arrival.

In the better light of the dining-parlor, Mary could more easily see that Colonel Fitzwilliam, while not handsome, was more sturdy and robust than he had seemed in the candlelight at Rosings. It made her wonder whether he was really the dilettante she had supposed him to be. He was, however, as he had proven the previous evening, most truly a gentleman despite his neatly trimmed beard that went decidedly athwart the current fashion for gentlemen of her acquaintance.

Mr. Darcy, who followed him into the room, looked and acted much as he usually did, paying his compliments to Mrs. Collins with his usual air of composed reserve and then sitting back to let his cousin carry the conversation.

The colonel, as before, was dressed as a gentleman rather than an officer, and he fulfilled her expectations by again opening the conversation with the readiness and ease of a well-bred man. After only a few minutes, however, Mr. Collins excused himself to his study, claiming the necessity of working on his sermon for Sunday.

Her husband's departure seemed to bring a noticeable change to Mr. Darcy's air since he settled back in his chair and became more comfortable.

"Do you hear anything from your letters regarding Mr. Bingley?" he said after some minutes. "You mentioned your sister is doing well, but I have heard nothing from my friend."

"Everything Jane says in her letters indicates he is as happy in his new life as she. Jane is wonderfully frequent in writing very long letters, and she tells me everyone in the neighborhood comes to call very often, and they receive frequent invitations to tea and to dine."

"I am very pleased to hear it, Mrs. Collins. I have written Mr. Bingley several times, but he has not responded. He has always been a rather indifferent correspondent, and I have simply been too busy to visit. But it seems as though he has been quite occupied himself. And your parents are well from what you said last evening."

"Indeed they are, sir, but thank you for enquiring," she said, looking at him curiously since he had always stood rather aloof from the inhabitants of their country neighborhood.

"But you are worried about your elder sister."

"I am," she said slowly, thinking this last question might be more significant than it appeared on the face of it. "But Elizabeth denies any physical infirmity in her letters, simply saying she is making up for the absence of Jane and myself by walking even more than she usually does. She has always loved wandering about the countryside."

Darcy nodded, saying he was relieved to hear it since her sister would not be so active if she were ill. Mary nodded in return, but she wondered what private motives had caused this most unusual interest.

I shall have to write Lizzy and tell her about this, she thought. *Though Mr. Darcy never showed the interest Mr. Bingley did, he did dance with Lizzy several times. And my mother was quite outspoken about soon having three daughters married and not just two.*

The gentlemen stayed for almost an hour and made their farewells most amiably, saying they would return regularly. That pleased Mary immensely since she had been gratified by their attentiveness. Their visit had certainly broken the monotony of life in the parsonage.

Chapter 20

//

*My heart no longer felt as if it belonged to me. It now felt as it had
been stolen, torn from my chest by someone who wanted no part of it.*

— Meredith T. Taylor, author

\\\

*Tuesday, April 16, 1812
Longbourn, Hertfordshire*

In mid-April, Lydia and Kitty returned from walking to Meryton in an acute state of despair. Elizabeth had forgone her walk earlier due to a sore ankle. She sat with her mother, trying in vain to read a book she had recently acquired, but she could not seem to concentrate.

It had been much the same since those tempestuous two months the previous autumn when so many of her preconceptions and hopes had been disarranged and then ruthlessly shattered. A shadow of her previous impertinence had barely started to resurrect itself, leading her to apply labels to different parts of the autumn. Pre-Darcy was the time before the tall, handsome, and utterly disquieting gentleman entered Hertfordshire, and she had abbreviated this first period as PD. The two months leading up to the ball had become During-Darcy and thus DD. And the time after he departed from Netherfield was, of course, After-Darcy or AD.

The present time was definitely AD. She wished she could somehow regain her carefree air and be the same person she was PD. But it was difficult. Charlotte had often tried to help since she had discerned enough of her dear friend's discomposure to know it concerned Darcy. That had been straightforward enough since she had seen most of the interactions between them. But even she had no idea of the true, soul-shattering impact this prideful man had made on her friend.

And Elizabeth was unwilling to say more, even to Charlotte. She still was surprised that she had bared her heart to Jane. She could never reveal her story to anyone else despite knowing she could completely trust in Charlotte's confidence. Recalling the devastating night she cried herself to sleep in Jane's arms, she could not bring herself to go through it again.

Elizabeth heard the loud, vulgar voices of Lydia and Kitty as soon as the front door opened, and she shook her head in exasperation at their complete lack of manners. But this occasion appeared somewhat unusual because there was little gaiety in their voices.

Both girls burst into the parlor, and Kitty said, almost in a wail, "You will not believe the distressing news we just received from Lieutenant Denny!"

"The regiment is leaving Meryton for summer quarters!" Lydia said.

"In Brighton!" Kitty said, and this time her voice was indeed a wail.

"Are they indeed!" Elizabeth said, her satisfaction plain.

"Lizzy, do not prattle on in your usual way!" snapped her mother, but Elizabeth ignored her.

She had barely been able to treat her mother civilly after the disastrous night at Netherfield. Since then, it had been difficult for Elizabeth to restrain her urge to scream her outrage and hurt at her mother. Most of the time, it was all she could do to force herself to turn away and ignore her mother's follies.

"They will be gone in a little more than a month," Lydia said in a rush, her anguish palpable. "They are to be encamped at Brighton. Where is that, Mama?"

"I only know it is on the sea, somewhere south of here," Mrs. Bennet replied.

"Do you think Papa would take us there for the summer?" Kitty asked excitedly. "Would you ask him?"

"I do not think my father would agree to such an ill-conceived scheme as this," Elizabeth said. "Such an endeavor would disjoint our family for good and all. Good Heavens! Look at how we have been upset by just one regiment! What would happen with a whole camp of soldiers?"

Both her mother and her sisters were quick to contradict her, certain their opinions were irrefutable. But Elizabeth only smiled at their fancies, for she knew her father better than they did. Despite his usual neglect in managing his family, he was logical enough to realize the foolishness of such a proposal.

And so it proved at the evening meal when her sisters raised the subject. Mr. Bennet listened to their arguments in silence, concentrating on his meal. At the end, having finished eating, he leaned back, patted his lips with his napkin, and smiled at them.

"I already knew I had two of the silliest girls in all of Great Britain," he said in bemused scorn, "and I listened to these frivolous arguments with as much amusement as I usually derive from reading my son-in-law's letters. On this occasion, however, I believe you two have bettered all previous marks for absurdity."

"But, Papa," cried Lydia, "it would hardly cost more to go to Brighton than to stay at Longbourn for the summer!"

"And on what, pray tell, do you base that assertion, my girl? I have never seen you pay the slightest attention to the many hours I spend laboring over my ledgers to ensure I do not exceed my income. Why, neither of you can even remain within the monthly pocket allowance I give you! You are always coming to me for more money, even with the little presents your mother lays in your hands." He turned to his wife. "Yes, yes, I know of your gifts, Mrs. Bennet! Depend on it, girls—and you also, Mrs. Bennet—taking the whole family to Brighton would be extremely imprudent. We shall not go."

"I should not have gone anyway," Elizabeth said, having listened without comment.

"I never expected you would, Lizzy."

But Lydia and Kitty could not understand their father's rejection of their scheme, and they were cast into extreme misery. They said nothing further since they were a bit afraid of their father. However, if they could not reproach their father for his lack of understanding, they vented their ire in what they believed to be a safer direction.

"How can you be so cold-hearted, Lizzy?" Lydia said. "How can you be smiling at a time like this?"

"Because, as my father just said, you are both being ridiculous," Elizabeth said matter-of-factly.

"Good Heavens!" Kitty said in despair. "What is to become of us? What are we to do?"

"You shall do much better than before this, I would think, without any red coats to drive you into frenzies." Elizabeth made no attempt to hide her smile as she made this comment.

But their affectionate mother joined with her youngest daughters and shared all their grief.

"I remember enduring the same misery when Colonel Millar's regiment went away, these five-and-twenty years ago. I cried for two days together, and I thought my heart should break."

"I am sure mine surely shall break," Lydia said mournfully.

"If we could but go to Brighton!" Mrs. Bennet observed, motivated similarly to her daughter.

But her husband only shook his head as he rose from the table. "Yet, I remain resistant to all this wailing and caterwauling. We shall remain at Longbourn."

So saying, he departed, leaving the least sensible of his family to their lamentations.

Tuesday, April 30, 1812
Longbourn, Hertfordshire

ELIZABETH'S FIRST INDICATION OF A REVERSAL—AT LEAST A PARTIAL ONE— of her father's decisiveness came a fortnight later as her sisters returned from their morning walk to Meryton for the few remaining days before the regiment departed and Lydia and Kitty's world came to an end.

She looked up as both girls rushed into the parlor where she and her mother sat, and Kitty wailed, "It is not fair! It is just not fair!"

"What is?" Mrs. Bennet asked, her interest roused by the possibility of some new and possibly even scandalous rumor from Meryton.

"Mrs. Forster, Mama!" cried Lydia ecstatically. "She has asked me to accompany her when the regiment goes to Brighton!"

"Oh, that is marvelous, my dear! Marvelous!"

Elizabeth rolled her eyes at another exhibition of her mother's foolishness, especially since it seemed to have inspired a similar lack of judgment in her youngest daughters. Only her desire to hear the details of this new scheme prevented her immediately leaving the room.

"She said I was her particular friend, and she would be devastated to go to a place where she knew no one else!" Lydia said. "Lizzy, you must congratulate me on my good fortune!"

Elizabeth was in no mood to do so and said so forthrightly, which brought the usual condemnation from her mother. She ignored this, being all too familiar with the very young Mrs. Forster who had only recently wed the commander of the militia regiment. It had been predictable that she and Lydia would become fast friends, since they both possessed the same exuberant humor and unrestrained, lively spirits. Lydia always called on her when she walked to Meryton.

"I cannot understand why Mrs. Forster should not have asked me too," Kitty said mournfully. "I have just as much right to be asked as Lydia."

"But you are *not* her particular friend!" cried Lydia, dancing about the room and accepting the congratulations of her mother. "You are just jealous!"

"But I am two years older!" Kitty said, sitting down and beginning to weep in disappointment and mortification.

Elizabeth could only shake her head. She knew Colonel Forster was a widower, his wife having died in childbirth some years previous to his arrival in Meryton. He was a man of middle years and possessed a modest wealth, and she knew he must have been lonely. Unfortunately, he had chosen, as so many men in his situation did, a young woman marked more by her youth and beauty than by her suitability to be the wife of a man of his station and responsibilities.

Meanwhile, Lydia's untamed raptures continued as she declared her need for new clothes since she would be attending all sorts of balls and dances in Brighton, and her mother voiced her complete and enthusiastic concurrence.

"Before you spend any of Papa's money, Lydia," Elizabeth said, "you had better realize he will not approve such a foolish excursion. Heaven's above! You are only sixteen! It is complete nonsense on the very face of it. He will not let you go."

"Of course, Mr. Bennet will approve of Lydia going with Mrs. Foster! You are just as jealous as Kitty. That is why you are so critical of Lydia's good fortune, yet you have not even the wit of Jane and Mary in securing a husband!"

Elizabeth went tight-lipped with fury at hearing such a thing from her mother's lips, especially in front of her sisters. Even more, just the oblique mention of Darcy's continuing absence sent a white-hot pang of anguish into her very heart. Wordlessly, almost trembling from her suppressed fury, she stood and left the room. Minutes later, the front door to Longbourn slammed as she left her mother and Lydia to their shared triumph.

"YES, LIZZY?" MR. BENNET SAID AS ELIZABETH CAME INTO HIS LIBRARY, her eyes much brighter than was usual these days. He had not the slightest idea of what might be causing the changes in her mood, her manner, and even her figure. He thought she was far too thin these days, almost certainly from the long hours she spent walking about the country.

"Papa, my mother has just told me you have given your approval for Lydia to go with Mrs. Forster when the regiment leaves for Brighton."

"Yes, you are correct," he said, putting his book down and looking at Elizabeth over the rims of his glasses.

"I think you are making a mistake—a very bad one. Lydia is far too young, too wild, and too unrestrained to be beyond the authority of her family."

"I agree with your description, Lizzy, but it is precisely the reason I consented when Mrs. Bennet came to me with this request. I suppose you know your mother looks on the excursion to Brighton with favor?"

"I do, but I do not share her opinion. Allowing Lydia to go to Brighton will be the absolute end of any possibility of instilling common sense in her. She is already known by everyone for the impropriety of her behavior. You know it as well as I, Papa!"

Mr. Bennet nodded but made no comment, so Elizabeth continued. "What possible advantage could she gain from the friendship of such a young woman as Mrs. Forster, who is almost as imprudent and undisciplined as Lydia? And Mrs. Forster would be the very person you are depending on to be Lydia's guardian while away from home. What can restrain Lydia's actions in the environs of Brighton where the temptations must be immeasurably greater than here at home?"

Her father listened attentively as Elizabeth finished her arguments before he spoke. "Lydia will never be easy until she has exposed herself in some public place or other. And we can never expect her to do it with so little expense or inconvenience to her family as under the present circumstances."

Elizabeth looked at him in astonishment, unable to believe an expression of such selfishness. But she determined to make one last attempt to make him see reason.

"Can you not imagine the very great disadvantages to us all that are certain to arise from the public notice of Lydia's unguarded and imprudent manner?" she said earnestly. "In fact, do you not know of the detriments that have *already* arisen from it? If you knew, I cannot but believe you would judge differently in the affair."

"Already arisen?" repeated Mr. Bennet with his usual wryness. "What, has she frightened away some of your lovers? Poor little Lizzy! But do not be cast down—"

He would have said more, for the words were on the very tip of his tongue, but he suddenly stopped as Elizabeth went pale as a sheet with anger, an expression of the most fierce and intemperate vehemence on her face.

Mr. Bennet usually enjoyed sparring with Elizabeth. She was the only one in the house with the wit to understand his allusions and quips. But on this occasion, his tongue stuck to the roof of his mouth at the reaction he had invoked.

"*Poor little Lizzy?*" Elizabeth hissed, her eyes ablaze with a rage he had never imagined to see from his favorite daughter.

"You dare to mock my suggestions and declare I could not have been harmed by Lydia's follies, dear father?" she said with fierce indignation, advancing to the front of his desk and staring down at him. "Have you not often tried to discuss the general malaise that has come over me and infected my mind with the most extreme melancholies and despairs? Can it be you have forgotten *that* when you call me *poor little Lizzy?*"

Elizabeth's fiery anger seemed to emanate from her whole body as she continued. "But then, why should I be surprised you would say such a thing? It is not only Lydia but all my family, save only Jane, who have been the instruments of holding all of us up to the general ridicule and contempt of others!"

She closed her eyes and visibly struggled to gain control of her temper, and her voice became calmer as she went on. "But I had originally intended to speak only of general evils rather than specific and personal ones. In that line, Papa, our family's importance, as well as our respectability, must be adversely affected by the wild volatility, the assurance, and the disdain of all restraint, which marks Lydia's character and which she displays so freely in public. This may possibly be the final opportunity of checking her exuberant spirits and teaching her that her present pursuits are *not* the business of her life."

She paused a moment before going on. "And the task of instilling a measure of restraint in your daughter is *yours*. If you will not check her, no one will, and her character will be fixed. At sixteen, she will be the most determined flirt who ever made herself and her family ridiculous! And she will ensnare Kitty in her wild improprieties, and both of them will soon be equally vain, ignorant, idle, and completely uncontrolled! Do you not understand that both of them will be censured and despised wherever they are known, and you, my mother, and I will also be involved in their disgrace?"

Though taken aback, Mr. Bennet saw Elizabeth's whole heart was in what she said. And since she appeared to have calmed down, he tried to take her hand in affection, only to have her jerk it away.

"Do not imagine you can pour oil on these troubled waters, Papa!" she said savagely, her anger so extreme that she spoke instantly, her voice raised in her anger and with none of her usual constraint and forethought. "I have had to stand aside while my mother became the very personification of discourtesy and bad manners wherever she went. The way she so blatantly shoved Jane at Mr. Bingley made our whole family a subject of ridicule! I heard the suppressed laughter and whispers you either did not hear or chose to ignore. You were there at Netherfield when she boasted of her two daughters who were soon to be married to rich men! If such ill-mannered and boorish vulgarities were not enough, you sat at her side as she said them and did nothing! Meanwhile, Mr. Darcy heard everything my mother said and formed a perfect opinion of our family!

"So do as you please, dear father. I suppose you will choose to preserve your tranquility and your ease instead of performing your duty. But when disaster strikes because you let your youngest daughter go to Brighton with nothing to restrain her other than her *particular* friend, do not say you were unwarned! Lydia will *not* be safe in such a situation! I have noted the looks she receives from many of the officers, especially Mr. Wickham, and they do not gaze on her as a possible wife! They have baser emotions in *their* minds!"

With this final rejoinder, Elizabeth stormed out of the room, leaving behind a father who was, at the same time, shocked—even angered—by her effrontery but also mortified by the truth he could not evade.

Above everything, Elizabeth had revealed that the improper manners and wildness of her family had aggrieved *her* and had done so in a particular and a severe way. She had also divulged, probably unconsciously, that the source of her hurt involved Mr. Darcy, whom her mother still hoped would return and renew his attentions.

He had been completely ignorant as to the source of Elizabeth's despondency until this moment. Mr. Bennet squirmed as he remembered his wife's gleeful boast of having one daughter settled at Netherfield and the other in Derbyshire. He remembered his amusement at his wife's silliness, but he had never even glanced at Elizabeth or Mr. Darcy. And he had never associated the "Derbyshire" comment with Mr. Darcy and his daughter.

Surely, if Elizabeth had heard his wife's boasts, then Darcy had also. He felt shame as he remembered that Darcy had appeared to be enjoying himself earlier in the evening but had left the neighborhood afterwards and not returned.

Oh, my poor girl! he thought wretchedly. *What have we done to you? What have I done to you? Darcy never returned! How selfish I have been! But what am I to do now? What amends can I make?*

It took several hours of thought before Mr. Bennet finally settled on two answers. First, he could do nothing to repair what had been done to Elizabeth. Sadly, it was too late, and he only hoped she could rise above her heartache one day and forgive him even if he could not make amends.

But second, he could avoid repeating his mistake. He rang for a servant and asked to have Lydia come to him.

Had Elizabeth Bennet remained downstairs, she might have found a measure of relief at her father having listened to her at long last; it was perfectly exemplified by Lydia's wails on being informed she would *not* be going to Brighton.

As the end of the regiment's stay in Meryton approached, all the young ladies in the neighborhood were in a mood of universal despair. Elizabeth and Charlotte alone seemed immune from the infection and were able to eat, drink, and sleep with a semblance of normalcy. Both Lydia and Kitty often reproved her for her lack of sympathy for their plight though Lydia had not an inkling Elizabeth had talked to her father about the matter. Instead, Lydia blamed her father alone, unable to comprehend how he could be so hardhearted.

In Lydia's imagination, a visit to Brighton would have involved every possibility of earthly happiness with the streets of the gay seaside town full of officers and herself the object of their attention. She lamented she would never see the glories of the camp with its scores of white tents stretching into the distance and all the roads of the camp filled with young and lively officers clad exclusively in scarlet. She almost wept at a vision of herself seated beneath one of those tents, tenderly flirting with at least six officers at once. And now it would never be, all because of her flint-hearted father!

Her mother's lamentations nearly matched her own since she had so looked forward to shopping for new clothes for her daughter. Had either she or Lydia known of Elizabeth's part in their shared woe, their anger would have been fierce.

Her sisters' cries of grief continued without ceasing, even when many of the officers dined at Longbourn on the evening before the regiment was to depart. Lydia and Mrs. Forster were beside themselves with despair at the possibility they would never see each other again. And Kitty could not contain her tears, certain she could not go on after the next morning.

For her part, Elizabeth remained composed at the keening of her sisters, secure in the knowledge that Lydia would be safe, for she still did not like the way Mr. Wickham so often looked at her youngest sister.

Wickham also came to speak with her and went so far as to ask about Mr. Darcy. But Elizabeth had been prepared for just such a question. She was well aware Wickham had been Darcy's boyhood companion and the favorite of the elder Mr. Darcy, so she was able to respond with a careless shrug, saying only that she had no news of him since the previous autumn.

Wickham responded that such information corresponded with what he had heard. "Of course, you know he is maligned among most of the neighborhood as well as in Meryton. Naturally, they did not know him as you did," he said with seeming casualness.

But Elizabeth knew Wickham and Darcy had had a falling out since their boyhood, so she gave another negligent shrug. "A few dances does not give one much of a chance to know another person very intimately. And Mr. Darcy does often display a reserve that makes him difficult to like."

"Yes, his manners are not nearly those of his friend Mr. Bingley."

"True," Elizabeth said with a calm nod. "But after talking with Jane, I think Mr. Darcy improves on acquaintance."

"Indeed!" cried Wickham with a look that gratified her, owing to his exasperation at not being able to defame his boyhood friend. "Does your sister say it is in address or civility that he improves? For I dare not hope he is improved in essentials."

"Oh no, Mr. Wickham! In essentials, I believe Mr. Darcy is very much what he ever was."

Wickham was clearly taken aback by these words, not knowing how to interpret them, and he looked uncomfortable and anxious.

"I suppose he may have been absent due to preparing for his match with Miss de Bourgh, which is much favored by his aunt, of whom Mr. Darcy stands much in awe."

Elizabeth answered only with a slight inclination of her head. She saw Wickham still wanted to engage her on the subject of his grievances, but she had no humor to indulge him previously and had none at all at the present time. So, seeing there was nothing to be gained, Wickham departed after a graceful bow and moved on to speak with others.

She saw him conversing and laughing during the rest of the evening, but he made no further attempts to speak with her. They parted at last with mutual civility and, almost certainly, a desire on both their parts never to meet again.

When the party ended, Lydia and Mrs. Forster gave each other one last, tearful embrace before the latter left with her husband for Meryton from whence they and the rest of the regiment were to set out early the next morning. Kitty and her mother also shed many a tear at the separation, and the three of them watched the last of the party depart from the front door.

Elizabeth saw none of this, having sought the sanctuary of her room despite the unhappy certainty that Wickham's talk of Darcy was going to plague her when she retired.

Chapter 21

//

It is best to love wisely, no doubt; but to love foolishly is better than not to be able to love at all.

— William Thackeray, British novelist and author

\\\

Monday, June 15, 1812
Netherfield, Hertfordshire

I shall miss you dreadfully, Jane," Elizabeth said, sitting in her sister's bedroom while Jane packed the last of her clothes, "but I cannot blame Mr. Bingley for buying an estate of his own. I know my mother must have been a terrible trial to both of you with her incessant visits. I tried to tell her so, but she simply would not listen. I cannot remember a single day when she did not visit at least once."

As was her nature, Jane was averse to criticizing anyone, so she merely shrugged. "I know she was only trying to help me manage this large house, but I believe she affected Bingley more than me. It is not like him to complain, but I am sure it explains his determination to find a suitable estate of his own."

"It will be difficult to visit you so far away as Derbyshire. I cannot make such a long journey alone, and my father is unlikely to escort me very often."

"It will be painful not to see you regularly, but Bingley is overjoyed to have found a suitable place only thirty miles from Mr. Darcy's home. From what he has said, Pemberley is a magnificent place, and the gardens are a marvel."

Seeing the change in Elizabeth's expression, one that might have gone unremarked by anyone less cognizant of her sister's unhappy moods, Jane stopped her packing and sat beside her sister, putting her arm around her shoulder.

"I am so sorry for what I just said, Lizzy. I know what you are enduring, and then I thoughtlessly made mention of Mr. Darcy's estate. I remember when I thought Bingley had left Netherfield forever. It was as though all my hopes had turned to ashes. I knew I felt a deep affection for him, but I had not known the depth of my love until I thought him lost."

"One blessing of that sad time was that you at last became enlightened to Miss Bingley's subterfuges and will not be fooled by her again," Elizabeth said, preferring to speak of something other than Darcy and his continued absence from Hertfordshire.

"I keep reminding myself not to be deceived again, now that she and her sister are attempting to renew our friendship. But it is difficult, Lizzy. Very difficult."

"You are too good for the rest of this world. As for Miss Bingley and her sister, just smile at them and be civil."

"I shall try my utmost."

"Do not worry overmuch about me. It is not as though Mr. Darcy ever showed me the preference Mr. Bingley showed you."

Jane knew Elizabeth was not being completely truthful with her, but she let her sister continue.

"In any case, I knew from the beginning that my desire for Mr. Darcy was doomed. But I will overcome this and become Elizabeth Bennet again."

"I worry you are overtaxing yourself. Mother says you sometimes leave in the morning after breakfast and do not return until late in the day. And you are much thinner than you used to be."

"It cannot be that severe, Jane," Elizabeth said with a smile. "My appetite is excellent, and I know I eat even more than I used to. I would not be surprised if I had gained weight instead of losing it."

Jane looked doubtful but had no desire to contradict such a definitive statement. "I am glad to hear it, Lizzy. And all the walking you are doing has to be making you stronger."

"Likely," Elizabeth said more cheerfully, and Jane returned to her packing.

"In time, I do hope you will be able to visit us."

"I certainly shall, but with Mr. Darcy living but thirty miles away, I will only visit if I am certain he is safely in town and might not make an unexpected visit."

Jane nodded in understanding. She knew Elizabeth would do anything to avoid the temptation of being in Darcy's presence. She had shown as much by staying in town when she and Bingley married.

"Speaking of visiting Derbyshire, I do have some interesting news. I just received a letter from Aunt Gardiner about our planned northern excursion, and it seems my uncle's business will make it impossible to go as far as the Lakes. But she does mention we might go as far as Derbyshire."

"I am sorry you will not be able to tour the Lake District, but I am cheered by the possibility that all of you might visit later in the summer."

She looked down and patted her abdomen, which was just starting to show she was with child. "I shall undoubtedly be in confinement by then, so a visit gives me something to look forward to."

"Yes, it does. Especially since a newborn child will make it impossible for you and Bingley to come to Longbourn for Christmas."

Jane looked up after placing her last item in the trunk. "You are likely correct. Bingley is very worried about this trip, and he has absolutely refused to allow our coach to travel more than three or four hours a day. I fear it will take more than a week to journey to our new home."

She embraced Elizabeth fondly though she had to wipe away a tear. "I have to confess I am excited to be going to a house that will be ours and not rented, but now I am starting to cry. You must promise to write often. I do so worry about you.

"Go and have many children, Jane, so I can come live with you and teach them to read and to play better than myself."

"Then you shall have to practice your fingering, Lizzy!" Jane said with a laugh, giving her sister a kiss.

THE IMMINENT DEPARTURE OF HER ELDEST DAUGHTER FROM HERTFORD-shire was quite distressing to Mrs. Bennet, who had so often told her friends of the pleasure she gained from visiting Mrs. Bingley and writing to Mrs. Collins. Deprived of half of those pleasures, she was not sure what was to become of her, and soon after Elizabeth returned home from Netherfield, Mrs. Bennet came into the front parlor where her daughter was taking tea alone.

"Well, Lizzy, what is your opinion of this sad business of Jane and Bingley leaving Hertfordshire? For my part, I cannot see why they should remove to the north when they could more easily stay among her friends in Hertfordshire. I am quite distraught."

"I believe Mr. Bingley very much desired to own his own estate, Mama," Elizabeth said coolly, wishing to be left alone rather than to listen to her mother's complaints.

"But why go so far away? Surely, Mr. Bingley could have found something closer to home."

"Netherfield is not Mr. Bingley's home, and Jane told me she does not care where she lives as long as it is with her husband. She also mentioned how excited Mr. Bingley is to have found a place so near his friend's estate in Derbyshire."

"Yes, yes, I know," Mrs. Bennet said, pacing back and forth in frustration. "Jane told me that also. But with Mr. Bingley leaving, how will Mr. Darcy ever return to Hertfordshire and renew his attentions to you? I was speaking of this with my sister Philips just yesterday, and neither of us can understand why you have not yet secured an offer of marriage from Mr. Darcy."

Elizabeth tried not to lose her temper at such a ludicrous statement, telling herself it was her mother's misery at having Jane move away that had prompted it.

"The simple answer, Mama, is that Mr. Darcy has not made such a proposal to me. In fact, I think you should face reality and admit he never intended to do so. It has been more than seven months since the ball at Netherfield, you know."

But Mrs. Bennet was in no humor for a logical statement such as this. "I still believe you could have accomplished this if you had been properly attentive to Mr. Darcy."

"Are you suggesting I should have thrown myself at Mr. Darcy?" Elizabeth asked, her temper slipping.

"Do you not realize the advantages of being married to a man with ten thousand a year?"

"Do you think I care a whit for his fortune? And even if Mr. Darcy had made me an offer, what makes you think I would accept it? I do not even like the man! I would rather stay with Jane and teach her children!"

"Nonsense, Lizzy! You are not—"

"Madam, I assure you Mr. Darcy has no interest whatsoever in me!"

Elizabeth said, interrupting her mother and overriding her attempts to speak. "He never has! All of this nonsense about him 'renewing his attentions' is a fancy living only in your mind and definitely not in the mind of Mr. Darcy!"

"How can you say that, Lizzy? He distinguished you out of all other young—"

"A few dances only, Mama! That is all! Please let the matter rest! I am actually glad Jane and Bingley are departing Netherfield since it means you can no longer cling to your delusion of Mr. Darcy returning there!"

"I am so disappointed in you, Lizzy! I know not how you offended him, but I suppose you are correct. There is not the least chance in the world of you ever getting him now. I suppose he will choose just as he pleases though both my sister and I will always believe he used you extremely ill. But he will be dreadfully sorry for what he has done when you die of a broken heart."

Harsh as were the words between them, they grew even angrier until Elizabeth fled the parlor and clambered up the stairs to her room. Once again, as she moved a set of drawers in front of her door, she lamented not having a lock for it.

ELIZABETH SAT ON HER WINDOW SEAT AS THE SUN NEARED THE HORIZON, wondering how her life had become so miserable. Clasping her knees to her chest, she rocked back and forth, her eyes closed and leaking tears, until she fell into a fitful sleep.

Dreaming, she imagined herself waltzing with Darcy, whirling about the dance floor in a most salacious manner. One by one, each of the other couples faded to wisps of smoke, leaving her alone in Darcy's arms, his hand about her waist as he pulled her close. In that moment, nothing else in the world mattered except the warmth of the smile on his face—the very one she had seen when they shared dinner at Netherfield. Her dress flew wide at the speed with which Darcy led her through the paces of the dance.

She gasped as if to complain when Darcy suddenly broke out of the dance, but her annoyance died on her lips as he scooped her up in his arms. Now all the other dancers were visible again, and they continued their steps while the man she loved so desperately carried her through the crowd and up to his room, bearing her as easily as though she were a mere sparrow.

In his room, Darcy set her on her feet. Then his face was above hers as she looked into his dark eyes. As his mouth descended on hers, Elizabeth gave a deep, throaty moan as she felt the sweet touch of his lips on hers—only to be ruthlessly torn from her dream by her mother pounding on her door, loudly demanding entrance.

Deprived of her sweet dream, Elizabeth burst into tears of frustration and shame. "Go away!" she screamed. "Leave me alone! After all you have done to me, can you not at least leave me alone?"

She pulled her legs up and clasped them against her chest as she tried desperately to retrieve and re-assemble the shreds of her dream. But as so often happened with dreams, especially when punctuated and destroyed by her mother's shrill voice and demands, the individual parts inevitably disappeared. The thought of yet another loss, trivial as it was, made Elizabeth cry harder at the way her whole family was betraying her.

Chapter 22

//

Every person has free choice. Free to obey or disobey the Natural Laws.
Your choice determines the consequences. Nobody ever did, or ever will,
escape the consequences of his choices.

— Alfred A. Montapert, American author

\\\

Mid-June through mid-July, 1812
Longbourn, Hertfordshire

I n the weeks leading up to the arrival of her aunt and uncle for the start
of their northern tour, Elizabeth was greatly relieved by the gradual
restoration of calm at home. When the militia first departed, the incessant complaining of her two younger sisters had precluded any vestige of
health, good humor, or cheerfulness at Longbourn.

As a consequence, since such whining had been an irritant to Elizabeth's
own ill humor, occasioned by her fitful sleep and recurring dreams, she was
quite fierce in checking the misbehavior of Lydia and Kitty. In this, she was
surprisingly aided by her father's occasional forays from his library, issuing
stern admonitions against offenses such as Lydia's bewailing his heartless-
ness or Kitty's general complaints on the absence of officers. The result was
a precipitous decline in such offenses. By the middle of June, both Lydia
and Kitty were sufficiently recovered to be able to enter Meryton without
tears. Combined with the return of the families who had been in town for
the winter and the resulting rise in summer engagements and finery, life at
Longbourn began to wear a happier aspect.

Even Mrs. Bennet was affected, going out of her way to avoid provoking Elizabeth after their fiery altercation around Jane and Bingley's departure. Moreover, Elizabeth now had her own upcoming trip to heighten her anticipation.

Her aunt's letters had provided the details on their abbreviated holiday, and the new plan was to tour Derbyshire as her aunt had hinted. In addition to a few days spent visiting the Bingleys, they would occupy the remainder of their three weeks with the other delights of the county, especially the town of Lambton, which had a particularly strong attraction for Mrs. Gardiner. The town lay near to Darcy's estate of Pemberley and was probably as great an object of her aunt's curiosity as all the celebrated beauties of Matlock, Chatsworth, Dovedale, or the Peaks.

Elizabeth did not join her aunt in wishing to visit Pemberley, especially in the summer when Darcy was more likely to be in residence, London being particularly hot and unhealthy. She was loath to withdraw from the excursion, and it required an express from Jane to quell her fears. It informed her that only Miss Darcy was in residence, the gentlemen remaining in town on business.

Surely, she thought in relief, *I may now enter his county and rob it of a few petrified spars without danger.*

Monday, July 13 through early August, 1812
Hertfordshire to Derbyshire

Soon, Mr. and Mrs. Gardiner appeared at Longbourn with their four children. Within the hour, Mrs. Philips arrived at Longbourn to help manage the children, it being an unfortunate fact that Mrs. Bennet's nerves would prevent her from being able to tolerate them by herself. Mrs. Philips felt otherwise, possibly due to her own inability to have children.

The Gardiners stayed only one night at Longbourn and set off with Elizabeth the next morning in pursuit of novelty and amusement. Mrs. Gardiner was pleased to see a decided renewal of Lizzy's usual optimistic spirits within a few days. Her niece could not help but be cheered by the present company compared to her own family.

They delighted in the remarkable places their party visited along their route northward, and they arrived at Mr. Bingley's yet-unnamed estate to find him exhibiting his usual good cheer, somewhat moderated by a high level of concern about his wife's confinement. After spending a few days with Jane, who bore her situation with far better spirits than did her husband, they pressed on to the little town of Lambton, the scene of Mrs. Gardiner's former residence. After her conversation with Wickham at Christmas, her aunt had learned that some acquaintances still remained, and they spent several days visiting.

Since the estate of Pemberley was only five miles away, Mrs. Gardiner renewed her desire to visit it as they had the other great estates, and her husband declared his willingness. But Elizabeth had no intention of accompanying them on this excursion. She worried that even staying at the inn in Lambton might be tempting fate. The thought of meeting Darcy terrified her, but she could not say as much in such an open manner, not with both her aunt and uncle being such excellent observers. So she merely said she was tired of great houses after touring so many and would prefer to stay at the inn, explore the town, and read rather than view more fine carpets and satin curtains.

Mrs. Gardiner did not press the subject since she and her husband had inferred that Elizabeth missed Jane's wedding for reasons pertaining to the owner of the estate, presumably some kind of thwarted love affair. So they left her at the inn the next morning when they boarded their carriage for the short journey.

Tuesday, August 4, 1812
Pemberley, Derbyshire

THE GARDINERS WATCHED FOR THE FIRST APPEARANCE OF PEMBERLEY woods with great anticipation since Mrs. Gardiner had heard so much of the great estate when she lived at Lambton. Both of them remarked on the fine aspect of the lodge when they made their turn, and they were even more charmed by the extent of the park and its beautiful woods.

When, at length, they found themselves at the top of a considerable eminence and caught sight of the great home on the opposite side of a valley, they both exclaimed at its handsome aspect and the natural way it seemed to blend into the woody hills and the lake and stream in front.

"That is a trout stream or I shall eat my Walton! Magnificent!" Mr. Gardiner exclaimed, for he was an ardent fisherman when he could indulge in his hobby. Fishing was not confined to the wealthier classes as hunting was, and one of his most prized books was *The Compleat Angler* by Izaak Walton.

"Though I anticipate no more problem touring the house and garden than at the other estates, I still have to doubt their hospitality will extend to an invitation to fish their waters."

"You are likely correct, wife," her husband said with a sigh.

"I am only sorry Lizzy did not wish to come. She would no doubt enjoy this aspect."

"We think we know her reasons, Mrs. Gardiner. And she certainly was not being completely forthcoming when she declined to accompany us."

"But we only *think* we know her reasons. When I know enough to hazard a more informed guess, you may be assured you will be the first to know. For now, we have heard no more than hints, and we both know how she has learned to keep her own counsel."

They soon drove to the door, and a closer examination of the house did nothing to change their original opinions of its magnificence. They were admitted into the hall while the housekeeper was summoned. They explained their desire to tour those parts of the house and grounds available to the public, and the housekeeper, who introduced herself as Mrs. Reynolds, was quick to agree.

The Gardiners were both impressed and a bit surprised by the respectable-looking, elderly woman. She was, at the same time, more civil and much less fine than they would have expected for such an elegant estate. They followed her into the dining parlor, which was a large, well-proportioned room, handsomely fitted but lacking the excessive ornateness so many of the great families seemed to find necessary in their domiciles.

As they passed on to other rooms, which were lofty and handsome, Mrs. Gardiner was entranced by the prospect she observed from every window. It seemed that, though the views of the surrounding hills, woods, and waters changed as she moved from window to window, every view was delightful to her excellent taste. Mr. Gardiner was more interested in the rooms themselves, their furnishings and configurations, and he much approved of them. Certainly, everything was suitable to the proprietor of the home but without being gaudy or uselessly fine. He thought there was more of real elegance than most other estates he had viewed.

At length, Mrs. Gardiner enquired whether the family was at home since she suspected such was the threat motivating Elizabeth's absence.

"Miss Darcy and her companion have been in residence all summer," Mrs. Reynolds replied. "It is much healthier here than in town at this time of year as you know. But Mr. Darcy and his American friend have been absent on business much of the time though they did return unexpectedly last evening."

Mrs. Gardiner merely nodded her understanding, but it was clear that Lizzy had been justified in her decision to remain at the inn to avoid seeing Mr. Darcy.

When the housekeeper took them into one of the rooms, Mrs. Gardiner called her husband over and showed him a miniature suspended among several others over the mantelpiece.

"Look, my dear, is this not a likeness of the Mr. Wickham we met at Christmas?"

"I believe it is," he said, leaning forward for a closer examination. "It looks as though it was rendered when he was perhaps nineteen or twenty, though he appeared to be in his later twenties when we met him at Longbourn"

Mrs. Reynolds joined him. "That is the picture of a young gentleman, the son of my late master's steward. My master raised him at his own expense, for he was very fond of the young man. He even paid for him at school and at Cambridge, but I am afraid the young man has turned out very wild. The last word I had of him was he has gone into the army." Her voice had a clearly disdainful air.

This is obviously not one of Mr. Wickham's admirers, Mrs. Gardiner thought, *and this information seems to conflict with Wickham's testimony about it only being the present Mr. Darcy who formed a dislike. Did he not say the housekeeper was very fond of him?*

"And that," Mrs. Reynolds said, pointing to another of the miniatures, "is my present master and is very like him. It was drawn at the same time as the other picture about eight years ago."

"I have heard much of your master's fine person," Mrs. Gardiner said, looking at the picture. "He appears very handsome, which agrees with what my niece has told me."

"And does your niece know Mr. Darcy?" Mrs. Reynolds asked in interest.

"I know they were introduced in Hertfordshire last winter though I am not sure of the extent of the acquaintance."

The mere fact of Mrs. Gardiner's niece having been introduced to her present master seemed sufficient recommendation to the housekeeper, who affirmed him a most handsome gentleman.

"In the gallery upstairs is a finer, larger picture than this. This was my late master's favorite room, and Mr. Darcy has kept these miniatures just as they used to be when his father was alive. My late master was very fond of them."

Mrs. Reynolds then directed their attention to a miniature of Darcy's sister, drawn when she was only eight years old.

"And is Miss Darcy as handsome as her brother?" Mr. Gardiner asked.

"Oh, yes!" Mrs. Reynolds said enthusiastically. "She is the handsomest young lady ever seen and is so accomplished! She plays and sings all day long! She was playing on a new instrument in the other room earlier in the day. It is a present from my master on the occasion of her upcoming birthday and was delivered just a few days ago."

"Is your master much at Pemberley during the course of the year?" Mr. Gardiner inquired

"Not so much as I could wish, sir. He is always going to town on business with his American friend, Major McDunn. He used to spend more time here, about half his time in the course of a year, but he is unfortunately too busy most times."

"If your master would marry, you might see more of him," Mrs. Gardiner said casually.

"You are indeed right, madam, but I do not know when that will be. I do not know who is good enough for him. I say no more than the truth, and everybody who knows him will say the same. I have never had a cross word from him in my life, and I have known him ever since he was four years old."

The Gardiners followed the faithful housekeeper, considering her words. This was praise, of all others most extraordinary, most opposite to what Wickham had declared, Mrs. Gardiner knew. She had assumed Mr. Darcy could not be a good-tempered man, but now she began to doubt her previous information.

"There are very few people of whom so much can be said. You are lucky in having such a master," Mr. Gardiner said.

"Yes, sir, I know I am. If I was to go through the world, I could not meet with a better. But I have always observed that they who are good-natured when children are good-natured when they grow up. And Mr. Darcy was always the sweetest-tempered, most generous-hearted boy in the world."

"His father was an excellent man," Mrs. Gardiner said for it had been common opinion when she resided at Lambton.

"Yes, ma'am, he was indeed. His son will be just like him—just as affable to the poor."

As they continued on, Mrs. Reynolds related the subject of the pictures, the dimensions of the rooms, and the price of the furniture. "I do apologize for not taking you to the lobby above where there are many pictures and several fine bedrooms you would likely find interesting. With the family in residence, however, you have seen everything open to general inspection."

She was clearly disappointed in not being able to continue her praise of the family but continued to talk as she guided them to the hall door. There she consigned them to the care of the gardener, who started to lead them across the lawn toward the river. Mr. Gardiner, however, stopped to look back, enquiring of their escort as to the date of the building, but the man had to admit his lack of knowledge. His expertise, he said, lay in growing things, not at all in bricks and mortar and wood.

The gardener now led his charges toward a beautiful walk by the side of the water, where every step they took brought forward a nobler fall of ground or a finer reach of woods. Everything seemed to fit together in a harmony that was unique in their experience. They were enjoying themselves immensely, exceedingly pleased to find the Pemberley gardens every jot as impressive as reputed and a brilliant match with the magnificence of the house itself.

The gardener next led them away from the river into the woods and along climbing paths to higher ground, which gave the eye a chance to roam among openings in the surrounding trees, affording many charming views of the valley, hills, woods, and streams. Mr. Gardiner was so enthused, he expressed a desire of going round the whole park, but his wish met the sly, triumphant smile of the gardener, who informed both husband and wife that the whole walk encompassed a full ten miles. Somewhat disappointed, they quickly settled for the accustomed circuit, which at length brought them over a bridge from which they could see the house in the distance.

This was, at last, too much for Mrs. Gardiner, who was not a great walker, and she declared her fatigue to her husband, wishing to return to their carriage as soon as may be. Mr. Gardiner declared his complete understanding, and the gardener led them toward the house.

Their progress was slowed by Mr. Gardiner's close inspection of the occasional trout in one of the many streams. He was talking to the gardener, asking the usual questions of a dedicated angler as the trio approached an archway cut through a tall hedge. They looked up suddenly when they heard the quick footsteps of a man running on the other side, and they were quite startled as a tall man suddenly burst through the opening in the hedge. Mrs. Gardiner gave a squeak of fright, and the apparition came to a sudden and precipitous stop not five feet in front of them.

"Sorry, sorry, sorry!" he said in a deep, anxious voice, clearly alarmed at having confronted them so unexpectedly. He was dressed in strange-appearing, loose clothing marked by dark areas of perspiration. His chest rose and fell with his deep breathing, but he did not appear at all distressed by his exertions.

"Please excuse me. I was just finishing my run, and I quite forgot there might be visitors touring the grounds."

He smiled broadly at the gardener. "Good day, Taylor. I hope I didn't frighten you or your charges."

"Good afternoon, Major," the gardener said, returning McDunn's nod. "It does seem you gave the lady a bit of a fright, but me? Glory be, no, sir. I am well used to our mad American by now."

The stranger grinned even more broadly and turned to Mr. and Mrs. Gardiner, who had regained their aplomb and looked at him in wonder, bemused by both his accent as well as his appearance.

"Yes, indeed, you may well look at the mad American in astonishment," he said lightly and in such a manner that both of them had to smile. "My strange attire is what I wear when I run since a gentleman's walking or riding attire would be highly uncomfortable."

"I daresay, sir," Mr. Gardiner said with a slight smile.

"Since I hail from the colonies, I am still learning the ins and outs of how people are supposed to be introduced, so I introduce myself to anybody and everybody without bothering to learn their proper status. Accordingly, my name is Edward McDunn. Darcy always introduces me as Major McDunn, giving me the courtesy of a military rank despite the fact that I'm no longer a serving officer. But I respond to either one as well as a variety of others, some of which can even be repeated in polite company."

Mr. Gardiner laughed out loud, clearly liking the forthrightness of this young stranger very much, and his wife hid her smile behind her gloved hand.

"My name is Gardiner, young American, and this is my wife. However, while I must admit you are a character quite out of the ordinary, you do not appear to be at all mad. But I do have to ask why you were running so fast and so hard since you clearly were not running from danger of any sort."

McDunn smiled at this amiable, middle-aged man who seemed much less stiff and reserved than most people he usually met either socially or as part of his business.

"I call it my daily three-mile run, Mr. Gardiner, except I have been prevented from indulging myself while Darcy and I have been in town. Business, you know."

"Darcy, Fitzwilliam, and McDunn!" Mr. Gardiner burst out unexpectedly. "I should have known it when you introduced yourself!"

"You recognize my name?" McDunn asked. "Have we met before?"

"No, sir, we have not, though I have met with your agents when I was arranging for the purchase and delivery of a large quantity of wooden rectangles for some project they would not discuss."

Mrs. Gardiner watched this amiable conversation, her initial fright ebbing away at the tall man's manner and her husband's recognition of his name. While his behavior was indeed out of the ordinary, she no longer felt any fear of him.

"Wooden rectangles," repeated McDunn carefully. "Could we walk on, Mr. Gardiner, madam? I was almost through with my run, but my muscles will cramp if I do not walk after running. Kind of like a horse."

"Certainly, sir, certainly," Mr. Gardiner said agreeably because he very much wanted to continue his discussion with this young man. His wife nodded agreement and took her husband's arm as they walked through the opening in the hedge toward the house.

McDunn continued. "You mentioned wooden rectangles, didn't you, sir?"

"I did. Your agents were quite determined that the measurements of the rectangles needed to meet certain stringent requirements, and since I received several additional orders, I surmise our product met those requirements adequately."

"They did, sir; they most definitely did," McDunn said, his face suddenly colder and grimmer. "We had a bit of trouble with other suppliers. They all seemed to think our measurements were mere suggestions, and not all the items they delivered met them. Yours were quite satisfactory, and we were pleased you were able to make additional deliveries."

"It did take almost a week to get everything set up just right before we started cutting. And then we had to soak them in that foul liquid your people provided."

"Wood tar—keeps the wood from rotting in the ground. Otherwise, we'd have to tear up the crossties and rails every four or five years and replace them. It's no way to run a business at a profit."

"I knew it must have been some important reason. But you mentioned rails, which leads me to wonder whether you needed our product for Mr. Darcy's steam locomotive."

"So you did not know what use your deliveries were being put to?"

"No, sir. Your agents would not give me a clue."

"That's because I didn't give *them* a clue, Mr. Gardiner!" McDunn said with obvious pleasure, "but I'm pleased we managed to keep the information secret. I've learned from experience that what a man doesn't know, he can't divulge. But I suppose the reason for such secrecy is mostly gone now, what with the reports in the papers."

McDunn suddenly stopped. "Look, Mr. Gardiner," he said earnestly, "I have no idea how you came to be walking these paths today, but Darcy and I were planning to call on you in town sometime soon. So meeting you today is both coincidental and fortuitous. Unfortunately, I have to bring up a sensitive subject since you are aware of our wish to keep parts of our business affairs confidential."

"And you wish to know if I can keep a secret—correct?"

"Exactly, sir. Parts of what we plan to do simply can't be bandied about in public."

"I am known as a man of my word to all my associates as well as my customers and clients," Mr. Gardiner said somberly. "You may trust my wife also. I am still waiting for the first time she has ever divulged a secret."

"I'm sorry to be so blunt."

"Think nothing of it, sir," Mr. Gardiner said with a dismissive wave of his hand. "I am not at all offended. I fully understand the need for secrets in the world of trade."

"Very well," McDunn said, nodding and holding out his hand. "Let's shake on it."

As her husband took the proffered hand, McDunn turned to Mrs. Gardiner with a crooked smile. "It's one of the reasons Darcy calls me his mad

American, Mrs. Gardiner. He thinks all Americans are wild to shake hands with everyone they meet. But I assure you I'm harmless."

"So it seems, sir," Mrs. Gardiner said, "though you do give some credence to what Mr. Darcy calls you."

McDunn laughed again and turned to resume walking. "You two make a comfortable pair, indeed you do. So, yes, you are correct. Your wood rectangles, which we call crossties, will be used in laying the rails for a steam railway—actually, steam railways, *plural*. You've probably read of our successful demonstration at the Wylam colliery, pulling heavy loads of coal with our locomotive."

Mr. Gardiner nodded, and McDunn continued. "One of the reasons we're so particular with our crossties is to keep the weight and the power of our locomotive from damaging the railway."

Mr. Gardiner was impressed by the easy command and confidence of this young man in speaking of the steam locomotive, which was being hailed as another triumph of the wealthy Fitzwilliam Darcy. He had been a bit doubtful such a wealthy gentleman as Mr. Darcy could have been solely responsible for the steam locomotive so glowingly described in *The Times*. His doubts were now at least partially confirmed. This young man had to have been equally or perhaps even more responsible, though his name had not even been mentioned in the newspapers.

They were now approaching the house, and McDunn saw Mrs. Gardiner leaning heavily on the arm of her husband. He pointed to one of the many benches scattered along the paths and urged her to rest.

"Thank you, sir," she said gratefully, sitting down with a sigh of relief. "I earlier asked Mr. Gardiner if we might seek our carriage soon. It appears I am not as suited for walking as I was in my youth."

"I can see that exploring Pemberley has taken its toll on you, Mrs. Gardiner. It's beautiful, but it's a stern objective to see as much as you'd like. However, when you feel up to it, could I talk you into returning to the house instead of going directly to your carriage? I would like to introduce both of you to Darcy, and then we might have a few words with your husband. I'll ask Miss Darcy to entertain you while we talk. She is a most excellent performer, as well as being every bit as sweet as I'm sure Mrs. Reynolds described her."

"Oh, that would be very pleasant. Mrs. Reynolds did praise her talents greatly."

"Excellent, excellent," McDunn said, smiling as he continued to walk back and forth. "Please excuse my walking."

"Yes, cramps, you said. Not at all," Mr. Gardiner said with a smile.

Darcy rose when he saw McDunn enter the room where Georgiana was playing her birthday present since a couple in their middle years accompanied him. He quickly appraised the visitors as being people of fashion though probably not wealthy enough to be true members of the gentry. The gentleman had a sensible, well-dressed appearance, and the lady, obviously his wife, looked to be a suitable match with the stamp of intelligence in her features.

"Ah, Darcy, Miss Darcy," McDunn said. "May I present Mr. and Mrs. Gardiner? They took a tour of the house and were being escorted through the gardens when I almost ran them down."

Georgiana gave a sudden giggle, and when everyone looked at her, she said, "He does that, you know. He seems almost to go into a trance when he runs. Quite odd, you know, these Americans!"

"So we were informed," Mr. Gardiner said.

"The reason I wanted you to meet them," McDunn said, "is that Mr. Gardiner put two and two together when he heard my name and associated it with yours, Darcy. It turns out he was responsible for delivering those crossties for our Wylam test."

"Ah!" Darcy said as he looked at Mr. Gardiner attentively. "That was a frustrating business, trying to get what we wanted. The artisans who work in metal are used to proper dimensions, but people who work in wood do not seem to be as far up what Major McDunn calls 'the learning curve.' My congratulations on doing the job correctly, Mr. Gardiner."

"You know, McDunn, before I met you, my life was so easy," Darcy said to McDunn with an expression Mrs. Gardiner could not really interpret. "I could go riding and shooting whenever I pleased, I could take the time to listen to Georgiana play, or perhaps I could spend the odd evening at my club. Now, everything is complicated, and I am so involved with the intricacies of our business, I hardly have time to listen to my sister."

McDunn nodded, and the smile the two men shared informed Mrs. Gardiner that Mr. Darcy had been teasing his friend. "You'll be glad to know this fortuitous meeting with Mr. Gardiner might save us a trip to town. My thought is to make it worth their while to stay on while we discuss a bit of business. We could offer them a little dinner either before or after we talk."

That startled Mr. Gardiner. "Pray, excuse me. I am afraid I have not the pleasure of understanding you."

"It's like this, sir," McDunn said. "You know our locomotive is head and shoulders above anything our competition has. And it won't surprise you to learn we plan to build more locomotives to haul coal and other freight. Eventually, we want to haul passengers, but we need rail lines built to do it, and we want them built to the same gauge—the width of the rails—as our locomotives. So we're negotiating for deliveries of iron rails in quantity."

Darcy looked directly at Mr. Gardiner. "We will also need crossties, Mr. Gardiner—crossties such as the ones you provided but in much larger numbers and delivered to the schedules we are planning. Might such a proposition interest you?"

At Mr. Gardiner's somewhat stunned nod, McDunn said, "Excellent! Then, perhaps you might come down to Darcy's study with us where we can discuss this in detail."

"Georgiana, will you inform the housekeeper that we will have two guests for dinner?" Darcy asked. "And do you think you and Mrs. Sturdivant might entertain Mrs. Gardiner while we talk?"

"Certainly, William," she said, sitting down at the pianoforte bench. Then she smiled sweetly at McDunn and said, "You see, Major? William calls me Georgiana, just as Richard does. I do wish you would stop calling me Miss Darcy. It makes me feel as though we have just been introduced instead of working side by side for so many months."

She spoke as though vexed, but she could not completely hide her smile from McDunn, who winked at her.

"I keep telling you I'm your protector, not your brother. So you'll remain Miss Darcy, just like the genteel and fashionable young lady you are."

Both the Gardiners were more than a little surprised at this exchange, especially when Georgiana stuck her tongue out at McDunn. But both her brother and the American just laughed.

"She thinks she can get away with anything because she helps me so much with our work," McDunn said cheerfully to the Gardiners. "Darcy's let me freeload on his hospitality for almost three years, and I've adopted Miss Darcy as my sister in place of my own. So she has two—no, it's three—brothers to tell her what to do. She's only sixteen at the moment, so she'll just have to put up with us for a few more years until we can get her safely married."

His comment drew a snort from Darcy, but his sister said quickly, "It is you for whom we must find a wife, sir! And my brother! Why, you are six and twenty, are you not? And my brother is two years older! You will both soon be...uh...what is the word for a gentleman spinster, Mrs. Gardiner?"

Both Gardiners laughed, and Mrs. Gardiner said, smiling ruefully, "I am afraid there is no such word, Miss Darcy. It is decidedly unfair that the gentler sex has to be burdened with such epithets, but there it is."

On that note, the gentlemen departed and left the room to the ladies.

IT WAS MORE THAN AN HOUR BEFORE THE GENTLEMEN'S BUSINESS WAS concluded and they sought the ladies, who were touring the gallery of pictures in the upstairs lobby. Mrs. Reynolds appeared to have taken charge, and she was explaining each picture to Mrs. Gardiner while she instructed Georgiana on the same subject, saying it was a necessary part of her education.

"It appears your discussions were successful, judging by your amiability," Mrs. Gardiner said as the three gentlemen joined the group.

"Quite successful," McDunn said. "Resolving this question is a big load off our shoulders."

"I will send our solicitor, Stevenson, an express to have him draw up our contract," Darcy said to Mr. Gardiner. "He will be contacting you—"

"That is enough business for the day, William," Georgiana said, interrupting him. "It is almost time for dinner."

Darcy nodded and Georgiana went on. "And you will never guess what I learned, William! Do you remember the young lady I met at Netherfield when Mr. Bingley's wife was so sick? Mr. and Mrs. Gardiner are her uncle and aunt! What do you think of that?"

"Ah, Lizzy and Jane," Mr. Gardiner said with a nod. "My sister is their mother. Lizzy has been touring with us, but she has seen quite enough large estates, so she remained at the inn with the intention of exploring the town and doing some reading."

Darcy was glad no response was required to his sister's information since he would have been quite unable to say anything. His voice seemed frozen with shock.

Elizabeth Bennet! he thought. *Here I have been sitting in the dark at night, trying to determine what I should do about this most disturbing young lady, and now she is but five miles away! I simply do not know what to do! Yet, I am convinced now I must do something!*

Then another thought entered his mind. *And she remained true to what she said at Netherfield. That we should not meet again. Ever. Why does the thought distress me so much now when it once seemed so sensible? Do I really want to meet her again? What would I have done if she had accompanied her aunt and uncle?*

This man—this gentleman—is the brother of her mother, Mrs. Bennet? It seems unbelievable, yet he admits it openly and easily. How can he be so sensible and well mannered, when his sister is so foolish and vulgar?

How did Elizabeth Bennet become so appealing in her manners, despite having such a mother? And her elder sister is the same! Every time I see Jane and Bingley together, so happy and contented, I am inestimably relieved I did not yield to the blandishments of Caroline Bingley and her sister to separate the two of them. I know I could have accomplished it since Bingley trusts my opinion, but had I done so, I would now greatly regret it. It would have been wrong and dishonorable.

Darcy made himself put these distressing thoughts aside and attend to his guests. But he knew he was going to have to resolve the turmoil inside him whenever he thought of the disturbing evening at Netherfield and Elizabeth Bennet's voice, dull and lifeless, *"Nothing will ever change. There is no hope whatever."*

"A MOST INTERESTING DAY," MR. GARDINER SAID TO HIS WIFE AFTER DIN-ner as their carriage started back to Lambton, and they took their leave of Pemberley. "In fact, 'startling' or 'astonishing' would probably be better words to describe it."

"By your comment, I assume the private conversations you had with Mr. Darcy and Major McDunn were rewarding?"

"Very much so. But no endeavor this important is going to be easy, and my whole business will have to change dramatically. I am going to have to sell my warehouse so I can concentrate solely on the Darcy, Fitzwilliam, and McDunn enterprise. The major said I would be a sole and trusted supplier, and it should be lucrative—very lucrative, assuming their railway business is as successful as their telegraph. As I say, it will be a big adjustment."

"I am sure you will be up to the task, my dear. I very much enjoyed my time listening to Miss Darcy play and talking with her companion. Miss Darcy was quite excited when she learned Lizzy is our niece, and she asked if it would be impertinent for her to write to her since she is only sixteen. I said our niece is only four years older than she is, so it would be quite appropriate."

Mr. Gardiner looked at his wife with a huge smile. "I had another surprise, dear. I happened to see Mr. Walton's book on Mr. Darcy's bookshelf, and it appears he is also a fisherman though he has little time to indulge in the sport these days. So he invited me back for a day of fishing tomorrow! And he suggested you might bring Lizzy to spend the day with his sister. He was absolutely astonished to find that she was our niece, you know. I have to wonder whether part of his amazement was not due to finding out Fanny is one of my two elder sisters. Clearly, he was acquainted with her though he made no mention of Jeanette. He likely did not meet her."

"And I wonder what Elizabeth will say when she learns what has happened today?" Mrs. Gardiner said seriously. "I will hazard a guess she will decline the invitation. I am more certain than ever that there is some kind of past acquaintance between her and Mr. Darcy, likely a romantic one, but I still have no idea of the details."

"I believe you make a valid point. Oh, Lizzy! She is so very secretive, is she not?"

"I am afraid that keeping her counsel is a requirement for her, given her family," his wife said sadly.

"A most interesting day," McDunn said, standing at the window in Darcy's study after watching the Gardiner's carriage depart.

"Very," Darcy said in agreement, but his thoughts hardly touched on his recent guests, being almost completely obsessed by thoughts of their niece. Learning this gentlemanly man was brother to Mrs. Bennet had been and still was difficult to believe. Two people could not be more different, but there it was.

But even this thought was nothing compared to those of their niece. What was he to do? He simply could not allow this distraction to continue, especially since he was now certain he would never be able to push thoughts of Elizabeth from his mind unless he did something to settle the doubts and unanswered questions that plagued his sleep with ever-increasing frequency. Impulsively, he suggested to Mr. Gardiner that he might bring Elizabeth the next day, but with more time to think on it, he felt certain she would devise some reason to decline. Of course, he might ride to Lambton and seek her out, but he instantly dismissed the possibility.

For all he knew, Elizabeth Bennet had stayed behind at the inn because the bitterness she had shown at Netherfield had changed into something quite malignant. She might hate him passionately for having caused her such grief, even if he had done so inadvertently. Emotions as strong as those she had shown were not at all predictable and likely to change. A meeting could not be chanced, not after having come to a business agreement with her uncle.

It now seemed incredible that he had once considered the events at Netherfield with satisfaction, thinking the best choices had been voiced and agreed on and he could get on with his life. Now, Elizabeth Bennet and her lively, playful manner plagued his dreams, and he increasingly remembered his bewitchment, which he thought he had put aside.

I cannot let her statement stand—that we should not meet again, he thought with sudden decision. *I will never have any ease if I do not determine why and how she is affecting me so. My distress cannot be the love she said she held for me. Nor is it the passion she also expressed. But one thing I do know: I have to resolve this. I have to!*

Suddenly, with the determination made, he could think on how to accomplish his resolution. He knew he could not simply ride to Lambton and ask to see her. But he also could not simply ride to Hertfordshire and knock on the door, declaring he wished to see and speak with Miss Elizabeth Bennet! No, it would never do! It was quite impossible!

Or is it? he thought suddenly as an idea came to mind.

I shall have to talk to Bingley.

Chapter 23

//

*To be ignorant of what occurred before you were born is to remain
always a child. For what is the worth of human life, unless it is woven
into the life of our ancestors by the records of history?*

— Marcus Tullius Cicero, Roman statesman and orator

\\

August–September, 1812
Hertfordshire

The maelstrom about to sweep through Longbourn began innocuously enough with the return of the Gardiners and Elizabeth from their tour of the north. The Gardiners had much to say about what they had seen during their excursion, not the least of which was the gracious hospitality displayed by Mr. Darcy when they visited his estate at Pemberley.

Mr. Gardiner mentioned none of his business discussions with Darcy and McDunn because of the need for confidentiality, instead preferring to speak of the joys of an entire day spent fishing with Mr. Darcy. And Mrs. Gardiner spoke more of the delights of hearing Miss Darcy perform than of any of their surmises regarding their niece and the owner of the estate, only mentioning Elizabeth's absence from the visit as being due to feeling somewhat ill.

Elizabeth said little, and she absolutely would not answer her mother's indignant demands as to why she had twice refused to visit Pemberley and see Mr. Darcy. In fact, Mrs. Bennet's vituperative questioning of her daughter brought Mr. Bennet from his library where he flatly ordered his wife to desist from plaguing her daughter and to attend to her brother and sister. And when he told Elizabeth gently that she might leave the room, she gave him a quick kiss on his forehead in gratitude for his understanding.

However, Mrs. Bennet had managed to gain enough information from her visitors before they left to enable her to return to her favorite avocation: finding a husband for her eldest unmarried daughter. She cherished the news she had gained and waited only for her husband's newfound temper to sink into its natural lassitude, whereupon she would resume her quest.

However, when her mother attempted to engage her a few days later on the subject, Elizabeth was completely unwilling to tolerate such vain and useless reprises of what she considered a closed subject and usually departed on a ramble or retired to her room.

It took a week for these abrasive interactions with her mother to begin to abate, only to be re-kindled when Mrs. Bennet received a letter from Jane on August 22. It contained the information that Jane and her husband had received a visit from Mr. Darcy, who asked if Mr. Bingley's lease on Netherfield was still in force. When Mr. Bingley answered in the affirmative, Mr. Darcy expressed an interest in residing at the house for a month or two until the hot weather subsided so he could more easily visit London without having to stay there.

The predictable result was that Elizabeth returned from a walk to have her mother meet her in the entry. She was highly excited and waving a letter in the air.

"You see, Lizzy!" Mrs. Bennet exclaimed happily, handing the letter to her daughter. "Jane has written to say Mr. Darcy is coming down from the north to live at Netherfield! This is what I have been waiting for, my dear child! It is perfectly clear he will soon be calling on you!"

"Mama," Elizabeth said, trying to reduce her mother's usual frenetic display whenever the topic turned to her favorite subject, "this letter says Mr. Darcy asked if the house might be prepared so he could more easily travel to town on business. It is already late August, and it will require a month, I am sure, to get Netherfield staffed and prepared. It will be cool in town by then."

"Lizzy, you must allow yourself to be guided by me in this matter," Mrs. Bennet said, warming to her subject. "The first thing we must do is to buy you new clothes. You have grown far too thin, and your dresses do not flatter your figure. And you must eat better and stop starving yourself if you want to secure Mr. Darcy!"

"I am not starving myself, Mama!" Elizabeth said in protest. "I weigh more now than I did last winter! And I have not the slightest intention of trying to secure Mr. Darcy! He is not interested in a young lady with no fortune and no connections!"

Since Mrs. Bennet would not acquiesce, Elizabeth threw up her hands and left the room.

Events leading up to the crest of the tempest now began to quicken apace since it was only a fortnight later that Mrs. Lucas informed Mrs. Bennet of Netherfield Park being opened in preparation for the arrival of Mr. Darcy and his sister. Mrs. Bennet was overjoyed by the news, but she had learned to avoid the subject with Elizabeth. Instead, on the eighth of the month, she expressed her excitement in a long letter to Mary in which she allowed her imagination even more freedom than she had with Elizabeth. As often happened, Mrs. Bennet was not prompt in posting the letter for several days.

As a result, Mary read the news from her mother barely a week later, outlining her mother's dearest wishes of a resolution to this long-delayed attachment soon being realized. She lost little time in informing her husband, who then hastened to Rosings to inform his patroness.

Mr. Collins ought to have given more thought to the usual reaction of Lady Catherine to news she did not wish to hear because, when he breathlessly informed her of the probable connection between her nephew and his cousin, her reactions were not at all as he expected. Instead of praise at keeping his patroness informed, he was rebuked. Her ladyship was not at all pleased that her objective of matching Darcy with her daughter might not be realized. Mr. Collins could only stand trembling, head bowed in abject submission, as this formidable old woman stalked through the room, gesticulating and screaming her ire, much of which seemed to be directed at him.

The culmination came when she summoned her butler and ordered him to have her large coach prepared.

"I wish to be on my way early in the morning!" she thundered before departing the room and leaving a much shaken William Collins, Esq. trembling in her wake.

Tuesday, September 15, 1812
Netherfield, Hertfordshire

"I AM SORRY, YOUR LADYSHIP," SAID MRS. ALBERTSON, THE NEWLY ENGAGED Netherfield housekeeper, "but your nephew is not here."

"Well, where is he?" demanded Lady Catherine de Bourgh.

"I do not know. He has not yet arrived from town though we expect him either today or tomorrow."

"I was told at his house in town that he had departed for Netherfield earlier in the day. It is not far. He should be here."

"But he is not, my lady." Mrs. Albertson's temper was growing frayed since this question had been asked and answered several times already. Even if this lady *was* the sister of an earl, she was a most rude and impolite visitor. It was difficult to keep her temper under control when confronted with such incivility.

This time, however, instead of engaging in yet another fruitless demand, Lady Catherine paused. Finally, she said, "Where is the estate of this Bennet family? It is nearby, is it not?"

"It is about three miles away in the direction of Meryton. The estate is called Longbourn and is about a mile past Meryton on the road."

Without so much as a "thank you," the old lady turned on her heel and left through the open door.

As she closed it behind this unwelcome visitor, Mrs. Albertson whispered a prayer under her breath that the old lady's immense coach might slide off the road into the ditch before getting to Longbourn. She was well acquainted with the Bennet family and considered most of them quite foolish. But not even foolish people deserved having such a woman inflicted on them.

Tuesday, September 15, 1812
Longbourn, Hertfordshire

MRS. BENNET SAT ALONE IN HER FRONT PARLOR, TRYING WITHOUT MUCH success to sew a new ribbon on an old bonnet and lamenting the absence of Jane these past two months. If Jane had remained at Netherfield, it would be more pleasant to visit her rather than attempting her present task. She had broached to her husband the subject of traveling to Derbyshire to be with Jane when the baby came, but Mr. Bennet had flatly refused to consider such a trip with winter coming on.

She also lamented the absence of Mary, who could always be engaged to perform such tasks for her, but she was also gone with her husband. Lydia or Kitty could not be prevailed upon to assist her since their skills were inferior to her own. And she supposed Elizabeth was gone on one of her long walks.

She is likely sulking after I tried to impart some sense to her yesterday, Mrs. Bennet thought. *Everything looked so favorable in November!*

The first indication Mrs. Bennet received of boredom ending at Longbourn came when she heard the front door open and close and saw Elizabeth sweep past the door to the parlor.

But it was the sound of horses and a carriage arriving in front of the house that made her immediately spring to the window in time to see a magnificent team of horses pull to a halt in a spray of gravel. They stood, streaming sweat and blowing white clouds of vapor in the coolness of the early autumn afternoon, while two footmen sprang to the ground to open the door to the coach and place a step in front of the door.

Just then, both Lydia and Kitty burst into the room with their usual lack of propriety.

"Mama, Mama, the largest, most magnificent carriage just arrived!" Kitty cried.

"It is a coach-and-four," Lydia said authoritatively. "It is too large to be a simple carriage. There are two footmen riding at the back, and there are four huge horses pulling it!"

Any further discussion was brought to an end by a loud, peremptory knock at the front door, and Hill shortly bustled into the room, an expression of unusual anxiety on her face.

"Lady Catherine de Bourgh, madam," she said, barely getting the words out before a tall, large woman with strongly marked features brushed past her into the room.

After Hill closed the door and left the room, the new arrival turned to survey the three Longbourn ladies with an air marked by overweening superiority without even a hint of conciliation. She was completely unknown to any of them, but her brusque and rude entry clearly demonstrated her disinclination to allow any of them to forget the inferiority of their rank.

Neither Mrs. Bennet nor her daughters could manage a word in the alarming presence of this fearsome woman.

"You are, I assume, Mrs. Bennet, mistress of this house? And these are your daughters, I suppose. Which of you is Miss Bennet? Miss Elizabeth Bennet?"

Mrs. Bennet was so intimidated she could only speak stumblingly. "These...these are my two younger daughters, Lydia and—"

"Then where is Miss Bennet?" Lady Catherine said, harshly interrupting her.

"She...she is above stairs, your ladyship. In her room, I believe."

"Then summon her immediately."

The old woman's tone was such that the already overwhelmed Mrs. Bennet could not even take umbrage at being ordered about in her own home. She meekly rang for Hill and asked her to have Elizabeth come down at once.

Lady Catherine had no interest in further conversation and turned away. She was so dismissive of Mrs. Bennet and her daughters that she did not even demand their withdrawal. Mrs. Bennet was so unsettled, she would have gladly done so, but she was incapable of any action not commanded by this formidable woman. Her two daughters, Lydia especially, did not seem at all in awe of this highborn lady. Instead, they wanted nothing so much as to witness what promised to be an exciting event and thus they sat down in chairs against the wall, trying not to be noticed.

WHEN ELIZABETH ENTERED THE PARLOR, HAVING COME DOWNSTAIRS ONLY because Hill had said a visitor had arrived who wished to see her, she found an unfamiliar woman standing at the window, looking out at the afternoon sun. She found it strange that her mother and sisters were seated, huddled together against the wall.

The woman immediately turned to Elizabeth and said with the utmost self-importance and lack of civility, "I am Lady Catherine de Bourgh. And you are, presumably, Miss Elizabeth Bennet."

Elizabeth was quite shocked at this arrogant and unseemly introduction. However, if this stranger hoped to intimidate her, she was not inclined to cooperate, so she only nodded and coldly so.

"I am the patroness—"

"I am well aware who you are," Elizabeth said, interrupting this rude visitor with equal incivility. "You are the patroness of Mr. Collins, who is married to my sister."

"I am not used to being interrupted, Miss Bennet!"

"Your attitude will make your situation rather pitiable, I am afraid, since

I am not at all disposed to meet rudeness with subservient politeness. Please state your business if you have any."

Elizabeth ignored her mother's gasp at her effrontery and kept her eyes fixed on this strange and uninvited intruder.

"Hear me in silence, Miss Bennet! I came here with the determined resolution of carrying my purpose, and I will not be dissuaded from it!"

Elizabeth said nothing to this, merely standing firm before this woman who towered over her. She wondered why she had come to Longbourn if only to behave in such an unseemly manner.

Lady Catherine, after glaring at her for a few moments, said in an angry tone, "I warn you frankly that I am not a person to be trifled with, Miss Bennet. A report of the most alarming nature reached me just two days ago, informing me that my nephew, Mr. Darcy, was intending to come to Hertfordshire and present you with the opportunity of a most advantageous marriage."

Despite her resolve, Elizabeth was stunned by this assertion, as was her mother, judging by her suppressed gasp. Never in her wildest dreams had Elizabeth expected such an openly expressed statement from someone outside her family, but hearing the words spoken aloud was so surprising, even shocking, she could not conceal her disbelief.

"Do not attempt to deceive me and protest you have never heard such a rumor, Miss Bennet!" Lady Catherine said angrily, incorrectly interpreting Elizabeth's expression. "You will not mislead or delay me on such a matter! I am known by all for my frankness, and I shall certainly not depart from it in a matter such as this! You cannot claim you are unaware that the nearby estate owned by Mr. Bingley is being prepared for my nephew's arrival."

Elizabeth only shook her head. "I have heard Mr. Darcy might stay at Netherfield to be closer to his business, but I certainly have no reason to believe he may have any intentions toward me. I have not laid eyes on him since last November."

Elizabeth spoke these words with icy formality and a deliberate omission of the woman's rank. She stated the truth as she knew it to be, despite the many unrealistic statements made by her mother. She had been so immersed in her attempts to heal the anguish in her heart that she had taken little time to hear of any news of the neighborhood, even from Charlotte.

"Such insincerity will not impede me from attaining my intention, Miss

Bennet!" declared Lady Catherine angrily. "I was informed of all this by your own sister's husband. Even though I knew what he told me had to be a scandalous falsehood, I lost no time in coming to call."

"If you knew that Mr. Collins's information was untrue, why would you waste your time coming to Hertfordshire? You must know, after all, that you have never been introduced to anyone in my family other than my middle sister. Coming to call at Longbourn in such a manner as this would tend to lend credence to what you declared a scandalous falsehood."

"I came to demand that you own to having industriously circulated this offensive rumor, Miss Bennet!" Lady Catherine cried shrilly. "Mr. Collins informed me that this gossip is known and accepted throughout the neighborhood!"

To this, Elizabeth only gave a careless shrug. She was becoming more and more irritated by this useless argument as well as by this overbearing and offensive woman.

I did not dispute Mr. Darcy when he referred to the social inferiority of my family, she thought irritably, *because he did little other than speak the truth. But he cannot take any pride in such a close relation as his aunt thrusting herself upon my family in such an arrogant and improper manner. Haughty old woman!*

"This is not to be borne, Miss Bennet! I insist you openly admit to having spread these untruths!"

"I shall make no such admission! I have heard no such news as you charge, and I certainly had no part in spreading it about the neighborhood! And I must tell you I am not at all disposed to continue an offensive conversation such as this with a person so wholly unrelated to me and my family!"

"Do you know who I am, Miss Bennet? I am almost the nearest relation my nephew has in the world! I am entitled to know all his dearest concerns!"

"But you are not entitled to know mine! And behavior such as you have displayed today shall never incline me to be explicit on *any* matter, much less one that appears to exist solely within your deluded mind!"

"I have not been accustomed to such language as this from anyone, much less a person who has the presumption to aspire to a connection so wholly beyond her station in life! Unfeeling, selfish girl!"

The sheer effrontery of having such a haughtily disdainful person make a statement so condescending and disparaging drove Elizabeth into a blind fury.

"I am not to be intimidated into any such unreasonable admission as you demand. However farfetched and ludicrous your assertions may be, I will only say this: I should not be quitting my sphere if I were to marry your nephew. He is a gentleman, and I am a gentleman's daughter. Our stations, in fact, are equal."

"You may be a gentleman's daughter, but who are your relations—your aunts and your uncles? I am all too aware of their condition in life: one uncle a lowly solicitor in a country town, and the other in trade in Cheapside! Besides, Mr. Darcy is engaged to my daughter. They have been intended for each other since their infancy."

"Then why have you made such a useless journey? If your daughter's engagement to Mr. Darcy were secure, then why would he make an offer to me? I suspect, your ladyship, that your professed confidence is a sham and Mr. Darcy has no intention at all of marrying your daughter."

"Impertinent, avaricious girl!" cried Lady Catherine. "You are only in pursuit of my nephew's fortune! An adventuress, a parasite! You care not that you will ruin him in the opinion of all his friends!"

Elizabeth smiled grimly at the success of her barb, and she was not even stung by Lady Catherine's insults. "If I were pursuing your nephew's fortune, then I think I would have found a way to put myself in his presence sometime in the last ten months. As a fortune hunter, it would appear I am a particularly inept one."

"That is what *you* say, but is it the truth? I suspect not! I believe you have been in secret communication with my nephew and have engaged your arts and allurements to draw him in and make him forget his duty to himself and to all his family! You have seduced and infatuated him so he comes to this unknown and insignificant corner of England in pursuit of you!"

Elizabeth laughed bitterly at this absurd statement. It was she who was entranced, but not by the wiles of her nephew. Darcy neither suspected nor imagined it. She did not have the option of pursuing Darcy and could only clutch her secret desires to her heart, crying herself to sleep at night.

"Miss Bennet, I insist on being satisfied! I will not be dissuaded from it! I will have your promise that you will cease your maneuverings and, above all, will not accept any offers of marriage from him. Will you give me your promise?"

"As I have said before, such an event will simply never happen. You demand I make promises to you when you insult my family and me and refuse to listen. Hear me now, then! Though you babble nonsense, I will make no promises of any kind to you. If your nephew calls tomorrow, ridiculous as it may be, and makes me an offer of himself and all his worldly goods, I will make my decision solely on the basis of what would constitute my own happiness. My decision would have nothing to do with *you* or any other person so wholly unconnected to me. I owe you nothing."

"And this is your answer? But I will not relent, Miss Bennet. I am not used to being thwarted in my intentions, and I shall not be disappointed in this case."

"You will simply have to become accustomed to disappointment. I am completely unmoved by your distress. It will have no effect on me. Now, I must demand you importune me no further on this subject and leave me in peace."

"Not so hasty, if you please, Miss Bennet. I am by no means finished! Is such a girl as you to be the mistress of Pemberley? Heaven and earth, of what are you thinking? Is the noble estate of my sister to be so polluted?"

"You can now have nothing further to say to me. You have insulted my family and me by every possible method! It is past time you leave this house!"

"You have no regard, then, for the honor and credit of my nephew, you heartless temptress? Do you not consider that a connection with you must disgrace him in the eyes of his peers?"

Elizabeth stood and glanced heatedly at her mother, who had witnessed the entirety of this attack without comment. "You know my sentiments. If my mother will not force you to leave our house, then I will do so."

Lady Catherine opened her mouth to continue her harangue, but Elizabeth stopped her with a raised palm.

"No! I will hear nothing further from you! The arguments you have made in support of your extraordinary and fanciful application have been as frivolous as they were ill judged. My character is such that I could never be worked on by such persuasions as these. I make no farewells to you, Lady Catherine. You deserve none."

Without another word, Elizabeth left the room and then the house, punctuated by the harsh slamming of the front door.

Lady Catherine stared at the empty doorway in frustrated anger at having achieved none of what she had planned. Mrs. Bennet stared also, hardly able to comprehend what she had just witnessed.

As for Lydia and Kitty, they stared at each other in delighted excitement. They could not wait until they were able to inform one and all of what they had seen and heard!

It was more than an hour and a half before Elizabeth had walked off her rage and thought of returning to Longbourn. She had been so driven by her anger when she slammed the door behind her that her only thought had been to get far away from the house and that infuriating old woman.

Only now did she comprehend how near the sun was to the horizon. To her alarm, she also realized an autumnal rainstorm had formed and was near to sweeping over her. The rain clouds were no more than a few miles away, and she hurriedly turned about and began walking homeward as fast as she could manage.

What a perfect end to a perfectly terrible day! she thought. *I will surely get soaked through before I get back to the house. I want nothing more than to have Sarah heat enough water for a hot bath before bedtime.*

Darcy's original intention had been to go directly to Netherfield so he could get a good night's sleep before calling at Longbourn the following day. But he and McDunn had decided to make a quick check of progress on their new locomotive, which took longer than expected. When the two men got started toward their initial destination, Darcy could not rid himself of the nagging feeling that going to Netherfield first had been influenced more by his anxiety about seeing Elizabeth and what he might say to her than by other arguments. The more he thought on it, the more convinced he became that he was coming down with a severe case of nerves.

Finally, he decided he would not be guided by his doubts. He would stop at Longbourn for at least a brief visit before going on to Netherfield even though the light drizzle had now turned into a steady, cold rain.

McDunn said nothing, only nodding in response to Darcy's change of plans, but Darcy thought something lurked behind his guarded expression. He made no effort to guess what it might be since interpreting his American friend's face was nigh impossible when he wished to keep his thoughts concealed.

The first indication of anything untoward came when the elderly housekeeper opened the front door at Longbourn. Before Darcy could even ask to see Elizabeth, the loud voices and the number of people in the hallway indicated considerable turmoil.

"I was going to ask for Miss Bennet," he said, looking over her shoulder at Mrs. Bennet waving her hands about while her husband attempted to quiet the crowd of family and servants. "But it appears something is amiss here."

"It is Miss Lizzy," the housekeeper said, wiping a tear from her eye. "She ran out of the house in the afternoon and has not returned though it is raining hard. Everyone is quite worried."

She gave way immediately as Darcy strode into the house, followed by McDunn. After joining the crowd about Mr. and Mrs. Bennet and trying to decipher what had occurred, Darcy gave up and cried loudly, "What is going on here?"

It took two further repetitions, each one louder than before, plus McDunn's booming command to "SHUT UP!" before anything approaching quiet replaced the chaos.

"Now, what is going on here?" Darcy repeated, and everyone gawked at him, wondering what these two tall men in rain-slick oilskin coats were doing at Longbourn. Finally, Mrs. Bennet recognized Darcy and immediately fled to him, pulling urgently at the sleeve of his wet coat.

"It is Lizzy, Mr. Darcy!" she cried plaintively. "She is somewhere out in the rain and has not returned to the house! I am certain she is going to die if we do not find her!"

Darcy looked at Mr. Bennet, who nodded without elaborating on his wife's information.

"And there is little time to find her," McDunn said, looking out a window at the rain-darkened sky barely illuminated by the setting sun. "The rain is ice-cold. Was she dressed for ill weather?"

Mrs. Bennet only shook her head and dropped her face into her hands while her shoulders shook from her sobs.

"Have you organized a search, Mr. Bennet?" Darcy said, having instinctively taken command of a situation marked by confusion and lack of leadership.

"I was trying to," Mr. Bennet said, licking his lips uncomfortably. "But we do not even know in which direction Lizzie walked."

"Where might she usually go? How many directions need to be searched?"

"She might have gone to Meryton," said the youngest of the Bennet sisters, whom Darcy remembered as Lydia. "She could have gone to stay with our Aunt Phillips."

"She was very upset by Lady Catherine's visit," the other sister said.

At Darcy's raised eyebrows, Lydia said in explanation, "Lady Catherine de Bourgh."

"What! My aunt was here? What was she doing here?"

Both sisters looked extremely sheepish and said nothing further though they did look at their mother, who was still sobbing helplessly.

"That is a question I would like answered, sir," Mr. Bennet said angrily. "Lizzy seems to have been made extremely upset by this inexplicable visit from Lady Catherine, and I want to know why."

Darcy had to repress the surge of anger he felt at this father who refused to command his own family, but his voice, while cold, was otherwise expressionless. "I will deal with my aunt after we find your daughter, sir. This is not the time for that discussion. Now, where else might she have gone?"

"Lucas Lodge," Lydia said. "It is very close."

"Oakham Mount," offered her sister. "Lizzy always liked the view from Oakham Mount."

"I know where it is," Darcy said with a nod. "It is farther away, and my mount is still relatively fresh. I will search in that direction."

"I know the way to Meryton and even have an idea where the Philips house is," McDunn said. "I'll go there and bang on some doors to find it. And Netherfield is only a couple of miles past Meryton. If I do not find her at her aunt's house, I'll check it out, though I have no idea why she might have gone there."

"Nor do I, but we must look everywhere we can think of."

Turning back to Mr. Bennet, Darcy said, "I would suggest you send a servant on horseback to Lucas Lodge. Could she have gone in any other direction? There are numerous branches in the road."

"I cannot think where she might have gone," Mrs. Bennet said through her tears. "I am so very worried."

"After I check Meryton and Netherfield," McDunn said, "I'll return here in case anyone has any further ideas." Turning to Mr. Bennet, he said, "Do you have any lanterns that will work in this rain? Sturdy ones that won't start leaking?"

"I…I am not sure. I think we may, but they would be in the stables."

"Then, Mr. Bennet, I suggest you send any servants who can ride to investigate other branches of the road," Darcy said. "As for me, I think it best that you roll up four or five blankets and wrap them in an oilcloth against the rain. If I do find Miss Bennet on the road, she will be soaked. I just hope she has not tried to take shelter in a thicket or copse of trees. With the growing darkness, I could easily miss her."

"And send to your stables for lanterns," McDunn said.

When no one started moving immediately, McDunn barked at the gathered servants and family in a voice trained by the harsh demands of discipline and combat. "Move it, people! A young lady may be freezing to death while all of you dawdle about!"

All concerned were instantly roused into action, and Darcy looked at Mr. Bennet. "Have those blankets brought to me immediately, sir. Your daughter may need them badly before this is over."

Giving the older man a cold nod, he turned and strode toward the front door and his waiting mount.

Tuesday, September 15, 1812
Hertfordshire

DARCY WAS MILES DOWN THE ROAD AND TRYING TO QUELL THE COLD HAND of worry gripping his heart as he continued through the rain. He had seen no sign of Elizabeth, and the darkness was almost complete. He kept riding, his eyes scanning the countryside for a place where she might have sought shelter from the freezing rain.

He was fifteen minutes farther down the road before he thought he saw something in the distance. His eyes squinted against the dark and wet, straining for a better look. It might be a human form, but he had seen similar apparitions several times in the last half-hour. Only when he discerned movement did he kick his horse into a gallop.

The figure he had spied through the rain became clearer as he approached, and the cold hand on his heart relaxed as he confirmed it was indeed Elizabeth Bennet trudging through the rain with her head down and her arms clasped about her chest against the cold. As he reined in his mount and jumped to the ground, Darcy could see her clothing was absolutely soaked. Still she trudged on, apparently aware of nothing except putting one mud-coated boot in front of the other.

297

"Miss Bennet," he said gently, placing the blankets and the lantern by the side of the road and stepping in front of her so he could grip her arms and stop her blind plodding. "At last I have found you. It is decidedly—"

A sudden bolt of lightning struck the ground close behind him with an explosive "CRAAAAAAAAKK!" It sounded as though the sky had split open and everywhere about him was illuminated by a harsh blue-white glare that left Darcy blinded.

When his awareness returned, he found himself flat on his back on the muddy roadway with Elizabeth motionless beside him. His thoughts were blurred, but a surge of energy went through him at the thought the lightning might have killed her.

He breathed a sigh of relief as his hand on her back detected the rise and fall of her chest, and he painfully climbed to his feet and pulled her up with him.

It was then Darcy recognized the full extent of the disaster that had overtaken him. He had dropped the reins of his horse to the ground as he dismounted, depending on the stallion's training to keep him motionless, but a quick glance told him the beast had not only bolted but was nowhere to be seen.

What in the world do I do now? I planned to wrap her in blankets and the oilcloth before we rode back to Longbourn. With my horse gone, we must find shelter—and quickly before the last shreds of daylight are gone.

He picked up the lantern, glad to see it was still lit even though the light it cast was rather pitiful. Then he picked up the blanket roll but made no move to unwrap it. Shelter was needed before he wrapped the dry blankets around Elizabeth.

Since she seemed able to continue if guided, Darcy began to walk up the road toward Longbourn in search of some kind of trees or brush. If he could find what he was looking for, he should be able to weave the branches into an arch to shelter them both, using the oilcloth and the ropes around the roll of blankets. During his younger years, when he and Wickham had tramped and hunted all over Pemberley, they had made similar shelters many times.

He was growing worried at how long he could keep Elizabeth walking before having to carry her when a promising thicket against a hillside loomed before him. The lantern was of little help against the near darkness, so he hurried toward it, pleased to see a number of dense-leafed, head-high bushes that might be used as well.

When he entered the thicket, the weak lantern light revealed the open mouth of what appeared to be a cave behind the bushes. He shoved his way through, pulling Elizabeth behind him, until he was crouched in total darkness that was gloriously dry.

He looked about with the lantern and gave thanks to his Creator to find himself in a rock cave that may have been low but was deep enough to hold them both. Quickly, he loosened the oilcloth and set the roll of blankets aside before wrapping Elizabeth in the rainproof cloth and settling her in the back of the cave.

His next task was to get a fire lit to warm the cave. Darcy knew any wood he found in the thicket was going to be water-soaked, but he also knew how to solve such a problem and soon pulled a number of promising branches into the dim light of the cave.

Using the knife in his boot, he quickly produced a pile of shaved kindling, pleased to find his skills had not deserted him, and lit a thin twig from the lantern. Within a few minutes, he had a small fire that he carefully fed with larger shavings and trimmed twigs until it was a small blaze going with a mix of kindling and drying branches while the wetter branches dried beside it. Then he could finally turn to Elizabeth.

Her eyes were closed, and he was certain her shivering was worse than it had been before. Clearly, he had to get her sodden clothing off so he could wrap her in dry blankets. It was a terrible breach of propriety, but he knew she would not live through the night if he did not get dry blankets wrapped around her. He would worry about trivialities like propriety later.

Propping her against him in a sitting position, he tried to work at her buttons, but his rain-drenched gloves made it impossible. Even after he took them off, it took only a few attempts with his cold-numbed fingers to realize the futility of trying to preserve Elizabeth's attire. He sighed, refusing to think of the implications of what he had to do and pulled his knife from his boot again. Then, again thankful for its sharp edge, he set to work, ruthlessly shredding Elizabeth's clothing and casting it over toward the fire to be used as fuel during the night. The sight of her bare skin induced no forbidden urges in him; he was too terrified by the blue tinge her wet, cold skin had taken.

When he had her completely naked, Darcy wrapped her in successive layers of blankets until she was completely bundled. Only her feet stuck out of the bottom inside her wet walking boots with the shreds of her stockings hanging down beside them. His fingers were still useless to unbutton her shoes, and he had to resort to his knife again, slicing the leather to ribbons before he could wrap her feet in the single remaining blanket and lay her on the oilcloth.

Now he knew he had to build up the fire and secure a sufficient supply of firewood to last the night. He desperately wanted to rest. His effort to find Elizabeth as well as his fears for her safety had almost exhausted him, but he knew he had to finish his preparations because to do otherwise and fall asleep might be fatal.

"Sooner started, sooner finished," he told himself, and he rose to his feet.

At last, with all he could think necessary completed, he sat down on the oilcloth beside Elizabeth's motionless bundle of blankets and gave a relieved sigh at the feel of the rough dirt floor and the rock wall behind his back. It felt better than the softest mattress at Pemberley, and he opened his oilskin coat and pulled Elizabeth onto his lap, wrapping his coat and the oilcloth about both of them while he stretched his feet toward the fire. Now he could relax and let himself go limp!

As he watched steam rise from his boots, he felt Elizabeth's shivering gradually decrease as the blankets and the warmth from the now merrily blazing fire helped drive away the harsh chill of the September night. Sighing tiredly, Darcy set his hat aside and laid his head on the rock wall. He knew he ought to feel as tired as the girl he held in his arms, but the thoughts flooding his mind would not allow him to sleep.

Chapter 24

Only people who are capable of loving strongly can also suffer great sorrow, but this same necessity of loving serves to counteract their grief and heals them.

— Leo Tolstoy, Russian author

Wednesday, September 16, 1812
Hertfordshire

The first rays of sunlight slanting into the cave brought Darcy awake, and he groaned at the aching pain in his neck from his contorted sleeping position. He had not fallen asleep until well into the morning hours as he pondered the events that brought him to this cave in Hertfordshire. What little sleep he managed had done little to refresh him. His eyes burned—they were gritty as he blinked them against the daylight—and he turned his head slowly, wincing as stabbing pains protested the movement.

When he looked down, he started when he saw Elizabeth's dark eyes staring at him intently. Her face bore an expression he could not interpret, but it made him distinctly uncomfortable.

"Good morning, Miss Bennet," he finally managed. "How are you faring?"

"Fortunate to be alive from what little I remember," was her polite reply, but the strange expression on her face did not alter. "I do thank you for saving my life, sir, but I must ask: What in the world are you doing here?"

Darcy busied himself for a moment by touching her forehead and was relieved to find no fever. Still, it was several moments before he answered.

"I found you plodding along the road in the rain, and—"

"No, no," she interrupted. "I know how I came to be in this cave. You must have brought me here and started this fire to warm me. And obviously, you wrapped me in these blankets.

"The last thing I remember is the icy rain that had me shivering so hard I thought I would never be warm again. But what I mean to ask, Mr. Darcy, is why are you here in Hertfordshire? Instead of at your estate in the north? Or in town?"

It seemed a long time to Elizabeth before Darcy said anything, and when he did, his answer was unrelated to her question.

"I cannot tell you how shocked I was by our encounter at Netherfield last November, Miss Bennet," he said slowly and seriously.

"That is not an answer, sir! What brought you to Hertfordshire so you could find me and save my life? I do not wish to seem ungrateful since I am well aware I should not have survived the night otherwise. But why do I find you here, sir? After that night at Netherfield, I thought everything was settled between us."

"And so I thought at the time," he said softly, and it appeared as though his eyes were focused far away. "But I have come to think such a determination may not have been a wise decision."

Elizabeth had been in a quandary ever since she awoke to find herself not only still alive but in the arms of the man she had never expected to see again. Now, after hearing him make such a statement, she was completely dumbfounded, and though her thoughts whirled about in her mind, she tried to find something tangible to grasp and bring sense to this strange morning.

A host of other questions tried to make their way to her lips, but it was clear that Darcy was following some convoluted path of reasoning only he could understand. Trying to question him now would likely impede, rather than accelerate, finding the answers she sought.

Darcy's face was intent and thoughtful, and Elizabeth could not keep herself from staring helplessly at the man she loved so desperately and so utterly in vain. Her chest ached with suppressed yearning to know how he came to be in Hertfordshire, but she ruthlessly forced herself to wait.

At long last, he said, "Everything seemed so clear at Netherfield. I agreed readily to what you suggested, certain it was the best course. Our spheres were simply too far apart for there to be any other resolution."

Elizabeth nodded since her thoughts were exactly the same, but she said nothing and let Darcy continue.

"Over the following months, I found myself unable to forget the depth of grief in your voice and your expression when you said, 'It is no use,' and 'Nothing will ever change.' Your words haunted me. My selfishness haunted me."

Elizabeth was immeasurably grateful that Darcy was not looking at her since she doubted she could control the emotion coursing in her heart and surely visible on her face—an emotion she thought never to feel again, not in all of her life—the possibility, the merest possibility, of hope.

"You were probably unaware of it, but I watched you often, even before the Netherfield ball. Increasingly, I found you...enticing. Though perhaps 'bewitching' would be a more accurate term."

Elizabeth felt as though the breath had been snatched from her lungs, and she could find no words with which to respond. Finally, her throat tight, she managed to say, "I did not notice any particular regard on your part at first, and I never imagined, never thought..."

Further comment failed her. Now, completely incapable of subterfuge or concealment, she could only look helplessly at Darcy. She knew he must be able to comprehend the longing within her, on her face...and she was frightened. Terrified. The hope she held so briefly could not be entertained; it must be ruthlessly suppressed. She could not bear the inevitable disappointment if she did not do so.

"It was the pain in your eyes that kept returning to me." Darcy closed his eyes as though in painful memory, and Elizabeth could not believe he could not hear the painful throbbing of her heart in her chest.

"My comprehension was slow in coming. It took months, and I resisted accepting it. Such thoughts were not at all pleasant to dwell on, and because I never intended to cause you pain, I could not be held responsible for your distress. Especially since I was content with the strictures my parents impressed on me regarding which young ladies were suitable choices as a wife, the woman who would carry the Darcy name."

Darcy's eyes finally met Elizabeth's directly. "When I met your aunt and uncle at Pemberley while you remained at Lambton, true to your declaration,

I decided I could not let matters continue as they were. I simply had to return to Hertfordshire and resolve…settle…the unfinished business between us one way or the other. I thought it was entirely possible you might now hate me for the pain I caused you, and I could not blame you. It was unintentionally done, but I knew it might matter little to you. If it were so, it would at least be a resolution to what plagued me."

Elizabeth was bewildered, and she could not respond to these softly spoken words. She could not believe they could possibly have any significance for her. She wanted to believe it, but it simply could not be true. She must have misheard or misinterpreted what Darcy said.

"So I decided to come to Netherfield, not with a defined purpose in mind, except possibly to find answers to what troubled me so I could go on with my life."

"So my mother was right!" Elizabeth heard herself say. "You *did* have Netherfield opened! I would not believe her. And I did not believe your aunt when she said the same thing."

"Which leads to a question of my own," Darcy said with a new and different tone in his voice. "What in Heaven's name was Lady Catherine doing at Longbourn?"

Elizabeth could not answer this simple question at first. To do so would require her to say things aloud she dared not say. Her cheeks colored, and she looked everywhere about the cave except at the man who so unbelievably held her in his arms. It was long moments before she could force herself to meet Darcy's eyes again.

"She came to…to demand a…a promise from me. A promise…that I would not accept an offer of marriage from you."

"Why on earth would she do such a thing?" Darcy said, showing none of the offense Elizabeth had been petrified he would. "No one knew what I planned except Major McDunn, and nothing could drag information from that man's lips that he did not wish to disclose."

"I can easily believe that!" Elizabeth said as the first slight smile of the morning played about her lips. "All I know is that my elder sister wrote to my mother to tell her you asked Mr. Bingley whether you might stay at Netherfield. And my mother wrote to my other sister, Mrs. Collins—"

"—who told her husband," Darcy said in a rush, "who then informed my aunt, who leaped to the conclusion that I intended to pay court to you and was coming to Longbourn to do so!"

"She was most abusive and intolerant," Elizabeth said, a quaver in her voice as she remembered the terrible confrontation. "I was terribly angry and hurt and confused. I tried to keep it inside, to control myself, but I finally could take no more. I simply had to escape, and I ran from the house to find relief as I usually did in walking about the country. You know just how poor a decision that proved to be."

"I shall speak with my aunt about this, and it shall not be a pleasant conversation—not in the slightest. I never thought a member of my family could conduct themselves in such an improper and outrageous manner. You could have died!"

"I *would* have died had you not found me," Elizabeth said, unable to repress a shiver at her memory of the bitter cold. She knew the ghosts of helpless terror had to be easily discernible on her face. "I was not thinking very clearly...or even thinking at all...when I left the house. I walked until I finally realized my peril and turned for home. But I had waited too late, and the rain began coming down in sheets. By the time you found me, I was shaking terribly from the cold, but I was too exhausted to care. All I could do was to keep walking since I knew if I collapsed, I would surely die."

"Only an impulse led me to change my mind and stop briefly at Longbourn before riding to Netherfield," Darcy said, his tone grave. "I found you gone from the house, and no one had any idea what to do. Your parents had no inkling of which direction you might have gone. It was mere chance that one of your sisters mentioned Oakham Mount. I knew the way, so I decided to search in this direction while McDunn rode to Meryton and call at your aunt's house."

"You came looking for me yourself?"

"Well, I had to," he said with a wry smile. "How would we settle things between us if you died of the cold? But I had not planned on my horse bolting into the night when lightning struck."

His face sobered suddenly, and she felt the intentness of his gaze. "Of course, we shall not be able to *settle things* as I had anticipated. Not now."

Elizabeth's brow furrowed. "What...what do you mean?" she asked, her words brittle and frightened.

"We have both been absent from Longbourn all evening, Miss Bennet," he said, the gentleness of his words soothing her fears. "There will be the assumption I spent the night having carnal knowledge of you in the most improper manner as my reward for saving your life."

"But…but you came out in a rainstorm to find me!" she said in consternation. "And you did! You did save my life! There was nothing improper in what you did!"

"Yes, I know, but I have been thinking on this much of the night. Perhaps we might convince your father of our innocence, but I know assumptions will be made by ungenerous people since we were not, of course, chaperoned in any way last evening."

"But with the rain and the cold, how could anything improper have happened?" she said, almost sputtering in outrage.

Darcy shrugged eloquently and smiled. "I did not say it was fair, Miss Bennet. I said it was a fact. All your neighbors will soon be aware of what has happened if they are not aware of it already. You have undoubtedly heard about rumors spreading like wildfire and twice as swiftly as the wind. Your reputation will be affected—perhaps ruined—and that of your family also."

"But…but…it is so unjust! You did nothing ungentlemanly!"

"Actually, it may not be the full and complete truth. I had to remove your wet clothing before I could wrap you in those blankets. Otherwise, I would not have been able to get you warm."

She stared at him as a sudden shock of realization came to her, and she said slowly, "Now I remember…at least a little bit."

"The fact cannot be concealed when I arrive at Longbourn with you in my arms and wrapped only in blankets. I shall have to walk since I am sure my horse will not return. In fact, I may never see him again. But the pertinent fact is that everyone, most especially your mother and father, will soon be aware that I have seen you completely unclothed."

Elizabeth blushed scarlet and averted her eyes. Finally, she managed to whisper, "Completely?"

"I had to remove everything, Miss Bennet. Even your shoes."

She wriggled her feet and ran her hands along her bare skin under the blankets as she realized the truth of what he had said.

"I could put my wet clothing on before I return home," she said in desperation. "We can dry it before your fire and—"

He shook his head contritely. "I had to cut everything off, Miss Bennet. You could not remove your clothing by yourself, and my fingers were too numb from the cold to assist you. I see a few shreds of cloth about the cave, but most everything went into the fire."

"Well, I can at least put on my shoes and arrive on my two feet, even wrapped in these blankets—"

"Doubtful," he said, holding up one of her shoes, which looked like a gutted fish ready for the frying pan.

"Just how sharp is your knife, Mr. Darcy?" she asked, her eyes wide at the complete destruction of her attire.

"Very sharp, Miss Bennet. It is a gift from Major McDunn, and I carry it in a sheath down my boot. As he says, 'You must always carry a knife since you will never need one until you need it very badly indeed.'"

She cleared her throat. "An interesting man, your Major McDunn."

"You do not know the least of it, Miss Bennet. As I was saying, as soon as we arrive at Longbourn, I fully expect your father to demand we marry and quickly. I cannot blame him. He will have no other choice."

"Marry?" she asked in apparent confusion, but the truth was she was totally nonplussed by the sudden surge of hope sweeping through her as though she had been struck by the same lightning that so frightened Darcy's horse.

"It is the usual mode of salvaging a damaged reputation for a young lady such as yourself, as I am sure you are aware. And I am not opposed to it myself, not any longer, though I was not aware during the night of just how you might react."

He looked directly into her eyes. "I could not know your present opinion of me. As I said, I could not blame you if you had formed a deep hatred of me. Even if I did not cause your grief, I was still the reason for it. But none of this matters any longer compared to our grievous breach of all propriety. We are going to be brought to task, and I see no alternative, no matter what each of us might wish to do."

He spoke gravely, and Elizabeth could see anxiety on his face.

"After my shameless behavior in the garden at Netherfield, Mr. Darcy," she said very softly, "can you have any doubt how I feel? Can you doubt the passion I felt then?"

"That was then, Miss Bennet, and this is almost a year later. I am well aware your opinion of me might have changed dramatically and in ways I cannot imagine."

She shook her head firmly at this, ignoring the desperate passion of her heart as she steeled herself to say what must be said in the interests of honesty. "My opinion has not changed—not at all. Whatever my own wishes might be, I shall not allow you to be forced into a marriage against your will."

"As I have said, I am not at all opposed, Miss Bennet. Anxious, of course, but not opposed."

"But...your view of a suitable wife," she said, with some trepidation. "Your parents—"

"Somehow, those objections seem to have been dispelled over the months," he said with a crooked smile that had more warmth in it than she had seen since early in the night at Netherfield. "I was not aware of it until early this morning when I was thinking long and hard on this. Perhaps it was the knowledge that neither of us has an alternative that would salvage our reputations. But whatever the reason, I found myself comfortable with a prospect that, given our past, is sure to leave you mystified.

"And I must marry, Miss Bennet, so would it not be much better for *me*—since you appear worried on my behalf—if the lady I married felt for me as deeply as you appear to feel? I am certain I will, in time, respond in kind and hopefully provide some solace for what you have endured."

Elizabeth looked up at him with an intensity he had never seen before. Her eyes were almost ablaze as she licked her dry lips, and the hope in her face was so desperate, it made his heart ache at the raw emotion he saw.

"I always knew my hopes...my desires...were impossible," she said. "I have dreamed a thousand times of being with you always, bearing your children, sharing your life, but I knew they were a hopeless illusion. Now, you say you will marry me—"

"I chose my words carefully to show how my opinions have changed, but they do not describe my wishes completely. Yes, we have no choice but to marry, else cruel whispers will follow both of us for the rest of our lives. I have dismissed many of the constraints my parents laid on me, and I am now certain you will be an excellent wife. You are, in fact, more than I deserve, and I am looking forward to learning more about you, making a life with you, all the things you just said—"

He stopped speaking abruptly since Elizabeth was squirming about in his lap, struggling against the blankets that swathed her in a cocoon. She finally freed her arm and reached up to lay her hand on his cheek.

"I cannot believe this is happening," she said, the expression on her face full of tenderness as her fingers explored the lines of his unshaven face. "When I awoke and saw you sleeping above me, I could not comprehend what was happening. I never expected anything like this."

Darcy took her hand, brought it to his lips, and kissed her palm. He heard her sharp intake of breath as he ran his lips over her smooth, soft skin. Her bare arm stuck out from the blankets to her shoulders, and he thought he had never seen anything so desirable. His lips moved to her fingers, just as hers had done months earlier, and he kissed each finger tenderly, running his lips along the slim, elegant line of each of the fingers of her small hand. Elizabeth laid her head back and closed her eyes in visible contentment as he continued slowly and thoroughly.

"I never dared hope to feel anything like the touch of your lips. Your touch…so gentle."

Darcy's throat tightened at the look of happiness on her sweet face. Elizabeth opened her eyes, and he was enthralled by the intensity of her gaze as she gently pulled her hand from his grasp and raised it to his neck, pulling his head down to hers.

Darcy was not the man of the world Elizabeth likely expected, but he was more than aware that her kiss was one of virginal innocence and exploration. The feel of her lips under his own kindled a passion in him, and he pulled her to him, even as her arm tightened around his neck. Their kiss deepened, and both of them lost track of the passage of time.

At length, Elizabeth's soft moans made him aware of the extent to which each of them was becoming aroused, and he reluctantly broke the kiss and raised his head.

"I think we should save any more kissing until we are safely married," he said playfully. "But it seems you have put my worries about your opinion of me to rest, and—"

"Just one more kiss," she asked beseechingly, and he lowered his head down to meet hers once more as he kissed her lips, her cheeks, and even her closed eyes.

Elizabeth's breath was ragged when they finally pulled apart. "I love you so! I wish we did not have to stop."

"It would seem advisable," Darcy said dryly. "We are not quite in control of our emotions at the moment. But it does seem as though all questions between us have been answered."

"I suppose you are right."

She nestled herself against him and rested her head against his chest, and Darcy felt it to be one of the most endearing and touching things he had known in his life.

"I cannot believe we will be married," she said, her voice muffled. "It is like a dream I never let myself have. I have no fortune, you know, and—"

"Hush, Elizabeth," he said softly, his finger on her lips. "I think we should start back to Longbourn."

"But…what shall I call you, sir? I love the way you call me Elizabeth. It is ever so much more intimate than Lizzy or Eliza, which are what most people call me. But I absolutely refuse to call you Mr. Darcy any longer, though I know many wives do so. I am too impertinent, you know."

"Georgiana calls me William though my given name is Fitzwilliam after my mother's family. But I do not like it—not at all. So call me William."

"Very well," she said, settling herself against him as he took her in his arms again, stood, and carefully scattered the embers of the dying fire about, grinding them into the waterlogged ground outside the cave. Then, careful of his burden, he began to make his way out of the cave and toward the road to Longbourn.

Wednesday, September 17, 1812
Longbourn, Hertfordshire

IT TOOK MOST OF AN HOUR OF WALKING BEFORE THEY SPIED A TRIO OF mounted grooms coming toward them from the direction of Longbourn. The road had been so muddy, Darcy had spent much of the time picking his way through the tall grass beside the road, but he had occasionally been forced to slog through the mud. His trouser legs were sodden to the knees, and both boots were so encased in mud, they felt as though they each weighed ten pounds.

The grooms were jubilant to see their master's daughter still hale and hearty, and one of them quickly galloped back to Longbourn to bring the good news while the other two assisted him to mount one of the horses before handing Elizabeth's blanket-swathed body up to him.

Darcy learned from Elizabeth's comments that he had been entirely disoriented the previous night. What he thought was the way to Longbourn had been incorrect, and if he had tried to find his way to the house in the dark, it was likely both of them would have been dead before morning.

"We seem to have attracted a crowd," he said, motioning with his chin toward Longbourn where a gathering of people milled about.

Elizabeth had been resting as Darcy held her close, lulled into a drowsy state by the motion of their mount. They had been proceeding at a walk with the unmounted groomsman leading their horse. Elizabeth's head had been tucked into his chest, but she turned to look toward her home.

"Oh, my word! You are right! Look at all of them!"

"I can recognize Sir William and his wife from here and your sisters along with your friend Miss Lucas, but no one else."

"There are my Aunt and Uncle Philips standing next to my mother. And then there are her friends the Gouldings and Mrs. Long along with Hill, our housekeeper. You were absolutely correct about everyone learning everything, William. What was my mother thinking?"

"Once the groomsman informed everyone you were alive, I suspect she decided to make sure as many people as possible knew of our grievous indiscretions. Now, she can be certain your father will demand we marry, especially with everyone thinking some variation of, 'Here comes the rake with the innocent young lady he spent the night ravishing!'"

Elizabeth had to turn her face into Darcy's chest to hide her laughter, and then she looked up at him reproachfully. "Are you going to make a practice of being right all the time?"

Darcy whispered out of the side of his mouth. "I had best control my words. Your father is coming to meet us, and he does not look nearly as complacent as your mother."

Darcy was unsurprised to see McDunn lounging against the wall of Longbourn wearing a broad grin, clearly enjoying the morning's events. Mr. Bennet approached as Darcy dismounted, balancing Elizabeth on the saddle until he could take her back in his arms. Her father looked closely at his daughter and then at Darcy, his relief clear though he still looked displeased.

"As you see," Darcy said, forcing his voice to be mild, "I found your daughter."

"I do see. And I am thankful to the Almighty to see her alive, but are you aware of the dilemma in which you have placed me?"

"I had intended to bring Miss Bennet back to Longbourn when I found her, but a bolt of lightning struck so close it left us unconscious and afoot when my horse bolted. Not being certain of the way in the dark and with your daughter still too weak to assist me, I had to seek shelter from the storm. I was able to get her wrapped in your blankets and get her warm. She has no fever this morning, which is the important thing."

Mr. Bennet waved about the drive at all the eyes on them. "I do not dispute your words, Mr. Darcy, but—"

"Papa, you owe Mr. Darcy a debt of gratitude for saving my life!" Elizabeth said forcefully and sternly, knowing for now and always where her loyalties lay. "If you want to be angry at anyone for what happened, then blame me since it was I who rushed down the road until I was too far away to return before the rains came."

Mr. Bennet was taken aback at the tenor of her words. "I know, child, but Mr. Darcy has placed me in a most uncomfortable position, and I do not—"

Her father stopped, looking back and forth between the couple and now comprehending the way his precious Elizabeth looked at this haughty stranger—as though she thought the sun rose in the sky because he wished it.

"I see," he said finally. "I suppose you are right, Lizzy, but this is not the place to discuss these matters, especially as it appears some things have changed during this terrible night. So perhaps there might be a silver lining to what I was deathly afraid was going to be one of the worst days of my life."

He managed a weak smile and gestured about the drive. "My wife appears to have summoned a considerable audience this morning to ensure I do my fatherly duty. I believe she anticipates some kind of dramatic event now you are safely returned home."

"A shotgun wedding, I would imagine," McDunn said cheerfully, having somehow materialized at Mr. Bennet's side. "Good morning, Miss Bennet. Good morning, Darcy. It appears your quest was more successful than mine."

Seeing Darcy's look, McDunn smiled broadly and said, "I'll explain this particular Americanism later, but you can probably guess its meaning."

"I daresay," Darcy said dryly. "I think it best that I take Elizabeth to her room. I have her well in hand, and I do not want to take a chance on someone dropping her before we have the opportunity to pay for our transgressions."

McDunn barked his laughter, but Mr. Bennet frowned at this improper familiarity. Only then did Darcy realize he had unconsciously used Elizabeth's Christian name.

"Papa," Elizabeth said urgently. "Mr. Darcy did nothing except save my life. Nothing at all ungentlemanly. I am as innocent now as I was yesterday."

"I know, I know, Lizzy. I would never believe differently. But I was just angered by—"

He waved his hand back at the drive. "Your mother, you see. She, well, she…she summoned them a half-hour ago and…"

Words failed him, and Elizabeth blushed as she saw her mother all but dancing with excitement. Turning to her father, she said, "So William was right, and we must marry?"

"I am afraid so, child," her father said consolingly. "Especially with your mother having summoned her friends."

"I was not asking for myself, Papa. I was asking for William. I do not wish him—"

"You know my wishes," Darcy said, his voice gentle. "I shall not consider ruining your reputation, so put your worry aside."

Elizabeth looked at him tenderly before she managed to say, "After Mr. Darcy and I are safely married, Papa, by—what was it you called it, Major McDunn?"

"Shotgun wedding," McDunn said happily. "A revered custom from my country's proud history."

"Yes, shotgun wedding," Elizabeth said doubtfully. "After that, Mama will have only Kitty and Lydia to worry about."

An older man, dressed in the black suit and white cravat that were almost a uniform for a clergyman who was not actually preaching, had just stepped to Mr. Bennet's side.

"Good day, Reverend Palmer!" Elizabeth said.

"Considerable excitement for so early in the morning, would you not say, Lizzy?" he said, wearing the slightest of smiles.

"Yes, I agree. It appears my mother will finally achieve her dream of getting another daughter safely married."

She smiled at McDunn and said softly, "But I do not believe your shotgun will be necessary, Major. Mr. Darcy says he wants to marry me, and I certainly want to marry him—more than anything else in the world."

"Why, then," Reverend Palmer said cheerfully, "there seems little left other than the formalities. And those would be best discussed in your father's library rather than in your drive."

"And I will take Elizabeth to her room now," Darcy said.

"I will show you the way, my dear," she said softly, not even aware of her father's grimace at her use of such an endearment.

As Darcy turned away, Mr. Bennet called to one of the crowd of servants by the front door and said, "Sarah, please accompany my daughter to her room and assist her in changing her attire. Also, a bit of breakfast and some hot tea, but do not prepare a bath. We have many things to discuss this morning."

As Darcy turned away, Elizabeth's mother had reached the group, and she fluttered about as he strode toward the door, uttering one meaningless endearment after another to her daughter, causing Darcy to roll his eyes. He looked at McDunn, who had resumed his position leaning against the house, but the major only smiled cheerfully. Darcy shook his head sadly as he entered the house.

Though that went better than I anticipated, I still want to marry Elizabeth before her family causes her any more pain. I shall make sure Mr. Bennet's parson agrees to issue a common license before he leaves this house. I want to give her the comfort and love she deserves. I do not believe I shall let her leave my bed for a week!

Darcy was in a much better frame of mind when Sarah opened the door to his future wife's room and he laid her gently on her bed.

Elizabeth forced herself to lie quietly until Darcy left, closing the door behind him, then she abruptly threw off the blankets and leapt from the bed, completely ignoring her nakedness and the wide-eyed stare of her maid. She disregarded the chill morning air as she told Sarah to bring a water basin and clean wash cloths. She simply had to wash away the smell of those blankets.

He wants to marry me! she thought in disbelief as she began to wash herself with the cold water. *He says it is so and even admits an astonishing depth of remorse for his missteps—such remorse as I never would have imagined possible! He wants to marry me! And he is so changed! How is it possible?*

She wondered at the near-overwhelming emotion tightening her throat and chest. *Could what I am feeling be simple happiness? But it is so intense, so deep reaching! Surely, there must be more! Or, could it be something else entirely?*

Relief was part of it, she knew—relief at seeing an end to the anguish that had been her constant companion for almost a year.

I shall have to mind how I act when I go downstairs, she thought as Sarah laid out her clothing, but she laughed again as she began dressing with Sarah's aid. She was now certain that this feeling could only be pure bliss.

She sat down so Sarah could attempt to replace the pins from her hair.

WHEN ELIZABETH WAS DRESSED AND STARTED DOWN THE STAIRS, HER mother awaited her in a state of almost complete frenzy. One part, but a small part, of Mrs. Bennet's mind was concerned with the damage to Elizabeth's reputation by the events of the prior night. But the major part of her, the part always obsessed at finding husbands for her daughters, was mesmerized by the possibility—nay, the certainty—of her husband forcing Mr. Darcy to marry Elizabeth because she had been with him all night.

Of course, she gave not a thought to her own part in her daughter's flight from Longbourn, nor did she have the slightest awareness of how she had failed in responsibility to her child by letting her stand alone in confrontation with the fearsome old noblewoman. She had not even had the wit to summon her husband to the front parlor!

Mrs. Bennet was in such a state, she could barely pass on her husband's request for Elizabeth to join him and Reverend Palmer in his library. But the message was ignored when Elizabeth heard Darcy's voice coming from the front parlor and brusquely brushed past her mother to join him.

The parlor was rather crowded with her mother's friends, and Elizabeth realized others had arrived while she was dressing, including her dear friend Charlotte, who gave her a wave and a cheerful smile.

But Elizabeth had eyes for only one person in the room, and she walked straight toward him where he sat drinking coffee with his American friend. Both men rose as she approached, and there was time for nothing more than the usual exchange of greetings before her mother was beside them, having followed her daughter into the room.

"Your father wants to see you directly, Lizzy!" she said, low and urgently. "And you too, Mr. Darcy!"

Elizabeth's eyes were bright with mischief. "It seems we are being summoned, sir."

"I was waiting for you to arrive, Elizabeth," he said gravely, holding out his arm to her.

Instead of taking it, however, she seized his hand instead, and every eye in the room locked on them in astonishment as they left the parlor.

This crowd didn't expect that! McDunn thought in amusement as he sat down by his coffee and signaled a maid to refill his cup while hushed conversations broke out about the room.

Most of these people probably think Elizabeth and Darcy spent the night making wild, passionate love, which is really stupid. It rained bitterly cold most of the night, and Darcy said the cave was terribly uncomfortable, with rock walls and all. How they could have managed anything improper is impossible to imagine!

Oh, Miss Jane Austen, how your characters have managed to put things aright, though not at all in the manner you wrote! None of the Austen fans in my world would believe any part of this could have happened as it did!

He was quite disappointed at knowing he never, ever would be able to discuss it with anyone from this world.

Neither Darcy nor Elizabeth was gone long, and they returned to the parlor with the parson and Elizabeth's father. Mrs. Bennet stood with everyone else, and McDunn was unsurprised to see her looking openly exultant. Her husband looked more composed though McDunn thought he looked a bit sad, presumably at the thought of his favorite daughter leaving his home forever.

Adding to Mr. Bennet's mood was his displeasure at having so many neighborhood families in his parlor, McDunn was sure, and he seemed even less pleased at social custom requiring him to make his necessary announcement in front of them. However, there being no alternative, he performed his duty, stating merely that his daughter Elizabeth would wed Mr. Darcy of Derbyshire in seven days. Having done what was necessary with as little effort as he could manage, Mr. Bennet faded back and disappeared, intending to do what he could to repair the tattered tranquility of his library.

Mrs. Bennet was now in her element, accepting the felicitations of her friends in what she imagined to be a genteel fashion. McDunn, however, thought she looked more like the cat that swallowed the canary. Charlotte gave Elizabeth a fond embrace with no insincerity in it. McDunn could tell she was happy for her friend, and she appeared even more so once she had

Elizabeth's assurance that the match was what she desired.

As for the Reverend Palmer, McDunn never saw him leave. He seemed to disappear at about the same time as Mr. Bennet and well before Darcy and Elizabeth came over to join him.

"Well, that didn't take long," McDunn said after Darcy had seated Elizabeth. The conversations throughout the room continued, but several in the crowd were already leaving.

Elizabeth giggled at McDunn's comment, and Darcy said, "Mr. Bennet was prepared to deliver the usual speech, declaring we had violated the norms of politeness and convention with only an immediate marriage being able to atone for our indiscretions. But Elizabeth stopped him immediately and told him she had loved me for most of a year without me ever knowing of it, that I wanted to marry her, and would everyone stop all the unnecessary nonsense and go about the required business to perform the wedding as soon as may be. Her parson said he would immediately issue us a common license."

"He did so want to draw everything out—reading the banns, which would take weeks," Elizabeth said. "Ours will be the most significant marriage he has ever performed, and he was looking forward to having it be a much talked of event. But William demanded a license be issued today, and Reverend Palmer was unprepared to oppose him, so he acquiesced after only a few minutes."

"Perhaps it was because you threatened to accompany me to town this afternoon without benefit of matrimony, Elizabeth," Darcy said dryly. "It seemed to jar him into agreement. It appears as though bargaining with you could be a lifetime's occupation."

I think you just made an accurate prediction, friend Darcy, thought McDunn, hiding his smile by taking a sip of his coffee. *Obviously, my beloved author captured Elizabeth Bennet's playful nature perfectly even if nothing else worked out as I would have expected from reading her novel.*

"I'm still learning about these things, you know," McDunn said, "but I expected the two of you would be married before sunset."

"Such a hasty ceremony is not possible, McDunn," Darcy said. "The usual custom is to have the banns read in church for three consecutive Sundays, but doing so entails a three-week delay at the least. We insisted the reverend agree to issue a common license, which still has a waiting period of seven days. It is the soonest a couple can be married."

"Unless one runs off to Scotland," Elizabeth said with a twinkle in her eye.

"Only in those border villages like Gretna Green," Darcy said. "But Scotland is a rather long journey, and I believe you would prefer to wait in comfort rather than to bounce along the roads to the north for a week or so. I would have preferred sooner myself because it is my opinion that the sooner you leave Longbourn, the better, Elizabeth. You have had to endure far too much here."

Elizabeth sighed. She could do nothing other than agree, and Darcy turned to McDunn.

"Which brings up another matter, and that is Georgiana."

"I was thinking I would go fetch her, but I wanted to wait until the Spanish Inquisition was over. I'm actually disappointed to see everything happen with so little insult. I had hoped to be a fly on the wall for the inter-familial combat."

He stopped and looked at Darcy inquisitively. "'Fly on the wall.' Do you say something similar here?" At Darcy's amused shake of his head, McDunn continued. "It means—"

"I can deduce its meaning, Major," Elizabeth said with a laugh. "I am just sorry to disappoint you."

McDunn returned her smile. "Actually, I'm relieved everything worked out so smoothly. As for my odd sayings, you'll get used to them in time."

"Along with those atrocious contractions he scatters through his conversations," Darcy said, motioning with his coffee cup while his expression remained calm.

"You'll have to," McDunn said, smiling at his friend's jab. "Unless Darcy throws me out in the street, of course."

"Which is highly unlikely, McDunn. I have too much of my fortune invested in you to allow you to go wandering about the countryside unattended."

McDunn only smiled at this, drained the last of his coffee, and bid farewell to the betrothed couple before leaving.

"He lives with you?" Elizabeth asked.

"He has since he arrived in England," Darcy said, looking at her seriously. "It is a long story, one that will take privacy to relate."

He kept his voice low and soft. "But even when we have our privacy, I have other plans for the two of us than discussing McDunn. Plans you can likely guess."

"I shall depend on that, sir," Elizabeth said though her cheeks did color slightly. She took his hand and held it tight.

Wednesday, September 16, 1812
Darcy Townhouse, London

"MARRIED? YOU CANNOT BE SERIOUS!" EXCLAIMED GEORGIANA FROM THE bench of her pianoforte.

"I am being dead serious, Miss Darcy," McDunn said with a smile. "Your brother will indeed be married. In a mere seven days."

Georgiana's look of stunned surprise was suddenly replaced by one of acute anxiety, and McDunn was quick to relieve her apprehension. "Don't worry. He's *not* marrying the sister of his best friend."

Georgiana flushed a little at having revealed the source of her concern, and it took no little time for her to collect herself. "To whom will he be married, then?"

"To a certain Miss Elizabeth Bennet."

"Oh, I know her! I know Miss Bennet!" After a few moments, her smile spread into one of true delight. "In fact, I remember recommending to William he should marry exactly that young lady!"

"I remember it well. And you might mention the fact often and rather loudly. A little humility wouldn't do Darcy any harm at all."

"Oh, I will, I will! Seven days, you said? Is it not rather sudden?"

"Sudden, in my experience, would have been this afternoon. But you Brits have some strange laws about marriage. I suppose I shouldn't feel so superior. America has some strange laws of her own. With a week before the wedding, there's no need for a speedy departure. We can leave tomorrow after you and Mrs. Sturdivant have had your trunks packed."

Georgiana nodded in acknowledgment, and McDunn went on. "After your brother and Miss Bennet are married, we'll have to come back here. The newlyweds will be remaining at Netherfield for at least a week, I'm told. Evidently, seven days is the usual period for a newly married couple of the wealthier classes to…ah, explore the intimacies of wedded bliss."

Georgiana looked at him with interest at his comment.

I'm not going to be the one to explain the birds and the bees. It's a topic best left to the discretion of Georgiana's new sister, he thought. *Another area that's none of my business.*

He looked at Mrs. Sturdivant, who seemed to be trying to hide a smile, and he gave her a friendly nod. Obviously, she was thinking of much the same topics as he was, but she said nothing as her attention returned to her sewing.

Georgiana had no idea what was running through McDunn's mind, and she chattered away about how delightful it was going to be to have a sister as amiable as Miss Bennet.

Chapter 25

Everyone says that love hurts. But that's not true. Loneliness hurts, rejection hurts, losing someone hurts. Everyone confuses these with love, but in reality love is the only thing in this world that covers up all the pain and makes us feel wonderful again.

— Unknown

Wednesday, September 23, 1812
Netherfield, Hertfordshire

During the short journey to Netherfield in Mr. Bennet's carriage, Darcy held Elizabeth close while she nestled against him, holding onto his coat firmly. He had become accustomed to her desire, her need, for closeness in the past week. At every opportunity, she wanted to be as close to him as possible. It was not considered proper as her mother had told them several times as they sat together on the sofa in the front parlor, but Elizabeth simply looked at her wordlessly until her mother left the room.

That rather saddened Darcy, but he knew how furious Elizabeth remained with her mother, and he could hardly blame her. During the past week, Elizabeth had gradually explained details of what her mother had done in the months after the Netherfield ball, including, he was horrified to learn, how her mother had so often been the architect of her miseries on other occasions besides her boasts during the disastrous evening at Netherfield. He did not know how long it would take Elizabeth to forgive her mother though he knew she would do so eventually. She was not made to cling to her anger as were some, but she could not pardon her mother at the present time. It was too soon. Her wounds were too raw. She needed time and other, happier experiences before she could begin to bury her ghosts.

They had few moments completely alone, even on their walks, because they were accompanied by either Lydia or Kitty and sometimes both. Mrs. Bennet, it appeared, had accepted the supposed improprieties when it was convenient to do so, but she wanted no more examples to inspire comment among her friends.

While he and Elizabeth usually laughed at her mother's antics, her behavior was wearying, and Elizabeth had grumbled a time or two about wishing Darcy *had* ravished her in the fire-warmed cave. That way, she had said, they would at least have something about which to feel guilty. But he brought her reverie to an end by reminding her of the discomforts of the cave, which would have made any amorous activities simply absurd.

Now, after the brief ceremony in the morning and the wedding breakfast following, Mr. Bennet's carriage was nearing Netherfield. Darcy's larger coach was needed to return Georgiana and Mrs. Sturdivant to London, while McDunn rode beside it on his favorite horse.

I am sure his magical pistol will be under his coat, thought Darcy. *McDunn does take his self-appointed role as Georgiana's protector seriously—every jot as much as Brown, who will be in his usual position behind the coach. It is quite pleasing to see how McDunn has developed quite a fancy for riding despite his initial reluctance.*

As the carriage turned onto the drive to the house, Elizabeth sat up and looked at him seriously.

"I still sometimes feel as though everything that has happened between us has been a dream, William. I have been terrified to go to sleep this last week. I longed to be beside you. I could not sleep at all last night."

His voice deepened and he lowered his lips to her ear. "You may sleep as much as you please during the next week, my dear—after I have my way with you."

Mischief sparkled in her eyes. "I am not totally ignorant of what to expect, but I shall require some tutoring.

"And I will be your most devoted teacher, Elizabeth," he said, leaning down to kiss her temple.

"I am all nerves right now. May we go to our rooms as soon as we arrive? I will require Sara's help."

Darcy quickly put her at her ease. "Certainly, but I do not believe you need the aid of a maid. I have already seen you unclothed, my love, and I think I can manage your clothing. If need be, I will simply cut it off."

"You would not dare!" Elizabeth said, laughing in delight.

"Though I do look forward to seeing you without the somewhat off-putting tinge of blue you wore when we spent the night in the cave."

She laughed softly at his jest before looking up at him. "I do think it would be best if we prepared for bed in the usual manner. I am a bit uncertain about managing your clothing, and I am certain you would have great difficulty managing mine. I will come to you as soon as I can."

Darcy leaned over and whispered a suggestion into Elizabeth's ear. She looked somewhat startled but certainly not offended, and he was amused to see a wicked gleam come to her eye.

"Coming to you wearing no clothing whatever does sound…interesting, and I am not opposed, but the simple approach might be best after this very complicated courtship," Elizabeth said as the carriage stopped with a jerk. She checked her bonnet instinctively before turning to him.

"We seem to have arrived, sir," she said, her voice calm. "I forgot to mention: my father sent Sarah to Netherfield earlier to be my personal maid if you do not mind. He admitted you must have an entirely adequate staff, but the servants at Netherfield are only temporary. He thought someone with whom I was familiar would be a comfort since he seemed to think we might be…otherwise occupied."

"Your father does have moments of insight."

At seeing the look of distaste on Elizabeth's face, he instantly interpreted it. "You shall have to forgive him, Elizabeth—and your mother too. I know you are upset now and for good reason, but I also know it is not in your nature to hold a grievance forever. Remember, your life is changed from this day. This morning you awakened as Elizabeth Bennet of Longbourn. Now you are Elizabeth Darcy, and we will face the trials of life together."

"I know, I know," she said with a sigh, "but I will have to apply some effort. Now, shall we go inside?"

When Elizabeth and Darcy entered Netherfield, she would have preferred to climb the stairs to their bedrooms immediately. However, as she suspected, the staff was lined up to greet them. She knew the necessity of acknowledgements could not be avoided. She had a new and unaccustomed role to perform, that of the wife of this wealthy and important man, so she tried to respond graciously.

She was rather surprised to find her fears were not as severe as she had expected. Much of the reason for it was the man at her side who seemed to know exactly what to say as they went down the line, leaving her only to nod her head at each introduction.

When the staff was dismissed to their duties, Elizabeth was ready to mount the stairs, but she never got the chance since the world suddenly revolved about her as Darcy swung her up in his arms effortlessly.

"William!" she cried in a muffled voice, surprise mingling with delight. She had never imagined the stiff, haughty Mr. Darcy of Pemberley would do anything so impulsive.

She kept her head tucked into Darcy's neck as he carried her up the stairs in much the same way he had carried her back to Longbourn a week earlier. As soon as Darcy set her on her feet outside her bedroom, he leaned down to whisper in her ear.

"Do not take too long, my darling." There was a dark edge to his voice but a warm smile on his face.

"No longer than necessary," she whispered back. "You shall not find a shy, reluctant maiden here. Maiden I may still be, but I am as eager as you!"

With that, she disappeared through the doorway into her bedroom where she found Sarah already awaiting her in the dressing room. The girl she had known for years had little difficulty managing the intricacies of Elizabeth's clothing, though they would have surely confounded Darcy if not baffled him entirely. Since she had bathed in the morning, Sarah had laid out the simple but elegant nightgown her Aunt Gardiner had brought from town as a gift.

Taking down her hair was a bit of a chore since her mother had instructed the maid to use a multitude of pins for fear a single strand might come loose. But it was soon accomplished under Sarah's trained hands, after which she brushed her mistress's long, dark hair until it cascaded down her shoulders.

"Thank you, Sarah," Elizabeth said, standing up. "You are dismissed for the evening."

Then she stepped to the connecting door to Darcy's room, gave a quick knock, and entered.

Darcy was clad in his dressing gown, a loose, knee-length garment made of cotton rather than the more usual satin, velvet, or silk damask. Elizabeth's nightgown, made of light, pale-colored silk, was far more fashionable than the more usual garments designed for warmth at night.

Darcy stepped toward her, a compliment on his lips, but she rushed forward and embraced him with an intensity unlike anything she had previously shown. He found himself startled that such a diminutive body could possess so much strength.

Once she was in his arms, he felt her shoulders heaving in sobs, and though he tried to hold her at arm's length to see why she cried, she absolutely refused to allow him to break their embrace and just shook her head against his chest.

"What is troubling you, Elizabeth? Tell me."

Keeping her face firmly pressed against his chest, her voice was choked with emotion. "I never believed this time would come, even after Reverend Palmer completed the ceremony and we signed our names! I was going mad with every little delay my mother or anyone else suggested when all I wanted was to be here with you. Alone."

"It did seem as though everything took a very long time," he whispered. "But you are worth the wait. You are enticing, Elizabeth. Bewitching."

His compliment drew a smile, and he wiped the tears of joy from her face.

"Aunt Gardiner brought this gown to me when she came. It appears she had it made for me weeks ago. She just smiled mysteriously when I tried to press her further."

"A very insightful woman. I like both your aunt and uncle very much."

"That is enough talk about my relations, husband," Elizabeth said sternly. "Is it not time to take me to your bed?"

"In a moment, Mrs. Darcy."

As she untied the belt of his dressing gown and worked it off his shoulders, he took in the swell of her soft breasts as they swayed with the movement of her fingers and arms. He had become aroused, and it was quite visible, even before his dressing gown fell to the floor.

Elizabeth's laughter was soft and alluring. "It seems you do not find me too unpleasant to look upon."

She ran her hands over his bare chest in exploration. "I was not aware men and women's bodies were so different, but I like the distinctions. I hope I do not seem brazen, and I assure you I will attempt to be more proper at other times but not tonight. I first knew I loved you at Netherfield, but I *desired* you long before that! Here. Like this. Tonight I want to be your lover. Your wife.

"But come, sir! You have not upheld your part! Here I have removed your dressing gown so you stand completely unclothed, and you have not even taken me to your bed!"

They laughed as Elizabeth tugged on his hand, pulling him toward the bed while he pretended reluctance, but she gave a sudden squeal of delight as he suddenly pulled her nightgown over her head and cast it aside.

"Lesson one in tutoring my new wife," he said, holding her at arm's length and turning her around. "Lose no time in removing her clothing. It will only get in the way."

Elizabeth gave another cry as he swung her into the air again. "You are exquisite, Elizabeth, but you are even more desirable than you were in our cave because now you are mine."

Darcy pulled her to him, and they kissed with an urgency that would not be denied. Her arms clasped strongly around his waist while his hands caressed the fine planes of her back. They gloried in the feel of their bare flesh touching without impediment.

Elizabeth gasped as he took hold of her bottom and easily lifted her until her face was level with his. He brought his mouth to her ear and whispered words of passion meant to send waves of desire through her.

She wound her legs about his waist to support herself as he walked over to the bed and climbed onto it. Then she released her hold and nestled herself next to him as he lay down. Their lips again met, and Elizabeth gasped with shock and pleasure as Darcy licked the seam between her lips and touched her tongue with his. She responded feverishly and their tongues danced together.

Pulling back, Darcy looked down at her seriously. "You may say you need tutoring from a man with more worldly experience, but do not think I am put off by your declaration that you desired me before you loved me. I could not be more pleased than to find myself married to a woman with passion in her soul."

Her voice was taken away as his mouth moved lightly from the nape of her neck down toward her breasts. His hands explored their velvety softness, and he rolled her hard nipples between finger and thumb, giving rise to a shudder of pleasure he felt beneath his hands.

Darcy gave a groan as her hands moved to his manhood, gripping it with a soft laugh of satisfaction.

"I look forward to furthering my education."

"You must release me and quickly, else I will not be able to continue your lesson without a pause to recover," Darcy said with some difficulty.

"Very well," she said, doing so reluctantly. In recompense, his lips were busy, moving from her cheek to her ear, as he used the soft pressure of his teeth on her earlobe.

"Please, let me—" she moaned, trying to sit up, but he only laughed softly and guided her back down on the bed.

"Slowly, Elizabeth, slowly," he whispered. "It will be much better for you." He touched her with intimacy, as though he had done it a hundred times before.

"But I am still a girl," she said her hand moving downward. "I want you to make me your woman."

"You will be my woman soon enough," he said softly. "Let me lead you. But deliberately, my love."

She was reluctant at first, but his fingers and his lips moved over her bare body, finding places to caress he knew would be pleasurable.

"Soon, I think," he said while his fingers moved down to the juncture of her legs. She eagerly opened her legs to his touch, moaning deep in her throat as his fingers slid over her sex and then dipped inside.

"I believe you are ready now, my Elizabeth. Surrender to me," he whispered, as he lowered his hips to hers, gently guiding his manhood to her moist femininity.

Elizabeth cried as he moved inside of her and gently probed deeper.

"Am I hurting you?" Darcy asked in sudden concern.

"Do not stop!" she cried again, her hands on his buttocks and urging him deeper. "It matters not! Oh, God, I love you so much, William! Please, please, go on!" She threw her head back and gasped.

He slowed his movements, and it was soon evident the pain of losing her virginity had either been diminished or had been replaced by other feelings.

Her cries and her burning hands drove him on as she instinctively matched his rhythm with her own.

WHEN DARCY AWOKE IN THE EARLY HOURS BEFORE MORNING, HE FOUND further evidence of his new wife's fervent attachment since she slept with her chest mostly resting on top of him as he lay on his back, her arms and legs wound about him. When he tried to look down at her in the dim light before dawn, she gripped him more firmly until she finally came partly awake and opened her eyes.

"I am just looking at you, my love. You are so very beautiful, you know."

She gave a soft sound of assent, moving herself about until she found a comfortable position with her arms and legs again entwined about him. Her breathing deepened, and she again slept.

Darcy looked down at her dark, tousled hair as she lay with her face on his chest, and he felt a rush of love and protectiveness surge within him. He had not been altogether sure what to expect when he wed this lively, intelligent woman. He smiled as he remembered the intensity of their lovemaking during the night and her cries as he took her to her peak

As he felt himself drifting off to sleep himself, his last thought was that this new marriage promised to be very interesting.

Chapter 26

//

The first bond of society is marriage.

> — Marcus Tullius Cicero quotes Ancient Roman lawyer,
> writer, scholar, orator and statesman, 106 BC–43 BC

\\

Monday, October 5, 1812
Pemberley, Derbyshire

The sun was an hour above the horizon when McDunn, his face barely moist in the cool morning air, turned a corner on one of his usual running paths in the Pemberley gardens to find Elizabeth Darcy walking toward him. She stopped still as soon as she saw him, and McDunn throttled back his pace to a trot until he came to a halt about five feet away from her, breathing deeply but not especially urgently.

"Good morning, Mrs. Darcy," he said, giving her both a bow and a warm smile. "You're up rather early. I usually have these paths to myself when I run."

"Good morning, Major," she replied, giving him a curtsy as she examined him.

"Yes, I know," he said, with a crooked grin. "You've likely never seen someone running around in such unfashionable clothing and sweating unnecessarily like I do."

"I was not aware you had arrived from town," she said, dodging his statement though she indeed looked rather startled by his appearance.

"Miss Darcy and I arrived last evening," he said in explanation, then his grin widened. "You likely were not aware of our arrival since you and Darcy retired rather early."

At Elizabeth's blush, McDunn continued. "I run when I can to try to retain at least a few shreds of physical fitness."

"Ah. I see. I believe."

McDunn laughed lightly and motioned to the path. "Might I prevail on you to walk with me? After I run, I need to walk to cool down." She nodded, and he turned to walk down the path in the direction she had been going.

"And I can't afford cramps since I'm sure Darcy will want to ride after lunch."

"I did not know you rode, sir."

"I had to be dragged into it, kicking and screaming, by the efforts of both your husband and his cousin as well as his sister. However, after almost three years of practice, I've come to enjoy it. It's completely unlike anything I've ever done before though I've been warned this period is quite dangerous for a relatively new rider. Evidently, I know just enough to be dangerous, and this is the time when I'm most likely to get myself killed."

"Let us hope it does not happen. Your company would be missed by my husband, and you and I have hardly moved beyond our first introductions."

"I'll try my best, Mrs. Darcy."

"I left William sleeping when the sun woke me because I was eager to see his gardens. They are so lovely, and they seem to stretch forever!"

"I know what you mean though I'm not as much of a garden and flower person as you appear to be. I'm an urban boy though the town where I was raised was rather small by comparison to the really big cities. But I never spent much time outside town until I joined the Marines, and they sent me all kinds of places—usually, unpleasant places."

"I just love to walk through the country," she said, looking about her with pleasure.

"You'll have a good time exploring then. I usually try to run about three miles, and I know there are many parts of this park I haven't seen in the three years I've been here."

"That is what Georgiana told me when she and Darcy visited at Longbourn. And William enjoys walking these paths as much as I do when we walk in the afternoon before it gets too cool."

"I think Darcy enjoys walking with you more than he enjoys the gardens. He's about at smitten as I've ever seen a man."

"I suppose it was a rather unusual courtship."

"And very short!" he said with a laugh. "That's what I want in the unlikely event I ever find an Elizabeth Bennet for myself—a short courtship—though I think I'll skip the excitement you and Darcy experienced."

"Perhaps you need some help, Major. I could enlist Georgiana to help me. Between the two of us, I am sure we could find you a suitable lady."

McDunn only shook his head slowly. He had a smile on his face, but there were dark shadows lurking behind his eyes.

"No," he said, after they walked a bit further. "I don't think I'm ready. Maybe I'll take you up on your offer sometime, Mrs. Darcy, but not just yet."

As they walked farther into the garden, Elizabeth remarked, "I really do not know much about you other than you are William's friend and you do not dance."

McDunn laughed merrily at this. "Actually, I do dance. At least, I do now. Darcy's sister made me learn. She was a stern taskmaster and even went so far as to hold practices with the staff and musicians to accompany us. A most assertive person, Miss Darcy."

"I wish I could see you tell my mother that. I am afraid she does not have a very high opinion of you. She does not understand why Darcy persists in keeping you as a friend."

"Because I'm not a gentleman, I assume. But it's okay because I'm really not. I'm perfectly comfortable just being Darcy's friend. He's certainly the best friend I've ever had though we're quite different people."

"He says the same about you, Major. I think you are good for him."

"I hope so. In any case, I really enjoy running here at Pemberley where everyone is used to me. It's too difficult to run in London without being terribly conspicuous. And I try to avoid being conspicuous."

"But why do you run?" she blurted. "I have never seen anything like the way you were running. It was as though you were running for your life!"

McDunn looked at her and smiled. "In a manner of speaking, Mrs. Darcy, I was. Tell me, have you heard of the Royal Marines? They serve on the ships of your navy."

She thought for a moment. "I have seen marines mentioned in *The Times*. I remember a story about something called a 'cutting out' expedition."

"I was an American Marine in...in a far off war. A very, very bitter and devastating war against tough, hardy enemies. We did physical exercise to keep ourselves ready for battle. We had a saying: better to sweat a little in peacetime than to bleed a lot in wartime."

"But you are no longer a…an American Marine, are you?"

"No, though old habits die hard. Darcy's cousin is in the army, and he rides every morning. And he rides hard. His horse is always well lathered when he returns. And he and Darcy practice fencing since it's also part of the colonel's martial duties. I suspect he will do it for the rest of his life. So I continue to run and occasionally do other exercises even though, as you said, I will never be a marine again. But so much of what I do these days seems to be done sitting at a desk that I need to do something to delay the onset of swivel-chair spread."

She looked at him in confusion. "What is it you said? Swivel-chair spread?"

"An American expression. As I said, you'll get used to them. Swivel-chair spread refers to getting a fat posterior from sitting too much."

"I see. At least, I have a glimmer of what you mean. But what of your family, Major? Are they in America?"

She was both surprised and shocked to see Major McDunn's face take on an expression of sudden grimness, one most at variance with his usual mien. The harsh lines carved in his face made him look distinctly…stern. He looked most alarming.

"I…I am sorry. Did I—"

"It was not you, Mrs. Darcy," he replied hastily. "It was me…I was remembering my parents and sisters, all of whom are now dead. And a very special woman who also died. Your question…well, it made me remember how much I miss everyone."

The expression on her face must have indicated her desire for more information since he forced a slight smile and shook his head slightly. "Not right now if you please, Mrs. Darcy. This lovely morning is much too pleasant for sad memories of an unchangeable past. There surely are more pleasing topics."

They walked on in silence again for a few minutes; then she spoke again. "I have not yet met William's cousin. Colonel Fitzwilliam."

"You will very soon. We expect him this morning. I like him tremendously, almost as much as I like Darcy. Colonel Fitzwilliam and I understand each other. He and I have shared similar experiences—experiences that give us an understanding Darcy comprehends but has never experienced personally. We have, as we used to say, both gone to see the elephant."

"I am sorry," Elizabeth said, her brow wrinkled in confusion. "I do not have the pleasure of understanding you."

"Roughly, it means gaining experience entailing considerable hardship and cost. We have both been in situations where people were trying very hard to kill us, and we had to do the same to them before they did it to us."

"Ah, I take your meaning although I have no idea what it would be like to be where you and Colonel Fitzwilliam have been."

"That's why we were there, ma'am," he said gently. "We were there to protect you so you and the other civilians wouldn't have to experience similar or worse horrors yourself. You've read of the Trojan War, I presume?"

When she nodded, he continued. "The warriors of Troy were doing the same for their women and families, but they failed. As a result, their women suffered all the horrors of being ravaged by the victorious Greeks."

Elizabeth seemed to be digesting this as they walked, then she suddenly stopped and faced him. "I long to know more about you, Major McDunn. I am certain there must be more."

"I realize that, Mrs. Darcy," McDunn said gently, "but we decided to wait until Colonel Fitzwilliam joined us before we explain everything to you. I warn you, some of it will be rather difficult to believe, and we wanted to allow you and Darcy some time to yourselves before we told you everything."

"Everything?" she asked in surprise.

"Everything we know—why Darcy kindly offered me his hospitality for as long as I wish, why he also offered his estate for my experiments, and why we—all of us—have formed a partnership for our telegraph and other inventions."

"I did not know you were partners," she said, looking at him in wonder. "I have heard much about this telegraph, but it was always mentioned as though it was owned by my husband."

"That's just as we wish it, as you'll learn. But be patient. We're waiting for Colonel Fitzwilliam so all of us who have been together since the first day will be there."

"All? Including Georgiana?"

"It most definitely includes her. Miss Darcy has been a part of it since she was thirteen years old."

Elizabeth mulled over what she had been told for a few moments before she sighed. "Well, I suppose I shall have to be patient until my new cousin arrives. It appears our walk is at an end since we have arrived at the house. But before we go inside, I want to say how much I have enjoyed speaking with you this morning. You may be an American, as you keep repeating, and you may not be a gentleman—as my mother accuses you though I would dispute the matter with her—but your manners and civility cannot be criticized. I have greatly enjoyed our walk as well as your amiable and intelligent conversation."

"This cannot be!" breathed Elizabeth, as she toggled the images on the computer tablet in her hands. On the table before her were one of McDunn's pistols along with his only remaining Krugerrand, a few other coins from his time, his wallet, and the pictures of his family. She had seen them all and listened to his story with eyes that had remained wide with astonishment the entire time.

Suddenly, she looked at McDunn apologetically. "I am sorry; I did not mean to question the truthfulness of what you have told me—"

"It's just so unbelievable, right?" McDunn said with a broad grin.

"Exactly so," Elizabeth said with a smile of her own.

Putting down the tablet, she leaned back in her chair. "Now everything makes ever so much more sense."

"And you see why we need to keep my involvement camouflaged as much as possible. Otherwise, some wise guy is going to start asking questions we can't answer, even if your husband is a bit unhappy with the praise he gets. But he deserves all of it, Mrs. Darcy! Can you imagine the leap of faith he made when he didn't have me run off his property three years ago? Now that really is unbelievable!"

"Yes, you have a point, Major," Elizabeth said, looking up at her husband, who colored slightly at McDunn's praise. "So, what do you plan next?"

"Build some more steam locomotives for a start. The demonstrations of our ability to haul large tonnages of coal at higher speed and for much less cost than our competitors give us a leg up on building more rail lines to start hauling freight and passengers." He shook his head ruefully.

"What is it, McDunn?" Fitzwilliam asked.

"I was just thinking of all the things we've had to learn. I remember thinking that I knew how to do all of this, both from my own knowledge as well as the historical and technical records in my computer tablet. Then we started, and as problem after problem cropped up, I had to repeatedly ask myself why it was so cursed difficult to make this stuff work as we planned!"

"I remember," Darcy said with a reflective chuckle. "Your language is usually rather restrained, McDunn, but I heard oaths definitely not fit for delicate ears."

"Well, he is a military man, Darcy," Fitzwilliam said.

"I remember stumbling on a saying from one of the most important inventors from my time," McDunn said. "He said, 'Success is one percent inspiration and ninety-nine percent perspiration.' Boy, was he correct!"

Georgiana looked up from the two computer tablets she had in front of her. "Both of these have passed all their self checks, Major. And they are fully charged. Shall I shut them down?"

"Until next month, Miss Darcy."

"Very well. But you know how much I would dearly love to spend hours and hours exploring them."

"I agree!" Elizabeth said feelingly. "The photographs alone are enthralling!"

"But you both know why we have to save them."

Georgiana mournfully stabbed the power-down soft key on the screen. "They are all we have and all we will ever have in our lifetime."

"Do not despair too much, Miss Darcy," he said consolingly. "I have some ideas about reducing the amount of smoke and coal ash coming out of the exhaust stacks of our locomotives, so you will need to do some research for me."

"When may I begin?" she asked eagerly.

"Tomorrow, I think. And if Mrs. Darcy wishes to help and learn at the same time, I see no reason against it."

"Oh, wonderful! I shall be delighted," Elizabeth said enthusiastically.

"As for right now, I believe it is time to sample some of my newest batch of blended Scotch whisky and pat ourselves on the back for discovering how to make it so much smoother. I'm glad our need to talk in privacy allowed us to get rid of your absurd habit of making the ladies leave when we menfolk imbibed the stronger drinks."

"Of course, this blending of yours is just as illegal as the whisky itself," Fitzwilliam said, curling the mustache he had kept in imitation of McDunn's when he shaved his beard. "That makes it taste ever so much better!"

Darcy only rolled his eyes as he crossed to McDunn's sideboard to pour himself a brandy.

"I still say it is filthy stuff."

Chapter 27

//

*In any moment of decision the best thing you can do is the right thing,
the next best thing is the wrong thing, and the worst thing you can do
is nothing.*

— Theodore Roosevelt, American adventurer,
war hero, and US President

Saturday, October 10, 1812
Pemberley, Derbyshire

As Darcy's comfortable coach rumbled along the road leading away from Pemberley, McDunn was daydreaming, half-lulled to sleep by the easy rocking of the well-sprung vehicle. Word had come earlier that Mrs. Bingley had given birth to a daughter, and all their party were on the way there when Elizabeth Darcy gave a sharp cry of alarm, bringing him upright.

"A man!" she cried, pointing out the window. "A man just appeared in the air!"

McDunn saw Darcy and Fitzwilliam look sharply at each other.

"Was this not—" Fitzwilliam began.

"Yes!" cried Darcy. "It was exactly here! Wainright, stop the coach!"

All at once, McDunn realized what Darcy and Fitzwilliam meant, and a sudden jolt went through him. "Today's October 10!" he exclaimed.

When the four occupants of the coach looked at him, he said, more softly, "October 10! The day you found me, three years ago to the day. And evidently right here from what you say!"

"What does it mean?" Elizabeth asked, trying to catch sight of the man who had fallen from the sky, but he was nowhere to be seen.

"I have no idea, Mrs. Darcy, but I had better take a look!" McDunn drew his pistol from beneath his coat as he jumped to the ground.

Fitzwilliam followed behind him, and McDunn turned as he heard other boots hit the ground. Darcy was assisting his wife from the coach while Georgiana waited eagerly behind her.

"Hey! Wait a minute!" McDunn cried.

"You cannot stop Elizabeth," Darcy said. "I have already learned better than to try."

Darcy saw that his sister also intended to join the rest of them, but at his stern look, she only shook her head and jumped to the ground.

Georgiana wrapped her arm through Elizabeth's. "Your wife will protect me," she said smugly. "I did not see Major McDunn arrive. I shall not miss this one!"

"At least let me go first," McDunn said, lowering his voice. "But if I yell to get down, then get down fast! Flat on the ground, and forget about modesty! Because I might have to start shooting immediately! Understand?"

When they all nodded, he turned about and cautiously began to approach a depression in the grass. He held his pistol in a standard two-handed grip though his finger was not on the trigger. A cartridge was in the chamber, and the safety was off. If his finger went to the trigger, he would be shooting in the next instant.

As McDunn moved forward step by step, the others carefully followed five paces behind. After he got close enough, he was able to recognize the familiar colors and patterns of the man's clothing.

"It looks like Marine BDUs," he said softly to the others, "so it's most likely one of my own. But who? Kaswallon said everyone was dead."

A closer look confirmed his guess. The man lying on his back was uniformed and equipped just as he had been when he arrived three years previously. McDunn could not recognize who it might be because the man's helmet had fallen forward over his face.

He halted about five feet away and waved the others to stop. He was not sure what he should do, but he knew he was *not* going to do what Darcy had done and touch the man's boot. Even his friend now admitted how foolhardy he had been.

Instead, McDunn said in a normal tone, "Marine."

It was as though the man had been waiting to hear something, and he slowly reached up to his helmet. McDunn tensed, wondering whether some barb had stolen a dead marine's clothes and somehow forced Kaswallon to send him after McDunn. Then the helmet lifted, and McDunn's world froze as utter amazement locked his muscles—and his mind.

"Gunny," Corporal Sandra Desmond said rather weakly.

"Dancer!" McDunn said breathlessly when he was finally able to speak. He found himself on his knees, having dropped down without realizing it. Acting by reflex, he put his pistol on safe and slid it back in his shoulder holster.

As energy seemed to flow back into Sandra's body, she slowly started to wriggle her arms free from the straps of her field pack, blinking against the sunlight and looking about her.

"Fancy meeting you here. Where'd you get the elegant suit? Boy, it sure is good to see you made it here okay! Wherever here *is*, of course."

"You were dead," McDunn said as though someone else controlled his tongue. "Kaswallon told me everyone was dead."

Now freed from her pack, Sandra rolled over and came to her knees right in front of him. Suddenly, he had her in his arms, clasping her so tightly she gasped.

"Hey! Go easy, big guy! Everything hurts from hitting the ground!"

McDunn murmured words of contrition and loosened his hold somewhat, which allowed Sandra to pull his head down until her lips touched his.

McDunn responded exactly as though Sandra was a long-lost lover, hardly remembering how he had forced himself not to think of her for the past three years since he could not have endured the reality of her lying dead with all the other marines of the regiment.

At last, the two of them drew back, and Sandra smiled up at him with an impish grin.

"That's better, Gunny. Much better. I've wanted to do that for a very long time. Even before we left the States."

"I never suspected," McDunn said, stunned by this surprising revelation.

"There was never any time. And you had your hands full."

Suddenly, a thought came to McDunn, and he leaned forward to whisper in her ear. "When I introduce you to everyone, don't show any surprise at their names—or the names of the places here. It's really a shocker, but be calm. I'll tell you everything later."

Pulling back, McDunn got to his feet and helped Sandra up. Then he turned to the others, who had drawn close when he holstered his pistol.

"Mr. Darcy, Mrs. Darcy," he said, drawing Sandra forward with his arm still around her, "permit me to introduce one of my fellow marines, Corporal Sandra Desmond. Somehow, although I have no idea how, she survived our last battle and was transported here in the same way I was."

He paused momentarily before he said, "She is rather special to me."

"She is the one you grieved for these past years!" Georgiana said with sudden insight.

McDunn looked startled. "Yes, Miss Darcy, she is."

He then introduced the others to her, pleased that Sandra was not responding in shocked surprise to the various names, as though they were not at all familiar.

And they may not be, he thought. *She's probably never read a single word of Austen.*

Sandra reacted to each introduction as she would have in their old culture, stepping forward with her hand outthrust. McDunn kicked himself for not expecting it since he had done the same. Darcy and Fitzwilliam shook her hand immediately.

Surprisingly Elizabeth never hesitated when the sturdy, uniform-clad woman did the same to her, though she did grimace a bit at the strength of the other woman's grip.

"Sorry," Sandra said contritely, then shook Georgiana's hand with more delicacy.

She beamed at McDunn. "So you grieved for me for years. Evidently, you've been here for a while."

"Three years. To the day."

"And I just got here! There's a story there, for sure."

"Which we should not discuss here, Dancer. Wait until we are safely back at Pemberley."

Sandra nodded in acknowledgement, and McDunn looked about him, noting Sandra's field pack and her two rifles, as well as a pair of canvas bags lying amid the depression in the grass where she had appeared.

"It looks like you brought a few things with you. Uh, anything valuable?"

"Oh, my yes," Sandra said, slyly. "I think you could say that."

"Then we had better get everything on your coach, Darcy. Uh…shall we continue on to Mr. Bingley's as planned?"

"I think not, McDunn. In light of this extraordinary event, I think it best to return to the house."

"Could you give me a hand with the heavier stuff, Fitz? We need to put it inside the coach. You remember how heavy my bags were."

Fitzwilliam nodded and bent down to pick up the two canvas bags, grunting at their weight, while McDunn picked up Sandra's pack and her two rifles.

"Hey! One of these is an AK!"

"And there's some AK ammo in my pack," Sandra said softly, so only McDunn could hear. "I wasn't sure where I was going to wind up though I told Kaswallon I wanted to go where you'd gone. I wasn't sure he could make that happen, but I guess it all worked out even if there was a bit of a time slip. But there was a lot more AK ammo lying about than anything else, so I grabbed one of the best looking rifles and as much ammo as Kaswallon and I could find."

McDunn nodded, knowing that he and Sandra had to talk about what had happened and how she had made it here though she had already cleared up a few questions in his mind.

When they got to the coach, Sandra looked at it rather skeptically. "Look, it's going to be crowded in there, and I'm really dirty, and I know I smell. Maybe it would be better if I just climbed up beside the driver."

"Nonsense, Corporal," Elizabeth said. "Pray enter. But, given what you say, you might sit by the window beside the Major."

Sandra laughed aloud and did as suggested while all her remaining gear was handed up to the footmen and tied down.

"You can get a shower once we get to the house," McDunn told her. "But discretion is the word."

He pointed up above where the driver and footmen rode on the top of the coach. "Security."

Sandra nodded her understanding. "Wait, did you say a shower? Do they have showers these days?"

"*We* do!" Georgiana said proudly, nodding at McDunn.

"Well, I have been a little busy these last three years. There's a pair of showers and two bathrooms on each floor except for Darcy's suite, of course. But we have running water to the showers, and with some time to heat up the boiler, even hot water."

"That sounds glorious!" Sandra said, looking down at her dirty, bloody, and torn set of BDUs.

"Well, it's the little things that make life comfortable."

"I'VE SPENT THE LAST THREE YEARS THINKING YOU WERE DEAD, DANCER." The others had gathered in McDunn's room, which was more like an office than a bedroom. It was where all their discussions were held, and it was the repository of all things best kept from prying eyes. His desk was a massive affair, with handmade locks much more modern than anything available.

With contributions from Georgiana, Sandra was dressed in Regency fashion. During the dinner they had just finished, she had eaten with the same gusto McDunn had shown on his first days at Pemberley, and now all assembled leaned forward to hear her story.

"It seems like only a few hours ago when Kaswallon sent me off. All of us were certain you were dead, Gunny, with the mortar shell blowing you through the air like it did. We didn't know anything about the cave then, of course."

"I was with Murchison up in the rocks at his sniper pit when the bastards came over the perimeter. He'd caught a round in the shoulder, and I was trying to patch him up when several of them came up the hill. He got a couple and I got the others, but they killed him. Throat wound, right over his armor. That was where most of the blood on my BDUs came from since he fell on top of me after I caught a round in the helmet that knocked me into la-la land."

"This United States of yours seems to grow some stalwart women, Major McDunn," Fitzwilliam said with admiration.

"Oh, you do have a way with words, Colonel!" Sandra said, chuckling. "But I'm just a regular marine, not a real warrior like the gunny."

"Your major explained what it meant to go see the elephant, and I know you have seen the beast yourself."

"Colonel Fitzwilliam has heard the elephant's trumpet himself, Dancer," McDunn said, and she nodded somberly.

She cleared her throat uncomfortably and directed the conversation back to its original topic. "Anyway, with Murchison on top of me and his blood all over me, the barbs must've thought I was dead, especially since we were well up the hillside. I'd seen it was hand-to-hand down below me before my lights went out, and the regiment must have taken out almost all of the barbs before they went under. Anyway, when I started to come out of it, everything was eerily quiet—until your pistol shots went off, that is. And I knew it was you since it's hard to mistake the sound of that cannon of yours."

"So you didn't see Kaswallon drag me into the cave?"

Sandra shook her head. "Even though I heard the shots, I wasn't really with it for a while, so I must've missed Kaswallon when he got you. But I saw him when he came out dressed in those weird robes. He was bending over, looking through stuff, so I was able to get down the hill and sneak up on him. Even then, when I got an arm around him and put my knife to his throat, I don't think he would have cooperated except he must have recognized my accent. Anyway, he told me he had you in his cave and was trying to find a rifle and some ammo for you."

"Then you must have been the one who found my pack and the other stuff! I never could figure out where everything came from."

"Yup. Kaswallon helped me, and we gave you half the gold and about a third of the ammo we found. I figured four bags of gold would give us a good start wherever we wound up."

Darcy and McDunn looked at each other with a smile, and McDunn said, "Well, it might come in useful, Dancer, and it was a good thought. But Darcy and I formed our partnership early on, and we've been making enough money to fund our other enterprises. I think virtually all of the money from the gold he sold for me is still sitting in savings. Apart from melting almost all of it down so we could sell it, we just put it into savings and haven't had to touch it. It's our rainy day fund should we need it."

After a moment's thought, McDunn asked, "Did you have any problem convincing Kaswallon to send you after me?"

"He didn't want to at first, but I convinced him. That was after we got you all set up and you vanished, which really made the hairs on the back of my neck stand up, I can tell you! While we were waiting until it was my turn, we wired up a bunch of explosives on a timer, so he could set them off when he used the Siege. He wanted to make sure everything, including the Siege, was destroyed so the barbs couldn't find it."

"So Kaswallon's gone, too," McDunn said with a sigh. "Along with our whole world. You're the only connection I have to what we lost, and I was shocked to my core when you peeked out from under your helmet."

"That's about it, Gunny. You and me, and you grieved for me, and I had to get tough with Kaswallon to have him send me after you. So, at the risk of shocking your friends, I have to ask how long it's going to take you to make an honest woman out of me."

In the silence following this last remark, Sandra never took her eyes off McDunn's, and he broke the silence by clearing his throat.

"What Dancer means is...that is..."

"I believe we understand her meaning, McDunn," Darcy said, the beginnings of a smile curving his lips.

"Well, it had to be said," Sandra said matter-of-factly. "With the fancy clothes everyone's wearing, I suspect it's not common for a man and a woman to start living together. But I have to tell you, Gunny, after what you and I have been through, I'm not inclined to wait very long."

Georgiana did not even bother to attempt to suppress her giggle as she looked at the dumbstruck look on McDunn's face.

Finally, McDunn cleared his throat again. "Patience never was one of your strong suits, Dancer. Not that I'm opposed, you understand—"

"You'd best not be opposed!" she said fiercely. "Who else would we have to talk to at night otherwise?"

"—but we're going to have to talk this question over with my friends. I'm kind of ignorant of courting customs here. The only one I've witnessed was, ah, a bit unusual."

Darcy and Elizabeth looked at each other before laughing.

"I apologize if I've offended anyone's sensibilities. No offense intended, but I knew I couldn't wait for the Gunny to work things through."

"And no offense taken, Miss Desmond," Darcy said. He cleared his throat and looked at Sandra and McDunn.

"I have given some thought to the subject ever since seeing the way you and McDunn greeted each other earlier, Miss Desmond, which was certainly enough to compromise your virtue. And assuming he feels the same—"

"I do," McDunn said firmly.

"My first thought was to advise McDunn to take you north to one of the Scottish border towns, where a license is not required. But I have had another thought. It was not long ago a man and a woman could get married simply by saying they wanted to be married in front of a pastor. So, since neither of you is English by birth and no one here knows what took place before you arrived, I suggest you simply declare you are married and carry on accordingly. Who will oppose you? Certainly not any of us or our staff."

McDunn and Sandra looked at each other very intently. "A common law marriage works for me, Gunny," Sandra said while McDunn could only nod.

"That was exceedingly clever and devious, darling," Elizabeth said, giving Darcy's arm a squeeze.

"Yes, indeed, brother," his sister said in agreement. "I had no idea you had the soul of a barrister."

When everyone stood to leave McDunn and Sandra alone, Sandra suddenly spoke up.

"Gunny, I mean Edward. I guess I'd better start calling you Edward. Could you give me and Mrs. Darcy a few minutes alone?"

McDunn gave her a puzzled look but said nothing, only nodding his agreement before leaving with the others.

When they were alone, Elizabeth looked at Sandra expectantly.

"Uh...well, this is kind of difficult for me," Sandra said. Then she straightened her spine and blurted out what was bothering her.

"I don't know what to do!" she said plaintively. "Well, obviously I know *what* to do, but I don't know what's expected in this era."

Elizabeth smiled at the courageous young woman who could so easily risk her life but now found herself in a situation that utterly bewildered her.

"This is your country, and you already know all about manners and stuff." Sandra began pacing nervously about the room. "I know I talked a good line when I asked Edward to make an honest woman out of me, but he's been here for three years! He knows what to do."

She stopped and looked at Elizabeth. "If we were back in our own time, I'd go to the bedroom and get myself all showered and perfumed, put on an enticing nightgown or else just take off my clothes and get into bed to wait for him to join me."

"Getting into bed unclothed would work well enough even in this ancient time. Let us go into the next room, and I will tell you what I know."

Elizabeth led the way to the door connecting to the other bedroom of McDunn's suite with Sandra following her. "This is the wife's bedroom, where she would usually sleep. A husband and wife of the wealthier classes would sleep in separate bedrooms, and her husband would ask admission when he wished to be more intimate."

Sandra nodded her understanding. "I don't think Edward and I will need separate bedrooms."

"Nor do William and I. In your case, it will work out well since you can see the major's bedroom is much more of a working office than a bedroom. On their first night together, the new husband would remain downstairs for a time while his wife's maid helped her undress, brush out her hair, and help her don some kind of sleep attire. However, I am not sure any of the sleep attire we can offer you would qualify as *enticing*."

"A new bride in my time would have access to a considerable selection of alluring night wear, made of very sheer fabrics which almost made a woman feel like she was not wearing anything at all."

"Oh, my. That is very different."

"But I don't have any experience with such clothing. I'm not a fashion plate. I've been a marine since I was fifteen, but right now, taking off my clothes and getting in bed looks like my only real option"

Both women laughed; then Elizabeth said, "Even on your wedding night, you will require something with more warmth. I suggest we talk to Georgiana. She is closer in height to you. I have a few nightgowns my aunt sent me that you might use. Light, simple, and comfortable to wear, as well as being a little bit enticing."

"I'll have to get my new husband busy figuring out how to do some up-grades to my Regency attire, which should include brassieres, or as we called them, bras. For up here." She motioned to her bosom. "Sarah said there's nothing like bras here. And we might think about some of those enticing fashions I mentioned. How about you and I form a partnership like our husbands, except we'll focus on lady's clothing instead?"

"You will have to let me examine one of these bras you speak of," Elizabeth said, "but I think I would enjoy working with you. I think you may have a very good idea, Mrs. McDunn."

"Sandra," she said with a firm shake of her head. "And I might as well warn you I'm not going to call you Mrs. Darcy much longer. Edward is the only one with the patience to learn all the proper terms and niceties. In the States, you call good friends by their first name, and you and Georgiana are my first friends here in England. I'm afraid you are just going to have to put up with my shortcomings."

"Of course," Elizabeth agreed with a smile. "I think you are going to be very good for the Major, Sandra. He tries to act more like a proper English gentleman every day. You will keep him from becoming too reserved and aloof."

As my husband once was, though he certainly is not at all reserved with me!

Chapter 28

Oh, the marriage of your spirits here has caused Him to remain,
For whenever two or more of you are gathered in His name,
There is love, oh there is love.

— Noel Paul Stookey, songwriter and singer,
from *Wedding Song (There Is Love)*

Saturday, October 10, 1812
Pemberley, Derbyshire

When McDunn entered his new wife's bedroom, it was illuminated by only a few candles, but he had no difficulty seeing Sandra. She stood in front of the window with the drapes thrown back and the light of a full moon streaming into the room.

He stopped suddenly and sucked in his breath. He thought she was nude at first since he could see the outline of her body with absolute clarity. Then she turned around, and he heard a swish and saw the thin fabric cling to her lithe body.

It took his breath away. Her simple nightgown may have been nothing like the ultra-sheer negligées he had seen advertised in his own world, but it enhanced the beauty of a woman's body more than he would have expected in this world of Regency England.

She must have borrowed it from Elizabeth Darcy, he thought as Sandra began to walk toward him, swaying gently in the graceful, feline prowl that was hers and hers alone. *That was the reason she asked her to stay behind. But wearing a borrowed nightgown is dangerous. I haven't touched a woman for so long, my fingers itch with the urge to rip it off her! My God! I never imagined she could be so beautiful! And so damned sexy!*

As she came close, he gazed on the young beauty who had so precipitously become his wife.

"I've never seen a woman as beautiful as you, Dancer," he said softly. "Never in my life. You're so unbelievably lovely."

"Thank you, Gun—Edward," she said, giving him a brief, amateurish curtsey.

McDunn stepped forward and pulled her to him, their lips meeting in a lingering kiss. Then McDunn trailed light kisses over her cheek to her ear. Sandra leaned her head back so his kisses could move down her throat.

He easily picked her up in his arms and placed her on the bed, shedding his dressing gown and climbing in beside her. They kissed again while Sandra shrugged out of the borrowed gown. His hands explored her bare skin while she ran her hands over the broadness of his back. Both of them had the hard bodies of warriors, but it only increased their desire for each other, for warriors they were, what they had been, and what they would always be.

In time, Sandra whispered endearments into her husband's ear as he plunged into her in the eternal manner of a man with a maiden. They were two vibrant, strong young people cementing the bond that would bind them both until the end of their lives.

McDunn still found it astounding that Sandra had managed to follow him to this fanciful place seemingly taken from the writing of Jane Austen, and they were the only refugees from the world they once believed was the only one there was or would ever be. Without saying the words, they knew, to the innermost core of their beings, that they were joined forever.

LATER, AS THEY LAY NAKED IN EACH OTHER'S ARMS, McDUNN SAID, "Now we can talk. You did really well when I introduced everyone to you, but you probably didn't realize who they—"

"Of course, I knew who they were, Edward! Darcy and Elizabeth from *Pride and Prejudice.* I *did* read the book you know."

"What! But you never said a word about it! And you always gave me a hard time about reading it!"

"But that's just because I loved teasing you. By the way, I have to tell you

I really don't like calling you Edward."

He glared at her for a moment until he realized she was only smiling in the dark as she teased him. Finally, he settled back down. "You could call me Ed, I suppose. That's what the men in my family and most of my high-school friends called me. Or you could call me Eddie. That's what the girls in the family called me."

"I like Eddie. I've heard enough about your mom and grandmom to know I'd be happy to be in their company."

"And I'll probably call you Dancer until the day I die."

"I know," she said softly. "It's another reason I knew of your badly hidden attraction for me. You were the only one to call me that."

"But *everyone* called you Dancer!"

"Nope. Only you."

"Really? I can't even remember how it started. I guess I'm not as good at keeping things hidden as I thought I was."

"Oh, with everything military or serious, no one could ever tell what you were thinking. But when you called me Dancer and when I caught you looking at me, I knew why."

"Hmm. Well, then that's all right, I guess," he said with feigned indifference, but his fingers were moving lightly over her ribs. He was pleased to find a ticklish spot, and he soon had her doubled up in helpless laughter.

"That'll teach you to tease me," he told her.

"Stop it! Play fair," she said between giggles. "I thought you were a real marine, Eddie, but you fight like a girl. You've gone soft, big boy."

"Truce! We'll call this one a draw. You've worn me out, woman." He lay back and relaxed, pulling her close to him, and she responded by snuggling even closer.

"But go on with knowing about Darcy and Elizabeth," he said.

"Well, as soon as I heard their names, I knew the Siege was playing some sort of game, sending us to a world full of fictional characters. But I had a little time to think about what Kaswallon said about how the Siege Perilous worked and all those alternate worlds and stuff. So, how close are things here to the book?"

McDunn shook his head sardonically. "The characters are a lot like Austen described, but nothing seems to have happened as it did in the book. For example, the very first time Darcy and Elizabeth met…"

It took more than an hour for him to relate most of what he had observed, bringing Sandra to laughter at times and tears of compassion and sadness at others.

"A shotgun wedding!" she exclaimed as he ended his tale. "You're kidding me!"

"Nope. And now we're hitched as common-law man and wife. Nobody, but nobody, back home would have believed how things turned out."

"That's the truth!"

"Now, back to Kaswallon. You say you found him looking for ammo?"

"Yup. Sneaked up on him real good, put my knife to his throat, and asked all nice and polite what in the world he was doing."

"Nice and polite. Yeah. I can see it all now—yow!"

Sandra had jabbed him between the ribs with a knuckle. "Be quiet, Eddie, or I'll never finish this. As I was about to say, he couldn't wait to start talking once he realized I was American. He jabbered some stuff about trying to save your life with this Siege thing, and he was trying to find a rifle for you, but he had to finish before your gate opened.

"Anyway, I didn't really know what to think, but I was thrilled you were still alive, so I helped him go through packs for ammo and stuff, including the medicines I had left and what I could scrounge from Commander August's tent. She went down fighting, by the way. Got what looked like a half-dozen or so of the barbs before they got her. All the wounded were dead already, probably dosed with all the morphine she had left. I could only scrounge a couple of styrettes from her tent."

"Like you said, a good egg," McDunn said in mournful remembrance. "They all were. God damn all those barbarian butchers!"

"I hope they burn in Hell. Anyway, when I'd scrounged everything I could find, including the gold, Kaswallon and me headed to the cave. Kaswallon was really strong! He carried three bags of gold, your pack, and your rifle all by himself. I'd brought Murchison's sniper rifle down the hill, so I carried it and my own rifle plus my pack. And the AK. Probably not even half the load Kaswallon carried!"

"I knew he was strong. He dragged me into the cave all by himself."

"I couldn't even see the outline of the cave, but Kaswallon pressed something, and part of the stone wall slid aside. When we got to the back part, there you were, sitting on that big rock like it was some kind of saddle. He checked and said you were still alive and seemed to be doing okay, so we went back to pick up what we couldn't carry on our first trip. Kaswallon carried the remaining bag of gold and another bag we filled with ammo. And I looked all over the place for anything else that might be useful. I was being all pack-ratty by then since I could only guess at what we'd need. Or what *I'd* need if the idea I had about going to the same place you went didn't work out.

"When we got back to the cave, Kaswallon was going on about alternate worlds and how the Siege would send you where you belonged, where you were meant to be. He said it was almost time, and we got your pack and stuff on you real quick. Then he waved me back and started chanting some stuff real loud in a language I never heard before. Then, so help me God, he raised this wood staff high and struck the ground real hard. And you were gone—just gone. No fanfare, no big flash of light—nothing. Not at all like the movies."

"I came partially awake when he started chanting, and I thought I heard a big sound like lightning."

"Maybe on your end, but all I heard was the sound of his staff hitting the floor."

"I was out cold before then. I vaguely remember being jostled about and even hearing voices, which I knew had to be my imagination. Then I was gone, and I hit the ground. Hard."

"Yeah, tell me about it."

"The next thing I knew, something nudged my boot."

"Colonel Fitzwilliam described it to me. The way you reacted really impressed him, but looking down the bore of your cannon impressed him even more."

"I wasn't pointing it at anyone," McDunn said mildly. "I just had it at the ready. One of Darcy's footmen had his pistol out but hadn't raised it. Luckily, Darcy settled everything down without any more excitement."

"I've had all the *excitement* I want for an entire lifetime, Eddie. I'm looking for some old-fashioned boredom!"

"Yeah, me too, Dancer!" he said feelingly. "So I was gone. What happened then?"

"I told Kaswallon I wanted to go where you'd gone, and he got all stubborn and said the Siege thing didn't work that way. I was sitting astride the stone, and I just took the safety off my little pistol, which was in my thigh pocket. He didn't like it at all, but he did dig out this huge, old book. The pages looked pretty fragile, and he was careful about turning them. He read for a while, going from place to place, and leaned down real close to read. Then he gave some kind of exclamation I couldn't decipher. Maybe it was another language. Anyway, he looked at me and said the Siege wouldn't send me to the same world you went to since it wouldn't be the world meant for me. But he said, kind of reluctantly, that there seemed to be a way around the way the Siege usually worked.

"He could make the rock send me on the same path you followed so I could join you. It seemed kind of a ticky-tack distinction to me, but it seemed to mean something really big for him. He started to mumble about there being something strange in his book, but I told him it was good enough for me and to send me on my way. He said there was no need to wait for my time since I wouldn't be going the usual way. He helped me load up with all my stuff and started chanting again, but it went on for a lot longer than it had with you. He also had to go back to his book a couple of times before he finished. I heard the sound of his staff striking the ground; then I was falling. No lightning strike sound, though. Then I hit the ground like a ton of lead, and I couldn't breathe for a while."

McDunn got up and poured them each a glass of wine. Then he climbed back into bed and snuggled down next to his wife.

"Okay," McDunn said, "I can understand you wanting the Siege to get you out of our dying world—and I'm not complaining one single bit, not at all—but I'm still stunned you would want to follow me. I thought you were so beautiful, it made my gut ache, but I never noticed any particular interest on your part."

She looked at him solemnly for a few moments. "I guess I've become so skilled at camouflaging my emotions that I didn't let anything show, though I sure knew you were interested in me! But if there'd ever been an opportunity, I might have surprised you. I wouldn't have needed this gown Elizabeth and I borrowed from Darcy's sister. I think you'd have gotten the idea if you'd found me naked."

Her face lost its mischievous look and took on the solemn tones they both knew so well, those inspired by the devastating heartaches they'd endured. "But there was never the time or the place."

"You were so damned sexy tonight, I almost ripped your nightgown off and took you right there on the floor!"

Sandra leaned forward to kiss him long and deep. Then she returned to the point she wanted to make.

"As for why you, Eddie—what better man than you to follow?" she said, her mood suddenly serious. "You know I'm an orphan, right?"

He nodded, and she continued. "I was in orphanages and one foster home after another. There was no stability to my life, and the way the foster home people kept moving me around made me feel like a piece of merchandise. Anyway, I decided to get out somehow. I'd gotten pretty streetwise by the time I was fourteen even if I hadn't been able to get much regular schooling. And I'd also managed to accumulate a little cash, which I kept well hidden—"

She saw the look on McDunn's face and pinched his cheek playfully. "No, Eddie, I didn't do anything immoral though it was definitely illegal."

He looked at her and cocked an eyebrow, and she chuckled. "Maybe someday I'll tell you. It wasn't all that bad, but it'll be my secret for now. So, I used my money to get a fake birth certificate made up for me. It made me a year older than I was; there were some really skilled forgers in New Orleans, by the way! And they also falsified the form a parent signed to let their kid enlist at sixteen—"

"My God, Dancer!" McDunn said suddenly. "You joined the Corps at fifteen!"

"I can't fool you, can I, Eddie?" she said, again giving her flashing, urchin grin he loved so much. "I knew those foster people would stop me if they found out, but I caught 'em by surprise when I disappeared so early. The Corps had me on the way to Parris Island before they even knew I was gone. And those foster officials didn't even have my right name! I'd told them I was Sharon Demming when they first plucked me out of the Catholic orphanage—thanks to Father Ramirez who told them I'd never had a birth certificate. He knew all about the scam those guys were running, moving the orphans around like peas in a shell game so they could grow their little empire, and he told me how to smear my fingerprints if they ever tried to take them, but it never came to that. I think they figured they'd keep me in their system until I was eighteen. I was lucky Davis had the law about voluntary enlistments changed as soon as he became president—"

"Davis joined the Marines early, too. At seventeen, I think, though his parents gave their permission. Just like mine did when I was sixteen, but I also had my high school degree by then."

"I did too, though mine was forged."

"Naturally," McDunn said dryly.

"Yup. Naturally. So I joined the Marines, and Davis also had made the Navy change the rules so the Marines could have their own corpsmen. So I went to the Navy Pharmacist Mate school and then eventually came to Bravo Company after a bunch of time in the hospital in San Diego. Bravo Company became the only home I'd ever known, and I was happy—really, really happy, Eddie. I was even happy when they sent us over here. It wasn't until the crazies back home nuked DC and New York in the Massacre that it started to get bad."

"Yeah."

"So anyway, Bravo Company was my home, and you were the Bravo CO after the captain bought it in the first firefight, and then I started to really lust after your bod."

"You what?" McDunn exclaimed.

"You heard me, Eddie, even if you were too slow to figure it out. I may not have had much experience, but I was going to trip you into a bed if I ever got a chance. But there was never a real opportunity, and the company kept getting smaller and smaller until the whole blessed battalion was about half the size of Bravo when we came over. Then we all got killed on the last day except you and me. So the weird guy, the Druid—"

"I keep calling him a Druid too, at least in my mind, but I don't think he was."

"Anyway, the Druid said he thought you'd be okay when you went through the portal. You might die of something once you got where you were going, but your wounds belonged to our old world, not the one where you were going."

"He was right, too. My clothes were bloody and ripped, but I was perfectly fine. I didn't even have scars."

"So, assuming you'd be okay on the other side of the Siege portal, you were the only part of Bravo left. The only part of my *home*. So, all I wanted was to go where you'd gone. You were my only chance, my only link to the only place where I was happy."

"You have a home now, Dancer," McDunn said, folding her in his arms and hugging her fiercely. "And if our courtship was exceedingly unusual and one of the briefest on record, it would be par for the course since I've been in this place. But I'm happier at this moment than I ever thought I'd be, despite all the exceptionally good luck I've had here. And I'll make you happy. Trust me on that."

"I do," Sandra said, her head on his shoulder, then she immediately sat bolt upright.

"Is there any possibility of getting fed in this place? I know I had a huge dinner, but satisfying your carnal lusts has left me famished!"

"So it's *my* carnal lusts, is it?" McDunn said.

"Now, don't be petty, Eddie," she said. "What about some food?"

"I think something might be arranged. Maybe some bread and water or something similar."

At her stricken look, he said, "Just kidding, Dancer. I'll ring for a servant."

"Great!" Sandra exclaimed, jumping out of bed in one of those lithe movements that had caused him to award her the nickname.

"Now, where'd my nightgown get to? You better not have ripped it, you Neanderthal!"

"Regardless of your low opinion of my skill in undressing women," McDunn said smugly, "you'd better put on one of my robes before a servant arrives. And there's your nightgown. You were lying on it, and it looks just as good as new."

He held it out to her and she snatched it out of his hand, examining it carefully, seemingly unconscious of her nudity. McDunn had the distinct feeling she was deliberately showing off for his benefit.

Well, if so, she'll have to wait for a while, he thought with a sigh as he got up and crossed back to his room where he found a pair of robes for both of them. *Not only is someone coming to answer my ring, but this woman has worn me out. I couldn't summon an ounce of energy if my life depended on it.*

However, as he watched the graceful way in which Sandra slid into the robe he held for her while smiling lasciviously over her shoulder, he amended his thought.

At least, I don't think I could...but then, who knows?

IT WAS, ALL IN ALL, ALMOST A PERFECT NIGHT AS McDUNN DID, IN FACT, recover a modicum of energy. The only mar to perfection came when fatigue finally drove him to slumber only to have it disturbed by his oft-repeated nightmare—of his distant relations trapped in a Britain seemingly doomed to the same cultural suicide that claimed his own lost world.

Chapter 29

What we obtain too cheap, we esteem too lightly: it is dearness only that gives every thing its value. Heaven knows how to put a proper price upon its goods; and it would be strange indeed if so celestial an article as freedom should not be highly rated.

— Thomas Paine, English-born American political activist
and one of the Founding Fathers of the United States

Sunday, October 11, 1812
Pemberley, Derbyshire

Over the next few days, McDunn and Sandra hardly left their rooms. It was not as if they spent the whole time making love, though they did that often enough as was usual for newly married couples. McDunn found Sandra as enthusiastic at sex as she was at everything she did though she had no hesitation in admitting her relative inexperience. Sandra was a happy, wholehearted lover, and both of them were very much in exploratory and discovery mode, as well as being happier—especially in Sandra's case—than they'd been in their lives.

They talked about their lives before joining the Corps and the events that had taken place while he was in this world for three years. They decided to call it the New World, to differentiate it from the one they had left behind—but only between themselves.

Sandra found McDunn's lengthy and detailed descriptions of solutions the main participants had found that were similar to those Austen imagined—but nothing like the way she had written them—were especially entertaining, and she had him repeat Darcy and Elizabeth's tale again and again.

McDunn explained in greater detail all the experiences he'd had in the three years before she arrived. He told her of the inventions he'd introduced with Darcy's invaluable assistance—from the telegraph to the steam loco-motive to the bicycle—and of his frustration that the multitude of details associated with making the locomotive profitable were preventing him from working on his next project.

"I'd like to work on something like an electric carriage for London since cleaning up after the horses is a problem, and it's going to get worse. However, I've got to find a way to generate electricity at low cost to make the idea at all possible. And I also have a prototype of a bolt-action rifle I made up that Fitzwilliam is lusting after, but it's not going to be very useful until I figure out a way to make cartridges for it. Even though Fitzwilliam's convinced such a rifle would be a really great idea for their infantry, there's just no money for it at the present time. And since I'm not going to sell it outside Britain, it's kind of a dead end for now."

He grew somber and was silent for a long minute. "One worry that won't go away is the length of time my computer tablets will last. I'm depending heavily on them as we consider which projects to work on and in what order. I've thought long and hard about finding some way to make a permanent record of a lot of important technical information, but I'm at my wit's end. The gap between today and a future world that takes computers for granted is just too great."

"Well, I brought my own tablet, the one they gave us enlisted pukes. It's ruggedized, but it doesn't have much free storage space."

"And that will really help. I know how to take care of the storage problem, Dancer. I had to erase all the useless stuff the Corps put on it before I could back up my personal tablet, which has all my technical data."

"And I also have Murchison's tablet, which evidently he bought himself."

"Really? That's great news."

"I didn't mention it before now, but his tablet isn't nearly as ruggedized as the Corps tablet, but it has a massive internal memory—most of which is filled with porn, by the way."

"Maybe we could take a look at it and get some ideas—ow!"

Sandra giggled at his expression as he rubbed his side. "Be careful, Eddie!

I'm not in the Corps any more. I'm a respectable married lady with nothing but the finest of sensibilities."

"Still, we better erase it immediately. We don't want Georgiana to stumble across it!"

"No, indeed. I wouldn't have guessed it of Murchison, but he was a good guy."

"Good marine," McDunn said, which was the highest compliment he could pay. "I didn't know him all that well. All the snipers were kind of loners. But it'll give us another backup of the tech database my parents gave me."

Pain showed on his face, and Sandra reached out to cup his cheek in her palm. "I know, Eddie," she whispered. "I'm here for you now."

"And we did it all to ourselves. But we *were* fixing things up."

"Our world just ran out of time, that's all," she said soothingly, but she was startled as he suddenly sat bolt upright.

His face bore a look much as if he'd just seen a miracle. "That's it," he said softly. "That's what we need to do."

"Do what, darling?"

"I know what we need to do, Dancer," he said as though he looked into a world only he could see. A world of miraculous things. "I know what we need to do—what we have to do to save this New World so it doesn't tear itself apart like our world did. It's not a perfect solution, and what I have in mind will likely have all kinds of problems, but it'll work! If we can just bring it about."

Then he told her, his words tumbling out as he described what had flashed into his mind virtually full blown. He knew it was the way intuition worked, that his subconscious had been chewing on problems of the future when he was concentrating on his current difficulties.

But it can be done, he thought triumphantly. *We can do it. Maybe it's not a perfect solution, but we know what happens if we let this New World trundle down the same path ours did. This is my world now, mine and Dancer's and my friends' and all our children's, and I will not stand idly by and let our descendants make the same mistakes we did. Not if I can help it. We'll likely find new mistakes to make, but we have to do our best.*

Monday, November 9, 1812
Pemberley, Derbyshire

IT WAS A QUIET NIGHT AT PEMBERLEY WHEN THE DARCYS, COLONEL FITZ-william, and Georgiana joined the McDunns in the room where they usually met. McDunn served his guests their favorite libation.

My friends, McDunn thought warmly. *More than friends—my beloved and trusted brothers and sisters. I've never loved or trusted anyone in the world as I do these gentlemen and ladies.*

They've come to believe what I've told them and what Dancer has confirmed. But I've got to give them more details and facts from the future in order to have any chance of convincing them my plan is something other than a pipe dream—especially since I'm planning nothing less than a conspiracy for a mere half-dozen individuals to change the entire future of the world.

"I know you're wondering why I asked you here with most of the staff off at the harvest festival and the rest given orders to remain in other parts of the house so we can have the strictest privacy. The concept of this kind of security is unknown at this time, yet it's unfortunately going to be a necessary part of our lives from now on. If, that is, I can convince you to join me in this endeavor."

"That sounds ominous, McDunn," Fitzwilliam said, sprawled in the overstuffed chair he loved. "But then, nothing about you has been exactly... ah, respectable. No, that's not quite right. *Predictable?* That's better, but it still doesn't quite capture the essence. I'll think of the right word by and by, but go on."

"If you think I've been unpredictable before, just wait. Because I come to you tonight as one of the lowest forms of life—as nothing less than a conspirator."

He looked around at them seriously before he continued. "And I want to convince you to join my conspiracy—to become conspirators too."

Elizabeth wrinkled her brow as she looked back and forth between McDunn and his wife, both of whom looked most unnaturally solemn and quiet. "A conspirator at what?"

"A conspiracy to change the world," he said simply and sat back to wait for the exclamations and questions to subside.

"More precisely," McDunn said, leaning forward earnestly, "I want to convince you to follow me and my secret plan to alter the future."

He gazed around the room solemnly again. "This is something I've been thinking on since I arrived here so suddenly. I kept thinking about what's likely to occur between now and two centuries in the future, and I wanted to figure out some way to keep it from happening. It's also something that has been causing me to have recurrent nightmares in which my distant kin were trapped in an England headed down the same path as my own world. In short, I'm convinced that, left unchecked, this 1812 world of ours is going to take the same path leading to those catastrophic debacles Dancer and I've described—a path that destroyed our world and resulted in the two of us being here with you tonight. Our goal is to make the future take a different path, one that I think offers a more stable and wholesome future."

No one said anything, so McDunn took another sip of his Scotch before continuing.

"I consider myself a patriotic American, one who should have died in a small, meaningless conflict that future historians would not even mention when they chronicled the utter downfall and extinguishing of our civilization—assuming any historians remain to write the story, which I rather doubt. The victorious barbarians are probably already busy cutting off heads everywhere, and that's the future I think the world—*our* world of 1812—is headed for in a little more than two hundred years. In addition, all of human life might be exterminated by the Blight, which was spreading when our regiment was sent to England. And it's what I want to change."

"But can the future truly be altered?" Georgiana asked quietly.

"I think so since the scientific innovations we've introduced, such as the telegraph and the new steam locomotives, weren't mentioned in the history of my time. Not by such an early date and not by us. Some people have speculated that time is not just a single path but a multitude of possible alternatives. Change a critical decision or event, and time forks and leads to a different outcome. And that's what I propose doing.

"We have to. I was proud of the direction my country took at its inception, which was a refinement of what the British had done in establishing the concept of the freedom of the individual. America's Constitution stressed freedom and the rights of the individual as well as limited government. But my country turned out to have fatal flaws in its makeup, ones that led to disaster. It had all the necessary characteristics and attributes of a country that could have led the world, and it turned away from its responsibility because it lacked the will to lead. It chose instead to think only of the guilt associated with its mistakes and to ignore the successes. It set off down a path leading to a political vacuum of leadership...and the barbarians I've described rushed in to take the role *my* America discarded."

"Heavy stuff, Eddie," Sandra said softly.

"Heavy indeed, Dancer, but you and I have discussed the subject to death during the last month. Now, all of you know that Dancer and I came here from the future, and I've already told you Great Britain and its allies are on the verge of defeating Napoleon. But those allies couldn't defeat him themselves. Napoleon simply is too good, both politically and militarily, and they needed Britain. So, let's accept the defeat of Napoleon as a given and move on to a point I don't think I've mentioned before. Your Great Britain is on the verge, over the next fifty years or so, of establishing an empire—a world-wide empire."

McDunn took in the incredulous looks on their faces. "It won't be an empire based solely on military conquests. There will be military victories, of course, but trade and maritime commerce, along with political determination, will have more to do with the formation of this empire than pure military prowess though the Royal Navy will dominate the seas for more than a century. And I'll be quite blunt in saying the history books in my world accurately pointed out that your empire wasn't perfect. There were injustices and cruelties at times, and the opinion of the world eventually turned against the whole concept of imperialism and especially against the British Empire."

McDunn leaned forward with his elbows on the table. "If events proceed as they did in my world, Great Britain will step away from imperialism and lose most of its power and influence. It will abandon its role as a leader, much as my America will do later."

"Interesting," Darcy said, raising his glass to his lips.

"But do you believe it?" McDunn asked.

"*I* believe it," Elizabeth said. "You could not know what you have told us if you did not come from the future you describe. Though I am convinced you have told us only a portion of what you do know."

"And I can see that the war with the Corsican has elevated the horizons of people in the military and in Parliament," Colonel Fitzwilliam said. "They are not simply thinking of bringing the war to an end. They are looking at the world at large in a much different way—taking a much grander and far-reaching view than they did when my father was a serving officer. He has even noticed as much and mentioned it to me a time or two."

McDunn nodded then said, quite slowly, "Did you know English influence was so extensive at one time that it was said the sun never set on the British Empire? More to the point, I have concluded, based on my readings of the time, that the end of the British Empire was a disaster for virtually every colony and territory it left. Virtually all of them were far worse off ten years later, which is a fact the so-called experts of my time—virtually all of whom, by the way, would disagree with me—refused to face."

Now McDunn looked more somber than any of his friends had ever seen him. "So I decided to form a conspiracy—with you, my closest friends and comrades—to make sure the British Empire does *not* fall, and to hopefully lay the groundwork to correct its more severe faults, of course, but to keep it going."

After a long, thoughtful pause, McDunn wondered whether he had pushed too far or too quickly because the others didn't meet his eyes.

Finally, Georgiana lifted her head. "Why Britain? Why not America? It is much larger, and from what you said, has much greater resources?"

"For one thing, because I'm here in England, which is also going to be the prime player in what will come to be known as the Industrial Revolution. America will remain a nation of farmers for quite some time though their industry will indeed grow over the next century. So it will be easier for me to introduce the scientific innovations I think will be needed to give Britain the lead over other countries as its empire grows.

"In the United States, I'd have to start all over, and there has always been a built-in reluctance in the American psyche against getting involved in foreign affairs. More to the point, America's industrial capacity is not at all up to England's at this time.

"In addition, the United States has another problem, a really huge one, and that's slavery. It's going to lead to an unbelievably savage civil war between the northern and southern parts of my country. Britain has already outlawed slavery, and the United States should have done the same when they wrote the Constitution. But they didn't, and they're going to have to pay the price for their omission. My plan calls for an enhanced British

Empire, armed to a level of military prowess that will seem almost magical to those in America, to step in, declare peace, and effectively bring the United States into the empire."

"Civil wars are always the bloodiest of wars," Colonel Fitzwilliam said, "and they lead to the most intense and long lasting hatreds."

"In the United States, the animosities between parts of the country, especially the different racial and ethnic contingents, were still a problem when I lived there, almost two hundred years later. The Empire can stop it and also bring the States into the Empire. I think both sides can be made to like it if the Empire has the political will to do what is needed. But the crux of my plan is for the British military to be so overwhelmingly superior to everyone that the mere idea of resistance will be dismissed as lunacy.

"That will be in part scientific, which is my specialty, but also partly due to superior tactics, strategies, and training, which Fitz and I will explore from my historical records. The day of cavalry is done though there will be some who will attest otherwise in my world almost a hundred years from now."

"I was afraid you were going to say that," Colonel Fitzwilliam said, the anguish in his voice palpable.

"Over. Finished. Done, Fitz. Horses will continue to provide an important transportation function for some time to come, but it'll be to get Imperial troops in position to dismount and bring high volumes of accurate rifle fire against the enemy—which is why I constructed that hand-made, bolt-action rifle. You and I have only fired it about a half-dozen times because of the lack of ammunition, but it works. And finding a way to manufacture more ammunition is a technical and manufacturing problem that can be solved in time."

"Superb firearm," agreed Fitzwilliam. "Simply superb."

"But it's only a first step. You've seen our other rifles, the ones Dancer and I brought with us, the ones able to fire semi-auto and full auto with telescopic sights to reach really long ranges. But our country—Britain—is never going to be able to acquire those firearms for our military if they have to be handmade. That's why we have to build the tools to fabricate the improved arms I believe will be needed by the Imperial military. And all of this needs to be done in the strictest secrecy! It won't do the Empire any good if its advantage is only transitory, as it would be if other countries are able to buy or steal our improved technology.

"I think that's going to be Mrs. Darcy's specialty, for reasons I'll get into later." He looked directly at Elizabeth and read the shock on her face. "But security is only one component of the function of Intelligence. We want to keep our stuff secret because our superior technology will be a big part of the Imperial military's dominance. We also need to know what any potential adversary is doing, and whether they make any sudden leaps in capability that might be traced back to leaks in our security, such as somebody stealing our stuff.

"I have to be absolutely, cold-bloodedly blunt here, ladies and gentlemen. We have to be ready to kill when necessary but also smart enough to know when not to kill. Our future Intelligence organization can't get a reputation either as pushovers or as ruthless murderers.

"That's why I've tentatively selected Mrs. Darcy to learn the business of Intelligence and organize and run Imperial Intelligence, though it will really be our own Intelligence for the foreseeable future, not the present government's. Our conspiracy will have to provide the funding for that as well as some of the military improvements. That's the reason I suggested Mrs. Darcy as the leader for this part of our plan.

"We simply cannot take a chance on British codes of honor when the future of the world is at stake, and the concept of chivalry and honor is almost exclusively the purview of gentlemen. Dancer and I have seen the future, and the number of people in our world who are going to die if we do nothing is literally incalculable. We want to avoid the path of doing nothing, and I believe Elizabeth Darcy has too much common sense, astuteness, and responsibility to refuse to face what needs to be done when it comes to the safety and welfare of her children, her grandchildren, and her country. The perfect spymaster."

Several of the others, especially Darcy and Fitzwilliam looked doubtful, but McDunn just smiled. "But the reasons I've just given, while important, are by no means the sole reason for my decision. Consider the general opinion of Mrs. Darcy with the people outside our circle. They might remark that she's intelligent, witty, a good judge of character, and most of all, a beautiful woman. She is not someone the outside world would consider a likely conspirator and a spymaster. On the arm of her husband, she would be seen as an attractive ornament for a very wealthy and important man. It would be the perfect cover for her to disguise the work she would do."

McDunn then turned to his wife. "As you and I discussed, Dancer, we're going to need you to lead the complete renovation of medicine in Britain and the Empire, especially when it concerns things like providing medical support to our combat troops. And medical breakthroughs are going to be treated as Imperial assets and will be neither given away nor sold to other countries. They will be protected by our Security. If other countries want access to Imperial medical care, they are going to have to meet the standards we're going to demand before we'll allow them to join the Empire. It may be heartless, but I do not want my new country to go the way of my old country due to misplaced altruism."

"I note you have made several references to 'my country' in this soliloquy, Major McDunn," Georgiana said.

"My country is dead, Miss Darcy," McDunn said flatly. "It committed cultural suicide though it's doubtful it could have stood against a world determined to do the same. I could never go back to that future time even if it were possible. And Dancer and Kaswallon made sure no one else will ever come here by blowing up the Siege Perilous."

"I understand the need for secrecy, Major McDunn," Elizabeth said quietly, though her eyes were stricken at the thought of such responsibilities, "and I think it will be necessary several decades from now. But is it really important at this time?"

"Ah, that's the interesting part of your assignment. We have to start organizing, and it's going to be rather difficult if we don't start right away. It was a truism in my time that Security was more a state of mind than a list of procedures to follow. We have to cultivate the proper state of mind starting right now so we can train and prepare people to carry on after we're gone."

"That will be rather challenging," Darcy said. "But I note you have outlined prospective responsibilities only for yourself, your wife, and my wife. Do you have plans for the rest of us?"

"I thought you would notice that! Well, I haven't quite figured out whether your cousin will be more valuable in the military or whether we should start grooming him to be prime minister. As for your sister, I think she's learned a lot of history, military history, and theory while helping me. As Fitz's wife, she can be his secret advisor."

"Eddie! Do you *ever* think about something before you say it?"

"Well, who could mistake what their intentions are, given the way they look at each other? And I couldn't give any explanation why Richard hasn't said something, given he's a man of action, so I submit they need a little guidance. I admit I was a little worried at first since they're first cousins and all, but that's not a problem here in England."

Colonel Fitzwilliam and Georgiana's eyes were downcast and both of them had flushed scarlet.

Good! he thought. *We need to get this arrangement formalized! We have work to do!*

"I left you until the last," McDunn said, returning his attention to Darcy, "because I'm even less sure about what would be the best role for you. I sketched out a number of roles, and mine is a combination of scientific invention—since I did train as an engineer—and business, which I'm still learning. But we all know I need to stay out of the limelight completely, so I suspect your role will be as an industrial magnate—the controlling force behind all the companies we'll want to form once Britain makes corporations legal. That's going to be challenging enough for you since you grew up in a world where wealth was measured by the ownership of land, but that world's already changing and will change even more.

"But you might well have to assume a different role, one I don't think will be to your liking. If Richard proves to be more valuable in a military role, we will need you in politics and statesmanship."

"No!" Darcy said, instantly and firmly.

"I'm afraid so, old friend," McDunn said sympathetically. "There are a number of areas that can only be addressed if we have a major player in the world of politics— for one thing, making preparations to support the growth of the Empire while also limiting the mistakes committed by private enterprises trying to take on the role of government. To be exact, wresting the control of India away from the British East India Company. In my world, the Empire didn't displace the Company until almost 1860, but more is needed and earlier than then—much earlier. India needs to become a full-fledged part of the Empire with self-rule so it doesn't revolt or get exploited as a colony. Britain lost India a century later because they didn't do it, which was the same mistake they made in the American colonies. Avoiding such mistakes can only be prevented through political means."

"I did not say no solely because I do not like politics, though that is certainly true. But I know myself, and I know I am not up to the challenge,"

Darcy said.

"I have thought this over very deeply, even before I came up with the points I've made tonight, Darcy. I am convinced you can handle the challenge, and I'd like you to read as much history as you can on my third tablet before it fails."

"So it is failing?" Sandra asked, taking his hand in hers.

"I'm afraid so, Dancer. Georgiana and I have been trying to stay on top of it. The diagnostic software is moving things around as much as it can, but eventually, information in the memory will start disappearing—if it doesn't fail catastrophically."

"Too bad! I'd hoped to get more out of it."

"There's nothing to be done, and we got three years out of it. You had two—no, three!—strokes of genius when you came into the cave after me. You brought your two tablets, and the medical supplies. The gold turned out to be nice but not absolutely necessary."

"You said *three* strokes of genius, Eddie," she asked, her brows furrowed.

"You brought yourself, Dancer," McDunn said softly.

She looked at him silently for a moment then leaned close and whispered, "Don't plan on getting much sleep tonight. You're going to be busy."

"See? It's no wonder I married you!" he whispered back, but not nearly as silently.

"That is enough, Sandra!" Elizabeth said firmly. "If you keep distracting Major McDunn, we will never find out why my husband needs to go into politics."

"To be perfectly frank, I think either he or Richard needs to be prime minister," McDunn said.

"Oh, my dear Lord!" Darcy said, an almost a plaintive wail in his voice. And Fitzwilliam looked equally stricken though it looked suspiciously as though Georgiana had seized his hand beneath the table.

"Of course. How else will you be able to force the country to adopt a constitution if you're not prime minister? It should be modeled after the United States Constitution—with modifications, of course. I know of some, but I'm sure you can help me find others. I don't know if we can implement this before the Empire intervenes to avoid the American Civil War and bring the States into the Empire, but we'll certainly have to do it then if we hope to convince the Americans.

"But Britain needs it just as much because there is a massive defect in the British parliamentary government, as good as it is. There's no written constitution guaranteeing the rights of the citizens and limiting what the government can do, and England in my time got to the point where Parliament could rule as a tyranny between general elections as long as they didn't lose a vote of confidence. Government is a necessary evil, but it needs limits on what it can do. The US Constitution is a good place to start, so future governments cannot simply redesign what the Constitution says until it's meaningless. That was what my country was trying to recover from when the final wars started."

"How on earth am I going to be able to do that?" Darcy asked.

McDunn had to hide a smile because he detected interest rather than instant rejection in his voice.

"In addition to studying technology over the past month, I also studied history, so I can point out some areas that will give us ideas." McDunn drained his Scotch then stood. "And that, ladies and gentlemen, is the end of tonight's speech. Think on what I've said, and we can talk later. But remember, Security with a capital 'S.' No matter how good my intentions are, a number of things I said tonight could be very dangerous if they got out. I would prefer our conspiracy, if you decide to join me, not come to a premature end because a servant thought we were plotting the overthrow of the King. Now if you'll excuse us, my wife and I have an appointment."

The remaining four looked at each other in silence after the McDunns left, arm in arm.

"Interesting," Darcy said at last.

"I thought McDunn was extremely bright and inventive for a military man," Fitzwilliam said. "But I never anticipated this! The concept is so far-reaching! It betrays a kind of...well, almost philosophical leaning on his part."

"I think he is right," Elizabeth said. "I looked in his eyes when he said, 'My country is dead, Miss Darcy.' I saw the truth and the horror in his eyes, and I think he is determined to take whatever steps are necessary to keep the same thing from happening to our country. And I will help him."

She turned to her husband. "As will you, my darling. Since I have no more idea how to be—how was it he put it?—a spymaster?—than you have to be a prime minister, we both can learn together."

"Until that tablet goes bad," Georgiana said, worry in her voice.

"He and Sandra have four others," Elizabeth responded. "And, if I understand correctly, several of theirs are made to a more rugged standard than the tablet that is failing, and they are keeping those in reserve. Our source of information and history ought to last long enough for us to get this conspiracy up and running."

She smiled after she said that. "If nothing else, Major McDunn has provided me with all sorts of new sayings. 'Up and running' is truly marvelous!"

"His best is 'up the creek without a paddle,'" Fitzwilliam said. "That was made for a soldier!"

"Actually, I believe he phrased it, at least once, a bit more earthily, Colonel," Georgiana said demurely. "And he mentioned being without a spoon rather than a paddle."

Unfortunately, at that moment, Fitzwilliam was draining the last of his Scotch with the result that it went down the wrong way, reducing him to a fit of coughing. Darcy started to move to Fitzwilliam's side, but his sister waved him away.

"You and Elizabeth go on to bed, William," she said softly. "I will attend to my cousin. In any case, I think he and I need a few words together."

Darcy paused a moment then nodded sharply. "To be sure," he said simply then left the room with Elizabeth on his arm.

Epilogue

//

Trying to predict the future is a discouraging and hazardous occupation. If by some miracle a prophet could describe the future exactly as it was going to take place, his predictions would sound so absurd that people everywhere would laugh him to scorn. The only thing we can be sure of about the future is that it will be absolutely fantastic. So, if what I say now seems to you to be very reasonable, then I will have failed completely. Only if what I tell you appears absolutely unbelievable have we any chance of visualizing the future as it really will happen.

— Arthur C. Clarke, British scientist,
science fiction writer, and futurist

\\

Monday, April 8, 2047
Imperial Suez Canal Zone between the
Egyptian Protectorate and the
Imperial Commonwealth Kingdom of Palestine

Governor General Sir Richard McDunn stifled a yawn as he watched the participants in the ceremonies take their places. He was not involved in any of those ceremonies, but as the representative of His Imperial Highness to the Egyptian Protectorate, he could no more absent himself than could the Prime Minister of the Kingdom of Palestine, who stood beside him with equal boredom.

McDunn was a bit more alert than his Palestinian counterpart since the denizens of McDunn's dominion were a surly, backward lot compared to those of Noam Mizrahi, whose countrymen had been full-fledged Imperial citizens for a century. The overwhelming majority of the workmen who had labored to complete the additional Suez waterways, which would more than double the commercial traffic between Europe and the Empire's dozens of dominions in Asia, had been Palestinians from the Kingdom. Those workers from Egypt, even those who passed the rigorous pre-hiring interviews and investigations, had not been good employees, and turnover and absenteeism was high. A number of untrustworthy Egyptian hires had managed to slip past the stringent screening process and had tried to sabotage the project.

We had to make the effort, I guess, McDunn thought. *And we did find a few good workers, many of whom may well immigrate to Imperial domains if they pass Rebecca's even more stringent screening process.*

He looked over at his American wife as she stood talking with Madame Mizrahi, admiring Rebecca's striking, high-cheek-boned features and dark complexion, gifts from her Cherokee ancestors, before moving on to carefully appraise the security for the ceremony.

A full battalion of Imperial Marines had drawn the assignment for today, given the number of important dignitaries in attendance, and eight Iridium-armored heavy tanks floated on contra-gravity at the points of a compass star about a half-mile in the distance. They were hard to discern, of course, with their camouflage screens powered up, as were the two squadrons of sting-ships providing aerial security.

He could also see the company of elite Royal Marine Commandos in various strategic locations providing close-in security, but that was only because he knew where they would be placed. They were just as difficult to see as the tanks due to the chameleon coating on their powered armor, but their combat readiness was clear. Most of the commandos had their mirrored, armor-glass faceplates down and locked, receiving electronic information from various fixed and mobile sensors. They crouched behind their barricades, facing outward with their pulse-ion battle rifles at the ready, the thick cables from their backpack power magazines in place.

Of those commandos who had their faceplates raised, McDunn could identify at least a dozen different ethnicities, representative of the many locales from which the IM drew their recruits. And he easily recognized the trained lethality of the commandos themselves since he had done nine years in the IM Commandos before embarking on a career in the diplomatic service. *Sometimes I wish I'd stayed in the IM,* McDunn thought wistfully. *I'd be at least a full colonel by now. And it would be nice to be anything close to as fit and trained as those young men.*

But then, he would not be married to Rebecca since she had made it clear she wanted to do something meaningful, not wait at home while he might be deployed half a world away on thirty minutes notice.

All in all, he thought, more than a trifle complacently, *I think I made the right choice. Life with Becca is never dull!*

He carefully extracted a handkerchief from his pocket and, with practiced subtlety, drew his hand across his face to wipe the sweat away. It was beastly hot for so early in the morning.

He looked back at his wife, and he did not know whether her ancestry or her American heritage had first brought her to the attention of Dame Darcy Harrison, the head of Imperial Intelligence. It was a fact that an overwhelming number of II operatives were female, and many were descendants of the first head of II, the legendary Elizabeth Darcy, as was the present holder of the office. And certainly Rebecca was destined for more responsible assignments after his term as Governor General was completed in a month.

I'll be very glad to kick the dust of this place off my shoes, McDunn thought sourly, seeing a familiar face in the Egyptian delegation. Hashad el Ramani's expression showed even more acrimony than McDunn felt, as the wiry Egyptian looked on the Palestinian representatives with open hostility. Alarm bells went off in McDunn's mind at seeing such openly displayed animosity.

The man ought to know better than to give rein to such visible hatred. There can't be anything suspicious in his files, or he wouldn't have been able to achieve any kind of responsible position in the Protectorate civil service. But being as cavalier as to show his hatred openly is a very bad mistake. Certainly bad tactics or, as Becca would call it in the intelligence service, bad tradecraft.

Rebecca, as the head of the local branch of the II, would be the one to take a better look at Ramani, and he thought he would direct her attention toward the man. But he saw her already inspecting Ramani closely though *her* tradecraft was so polished he did not think anyone other than himself would have noticed her interest or her assessment that Ramani was too blatant in his malevolence toward his ancient enemies. But the Palestinians were Imperial citizens, and Rebecca possessed the same streak of ruthlessness as had Elizabeth Darcy when it came to the well-being of the Empire.

Too bad, Ramani, he thought wryly, knowing the other man had not the slightest suspicion of how badly he had betrayed himself. Nor did he guess he was likely to disappear quite soon.

I hope you enjoy tending your little garden on Elysium. That's assuming you don't do something rash, like resisting the grab squad. We Imperials may be well mannered, and we may not look particularly cold-blooded, but we've been well trained to put the welfare of the Empire only slightly behind that of the Almighty and family.

I've read the ultra-secret family papers. Though I'm a direct descendent of two Founders, Edward McDunn and Field Marshal Sir Richard Fitzwilliam, it almost took an act of God to get permission. According to what McDunn wrote, the Empire has already lasted a century longer than it did in the future from which he came. And it has been successful in more than simple longevity. I deduced this from my ancestor's writings when he described the purpose of the Founders and warned of the errors made in his future and the dangers we would face. In the more than two hundred years of the Empire, there have been no major wars and no minor wars of any significance—no world wars with their uncounted millions of dead, certainly!

One chill after another went down my spine while I sat in that vault two hundred feet under Pemberley Manor and read his messages to his heirs. The prospective combatants haven't enjoyed a visit from the Imperial military, of course, as they were sternly informed wars would not be fought as a matter of Imperial policy. Period.

Certainly, the Americans hadn't been pleased when the Imperial fleet anchored off New York, Boston, and Washington, and our envoys, complete to brigade-sized Imperial Marine escorts, informed their president and congress that slavery would be ended, their military would disarm, and they would become members of the Empire one way or the other. Yet the Commonwealth of North America is now more staunchly Imperial than almost any other area except possibly the Commonwealth of India. More than one Imperial Prime Minister has been born and raised in those distant parts of the Empire.

And now we have three thriving lunar colonies and a pair of fledgling colonies on Mars and Ceres. Most important of all, our Empire will not commit suicide by refusing to face facts. As Founder McDunn wrote, "Truth is always the first casualty of political correctness."

He smiled at his wife as she came over to stand beside him while Prime Minister Mizrahi moved to join his wife. McDunn and Rebecca exchanged kisses to their cheeks, which was the accepted form of public greeting for people of their standing.

After a minute, McDunn leaned over and whispered, "Poor Ramani."

Rebecca nodded, but her voice was emotionless. "He brought it on himself, Richard. Anyone reckless enough to let his hatred show so clearly at an occasion such as this is clearly on the edge of outright violence."

"Elysium?" McDunn whispered, and Rebecca gave him the barest of nods.

Lucky you, Ramani, he thought. *If Becca thought you were really dangerous, you'd still disappear, but you wouldn't be tending a garden.*

She caught him casting a look at the camouflaged commandos and smiled sympathetically. "Do you miss that life, Richard?"

"Not much," he replied with a shrug. "I was just checking things over by reflex, not yearning for the old days. Anyway, I was close to having to leave the commandos and go back to the regular IM when I tendered my resignation. All in all, I'd rather be married to you than to be a colonel commanding an IM regiment. But I won't be sorry to leave *this* post behind."

"True, true," his wife said out of the side of her mouth.

"I haven't had a response to my request to know my next posting," he said, and his interest perked up as his wife smiled.

"That's because you'll be *my* consort next, Richard. Dame Darcy needs a new aide, and she's offered me the job. They're going to appoint you to a job in II also because we both have to be under the same level of protection. That's why we'll be returning to London in the admiral's cabin on the *Georgie* when it pays a visit to Cairo next month. Dame Darcy said the fleet flagship ought to be safe enough for the two of us."

McDunn's eyebrows went up at this news, surprised and flattered at the opportunity to travel on the new, super-secret fleet carrier, *HMS Georgiana Fitzwilliam,* named for the wife of the first head of the Imperial General Staff and the sister of the first Imperial Prime Minister, Fitzwilliam Darcy.

Of course, the fact that Georgiana was as much a Founder as the others probably played a part, but only the inner circle of the family, those privy to the knowledge that there even were *Founders, know that!* he thought,

"Yes, the *Georgie* should be quite secure, but I still wonder what I'll be doing."

His question was an idle one since he was not at all disappointed that his career as a diplomat was at an end. It had not been as desirable as being a commando or a marine in any case, but it had been a way he and Rebecca could be together.

"There was a request from Military Threats and Intentions to have you join their shop. I think it would be a good fit, don't you?"

"Likely so. After all, once a marine—"

"—always a marine!" Rebecca said with a chuckle before they turned and came to attention as the opening bars of the Imperial Anthem sounded.

God save our imperator,
Long live our sovereign lord,
Stand beside him,
And guide him
Through the night, with the light from above!

From the oceans,
To the mountains,
To the cities,
Bright with hope!

God bless our noble realm,
Our home, sweet home!

O Lord our God arise,
Scatter our enemies,
And make them fall!

Confound their politics,
Frustrate their knavish tricks,
On Thee our hopes we fix,
God save us all!

FINIS

Printed in the USA
CPSIA information can be obtained
at www.ICGtesting.com
LVHW101228170823
755277LV00001B/61